DIARY OF A PALMIST

The life and times of William John Warner, World famous as "Cheiro".

BY

Stephen Dundon-Smith

ANTEONI
PRESS

For my grandmother Vera,

The light continues to shine.

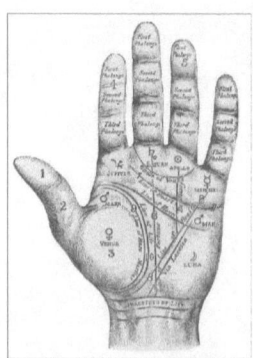

Author's Note

Anyone encountering the charismatic, William John Warner, could tell you a story or two. In bygone years, members of my family knew him well, and their recollections inspired this book.

As a child, riding to my grandmother Vera's house on a Sunday, was a regular event. My father's mother was in her late 80's, lived alone, and I remember well, her gentle smile when a bunch of flowers emerged from the bicycle basket. After eating a sumptuous meal, she'd recount stories once shared with her mother, Marian. It was important to document my ancestor's lives and preserve the information.

My grandmother was born in London at the end of 1903, and just before her tenth birthday, she emigrated to Australia with her parents. In the late 1890's, Marian was involved with the Theosophical society and the London school of Chirology, and Cheiro's name was first mentioned in relation to these organizations. What followed were countless tales regarding this famous London palm reader, and by all accounts, my great grandmother was well acquainted with Cheiro's affairs until she left England in 1913. My Australian grandfather's family were involved in the theatrical world during the Victorian Era, and knew the actors Wilson Barrett and Maud Jeffries when they toured Australia in 1898. Maud married a pastoralist in 1904 and retired from the stage two years later. The former star, visited Sydney frequently from her property 'Bowylie', near Gundaroo, New South Wales. Maud remained good friends with Marian and Vera until her death in 1946, and the topic of Cheiro was often discussed because of their shared association. Researching the history and sifting through family memorabilia gave credence to the stories.

Cheiro's own memoires present his life as glamorous and legitimate, but many of the claims described in these scenarios are false. Reaching into his shadowy past with new information, has uncovered the truth.

S.D.S.

Table Contents

Chapter One

1882-1885

My early years in Ireland / How I came to England / I share a house with the artist Frank Miles in London / My stage work with the designer Edward Godwin / Henry Irving's Theatre Co / Wilson Barrett's Theatre Co.

Chapter Two

1886-1889

I tour America with the Wilson Barrett Co / My meeting with Walt Whitman / I leave Wilson Barrett Co / Hard times in London / A theatrical disaster / Bloody Sunday / My friend Robert Hichens comes to the rescue / I find a job at Terry's Theatre as a stagehand / I study acting at Ben Greet's School / Edith Halford Nelson.

Chapter Three

1889-1890

I begin writing short stories / The Golden Dawn / The Star newspaper and Harry Dam / I travel to Paris with Oscar Wilde / The Cleveland Street scandal / Katharine St Hill and The London School of Cheirology.

Chapter Four

1890-1892

Duchess Blair and the Duke of Sutherland / I begin writing my own works on Palmistry / Princess Mary Adelaide and her daughter, Mary of Teck / I open my rooms in Bond Street / Lady Arthur Paget and Edward VII / Maud Jeffries.

Chapter Five

1893-1895

Blanche Roosevelt's dinner party/ May Yohe and the Hope diamond / Lord Alfred Douglas/ Chicago World fair/ Assassination attempt in New

York/ Wilde Trial/ Crawford House New Hampshire/ American lecture tour/ Chicago Spiritualist lecture with Betz Hermann.

Chapter Six

1896-1897

Emma Calve/ Saharet/ My father dies in Ireland/ Return to London/ Lady Colin Campbell/ The Devonshire Ball/ The Thought machine.

Chapter Seven

1898-1899

Frank Shackleton/ Katie Bilsborough reading/ Robert Hichens collaborations with Henry Irving & Wilson Barrett/ Blanche Roosevelt's death/ Duchess Blair's Diamonds/ Oscar Wilde in Paris.

Chapter Eight

1900-1910

Parisian Diamond Company/ Living in Paris/ American Register/ Entente cordiale/ Marquise DÓyley/ Nellie Meier-Simmons/ Czar Nicholas II/ Russian connections/ Irish crown jewels/ Troubles in France.

Chapter Nine

1910-1920

Ernest Shackleton/ Prince Yusupov/ London under attack/ My marriage to Mena.

<u>Prologue</u>

"So, you'd like me to tell you a story,

If I've anything strange or new;

You won't mind if it's not of glory,

Or deeds that all heroes do.

For to-night my thoughts keep turning

To a simple tale that is true."

Cheiro 1895

10th November, 1935, 7417 Hollywood Boulevard, Los Angeles, California.

A creature devouring itself. The eye of the ouroboros watches from its elaborate frame as I write. Why does this image of a serpent eating its tail hold my attention this evening? I've been familiar with the ancient design for years, but tonight, the cyclic symbol of life, death and rebirth appears different. Perhaps it's because I've celebrated my 69th birthday and will not see my 70th. According to the lines on my palm and numerological calculations, I'm entering the last year of life. The grandfather clock strikes the hour, and the ticking becomes annoying. I stop the pendulum in a vain attempt to control time.

The passing of years has altered my views on many things. When I depart this world, the truth of my life should remain for those who are interested. An old diary with its tattered cover rests on my desk, and the pages within hold details of events long gone. My home is a magnificent old mansion nestled amongst the metropolis of Hollywood, California. In 1929, when my health began failing, I relocated from England to a warmer climate. Emigrating allowed me to escape other dangerous forces in London as well.

I expect the last chapter of life will play out here amidst the bright lights and palm trees. My eyes rest on an exquisitely crafted Buddha, almost certainly stolen from an ancient temple. The deity sits in silence, a redundant piece of interior decoration no longer venerated by countless devotees. In bygone years, I too was adored for my mystical predictions and handsome features, but time has depleted both. I try to forget the past and the memories which belong to a world no longer in existence.

The full moon casts its eerie light over the garden, and my faithful companion, an aged Alsatian, rests his head on my foot. Like myself, he seems content to pass his days relaxing and eating. Opening a drawer, I find my favourite pen; a gift in gold and diamonds from the Czar of Russia. I recall with sadness the fate of the man who placed the intricate object in my hand. Czar Nicholas II was one of many individuals who sought my guidance and whose destinies were fated to end in disastrous circumstances.

Over the years I have for the most part, been blessed by good fortune and success, however, these highlights haven't protected me from tasting the bitter fruit of rejection and despair. I've suffered the contempt of those who don't understand me and the changing loyalties of those who no longer need my services. I've caressed the hands of brilliance, and observed those of the most sinister and depraved of this world, making no distinction or judgment on those seeking my advice. It was never my practice to reject individuals based on their social standing or background, nor was it my way to judge or condemn those who'd confided in me. Like a priest, I heard many confessions. This is something I've learnt to live with and process in my own way. Some of those revelations have left me emotionally burdened. Along with my physical body, this knowledge has grown heavy with the passage of time. I've come to respect those brave souls able to reveal private thoughts to a total stranger. It must be a highly evolved individual who can deal with the weight of someone else knowing its darkest secrets without fear of retribution. In a life of endless social intercourse, I've encountered few who ever possessed such qualities.

In the past, I've written about my exploits in an entertaining fashion. Now, the inner part of my conscience demands release. I realize, the true incidents of my life are just as interesting as the false ones invented. Purging unspoken events has become a priority, as the light drawing me to my new home grows brighter. I no longer fear the danger of revealing certain facts haunting me, as enemies have grown older and weaker.

Many of the individuals who played a part in those affairs, have gone before me to their spiritual dwellings. In my visions, I see their spectral arms beckoning to me, and I'm at peace knowing these souls won't be touched by the controversy my stories will bring. Others earthbound like myself, continue to work through our individual destinies before we make the great transition. To those still living, I make no apology for the inclusion as I predict the publication of this memoir will not eventuate until after their deaths. Karmic obligation dictates I complete the authentic details of my life without the embellishments. Revealing the true path of my spiritual knowledge and success will be the final chapter in the story.

~~~~~~~~~~~~

Chapter One

I was born as Venus rose across the Irish sea on the 1$^{st\,of}$ November 1866. When the planet aligned the ascendant, it bestowed good looks and charm, but failed to grant the aristocratic family I'd alluded to. The handful of exotic names used throughout my career were fictional, my true name being William John Warner. Never comfortable sharing it with my father, I used Louis after moving to London. It sounded less common and distanced me from the world I'd left behind. It was the first change, but not the last.

Early life in the coastal Irish town of Bray was uneventful. I craved stimulation and found it difficult to remain focused on my schoolwork. My father was well educated, and worked as a teacher in the local schoolhouse. Complex mathematical problems were dished up with the evening meal. Despite my mother Margaret's melancholy nature, I remember her fondly. Unfortunately, the death of my younger sister Sarah Elizabeth as an infant, plunged her into a depressive state. Our life was mundane, and I'd fantasize about having wealthy parents from notable families. In my dreams, there were invitations to balls and important government ceremonies, and these imaginary visions helped to cope with the boredom.

Observing the privileged classes parading on the promenade of Bray's seafront, provided some distraction. Latest designs from Paris and London added to the sophisticated atmosphere with feathered hats and silk dresses fluttering in the breeze. The exotic couture only increased my desire to visit the world from which they'd come.

Aristocratic families visited during the Summer, to explore the scenery of Bray Head. The mountainous peak with its winding trails, was a popular destination for tourists. At times, I'd climb to the cliff top, and spend moments in quiet contemplation. Looking over the water, I'd imagine the lands beyond, and the wonderous things there. I was confident of departing Bray's shores one day, and living the life of my dreams.

Our house was located amongst shops on Castle Street in Bray, and in June of 1881, I came across an employment notice in one of the windows. This was the beginning of my journey to independence. It read.

'Young lad required for immediate start. General duties and training will be provided for the right, well-presented applicant. Apply directly to The International Hotel, Bray.'

I often watched the carriages arriving at the hotel entrance, and the smartly dressed porters helping the occupants. What lay beyond those front doors? Having attained the position of hotel page, I soon found out. The uniform reflected the hotel's high standard, attracting amorous glances from guests. Passing by mirrors, allowed me to reflect on the handsome image. Why couldn't I become a professional thespian? A dream materialized more appealing than carrying bags, delivering messages, and picking up parcels.

***

A day can begin without any indication destiny has it marked for you. A chance meeting can change one's path at any moment. In early December 1881, I was sent to collect a parcel from the town hall, and welcomed the chance to escape the confines of the hotel. Ominous clouds gathered, casting strange shadows over the Brabazon fountain outside the town hall. The recently completed water fountain attracted criticism. Atop the structure, a large wyvern or dragon looked down on the people, and stories of bad luck and ill health affecting those who drank increased. The superstitious tales didn't deter me from satisfying my thirst, and as I drank a crow landed on the head of the wyvern. Its screech caused me to jerk back and walk into a man, as thunder resounded, and rain fell.

"Excuse me Sir." I apologized, running off.

At the town hall portico, I brushed the rain from my clothes. On a notice board, an advertisement for a performance of a travelling Italian opera company caught my attention. When reading the details, a hand adorned with a scarab ring pointed out the name of a performer.

"Ah Signor d'Amico. A brilliant voice. What a shame I'll not be here to see him." He sighed.

It was the man I'd previously collided with at the fountain.

"Have you heard him sing?" I asked.

"Oh Yes. He's wonderful. The voice is deep and soulful. Mediterranean's have a special quality when it comes to the expressive arts."

The tall character stood with a gold tipped cane. Flicking back long strands of his dark hair, he smiled. I'd decided the cane was a fashion accessory, as the owner was neither elderly nor incapacitated, estimating him to be in his late twenties or early thirties. There was something unusual and entrancing about this person. His eyes were quick to detect my studious observations.

"The name is Oscar." He told me, extending his hand in a regal fashion.

Mimicking his behaviour, I shook the soft appendage, and replied.

"Pleased to meet you, the name is Louis."

The lie rolled naturally off my tongue. Louis was an appellation conjuring the pomp and pageantry of France, and the name of countless kings and nobles. It was a suitable alias for one who claimed to be of Norman descent.

"I see you are employed at the International. Are you fond of the work?" Oscar smiled.

"It suits me for the moment." I replied.

"So, you have aspirations to do something else?" He asked, flicking the hair and crossing his right shoe over the left.

"I'm hoping to go to London and work in the theatre." I replied.

Hearing the words made the plan real, and in the company of such a person, attainable.

"That's an admirable dream. Perhaps I can help you realize it." He said.

I remember the words with mixed emotions. Oscar's promise opened up a new world for me. We met the following day at his lodgings, and discussed the details of London. The level of elation after this second meeting with my newfound friend was immeasurable. In life, there are signs which aid us, and others to warn us. Are the omens clear or lost in murky obscurity? Could a screeching crow or a heavy downpour be seen as a warning? To one who was sensitive to such things and prepared to look beyond, yes. There are those of us who dislike being controlled when it comes to making decisions. Whether the interference comes from mortal or immortal realms is irrelevant. Such people prefer to make their own destinies, and if these individuals choose to dance with the devil, then so be it. It's naïve to think freedom from the shackles of mediocrity comes without a cost.

***

After saving enough for the passage, I boarded the boat to Liverpool with a letter of introduction to an artist friend of Oscar's, Frank Miles. He shared a house on Tite Street, Chelsea with him, and as Oscar was embarking on his lecture tour of the United States, he thought I might replace him. Another letter was for Bram Stoker, a friend from his early days in Dublin, and manager of the Lyceum Theatre in London. Oscar assured me, Mr. Stoker was of good character and I'd be given the necessary training. Full of excitement, I knocked on Frank's door, and was met by a scantily clad woman.

"Hullo luv. Can I help ya with somethun?" She asked, seductively.

"Who is it?" Shouted a voice from the hallway.

"Ere, what's ya name then?" She asked.

"Louis Warner, looking for Mr. Frank Miles." I told her.

The shadowy figure moved down the hallway.

"I'm Frank Miles. Are you the young acquaintance of Oscar I've been expecting?" He asked.

Frank edged the woman away.

"Yes. I've a letter for you." I told him, removing it from my trouser pocket.

"Ah, a letter from Oscar. Something one waits for with delicious anticipation." He grinned.

"Oh, and it's still warm." He smiled, holding it to his cheek.

The woman rolled her eyes, and walked down the hallway into an adjoining room.

"Welcome my boy, come in," Frank beckoned.

"Please excuse the mess, I've been working with Emily on a new portrait."

Entering the parlour, I was overcome by the smell of oil paints. A large canvas rested on a wooden easel surrounded by an array of brushes, knives, spatulas, and half squeezed paint tubes, forming a montage on a table beside the easel. The canvas; a near finished work of a naked woman holding nothing but a red feather over her delicate parts, was mesmerizing.

"Do you like the portrait, Louis?" Frank laughed.

"Of course. I replied, blushing.

The erotic image remains embedded on my memory to this day.

***

Frank introduced me to the decadence of London, and the more time I spent with the bohemian types, the more comfortable I became. After meeting with Mr. Stoker at the Lyceum theatre, I began working on scenic designs under the watchful eyes of the talented artists Walter Hann and Edward Godwin. The skill and dedication of these craftsmen amazed me, and filling in the outlines of their masterpieces of theatrical design was inspiring. Employed backstage, allowed me to observe the acting talents of the day. The Lyceum was the home of the exceptionally talented actor Henry Irving, and his company was at the forefront of quality theatre during those years, producing master works from Shakespeare and other contemporary writers. It was in March of 1882 during the production of "Romeo and Juliet", I met Ellen Terry and George Alexander. These generous people demonstrated their acting techniques during our breaks. One evening, Ellen told me she was romantically involved with Henry, and also had been in a relationship with the head designer, Mr. Godwin. The three managed to remain amicable despite the history. Eventually, the illustrious Henry Irving took an interest in his stagehand. In early 1884, the final rehearsals for Shakespeare's, 'Twelfth night' were over. I'd just completed painting the last section of Mr. Hann's backdrop, when a voice came from the wings.

"It is Louis, is it not?" Mr. Irving asked.

"Yes, Mr. Irving." I replied, pleased he remembered my name.

"You may call me Henry. How are you finding your time with us?" He asked.

"I'm enjoying it. It's a privilege to work with such talented people.

"Yes, I have noticed how well you interact with everyone,

especially the actors. Would you like to come out from behind the scenes, and become a performer?" He smiled, inspecting the artwork.

"I'd welcome any opportunity to develop my dramatic skills." I told him excitedly.

"Well, becoming a noted actor takes a good deal of hard work and patience. Possessing pleasing looks can sometimes be a burden, rather than a gift. Our manager Bram, tells me you came to us through our friend Oscar Wilde. In the realm of theatre, there is no denying the man has talent, but one has to live in the real world as well. I'm not confident he is the right man to guide you in this area. You need to choose your associates carefully Louis."

Hiding my disappointment was difficult. Seeing this, Henry invited me for tea the following afternoon at his home. Although I'd failed to achieve my dramatic ambitions, socializing with someone of Henry Irving's standing, could prove advantageous.

***

Hansom cabs darted in and out of the cartage wagons up Bond Street. Strolling along the sidewalk, the stench of the roughly dressed men unloading them was overpowering. At the corner of Grafton Street, colossal glass windows dominated the thoroughfare. Framed by narrow columns, an array of sophisticated baggage was displayed, with leather and timber travelling trunks beautifully arranged. What adventures lay ahead for those individuals able to purchase the luxurious travelling pieces? Turning into Grafton Street, I found Henry's house number above a dark doorway, and rang the bell.

"Yes, may I help you?" asked the housekeeper.

"I'm here to see Mr. Irving. The name is Louis Warner."

"Yes, please come this way. Mr. Irving is expecting you."

The officious woman led me to a dimly lit room, where

coloured leadlight windows created a sombre glow. A massive timber fireplace dominated the room.

"Mr. Irving will be with you presently. Please make yourself comfortable." She told me and left.

In a bookcase, numerous ancient works unrelated to the theatre filled the shelves. Henry's interests extended beyond those of the dramatic world. Neatly arranged books on astrology, numerology, palmistry, phrenology and cartomancy were displayed. Witchcraft and mysticism resided in another dark cabinet. A crow with outstretched wings, sat fixed to a wooden plinth atop the cabinet. Looking into its eyes, I admired the skill of the taxidermist.

"Good afternoon, Louis. I see my feathered friend has caught your attention." Henry smiled.

"I've never been this close to a crow before. It appears much larger. Is it the same as the common ones we have in London?" I asked him.

"Yes, it is definitely common, nothing unusual about this specimen. The full scale of a creature is often gained when one becomes closer to it." He replied, moving nearer.

"Quite amazing." I whispered.

"And what do you make of my collection of old books?"

He asked, reaching up for a dusty copy.

"It's certainly an interesting collection."

"Come sit by the fire. My housekeeper will bring tea presently."

The tall, thin figure gestured to take a seat. Henry's long fingers unfolded from his palm, while a Scottish terrier appeared at his feet demanding attention. He gave him a quick pat, sucked on his pipe, and exhaled a cloud of fragrant smoke in my direction.

"As you can see, I've quite a collection of theatrical memorabilia." He proudly declared, waving a hand towards various objects in the room.

"A cross Edmund Kean wore in Richard III, and there, a sword he used in Hamlet. In the small glass case, a ring belonging to David Garrick. An exquisite piece of workmanship. It has a miniature of Shakespeare in its setting. Most people who come to my rooms are usually drawn to these items, but you were more absorbed in my library were you not?" He asked.

"I found the theatrical memorabilia interesting, but the topics in your book collection fascinated me." I replied.

"You must be honest with me Louis. I take my time observing others before making judgements."

The conversation was interrupted by the housekeeper returning with a tray of tea and cakes. The terrier jumped and wagged his tail in anticipation of a tasty morsel.

"Thank you, Mrs. Ross."

Henry rose, and dismissed the servant.

"Some tea and cakes Louis?" He asked, holding a plate of pastries.

"Thank you." I replied, eyeing the delicacies.

As we drank and ate, Henry's face relaxed. The dark eyes softened, and he appeared younger.

"Miss Terry and Mr. Stoker have told me of their conversations with you. They tell me you've an interest in topics unrelated to the theatrical world. Namely, those of a mystical and esoteric nature. Are these areas you would like to know more about?" He asked.

"I admit, these subjects do stimulate my curiosity." I told him.

"Excellent, I thought as much. Well Louis, I would like to invite you to a gathering of others who share our interests."

By the end of the afternoon, it became clear why I'd been invited to the thespian's domain.

***

Through Henry, I'd become a member of the Jerusalem Masonic Lodge. At one meeting, our theatre manager Bram Stoker, approached me.

"Good to see you here, Louis. Let me know if you need help with anything won't you?"

Bram's offer was appreciated, as Henry was usually busy with new initiates. A few months later Henry came to me with another member.

"Ah Louis, I'd like to introduce you to Alfred Vout Peters." Henry declared.

"Pleased to meet you, Alfred. Louis Warner here."

When shaking Alfred's hand, a strange sensation passed through my body. There was an unusual aura about this frail fellow.

"I will leave you two to get acquainted." Henry smiled, scurrying away.

"How long have you been a member?" Alfred asked.

"I'm relatively new, still learning what the Masons are all about." I replied.

"How do you find living in London? Don't you miss the green hills and that special cliff overlooking the water?" He asked.

I hadn't told a soul about my village in Ireland, or the times gazing over the sea atop Bray Head. Who was this young man with enormous eyes?

"No, I don't miss home. I'm enjoying the wonderful sights and sounds of London. There's always something happening here. That's what a restless spirit needs. What do you mean about my special cliff?" I asked.

Alfred grinned. Looking beyond me, he began to sway as if

falling asleep.

"Your special place is an ancient precipice overlooking the sea. I see you there, unhappy and longing for adventure. You dream of wonderful things and demand the universe provide them. You can attract others to achieve your desires, and your mind's eye foresees events, penetrating the souls of many. Transforming yourself, you become what you desire, but fail to find the peace and happiness your soul requires."

"Please stop. I don't want to know my future. You've a gift for sure, but I'm not interested in knowing what lies ahead." I told him.

"Oh, but you are interested. Your future will be inextricably wound up in the foretelling of it for others." Alfred replied, opening his eyes.

"My future lies in the theatre, Alfred." I said.

"We're kindred spirits you and I. Cut from the same etheric stone. You cannot hide from your destiny Louis. None of us can." He told me, walking away.

I'd never met anyone like Alfred. Questions come to mind when looking back on the experience. Would my tree of life have grown without Alfred's predictions? Was he sent to plant the idea of becoming a diviner of the future? If I'd never crossed paths with Alfred, would the call of the mystical been answered anyway? Soon after the meeting, the roots of my occult tree grew strong, and the countless options became confusing. Not too far in the future, fate intervened and showed which branch to follow.

***

Work continued at the Lyceum even though my focus was on the mystical side of life. Henry allowed me to borrow his books and participate in ancient rituals and practices of the order. Many religious ceremonies are theatrical, and the Masons were no different, wearing ornate outfits and reciting memorized passages.

A newly published work, '*Chiromancy or the science of palmistry*' by Henry Firth and Edward Heron-Allen, became invaluable. Practicing on the hands of the Lyceum employees helped me to retain the information, and before long, my reputation as a gifted seer was established. I admit, intuition played a large part in my early readings. As time went by, I realized a career as a scientific palmist offered more benefits than a stagehand.

***

I believe our minds have the power to attract those of benefit to us. I've witnessed it in my own life, and numerous others. Returning home one afternoon, I met a person who'd play an important part in my future. Outside the house, a driver waited in a hansom cab smoking a clay pipe, and I surmised he'd been there for some time as the horses were free of sweat. Was Frank entertaining another young lady? Entering, I heard the laughter of a woman and the grunts of a man. I moved closer to the parlour door.

"What are you up to Louis?" Came a voice down the hallway. It was Frank.

"I wondered who was here?" I replied coyly, after being caught in a compromising position.

"Did you now? What are you doing home so early?" Frank asked.

"I'm working late tonight, so Mr. Stoker gave me the afternoon off." I told him.

The door opened revealing Edward, Prince of Wales, and a young woman. The surprised royal glanced at me with concern, as the girl continued fixing her hair and attire. Frank assured the prince all was well, and he left, followed shortly after by the girl. The angry expressions of my artist friend sent me scurrying upstairs. Later in the evening Frank explained he'd known the prince for some time. In the past, commissions were obtained to paint several members of the British aristocracy, as well as individuals from the theatre. In doing so, Frank's abode provided a convenient place for Edward to indulge his passions for art and beautiful actresses. The girl with him, was the up-and-coming actress, Emmeline Ormsby, and sworn to secrecy, I never did speak of it until fate intervened at a later date. Destiny plays a part in the lives of some more than others. There are fated souls who come into this world with a purpose, and certain lines on the hand identify these people.

***

In the summer of 1884, I was invited to a soiree at Queen Anne's Gate. The abode belonged to Charles Hamilton Aide, an older gentleman of around sixty years who'd lived as a bachelor all his life. He was a prolific writer of novels and plays, and member of Henry Irving's intellectual circle. It was his talent for poetry which fuelled the literary evenings, and those invited were honoured to hear the recitations. He was famous for his generosity to young gentlemen wanting to further their literary careers. It was at such an evening I met Robert Hichens, who'd become an exceptionally good friend of mine. Robert was in his early 20's and came from a good family in Speldhurst, Kent, providing him the luxury of following whatever path he desired. The financial support provided by his family was by no means abundant, but adequate. At that time, he was following a musical vocation, studying at the London School of Music, writing song lyrics, an unpublished novel, and poetry. Hamilton was a great mentor for aspiring writers of all genres, and encouraged us to purge our emotions in prose and song. Along with the various recitations and readings, the conversation would sometimes turn to the esoteric and mystical, as many of us were heavily engrossed in these subjects. I remember one poem he wrote dealing with the question of life after death. The last stanza of his poem read.

'It cannot be. The things we here deem mortal, have in them often more of heaven than clay: Those links will not be snapped, when through its portal, the soul is swept from this dear world away.'

After Hamilton finished reading, the room was silent. The recitation touched us deeply, especially those who'd lost loved ones. It encouraged us to live in the present, for often death steals the young. Constantly being subjected to narrow religious doctrines was frustrating, and waiting for the afterlife was tiring. The calculated fear used to control people's lives made us aware of how important it was to be true to ourselves and our own spiritual beliefs. This included never breaking those ties which bind us to our loved ones, no matter what path they follow. It was a comforting thought to many of us who were often made to feel inferior to our contemporaries. Oscar Wilde made his entrance at Hamilton's later in the evening. He apologized for the interruption, sitting on the nearest chair. Watching him carefully, I waiting for him to notice me. Another poet delivered his lines to the group, and after a few minutes, Oscar's eyes shifted to my corner of the room. A nod of recognition was followed by a smile, which was returned. After the last reading of prose, he approached me.

"Louis, my dear boy, what a nice surprise to see you here. How are you? I've been hearing some interesting things about you from my friend Bram at the Lyceum."

"All is working out for me here in London thank you Oscar. How well you look." I told him.

The fashionable and flamboyant attire was even more decadent than usual.

"Yes, thank you, it must be married life agreeing with me." He replied.

Had I heard correctly? It was true. Oscar recently returned from Dublin after lecturing at the Gaiety Theatre. During this time, he'd proposed to a young woman, Constance Lloyd, the daughter of a wealthy Queen's Counsel. She'd accepted him, and they were married soon after in Paddington.

"We have been acquainted for some time." He continued.

Knowing him, marriage was not something I'd expected.

"I'm happy you've found someone. A solitary life doesn't suit everyone, especially a person born under the sign of Libra." I responded.

Astrological studies told me, Librans didn't cope with the isolation of living alone.

"You're right. Why waste all my witty rhetoric on an empty room."

The hair flip made its appearance again.

"I expect we'll be seeing more of each other, as Constance and I are moving into a new house on Tite Street. Edward Godwin has designed the space. You know him from the Lyceum."

"Yes. I've helped out on his productions with Mr. Irving. I'll be working with him again soon."

Oscar wished me well and returned home to his new wife.

*****

Around this time Henry and his actors were planning a tour of the United States, and I'd not be accompanying them. A conversation with Ellen Terry helped clarify the reasons behind the rejection. Henry had no intention of allowing me to advance as an actor, as my knowledge of the metaphysical was becoming too disruptive. He delighted in finding something for me to do whenever he caught me reading hands, and never allowed me to look at his. Perhaps I was getting too close to the actor and any secrets discovered may prove disastrous for his reputation. It was time to move on, and in October 1884, after the final performance of Irving's Farewell tour, my employment with the company ended. Along with other scenic painters and stagehands I began work with the actor, Wilson Barrett at the Princess Theatre. I'd no idea what lay ahead with this new company, if I had, I'm certain my choices would have been different. The first meeting with Wilson Barrett was brief and impersonal. He nodded and barely made eye contact, moving to another area of the stage where the actors waited. I wasn't important enough to converse with, when rehearsals for 'The Silver King,' were taking place. The play, written by Henry Jones was extraordinarily successful, running for some time to great acclaim. Barrett played the main role and his leading lady, Mary Eastlake, soon became a close friend. An established actress, Mary supported my dream of becoming a stage performer when others dismissed the idea.

The atmosphere of the Barrett company was completely different to Irving's. Barrett was a hard task master, and his boisterous personality was the antithesis of the etheric and dreamlike energy of Irving. Even their physical appearance was at opposite ends of the spectrum. Irving was tall and wiry with sharp angular features, whereas Barrett was short and stocky. Dictatorial and intolerant of incompetence, he ruled with force. Observing the short, thick fingers with spatulate tips, explained his dynamic personality. These individuals find it difficult to relax, and are impulsive and controlling. Barrett came from a farming family in Essex, and his success was achieved by sheer determination and persistence. Irving also struggled before finding his triumphs. The styles of acting differed greatly, with Irving's macabre malevolence leaving the audience captivated. Barrett's method was to seize the stage using his compelling and resonant voice. As a theatrical entrepreneur, Barrett was concerned with profits and money. Independent and aloof, he found it difficult to trust others with his creative vision. Even Godwin, who designed with skill and mastery at the Lyceum, was forced to succumb to Barrett's requests regarding costume design and scenery.

Working on the production of Henry Herman's 4th Century epic 'Claudian' was difficult. Assigned to the backstage operations of the scenic backdrops and paraphernalia was demeaning, and whenever the actors came onstage for a dress rehearsal, I became distracted. After watching the emotionally charged performance of a young woman playing the slave Serena, it was difficult to concentrate. I was certain I'd seen her before. After the earthquake scene where I pushed giant columns on to the stage, I spoke to her.

"I was hypnotized by your performance." I said.

The young actress paused for a moment, then exhaled in frustration.

"Well thank you. It's gratifying to receive compliments, wherever they come from." She replied, walking to her dressing room.

The rebuff was hurtful. It's interesting how quickly some actors move on from their characters. In this instance, a lowly slave onstage became the Queen of Sheba offstage. Her attitude did little to alleviate my feelings of inferiority. Later, when this young girl was devoid of makeup, all became clear. She was the one dallying with the Prince of Wales at Tite Street. Leaving the theatre, I found Miss Ormsby waiting for a hansom cab, and as it arrived, I rushed to open the door. Although surprised, she continued into the cab without so much as a thankyou or smile.

"Where to Maam?" The cabby asked.

"Yes, where to my lady? Perhaps a late-night portrait sitting?" I said, before she could reply.

The cab drove away, and Emmeline's expression left no doubt she'd recalled our former meeting.

Returning home, I wondered if the Prince of Wales and Miss Ormsby ever met again at Frank's house. In the salon, my flatmate was sipping a glass of cherry brandy.

"Louis, won't you come and sit for a while." He asked.

I welcomed any interaction with Frank as we were becoming distant, due to my work schedule.

"I believe you met Oscar the other day?" He asked, staring strangely.

"Yes, he was at Hamilton Aide's." I replied.

"So, what do you think about this marriage business? I couldn't believe it when he told me. I thought it another of his macabre jokes."

He reached for the crystal decanter, pouring more brandy.

"Would you like some?"

"No thank you."

Clumsily, he returned the decanter to its tray.

"To think he's moving here with his new bride, so close to our old life. You realize he's redecorating with her money?"

Frank was becoming agitated, and a change of subject was needed to diffuse his drunken hostility.

"What painting are you working on at the moment Frank?" I asked.

The ploy worked, with his expression changing from a frown to a smile.

"I'm glad you asked Louis. I've wanted to discuss it with you for some time. I needed to be in the right, or some would say, the wrong frame of mind, before beginning." He giggled.

"Who is it to be this time?" I asked.

Placing his empty glass down, he continued.

"I want to paint someone fascinating. I'm weary of aristocrats demanding I preserve their privileged faces. Money doesn't make one interesting, and titles are certainly no prerequisite to beauty. Physical attractiveness is the ultimate force in nature, it transcends all else. It matters not what lies beneath the flesh, if a glorious countenance exists. Only when loveliness fades will the real soul become apparent. While beauty is fresh it should be entrapped and preserved for eternity in a work of art. Louis, I want to paint you. I 've seen the power you possess. People gaze at you when they believe no one is looking, and the lust in their eyes betrays what their hearts yearn. I want, I need to capture that on canvas. Imagine the power of such a painting, and the thrill of possessing it forever."

Frank's eyes were wild, and I dared not refuse his request.

"Of course, if you want to paint me, I've no objection." I responded.

"Wonderful Louis, I'm quite tired now, we'll talk about it later, and work out the sitting times." He whispered.

After his rant, Frank closed his eyes and relaxed, exhausted. His voice trailed off and he fell asleep. Back in my room there were mixed feelings about the proposition. Flattered by the words, I ignored his disturbing behaviour. What would Oscar think of Frank's plan to capture me in oils? As a reputed leader of the aesthetic movement, he should be informed of any artistic activities occurring within our circle. Next time we met, I'd relay the details of Frank's new project.

***

The following weeks were extremely busy. Barrett continued driving everyone to the point of exhaustion. The interactions with Miss Ormsby were less abrasive, no doubt due to my knowledge of her activities at Tite Street. One evening in her dressing room, she added me to her list of conquests, and the power struggle between us was resolved. She no longer looked down on me as a stage hand, but considered me a young lover able to satisfy her enormous ego.

During the performances of Claudian another actress was beginning to shine. Her name was Helen Vincent, and she played the role of Edessa, one of the daughters of Alcares. After reading the glowing reviews, her personality changed, and vanity reared its ugly head. As a stagehand I was beneath her, but as a lover I was more than capable of satisfying her. Competition between Helen and Emmeline for my attention created problems. Helen fell out with Barrett when demanding more money, and with myself, when requesting more loving. At this time, stories were circulating about my interactions with members of the cast. This annoyed Barrett who preferred his ladies to fall in love with him. Married to an older woman, Barrett spent long hours at the theatre, and rumours of liaisons with female members of his company were plentiful.

As the months passed, I continued studying palmistry books and observing the hands of those encountered. Reading late into the night was a regular occurrence while Frank worked on his painting downstairs. He never showed his works until completed, and the curiosity was growing. When the final sitting arrived, I entered the salon to find Frank naked, putting the final strokes on his masterpiece.

"Good morning, Louis, come sit. I've only a few things left to finish."

I remained unflustered.

"How much longer before you're done Frank?" I asked nervously. It was difficult not to be distracted by the sight of Frank's body, especially when his private parts began to grow.

"I need to be at the theatre a little earlier today." I lied, trying to keep my eyes from wandering.

"Almost done." He smiled.

Frank added final strokes, and placed his brush on the palette. Standing, he walked back to scrutinize his work from a distance. The new position allowed a full view of his body.

"Do you want a closer look?" He asked.

Torn between the curiosity of what lay on the canvas, and the danger of being near to Frank's body, I approached.

"Is that really me?" I whispered.

The colours of the skin and lips contrasted with the dark hair. The long lashes highlighted the vibrant blue of the eyes, and the face radiated an unnatural energy. Frank's portrait was intoxicating.

"Yes Louis, I've captured the essence of your power." Frank whispered.

His hot breath was on my neck. Entranced by the painting I came to know the artist intimately. At times, erotic images of the lustful encounter come back to taunt me.

***

By the end of 1885, Frank's unpredictable behaviour became unbearable, and I moved into a boarding house not far away. In November, a dinner invitation from Oscar led to an interesting evening.

"Welcome Louis, wonderful to see you. What beautiful flowers." Oscar said.

"I bought them from the woman on the corner." I told him.

"Oh yes. She's a sorry looking woman. I believe she sells flowers during the day, and herself at night." He smiled.

Oscar showed me into the newly decorated salon. His wife sat by the fire.

"Constance, this is Mr. Louis Warner."

"Oh yes Mr. Warner, Oscar has told me many things about you." She replied, with a worried smile.

"Please call me Louis." I said, presenting her with the flowers.

"Why carnations, how beautiful they are, I can never find them when I want them." She spoke with a curious expression, moving to a table with a vase filled with gardenias.

"Perhaps I can find room for them here."

She began placing the stems in the vase.

"No, it seems not. I will have Molly find another home for them."

"Yes, my dear. Let me take them off your hands. I will find her while you entertain Louis." Oscar seized the flowers, and scurried off to find the maid.

"Pray sit Louis, tell me about yourself. How did you come to know Oscar?" She asked.

Constance was an intelligent woman, not a mere adornment for her husband. The suspicious tone made me uncomfortable.

"Oscar helped me to come to London. He introduced me to Henry Irving's theatre group, and to Frank Miles." I explained.

Constance was about to ask something when Oscar returned.

"Please excuse me, while I check on our dinner." She said, leaving the room.

"Did I hear you mention Frank, Louis? He tells me, you have left our street." Oscar asked, flicking his hair.

"It was time to move on. I 've found other lodgings." I replied.

Oscar sat on the large settee, crossing his legs.

"I went to see Frank the other day. He is not doing well." Oscar informed me, with an accusing tone.

"Oh really?" I responded.

"I have seen the painting of you Louis, simply superb. How could you keep such a secret from me?" He asked.

"I was going to tell you the next time I saw you. Time just slipped by."

Oscar waved his hand in a dismissive manner.

"Frank has shown it to no one. He keeps it beside his bed now. He is obsessed, almost to the point of lunacy. I am very worried."

At this point Constance returned.

"Who are you worried about Oscar?" she asked.

"Our artist friend Frank Miles my dear. He has not been the same since finishing a portrait of Louis." He explained.

"Frank has painted you, Louis? What a compliment, you must be thrilled?" She asked.

"It's a masterful piece." I replied, sheepishly.

No sooner had I finished my sentence when the doorbell rang. Oscar looked at his watch and jumped up.

"Oh, I almost forgot. We are having another guest for dinner. I believe he may be of special interest to you Louis?"

Oscar left the room to greet the unknown guest.

"May I ask you something Louis?" Constance whispered.

"Of course, anything."

"When you…."

The question was cut short when Oscar returned.

"I will let Molly get the door." He smiled.

A few moments later a young man in his early 20's entered.

"Constance, Louis, I would like you to meet Mr. Ed Heron-Allen." Oscar declared.

It was none other than the author of the palmistry book I'd been studying for months.

"What a surprise." I said, shaking his hand enthusiastically.

"You're too kind." He replied.

"I'm an avid scholar of your book on chiromancy." I explained.

Oscar led his guest to an oriental sofa.

"Have a seat Ed. Can I get you a drink?" he asked.

"A brandy please."

As Oscar poured Ed's drink, Constance departed.

"Please excuse me gentlemen. I'm going to check on our little son, Cyril. He can become restless at this time of night. I want to be sure he's settled."

Ed and I stood as our hostess left the room. Oscar continued to pour Ed's brandy from an ornate crystal decanter.

"Constance is a wonderfully attentive mother. She is marvellous with Cyril. Ed is going to cast Cyril's chart for us Louis. Our guest is not only an accomplished palmist, but an astrologer as well." Oscar declared.

Oscar handed Ed his drink.

"Many thanks Oscar."

"Our young friend Louis is a budding chiromant. He is quite engrossed in the study at present." Oscar informed Ed, sitting beside him.

"That's wonderful. I trust my book has been helpful to you Louis. The whole science is gaining popularity at present. I'm about to leave on a lecture tour of the United States. I'm told the bookings are doing well." Ed boasted.

Oscar put his hand on Ed's knee.

"You will have a wonderful time Ed, believe me. My lecture tour of 82 was a whirling adventure."

"Yes Oscar. Your experiences convinced me to undertake the trip."

Constance returned from checking on Cyril and informed us dinner was ready. We made our way to the dining room and spent a pleasant evening discussing everything from Eastern religions to the price of butter. Meeting Ed and hearing his plans, only strengthened my desire to continue with the current studies.

Ed was a remarkable young man. Only five years separated us in age, and this encouraged me. As a qualified solicitor, he'd chosen a different path, following his passions for esoteric knowledge.

Already a published author, he was about to begin a grand adventure lecturing on a subject which fascinated him. There was nothing to stop me from doing the same. It was true, Ed had been born into a family with greater financial resources than my own, but Frank's portrait had shown me the advantages I'd been given. I intended to make full use of those gifts in order to achieve my objectives.

<u>Chapter Two</u>

Around the beginning of 1886, whispers circulated amongst the actors and crew about Barrett's finances. The dark cold of London's winter did nothing to improve our mood. Barrett's expenditure on scenery and costumes was exorbitant, resulting in lost profits, and we feared the worst when he called us together. Instead of losing our jobs, we were told we'd be touring the United States. The actors cheered, when the summer itinerary was delivered. New York, Boston, Chicago, and Philadelphia, were cities we'd visit. I'd been in this situation before with Henry Irving's Company, and waited nervously to hear more details. To my relief, I was included. The United States tours were financially lucrative, and the press were quick to inform the public of the details. We counted the days until our adventure began.

***

The farewell performances ended on July 19th. Warmer weather brought people out to the theatres, and the shows were well patronized. Barrett's performances with Mary Eastlake were dynamic. With the financial situation improved, a new vitality permeated the company. One night after a performance of 'Hoodman Blind,' Mary appeared distressed, crying in the wings. In the play, her character Nance, is manhandled by her husband Jack, played by Barrett. There were gasps from the audience when the violence increased. Concerned, I came to her.

"Are you alright Mary?" I asked, placing a hand on her shoulder.

Sensing she was about to confide in me, I hugged her.

"You can trust me, Mary. Tell me what's troubling you."

There was silence as she pondered whether to reveal her secrets.

"It's Wilson. Please keep this conversation between us." She said, wiping away her tears.

"I'm attached to him, and mistakenly thought he felt the same. I'm just a player in his company, and shouldn't aspire to anything else. His wife is much older and I'm told, terribly ill. I foolishly allowed myself to believe there was a future in our relationship. We've been intimate for some time."

The nature of Barrett's interactions with Mary came as a shock. Knowing the complexities of the relationship, I'd nothing but admiration for Mary. It made her explosive scenes with Barrett more tortuous, and emotionally draining.

"Has Wilson made any promises to you Mary?" I asked.

"Well, not in so many words." She replied.

"What do you mean?" I asked.

"As actors, we drown ourselves in words. Someone's touch or caress can say more, and he certainly made promises on that account." she explained.

Mary's face reddened. She straightened her dress, still askew from the violent scene.

"He was angry tonight. He was really attacking me." She cried.

"Perhaps he blames you for his wife's illness. Maybe he's feeling guilty for the betrayal." I told her.

"I never wished her any harm." She protested, looking perturbed.

"Not consciously, but the unconscious is yet to be fully understood." I smiled.

Mary straightened her tousled hair.

"It's alright. He won't hurt me again. I've worked hard to become an actress, and I've a career to think about. Thank you for listening Louis."

Overcoming her emotions, Mary strode away. Like myself, she dreamed of something better. Her goal was to become Barrett's wife, mine to perform on stage. Was Mary's dream of marriage enough for her? Would she continue as his leading lady if they did marry? Perhaps she was only interested in capturing the heart of a seductive Hamlet. Barrett was a charismatic thespian who'd found comfort with a starstruck woman. In those times between rehearsals, he'd satisfied his own needs at the expense of another. I spent more time with Mary, helping her overcome the disappointment of a broken promise. During this period, she tutored me in performance and stage crafts. Our relationship became intimate one night after a torrid scene with Barrett in 'Romany Rye' left her distraught. Performing the emotional scenes with him was tearing her apart. Weeping, she collapsed into my arms, and kissed me passionately.

***

The journey aboard the SS. Wyoming lasted little over a week. I remember vividly the entrance to the great metropolis of New York. The breeze was fresh with the scent of approaching land, and the decks filled with travellers eager to catch a first glimpse of America. During the voyage, I'd spoken with many of the immigrants, including a group of Mormons from Scandinavia making the journey to Utah. The Elders from England preached their beliefs to the passengers during the trip. An older gentlemen rested beside me, and spotted a dolphin gliding on the wake of the ship.

"Look there, we have a welcome." He declared.

Leaning over, I caught a glimpse of the creature before it disappeared. Looking across the water, the glow of a lighthouse reflected in the dawn.

"That must be Fire Island." I announced.

A crew member told me this flashing beacon was the first sign of the coast. As the sun rose, we sailed past Sandy Hook Bay and the newly completed statue of liberty glistened in its gold skin. I glanced around to see if any of my fellow theatricals were on deck, but none could be seen. Interestingly, Barrett and others kept to themselves during the trip. It was Barrett's philosophy, not to become too familiar with the 'production workers' in his company. We were there to serve the great performer and support the cast. I did interact with a couple of people during the trip. George Kersley, a talented young poet and acquaintance of Oscar, acted minor roles with the company. Kersley was good friends with Barrett's secretary, Silvanius Dauncey who was the brother of the playwright, Henry Arthur Jones. Dauncey's real name was William John Jones. Barrett and Henry worked on many theatrical projects together in the past.

The two were great company, and I intended to spend time with them on the tour. One evening on the voyage, I practiced my palmistry skills on Dauncey. I'd been studying the position of headlines on the palm and noted Dauncey's swept much deeper and longer into the mount of the moon than was usual. Not considered a favourable position, it denotes someone who finds it difficult dealing with the realities of life. Such a person often retreats into the realm of fantasy and illusion, escaping from the harshness of the real world. I explained the position as best I could, not wanting to add another burden to his lot. Years later, Dauncey committed suicide. Sadly, not everyone can overcome the challenges which destiny delivers.

Arriving at our destination, the quarantine inspections took place. Dauncey, Kersley and I were processed through 'Castle Garden.' As our documents were checked, a commotion erupted nearby. Many of the Mormon immigrants were being refused entry as paupers. This was because many were unmarried and relied on the charity of the group. The United States followed a strict protocol of eligibility and the prospective entrants needed sufficient funds before they were allowed into the country. Women were crying on their knees, begging the authorities to let them stay, while the elder's pleas were ignored. The Mormons' history of discrimination resulted from their beliefs in plural marriages. It was not uncommon for corrupt officials to accept bribes in these situations. Kersley was not at all interested in the plight of the passengers.

"What a noise these people are making." He declared.

"Have some compassion for the poor souls. I've never seen such desperation." I exclaimed.

"Oh Louis. Why don't you go to their rescue, if it concerns you so much. Promise to marry one, two or three of them." Kersley joked.

"You're so amusing. I wouldn't want one wife, let alone three." I replied.

After processing, we headed to the lodgings Dauncey organized. Barrett and the other actors went to their respective hotels, with our illustrious leader staying at the well-appointed Brevoort Hotel at the corner of Fifth Avenue and Eighth street. Kersley, Dauncey and myself stayed at a modest boarding house in Lafayette place. Although Barrett provided hampers for the actors during their performances, the stagehands were not so fortunate. We found a grocer nearby, and bought a supply of food to keep our stomachs content. Our rigorous schedule at the Star theatre started at 10am, and finished at 2pm, and we needed to be back at Broadway and 30th Streets by 6pm, to prepare for the evening performance. Barrett's technical productions were exhausting for the backstage staff, and many times, I went to bed without a proper meal. Often, after a good sleep, I'd meet Kersley at a nearby café, where we saved money by ordering one meal, and sharing it.

***

On a free Sunday, Kersley, Dauncey and myself explored the city. We travelled on the elevated railway, as well as horse drawn trams. In a discarded newspaper, a favourable review of Barrett's 'Claudian', featured. Information regarding the Mormons on our voyage was also detailed, and all but five, were allowed to stay.

"Not that you're interested, but it seems those Mormons on the Wyoming were allowed to stay after all." I told Kersley.

"This really is the land of opportunity." Dauncey laughed.

Kersley huffed and pointed to a building across the street.

"Look, Turkish baths. Shall we indulge ourselves lads?" He asked.

Dauncey seemed interested. I was unsure.

"I've never been to a Turkish bath. There was an opulent establishment back home in Bray." I told them.

Dauncey became excited at the prospect.

"We really must go. Come on, we have time." He insisted.

The towel wrapped around my waist felt seductively soft. The ambiance of the bathhouse invoked images of exotic decadence. Sitting in a steam- filled room, wasn't something I'd imagined doing on our sightseeing adventure.

"What do you think Warner? Do you feel relaxed?" Dauncey asked, reclining.

I'd never been surrounded by so much naked flesh. Americans had few inhibitions when it came to their bodies. I wondered if the patrons in the Turkish baths back home paraded around without towels. Rather than feeling relaxed, I felt uneasy with the amount of attention I was receiving, and avoided looking at faces, or making eye contact. Streams of perspiration ran down my abdomen, trailing the line of hair to the matt below. Dauncey and Kersley smiled at each other.

"It's a wonder Oscar hasn't introduced you to the baths in London. You've a fine body, Warner." Kersley said.

I repositioned the towel.

"I think I've had enough. When are we leaving?" I asked.

Dauncey looked annoyed.

"Relax, we deserve some time to ourselves." He replied.

"Well, I'm off to find my clothes." I told them, standing up.

As I walked away, Dauncey pulled the towel away, exposing my manhood.

"That's not funny chaps." I said, angrily seizing it back.

Dauncey and Kersley's eyes were fixed on my groin.

"Behold, the source of Mary Eastlake's infatuation." Kersley laughed.

I left to find my clothes. Kersley's comments about Mary, showed there were others who knew of our liaisons. Had Barrett become aware of the relationship also? I preferred not to think of the consequences. Eventually, Kersley and Dauncey emerged from the Bath house, and we finished our sightseeing.

***

Mary was staying at the Hotel Dam in Union Square. The walk to her hotel gave me time to gather thoughts about our situation. As I crossed the street, Barrett exited, and entered a hansom cab. He stared, as it drove away.

Barrett's expression left little doubt he knew the reason behind my visit. Rather than fearing the worst, I was relieved. As a vital component of the tour, it was too late to replace me with another stagehand unfamiliar with the technical workings of Godwin's sets. Barrett was forced to control his actions, in order to preserve the integrity of the whole production. Professionally, he needed me, privately he despised me. He had the profession I longed for, but I had Mary. My visit only confirmed what he must have suspected. The reason behind the change in Mary's affections was clear, and I wondered how the next chapter would play out.

The company left New York for Boston the next day. Barrett became infuriated after a review compared his acting style to

Henry Irving, and a critic wrote of his constant posing. Others noted his short stature, ridiculing the platform shoes he used to gain height. News of his wife's ill health and the problems with Mary, contributed to his volatile outbursts. He watched me quietly. This was disconcerting, and I felt sure he was waiting for a chance to strike. Vengeance was a common theme in his productions, and I soon discovered how entrenched this emotion was in his psyche.

***

The train journey from New York to Boston allowed time to ponder my future, and what lay ahead after leaving the company. At the Globe theatre in Boston, and the Columbia theatre in Chicago, we played to full houses. In March, we arrived in Philadelphia, where I met the poet, Walt Whitman. Dauncey and Kersley travelled to his home to collect him. Kersley worshipped the great poet, attending to his every wish. I was introduced to this icon of American literature after a performance of 'Clito,'. Prior to my introduction, they'd met Barrett in his dressing room. The old poet clutched a signed photograph of the actor by his side. From his appearance, one could be forgiven for believing the man had fallen on hard times. His clothing was basic, and needed washing, and his withered face was hidden by a white beard and bushy eyebrows. The ancient eyes surveyed me.

"This is Mr. Louis Warner, our capable stagehand and sometimes friend." Dauncey announced.

I acknowledged the greeting, holding the withered hand. Before I could make any assessment, the cold and bony appendage was drawn back. Perhaps Kersley told him of my interest in palmistry.

"Why is it, so many fine specimens of humanity are to be found in the theatre?" The poet asked, wistfully.

"I see you've taken a sample away with you." I answered, looking at the photograph of Barrett.

"Oh yes. Mr. Barrett's star brightened my day."

Our elderly guest was clearly captivated by Barrett's performance.

Holding the photograph up, he edged closer to me.

"I will take home a piece of magic from today, and ponder on the vigour and frailty of one's age." He said, with a smile.

"Mr. Barrett does have a charismatic aura about him. Many have fallen victim to it." I replied, without revealing my malice.

Whitman looked intense.

"Beauty must be tempered with intelligence and poetry." He declared.

"I agree. The writing of poetry interests me greatly." I replied.

"You're wise my boy, to understand the importance of this, for someone like yourself."

Whitman's eyes grew lively, and he began to recite some of his poetry.

"Stop this day and night with me and you shall possess the origin of all poems,

You shall possess the good of the earth and the sun

You shall no longer take things at second or third hand, nor look through the eyes of the dead, nor feed on the spectres in books,

You shall not look through my eyes either, nor take things from me,

You shall listen to all sides and filter them from yourself."

"Wonderful words Mr. Whitman, you've inspired me, thank you." I told him.

That evening I drifted off to sleep feeling calm and centred.

I published my book of poetry 'If we only knew' in 1895. The memory of the meeting with Walt Whitman motivated me to write it, fulfilling a literary dream.

***

In April we returned to New York to finish the tour. The plays performed in America were Othello, Hamlet, Clito, Claudian, Lady of Lyons, Hoodman Blind, Chatterton and The Miser. Avoiding contact with Barrett for the last weeks of the tour, kept tensions to a minimum, as things were far from resolved.

Barrett's play, 'Claudian', was the last performance of the tour. It enabled him to wear a short tunic exposing his muscular legs, providing the opportunities for the poses he loved. The execution of the earthquake scene was a theatrical triumph, with the scenery collapsing around Barrett and the audience riveted in suspense. Eventually, he rises from the ruins like a God, revelling in the applause and adoration. On the final night, I planned to rob him of those accolades by rigging the scenery to fall directly on him. Although the set was substantial in size, there were smaller pieces which posed little risk, and the only injury would be to his pride. I hadn't told Mary of the plan.

The house lights faded as Act II Scene III began. Mary entered as Almida the daughter of Alcares a wealthy farmer. Barrett as Claudian, is infatuated with her. If he persists in his love, the hermit seer of the waste prophesized the relationship would end in doom. Almida continues to profess her love for Claudian, who after some hesitancy, gives way. In his speech, he ceases to yearn for death, and prays only to live for Almida and love her. Barrett relishes the scene, playing with Mary's emotions. The pain in Mary's eyes convinced me to carry out the plan. From the wings, I waited behind a column. After Barrett's speech, he cast a hostile glance at Mary, prompting her to launch into an unscripted monologue, changing her character's intent. Almida comes to her senses, realizing she must end the love. Departing from the original script, she's aware of the prophesy of doom which will follow, if the relationship continues. Barrett is visibly furious after Mary's covert message. He's been denied love by Almida, and his leading lady, in front of an audience. Both Almida and Mary are no longer under his spell. Despite Mary's departure from the script fracturing his ego, Barrett continued with the scene clasping her in his arms. Instead of holding her lovingly as rehearsed, he grabbed her roughly, and began squeezing her wrists.

Mary stood on Barrett's foot with hard sandals, pulling away from him. Abandoning the original plan of sending smaller pieces at Barrett, I positioned myself behind a huge column. Usually, the column is pushed to fall away from Barrett during the scene, but that night, Mary's distress caused me to aim it directly at him. Mary screamed as the column fell on Barrett knocking him to the stage where he lay stunned amongst the devastation. The audience were enthralled, unaware the screams and terrified looks were real. Visibly shaken, Barrett continued the play until the end. The reviews made no mention of the actor's facial bruising when taking his farewell bows, or the marks on Mary's wrists.

This dramatic scenario ended my time with the Wilson Barrett Company. I'd never work with the man again. A return passage to London was booked for the following week, and my wages were finalized by Dauncey. I planned to visit Mary the next day.

***

When I enquired at Mary's hotel, I was told the actors had left for a tour of the Statue of Liberty. The event had been specially arranged for Barrett and his company, to publicize its opening. Not wanting to miss this rare opportunity, I hastened to the pier, as the ferry was about to depart. The actors were aboard when I arrived. Daucey, Kersley were at the stern of the vessel, and Barrett was having a photograph taken at the bow. Mary was with Henry Cooper-Cliffe and the young Belmore girls. Walking to the gangway, a guard stopped me.

"Can I help you sir?" He asked.

"Terribly sorry I'm late. I'm part of the Barrett Company." I replied.

The guard waved me aboard. Daucey was the first to see me, and was soon at my side.

"Well, hello. You're a brave one turning up here after last night." He said.

Kersley joined us.

"If it isn't Louis. We thought you'd left already." He laughed.

The rest of the company looked fearful after noticing me. Whispering to each other, they turned their attention towards the front of the boat where Barrett was occupied.

Mary made her way to me.

"Louis, what are you doing here? Wilson is furious about last night. He had to apply copious amounts of makeup this morning to hide the bruising. You must get off the boat. I dread to think what he'll do if he finds you here." She begged.

I looked at her tenderly. The boat's lines were set free and we pulled away from the wharf.

"I can't go back now. Are you alright? I couldn't help my actions last night after I saw what he did to you." I explained.

Mary became irritated.

"I've told you before, I can look after myself. Do you realize that column almost hit me?" She said, angrily.

Surprised at Mary's attitude, I moved away.

"I'll be on the other side of the ferry keeping out of trouble." I replied.

As we approached the Statue, reflective shafts of sunlight forced me to shade my eyes from its beauty. It was another omen I chose to ignore.

After the ferry docked on the island, I waited until all the passengers disembarked. The Barrett group was led away to a lecture on the history of the project. Staying well clear of the group, I heard the guide explain the 162 steps inside to the crown. Exhausted from performing, most of the actors chose not to make the climb. Barrett declared he was going up with Mary. Protesting strongly, she turned to walk away with the rest of the company. Barrett grabbed her by the arm and pulled her towards the statue.

"Come now Mary, we don't want a scene with all the press here." He muttered.

"Can't you leave me alone? Haven't you done enough to ruin my life?" She cried.

Mary was too exhausted to fight, and they entered the base of the statue. Having observed the altercation, I followed. There were no other climbers at the time.

Mary continued protesting.

"Must you always have your own way. I'm tired. I don't want to climb all the way to the top." She implored him.

The statue's double helix staircase was designed for people to go up one way, and down the other.

Climbing, Barrett's voice became more frustrated with Mary.

"You won't ever make a fool of me on stage again." He shouted.

There was fear in Mary's words as she struggled with Barrett.

"Stop. What do you mean? I'm not going any further, do you hear?" She shouted.

"Oh yes you are Almida. You do love me, and you will follow me." He answered.

Mary began whimpering.

"Wilson, I'm not Almida. I'm Mary, your leading lady, and mother of your child." She screamed.

The words cut like swords. What was I hearing? Mary had a child with Barrett?

"How easily you could fall from this staircase Mary. A tragic accident. Your end would be an end to all my suffering and torment. "He cried.

Hearing the ominous words, I rushed up the staircase to rescue her from the hands of a madman. Aware of other footsteps, Mary resumed her struggle.

"Help, please help someone." She shouted.

Barrett wrestled with Mary, trying to silence the screams by covering her mouth.

Shocked by my presence, his face contorted into an explosive rage.

"Not you. Go away you bastard." He seethed.

"Let her go." I demanded.

"Never, she's mine, for as long as I've need of her. She may have been distracted by a pretty boy for a while, but our souls are intertwined by forces you've no concept of. It's the love one great actor has for another. Something you don't understand, for you are neither an actor, nor great. You work in the shadows with the other talentless hopefuls, waiting for your time to strike. Let me tell you Warner, the theatre is full of snakes like you. Over the years I've learnt to control them all." He warned.

"Here is one serpent you'll never restrain." I shouted, lunging forward to grab Mary.

Wrestling Barrett, Mary lost her balance and fell over the side of the staircase. She grasped the railing, while her legs searched for a footing.

"Wilson, please save me, I love you, I'm sorry." Mary screamed.

We both grabbed for her arms, but Mary's gaze was fixed on Barrett, and it was his hands she reached for.

After lifting her onto the staircase, she collapsed into his arms. Barrett kissed her lips passionately, begging forgiveness. Mary returned the affection, and I left them. Had she been in love with Barrett all those weeks we were together? I felt used and betrayed, knowing I'd been a frivolous diversion. The young boy she visited at her cousins' home, was actually her son. By the time I reached the bottom of the staircase, the whole story was clear to me. Daucey and Kersley were making their way to the statue after contemplating the climb after all.

"Louis, you look startled. I heard the view was something extraordinary." Kersley commented.

"Yes, everything up there is clear now." I replied.

Two days later, I passed Liberty on the return voyage to England. The clouds filtered the rising sun, and there were no rays to blind me. The events inside the confines of her metal skirt were still raw. I'd never trust my eyes with my heart again.

***

It was strange to be back in London without a home to return to, or loving family to welcome me. Having limited funds, a boarding house in the East end proved acceptable. After paying the landlady, an exploration of the area began. Along Whitechapel Road, numerous shops and residences lined the street, and in the back lanes, the inhabitants looked destitute. I was approached numerous times by unwashed children in their rags. This was the darker side of London, and I realized how fortunate I'd been to find decent places to live in the past. I contemplated calling on Frank Miles, but the memory of his strangeness was fresh. Believing my circumstances would improve after finding employment, I put the idea from my mind.

Over the next few weeks, palmistry books helped occupy my time. I continued studying the numerous lines and interpretations of Heron Allen's book. Barrett's vindictive streak infiltrated the theatrical circles of London, and I was turned away from every establishment visited. The actor used the events of the American tour to blacken my name, and his reference was poisonous.

Finances were low, and many times money was offered by those wanting physical gratification. I avoided walking in areas where desperate men and women sold their bodies for cash. After one of these encounters, I returned to Tite Street to visit Frank, hoping to find him in a better frame of mind. The doorway looked dirty and neglected, but desperation prevented me from turning away, and I knocked. After a short while the door partially opened.

"Who is it? What do you want?" Frank asked, suspiciously.

"Frank, it's Louis Warner." I replied.

Silence.

"Frank are you alright?" I asked.

Sobbing, he slowly opened the door. Frank was a shadow of his former self. The hair was long and unwashed, his face drawn and unshaven. He wore a flimsy night shirt, and was bare footed.

"Louis my boy, won't you come in?" He asked, pensively.

Frank's demeanour was weak and fragile.

"I was just passing and wondered if I might call on you."

Garbage filled the salon. Paints and brushes were thrown over furniture and uneaten food littered the Persian carpets. Something was wrong with Frank. His eyes rested on me, and tears formed.

"You are still as lovely as I remember Louis. I was wrong though. Beauty doesn't last forever. Some things cannot be preserved." He declared.

"What's happened to you? Are you ill? Do you need help?" I asked.

"Yes, I'm sick. Tired of it all. I've lost my talent and can no longer capture beauty. My creations are morbid and sinister. Louis, you're the palmist. Are these not the hands of a diabolical creature? They have created a vision of evil. I will show you." He shouted.

Frank leapt up and seized a draped painting from an easel in the corner of the room. Keeping it covered, he brought it to me.

"Unveil the work, Louis. See what I've done." He demanded.

Pulling the cloth away, my once glorious portrait was revealed. Frank's macabre reworking of the painting shocked me. The new image displayed a twisted and deformed nose, lips blistered with sores, matted hair, and sallow skin covered in festering lesions. What possessed Frank to hideously transform the painting?

"See the real you, Louis. Behold your soul. "He laughed, hysterically.

Frank's eyes rolled back, clearly insane, his lunatic behaviour sent me rushing out, never to return. Walking down Tite street I passed Oscar's home, but couldn't face him after the encounter with Frank. He would have heard the gossip regarding the Barrett Company and the events in America. After all his help, I foolishly believed I'd let him down.

***

The following week I crossed paths with John Taylor, who worked with me backstage at the Princess theatre. I was walking down Shaftesbury Avenue contemplating my next move when he approached me.

"Hello Louis." He smiled.

"Well, hello John. How are things with you?" I asked.

It was a relief to talk with someone who knew me. I'd been walking in silence, surrounded by strangers for days.

"Things are going well at the moment. What about you Louis? Are you working?" He asked, tentatively.

John's expression told me he knew about the issues with Barrett.

"I've been trying. Nothing has come up so far." I replied, solemnly.

"Yes, not surprising. I heard about your dramas with Barrett. You did something many of us wished we'd done. Have you heard his wife just died and he's taken time off? I'm working at the new Theatre Royal in Exeter outside of London. They're producing Barrett's favourite play, 'Romany Rye." He told me.

Death removed the main obstacle to Mary's ambition of becoming Barrett's wife. I refused to think about it, keeping my thoughts focused on employment. Would Barrett's negative press extend to the areas outside of London?

"Is there anything there for me?" I asked, hopefully.

"There could be. Come by the theatre, and we can talk to the stage Manager." John replied, encouragingly.

The chance meeting gave me something to look forward to. Exeter was a distance from London, and Barrett's venomous poison may not have reached the heart of this country village.

***

It was the afternoon of September 5th when I entered the impressive Theatre Royal in Exeter. The new theatre was rebuilt after the former building was destroyed by fire. Entering through the backstage, I met up with John, who told me we needed to see James Sidney. James was a scenic designer by trade, and was given the position of stage manager due to a staff shortage. He was clearly uncomfortable with the responsibility, strutting about the wings shouting at workers when we approached him.

"James, this is Louis Warner. He's an experienced stagehand, and was hoping to pick up some work." John explained.

The flustered stage manager cast his eyes over me.

"Oh Mr. Warner, I'm sorry. Your reputation precedes you. I've enough stress with this production without inviting more onboard." He told us, walking away without a backward glance.

John placed a comforting hand on my shoulder.

"Rude pig. I'm sorry Louis. James has let power go to his head. He was a nicer person when he painted trees and clouds." He said, concerned.

"It seems there's no limit to Barrett's influence." I sighed, deflated.

"I'm upset you've made your way here from London only to be disappointed. Come back later when the play starts, and I'll let you in. You can stay at my lodgings tonight after the show." He told me.

Crossing the street to the theatre, the town clock struck 10pm. The backstage door was manned by a worker who'd been told to look out for me. As the second half of 'Romany Rye' played out, I found John busy at work with the flies.

"Louis, we could've used you here tonight. An extra pair of hands would've been welcomed. We've made a few blunders already, but the crowd doesn't seem to mind. I'm not looking forward to explaining it to James later." He smiled.

At the front of the wings, I peered out at the audience who were engrossed in a scene with the actor Fred Moulliott. The pit and dress circles were full, and the upper galleries were also well stacked with patrons. The backstage area was congested with scenic cloths and flats not related to 'Romany Rye', and the air was thick with the smell of drying paint.

"What are all these other cloths John?" I asked.

"James has been working on them for the pantomime performances. It's hard enough to move around here as it is, without all this extra scenery. Can you help me with this next scene drop coming up?"

I nodded, asking what came down next. John pointed to a cloth, moving the mechanism to release it, and muttered something.

"What's the matter?" I whispered.

"Damn thing is stuck. Go to the edge of the cloth and give it a tug. See if it moves." He told me.

Up a ladder and into the flies, I grabbed the scene cloth. It had been hung close to a sixty-burner gas batten, and this would never have been allowed in the theatres I'd worked in. I hesitated, concerned by what I'd seen.

"Come on Louis, give it a pull. The scene is coming up." John implored me.

I pulled on the edge of the cloth.

"Not releasing." I told him.

John looked frantic.

"Pull it at an angle instead of straight down, and that might free it."

Reluctantly, I pulled the cloth backwards a few times to no avail.

"Forward, pull it forward." John insisted.

Leaning toward the front of the stage, the cloth partially released. It now hung at an angle close to the gas flames. The edge of the cloth caught alight and erupted into a sheet of orange before our eyes. I stood on the ladder, paralysed by the unfolding horror. No words passed between John and myself as the fire took hold. Panic set in as it spread fire to the other cloths, erupting into an overhead inferno. The actors who'd finished their scene, were shocked when they came backstage and ran to the back of the building. John chose to lower the act drop hoping to contain the flames. It jammed about two feet above the stage floor, leaving Moulliot wondering what was happening. Embarrassed by the situation, he stormed off the stage, leaving the audience roaring with laughter, ignorant of the catastrophe unfolding behind the drop curtain. The orchestra began a musical interlude, and for a moment I imagined all would be well, and people would calmly make their way out of the theatre before the flames reached them. At the back of the stage, other crew members panicked around the rear doors as John shouted to keep the area closed off, preventing a draught to feed the flames. Moulliot and others ignored his pleas, and flung the doors wide open. My last vision of John, was his look of terror when the doors were unlocked. The act curtain billowed out like a sail over the audience revealing the hellish scene behind, and the screams of terror were immediate. I joined the other escapees on the street and never saw John again. Help arrived swiftly in the form of ladders to the dressing room windows, and all the actors were saved.

The scene at the front of the theatre was indescribable. Those trapped threw themselves off balconies to escape the intense heat, and bystanders were sickened by the sound of bodies hitting the pavement. The torrents of water from the fire trucks did little to ease the ferocity, and in the end, countless people were crushed in the panic, dying before the flames reached them. It's ironic, this calamitous theatrical disaster was caused by the hands which write this tragic story.

***

The following weeks after Exeter were vague. I returned to Whitechapel and tried to put the awful scenes from my mind. Inevitably, they returned, especially at night.

A wave of desperate people arrived in the East end as employment prospects in the countryside vanished. Crime increased, and it became dangerous to move about after dark. One evening in December, I left my room for fear of going mad. Walking along the narrow streets around Whitechapel, young women wanted to sell their charms. Despondent face after face appealed for help. Could their predicament be any worse than mine? The outstretched hands, allowed me to analyse their owners based on my studies, with many classified as pointed. This type of hand was intuitive in nature, and gave the owner skills to see into someone's heart. Choosing the wrong person to go with, could end in disaster for these girls. Perhaps that's why the survivors with this type of hand still worked the streets.

"Sir, could you spare something for a nice time?" A young

woman asked.

The pleas were met with sorrowful glances, and I was never asked a second time. Perhaps one hungry soul recognizes the yearning for food in another. Anonymous cloaked figures moved amongst the dark buildings. High born gentlemen walked the same paths as the low born criminals in search of gratification. That Winter's night I encountered one of those shadowy forms, after following a kitten down a laneway. I'd been compelled to find its mother, after hearing the mournful cries. The rough, uneven surface made it difficult to walk in the darkness, with the only light coming from a faraway window. Not a soul was to be seen, and the buildings were silent. The courtyard was cold and eerie, and the cries of the kitten became louder.

"Have you lost your cat?" asked an educated voice from the darkness.

Out of the blackness a man emerged, holding the kitten in one hand and a silver tipped cane in the other. An ebony cloak concealed the strange figure, wearing a large hat, and a scarf wrapped around his mouth and nose disguised his features. The narrow eyes glistened in the lamplight.

"No. It's not my cat." I informed him.

There was no reply from the cultured gentleman. He dropped his cane to the ground and made no attempt to pick it up, expecting me to retrieve it. Every bone in my body warned against shifting my gaze from his eyes. Eventually, he realized I wasn't going to recover it. Bending down he grabbed the stick, revealing the ungloved hand of evil. A large clubbed thumb wrapped around the silver head of the cane, showed the homicidal traits of its owner. Thick spatulate fingers told of the impulsive, aggressive nature of the individual. My eyes met those of a murderer, who despite his affluent appearance, displayed the hands of depravity. This was a person destined to satisfy an insidious lust for extinguishing life, and his eyes widened in expectation of a kill. The kitten let out an unholy screech clawing its way to freedom, and the silver flash of a blade sent me following. Over the next few months terrible murders were committed in the area. I believe I encountered 'Jack the ripper' that night in Whitechapel. The infamous madman was waiting in the shadows for his next victim, and I consider myself fortunate to have escaped the individual responsible for some of London's worst crimes.

***

On 13th November, tempers erupted in Trafalgar square. It became known as 'Bloody Sunday, 'when the frustrated unemployed and key figures from the social democratic league, clashed with police at a demonstration for the release of the MP William Obrien. The member of parliament was imprisoned for incitement, resulting from an incident during the Irish Land War. Finding myself surrounded by fellow Irishmen at the protest was strange. My absence from the emerald shores, made it difficult for me to relate to the people. The savagery of the altercation was frightening. The Irish with their Shillelagh clubs clashed with the police and their batons, resulting in bloody faces and broken limbs. Annie Besant, a key figure in the theosophical society, spoke out demanding to be arrested. William Morris, a designer acquaintance of Oscar, was another participant. While innocently crossing the street, an officer raised his blood-stained baton to strike me. The world was chaotic, and I began to lose hope it would ever improve.

The cold snow drove the East Enders indoors to wallow in their desperation. My finances were at an end, and the pangs of hunger were growing stronger. An inner voice forced me outdoors as the new year approached. I returned to the beautiful streets of the West End, catching a glimpse of my sad reflection in the festive shop windows. A tear ran down my cheek as I imagined someone calling my name.

"Louis, Louis Warner. It is you, isn't it?" The young man asked.

Turning from the window, I was greeted by the concerned face of someone I'd met four years before. When he put his gloved hand into mine, I knew it wasn't an illusion.

"Robert Hichens. I met you at Hamilton Aide's a few years ago." He explained.

"Oh yes Robert, how are you?" I replied, ashamed at my state of affairs.

"I'm well thank you. And yourself?" He asked, with a worried look after noticing my wet cheek.

I don't recall how the meeting progressed, but I do remember breaking down during our conversation, and Robert inviting me back to his home at Phillimore Place in Kensington. Robert was an intuitive soul, and before long, I was eating a meal of soup, fresh bread and enlightening him on my predicament. His kind offer of food and a place to stay gave me the incentive to carry on. By the time the new year arrived, I was a changed man. Looking back to those terrible weeks at the end of 1887, I realize what a heaven-sent gift Robert Hichens was. I believe he was directed to me by a higher power who knew of my desperate situation, as no two souls meet without some purpose. Fleeting exchanges occur daily, and for the most part we are unaware of their significance. Nothing occurs separated from the greater plan.

As the weeks passed, traits arising from our common zodiacal sign of Scorpio became apparent. We talked for hours about the mysteries of life and human nature. We delved into unknown corners of our existence and those forbidden places religion dictates are evil. These are the worlds a Scorpion finds himself drawn to. We penned thoughts in poems and song, and soothed our souls from a shared pain. How gratifying it was to have a fellow companion to confide in, and explore the unanswered questions of our time. In our small apartment, we created our own microcosm of peace and creativity, but it was never meant to last. As time passed, Robert's attitude towards his studies shifted. He acknowledged he was musical, but not a musician. There was a difference. His creative inspirations were driven by words, rather than notes of music.

In order to study at the London School of Journalism, Robert needed his father's approval. Once again, he found himself with a frustrated parent, who engaged him in a heated interrogation. Finally, his father agreed to finance the new career path. I on the other hand, needed to find work. A stagehand position at Terry's Theatre, broke the spell cast by Barrett.

By the Spring of '88 Robert was attending his Journalism School during the day, while I worked nights at the theatre. The time we spent together diminished considerably, but we continued to share our daily experiences in those precious hours when together. Robert was at last on the right path, and my ambition to act was unchanged. The uncertainty of a dramatic career weighed heavily on my decisions, as the recent taste of poverty was fresh. Working at Terry's Theatre gave me security, allowing me to plan the next move. The stage manager William Nelson, suggested Ben Greet's Acting School, and soon after, I began my formal training. William's fiancé Edith, was currently attending and spoke highly of the place. Elocution and speech classes modified my Irish accent for Shakespearean performances. Robert was subjected to extracts from Hamlet and Macbeth, while I reviewed his short stories and pieces of journalistic prose. We discussed the characters encountered during our work and studies. Edith's misplaced sexual advances led to uncomfortable situations. Robert considering the woman emotionally unstable, warning me to avoid her at all costs. Future events confirmed his suspicions.

***

Chapter Three

(1889-1890)

Gossip about the School of Journalism and its principal David Anderson, kept us entertained for the next twelve months. Students regularly contributed to its periodical *'Mistress and Maid,'* and this encouraged Robert to write numerous fictional pieces. Reading his work inspired me to write my own short stories. In September, I finished my studies with the *'Ben Greet Acting School'*, and felt confident speaking to an audience. After Edith Nelson's obsession became intolerable, I left Terry's theatre. Changing the class time with Ben Greet solved the problem of meeting her there, but not at the theatre. The visits to William gave her an excuse to approach me.

I enjoyed conversing with Edith when we first met. She claimed interest in the spiritual side of life, and we spoke comfortably in those early days. Before long, the true nature of the woman revealed itself. After learning of my imminent departure, she cornered me backstage one evening.

"You can't leave after all we've meant to each other. We are bonded by time. In our previous lives in ancient Egypt, you were my lover. We must continue the connection." She protested.

"Edith, you're delusional. Come to your senses. If you expect me to believe such a story, you're madder than I thought. You forget, I've observed your hands, and I'm not easily manipulated by those who use esoteric rhetoric to gain power over others." I told her, angrily.

Edith's face darkened, and her fingers retracted like spider's legs when attacked.

"I realize your mastery is greater than mine. It won't stop me from completing the karmic debt we share with each other." She cried.

"My spiritual accounts owe you nothing Edith." I told her, walking away.

***

It was important to leave Terry's theatre without any issues. I never enlightened William on the escapades of his fiancé. Who knows what Edith's explanation to her betrothed would have been had I told him. I couldn't risk another bad referral. A new production at the Drury Lane theatre promised work, but the manager Augustus Harris, wasn't able to offer anything. As I left by the backstage door, a young stagehand peered out from behind a prop.

"Looking for work, are you?" He smiled, moving closer.

As his intensely blue eyes scanned my body, I made my own observations. The fair hair and complexion gave him a youthful appearance. The hands were large and artistic in type, and the spatulate fingers indicated a dynamic creativity. A raw sensuality radiated from his athletic frame. His Irish accent was unmistakable.

"Yes. I've just met with Mr. Harris." I replied.

"How did that go?" He asked, smiling wider.

"Nothing at present. Something could change in the future."

"You interested in other work? I might be able to help, if you are. I couldn't survive on theatre work alone. Take this card and come by when you can. The name is John Saul."

"Louis Warner." I replied, taking the card.

"Pleased to know you, Louis." He grinned.

"What's the nature of the work?" I asked.

"Well, that depends. It's with the General Post Office delivering messages. I've another business associated with the GPO. It may be of interest to you." He explained.

A lustful look entered John's eyes. A hand adjusted the growing bulge in his trousers. I pretended to be unaware of it.

"Thank you, John. I'll think on it, and let you know if I'm interested." I told him, exiting.

"You won't be regretting your decision." He yelled.

***

Driven by intense curiosity, I arrived at the door of 19 Cleveland Street a few days later. The house was unremarkable, nestled in a narrow throughfare amongst rows of houses and shops. Before I could knock, the door was opened by gentleman on his way out.

"Are you going in?" He asked, holding the door ajar.

"Thank you, yes." I replied.

The door closed and the pungent smell of burning incense filled my nose. The walls of the long hallway were decorated with pre-Raphaelite art, dimly lit with exotic lamps. At the end of the passage, a large room sectioned into compartments with heavy velvet curtains appeared, and the muffled conversations of male voices could be heard. The atmosphere made me uncomfortable, and as I turned to leave, a curtain was drawn back.

"Well, hello my friend. I'm glad you stopped by."

It was John Saul. Behind him, an embarrassed gentleman continued dressing.

"Come this way, Louis. It was Louis, wasn't it? Not that names matter here." He laughed.

Suspiciously, I followed. All was becoming clear. John was working as a rent boy or a professional 'Mary Ann.' Oscar used the term once, enlightening me on its meaning. The only difference between John and the other 'Mary Anns' I'd encountered in Whitechapel, was the location and richness of décor. I stopped following John.

"I thought I'd call in and talk about the work. I'll be honest with you John. I'm not interested." I told him, frustrated I'd wasted time.

"That's a shame. Maybe you'll change your mind after I tell you more? A day's pay here is equal to a month at the theatre, and the work is easy and stress free. I meet all kinds of people. You'd be surprised the people I know." He told me smugly.

"I wouldn't be at all surprised by your acquaintances John. I'm aware how easily the rich and powerful can be seduced with certain favours. Your lifestyle doesn't interest me, no matter how much you earn. There is no need to sell my body; I've other things people will pay for." I declared.

I left John and his Cleveland Street establishment. In my view, there was nothing more degrading than a 'Mary Ann'. I would rather starve to death than sell someone the right to use my body for their own pleasure. At the end of the street, fate decided Oscar and I should cross paths.

"Louis, my boy, how are you? Fancy seeing you in this part of town. What are you up to?" He asked.

"Hello Oscar. Just been, seen, met." Surprised, I stumbled over the words.

Oscar looked down the street towards John's establishment and smiled.

"Well, no matter. It's good to see you. Only yesterday you were in my thoughts. I was wondering how you've been getting on since we last met. I had the best intentions of catching up with you, but it's difficult to know where you are these days. Few people have seen you since you left Barrett. Anyway, working at 'Women's world' has kept me busy. He told me.

"Women's World. Are you writing for them?" I asked.

"I'm the editor my boy. You are out of touch. Where have you been hiding anyway? "He asked.

"I've a friend studying at the London School of journalism. We share a flat together in Kensington. Do you think he might call on you at your office and discuss any work for your magazine?" I asked, cheekily.

Oscar looked at me intently.

"Oh, the London school of Journalism, yes. I have heard of the establishment. Well of course he may call. What about yourself Louis? Where are you working?"

"I'm unemployed at present. I've been working at Terry's theatre, but that finished last week." I told him.

"Is that nasty Barrett fellow still causing you grief?" He asked, flicking his hair.

"The mere mention of his name." I stopped myself.

"So, you are a free agent at present?" Oscar put his hand on my shoulder.

"Yes. I've been occupying myself with palmistry studies. I've completed acting classes with Ben Greet since we last saw each other." I informed him.

"Elocution, that's it. I knew there was something different about you. You are becoming quite the gentleman Louis. I've a proposition for you. Would you like to accompany me as an assistant over the next few weeks? I'm off to Paris for the World Exposition." He explained.

"The World Exposition. What an opportunity. I accept."

After leaving Oscar, I headed to Piccadilly Circus to meet Robert. The Shaftesbury Avenue café where he sat drinking coffee, was almost empty.

"Robert, you'll never guess who I bumped into today. Oscar Wilde. Did you know he's the editor of 'A woman's world.' After singing your praises, he agreed to meet with you."

Robert closed the book he was reading.

"You seem to frequently cross paths with Mr. Wilde. What would the mystics say about it?" He asked, suspiciously.

"I expect they would say it was a lucky break. Let's not get too esoteric about things Robert. I've something else to tell you. He's asked me to the Paris world's fair as his assistant." I told him, excitedly.

"As his assistant? A wonderful offer. Are you going?" He asked.

"What do you mean am I going? Of course, I'm going." I answered.

"How long will you be away?" Robert asked, pensively.

"I'm not quite sure. It will be a couple of weeks, I imagine. Have you heard about the Exposition? There's much to see."

"Yes. I've been told." He replied, solemnly.

Robert finished his coffee and we left. Something was troubling him. As we walked in awkward silence, a laugh erupted from behind us.

"Fancy meeting you two." The voice chuckled.

It was John Saul.

"My old friend Robert, and my new acquaintance, Louis. Here together." He grinned.

Robert and I exchanged guilty looks.

"John. It's been some time. You've met my friend Louis then?" Robert asked, glaring at me.

"Oh yes. We saw each other this morning." He smirked.

John mischievously let Robert believe his suspicions were warranted. I clarified the situation.

"I met John the other day at Drury Lane theatre. After finding nothing available backstage, he offered me a job at his other place of employment. Today I visited the other establishment. I found the position unsuitable, and left." I smiled.

John's grin disappeared. It was my turn to unravel the truth about Robert's connection.

"What about you Robert? How is it you know John?" I asked.

"John and I met a few years ago, when I first came to London." He explained.

"It seems like yesterday." John smiled.

Robert farewelled the cocky 'Mary Ann'', and we headed home to Phillimore Place. Later that evening, he explained the connection to John. After hearing of Robert's literary skills, the rent boy wanted help writing an erotic novel based on his life as a male prostitute. After reviewing the content, Robert declined the offer. I never did find out the circumstances of their initial meeting.

***

"This way please. All aboard." Shouted the deckhand.

In September 1889, our barge departed for France. According to Oscar, a smaller vessel with less people would make for an entertaining passage. We disembarked at Dieppe on the coast, and boarded a coach to Paris. The spectacle of the French capital adorned for the World Exposition was something to behold. It was unlike anything I'd seen. The wide avenues, lined with trees and flowers provided a network for carriages carrying visitors from all over the world. In cafes, artists and poets sat drinking their coffees and talking with foreigners. Oscar applauded as the Eiffel tower came into view.

"Wonderful. Can you see Louis? Gustav Eiffel's remarkable

design. Much has changed since I was last here." Oscar said, waving a hand across the skyline.

This wasn't his first trip to Paris. Familiar with its sights and hidden gems, he promised to educate me on the delights of France.

"I've seen his framework inside the statue of Liberty." I proudly stated.

"Why of course. For once you have something over me, Louis. Did you make the climb inside?" He asked.

"Yes. An unforgettable experience." I replied, recalling the drama with Barrett and Mary.

"Take note. We are about to come to the Place de la Concorde. Here you will find an Egyptian gem." He declared.

Not far from the banks of the Seine, an obelisk surrounded by ornate lamps and fountains dominated the skyline.

"Amazing. How did they move it?" I asked.

"The piece was removed from its partner in front of the Luxor temple. The other still remains. After years of experience, the French, like the English and Germans, are skilled at transporting artifacts from the ancient world. The obelisks are gathered as symbols of power. Nothing has changed through the centuries."

"I believe the design has a mystical element."

Oscar flicked his hair back.

"Perhaps you're absorbing too much of the esoteric Louis. Art does have a vibrational quality, but to think an artist is conscious of this when he creates a work, seems overly optimistic. We should concentrate on the aesthetic rather than the spiritual value."

As Oscar's assistant, I remained silent. He considered himself the ultimate connoisseur of beauty, and his views on art and design were best left unchallenged. In the past, I'd witnessed the fate of those who disagreed with him.

We arrived at The Grand Hotel Terminus on the Rue Saint Lazare. The opulence of the building was breathtaking. Inside the foyer, guests admired the newly finished hotel. Marble columns complimented the arches of the design, and ornate ironwork divided off sections and provided safety on the various levels. As we climbed the stairs, I became nervous about the sleeping arrangements. A young porter struggled with Oscar's luggage while I insisted on taking my own. Memories of carrying heavy bags at the International Hotel in Bray allowed me to empathize with the boy.

"Thank you. Just put my bag over there." Oscar ordered.

The young Frenchman placed Oscar's belongings beside a double bed.

"Can I take your bag, monsieur?" He asked, smiling.

"No thank you." I replied, with a grin.

Surveying the room, a single bed was made up in another area. Relieved, I placed my bag down beside it.

Oscar and the porter stood smiling.

"Will that be all monsieur?" He asked.

"Yes, thank you." Oscar replied, handing him a coin.

After the porter left, we freshened up and headed to the hotel's elaborate dining area. The sumptuous room sat under a huge skylight. The intricate leadlight design dominated the overhead ceiling, and crystal chandeliers illuminated the rich colour scheme. Large palm filled jardinières softened the timber walls. After we were seated, Oscar surveyed the other patrons. His eyes rested on a corner table where two women sat with a young man of about nineteen.

"A very chic crowd I must say." He whispered.

I ignored Oscar's people watching, noting where his eyes rested.

"This hotel is really something. The French certainly know how to create luxurious spaces." I commented.

"They certainly do." Oscar replied, continuing to observe the table with the young man.

Obviously, the group were from the upper echelons of French society, and the fashionable clothing adorning their slim figures cut a dashing scene. As they laughed and ate, Oscar continued to stare. These were the type of people who interested him. Strong intellectual women may stimulate his mind, but young well-bred men in their tailored outfits tantalized his body. It was comforting to know, the fairer the colouring of the individual, the more attractive they became to Oscar. My dark complexion gave me some degree of protection. Deflecting energy of a sexual nature in Oscar's presence was something I'd mastered. The relationship was one of mutual understanding; our Celtic traits binding us in a common brotherhood. After dinner, we returned to our room. Separate in our thoughts and distant from our desires, we retired.

Our first day at the Exposition did not disappoint. The Eiffel tower dominated the entry area. Here we found the pavilions of Mexico, Venezuela, Chile, Bolivia, and Argentina. We enjoyed partaking in the Spanish delicacies of these countries. We didn't linger, as Oscar was impatient to visit the hall with the art objects. Along the causeway we passed displays from Uruguay and Paraguay, and at the pavilion of India, we indulged in incenses and exotic oils. An old man dressed in white robes sat in the corner watching like an eagle as I moved closer.

"Come Sir. Come sit. Let me read palms for you." He beckoned.

The Indian palm reader offered a chance to investigate an Asian method of divination older than the stars. I didn't hesitate. Oscar was occupied, talking to a dance troupe performing behind a snake charmer. Sitting on a carved bench, I placed my hands on a table engraved with a cobra. The old man studied the lines carefully, his eyes widening as he delved deeper. What information was he uncovering? My impatience grew, and after a time he spoke.

"I am sorry, I cannot read your hands." He told me.

"What do you mean? Why can't you read them?" I asked, stunned.

His black eyes stared.

"I am sorry. For some, it is forbidden." He replied.

"Forbidden? By who? Why can't you tell me what you see?" I asked, frustrated.

My expectations were crushed.

"Why won't you tell me?" I continued.

The Indian leaned forward and whispered.

"Do not be unhappy my friend. We have been blessed with the same power. It is a gift from the Gods and must be cherished and used for good. Those who use their abilities selfishly are wicked. They make the deities angry." He shouted.

The guru's eyes rolled back exposing the whites, and his mouth dropped open. A woman behind screamed as saliva ran down his jaw. Others came running shouting in Hindi. Pale and shaken, I left to find Oscar, informing him of the events.

"How extraordinary. He divulged nothing of what he saw?" He asked.

"Nothing. He refused to say anything, except a few things about angering the Gods." I replied, indignantly.

"While I conversed with Indian princes, you were having a supernatural experience." He smiled.

"I can do without such incidents. I'm still shaken by it, I have to say."

We continued through the pavilions of Morocco and Egypt, before finding our way to the great hall. Here, we spent the rest of the day marvelling at the latest designs in furniture and accessories. The French clock exhibit was exquisite.

In the evening, we dined at a café off the Bois de Boulogne. The experience of the Indian pavilion was not easily forgotten and the words of the old man played over in my mind.

"Louis, did you hear what I said?" Oscar asked, leaning across the table.

"Sorry Oscar. I'm a little preoccupied." I apologized.

"Was it not a superb day? If only there were an exposition every year." He exclaimed.

"Surely the novelty would wear off." I replied.

"Not for me. What are you thinking about? You are not still fretting over that old Indian, are you?" He asked.

"Well, yes. I'm trying to make sense of it. How often would such a person refuse a paying customer?" I asked, bewildered.

"In that line of work, I would say not too frequently." Oscar joked.

"Exactly. It's puzzling."

"You are puzzling Louis. I'm not at all surprised it happened to you." He announced.

"What do you mean?" I asked.

"You do have a strange effect on people. Vain to deny it. Can I tell you something Louis. You are the inspiration for a story I've just completed."

"Really?" I quizzed.

"The story revolves around an artist and his subject. The sitter for the portrait is a young and incredibly good looking fellow.

All who meet him are charmed by his irresistible combination of intellect and sexuality. Tragically, the artist himself succumbs to the spell." He explained.

"Go on." I told him.

"After the portrait is complete, a flippant remark sets in motion a tragic chain of events."

"What kind of remark?"

"This is where artistic license comes into play." He boasted.

Oscar was interrupted by the waiter.

"Monsieur, may I get you some dessert?" He asked.

"No thank you. I've had quite enough sweetness for today." He replied.

"Pray continue." I demanded.

"The young narcissist falls in love with himself after looking at the portrait. Instead of the painting remaining perfect, he wishes the artwork could age while he forever stays youthful. The devil grants his desire, in return for his soul." He elaborated.

Nervously, Oscar flicked his hair back.

"You do have a macabre imagination at times Oscar. It's an interesting concept." I told him.

"Would you ever make such a pact Louis? Would you sell your soul to retain the power you have over others?" He asked.

"Have you had enough?" I replied.

Oscar froze.

"I mean, of your food. It's late and we should be getting back to the hotel, don't you think?" I continued.

"You've never asked to see my hands? He told me, seriously.

"You've never offered them to me." I replied.

"This seems an opportune time don't you think?"

"Very well. If you're game to hear what secrets lie therein."

"I know my secrets are safe with you Louis." He smiled, placing his hands on the table.

"The difference in your fate line from the left to the right is glaring. The right hand or what we make of our life, ends in a cross. This is an ominous marking. No such marking is found on the left. You alone are responsible for the events which unfold in your destiny. Shall I go on" I asked.

"You are right, Louis. We've another day of adventure tomorrow, and our strength should be conserved." He smiled.

Waiting for a cab, I wondered if Ed Heron-Allen ever read Oscar's palm. I wasn't prepared to ask, as I was still angry about the nature of his latest story.

"You know Oscar, I've been meaning to visit Frank Miles. I've not seen him for some time. I'll make a point of calling on him when we return to London."

My words were met with a cold look.

"I expect you'll find the visit enlightening. You're obviously not aware, Frank no longer resides in Tite Street."

"Oh, where has he moved to?" I asked.

"He was committed to Brislington House Lunatic Asylum two years ago."

We returned to the hotel without further conversation.

Paris continued to provide endless surprises during those final days before we returned to London. The experience of the Exposition was unique as it allowed tourists to travel around the world, savouring the best of different countries. The experience gave me the information to pass myself off as a seasoned traveller.

Back in London, I was eager to return to Phillimore Place.

"Thank you again for giving me this opportunity." I told Oscar before leaving.

"Don't mention it, Louis. I've enjoyed seeing Paris again through your eyes. You must come around for dinner next Tuesday. I'm inviting Ed Heron-Allen as well."

Wanting to surprise Robert by returning unannounced, I opened the door.

"Louis you're back. We have a visitor." He nervously told me.

In the sitting room, a well-dressed gentleman was finishing his tea.

"Louis, this is Mr. Alexander Hood." Robert announced.

There was something familiar about Mr. Hood, and I felt sure I'd seen him somewhere before.

"Pleased to meet you Sir. Louis Warner." I told him shaking his hand.

"Robert has been telling me about your trip to the Paris Exposition with Mr. Wilde. Was it all you'd hoped it would be?" He asked.

"Oh yes, and more. Paris is an amazing city. My head is still reeling from the wonderful experiences." I replied.

"I'm glad. Mr. Wilde must have been an entertaining travel companion?" He smiled looking at Robert.

"Yes, there's never a dull moment. We gathered copious amounts of information for his reviews."

"Robert tells me you are a student of palmistry. You must have a look at my hands some time, if you are agreeable?"

"Yes of course. You'll have to excuse me, as I need to unpack. It's been a pleasure meeting you."

"Of course, my boy, no hurry. Whenever you wish. I must also make haste Robert. Thank you for a delightful afternoon. The conversation as always, was stimulating."

Mr. Hood departed and I began unpacking.

"You must be tired Louis? Do you want to rest for a while?" Robert asked, after seeing his guest out.

"No, I'm not feeling too bad. Tell me about this Mr. Hood fellow?" I asked.

I wanted to know where I'd seen him before? Robert put coal on the fire, and we relaxed into the armchairs.

"Alexander Hood is the 5th Duke of Bronte, and is well connected. His influence extends to the Royal family."

"What's your connection with him?" I asked.

"I've known him for some time. It was Alexander who introduced me to John Saul." He grinned.

"I see. No further explanation required. What was he doing here today?"

"While you were away, John and his associates at Cleveland Street have become embroiled in a scandal."

"Really, what's happened?" I asked.

"One of the telegraph boys exposed the brothel and its connection to the GPO. Alexander believes there will be implications for many."

"I've just remembered why your friend was familiar. I caught him partaking in the pleasures of the brothel when I visited."

"No. Are you certain?" He asked.

"Quite certain. I never forget a face, particularly when it's embarrassed. He was with John." I explained.

"Well anyway, he told me in confidence some of the names passed on by John."

"It doesn't surprise John Saul would brag about his clientele."

"Can you believe the names. Henry James Fitzroy, Earl of Euston and Lord Arthur Somerset, Equerry to the Prince. Even Prince Albert Victor has visited."

"What do you imagine is going to happen?" I asked.

"Alexander admits there's cause for concern. The MP Henry Labouchere, amended the homosexuality criminal laws a couple of years ago. He believes they're going to make an example of the Cleveland Street crowd."

"John Saul will be intolerable on the witness stand if he has protection." I told him.

"Yes, that's true. He's not worried about his reputation. The same cannot be said for his clients, the so-called pillars of society. They'll do anything to keep their names free of scandal."

"I expect a great exodus from London has begun." I told him, looking out the window.

"Yes. Alexander says many have fled to the continent already."

"They're probably in Paris enjoying themselves, and there are worse places, believe me." I laughed.

John Saul's power to destroy several prominent lives overnight was troubling. By merely naming these people, their destinies would be forever altered. What was John's karmic connection to these souls? Could there be signs on his hands explaining why he'd chosen an unconventional path? The thought intrigued me. I was glad to be meeting with Ed Heron-Allen at Oscar's the next week, as it was a subject, I hoped to discuss with him.

The night of Oscar's dinner arrived. It was strange to walk past Frank's former home, knowing he no longer lived there.

Clutching a bunch of fragrant carnations, I entered Oscar's domain. I brought the flowers for his wife, Constance, but found she's left unexpectedly to visit family. Ed Heron-Allen was settled on an armchair in the salon sipping brandy from an elaborate glass. He rose to greet me.

"Louis. Good to see you again." He smiled.

"Likewise, Ed." I returned the smile.

Oscar flicked his hair, signalling the banter was about to begin.

"Yes Ed. Louis is fast becoming a rival of yours in the palmistry field. He has undertaken a thorough study of the subject, which of course, has included your own work. I became quite engrossed in conversation with him about it during our recent trip to Paris." He explained.

"Of all the works I've researched Ed, I found yours the most helpful. The last time we met, you were about to embark on a lecture tour of the United States. I've not long returned myself. How did you find it?" I asked.

"The trip was successful, but I was glad to come home. I'm moving on to other areas now. I don't see myself continuing to lecture on chirology, or working as a practicing palmist. Dealing with individuals and their problems can be taxing. One must have the right temperament for such work." He explained.

Oscar poured me a drink, and sat on the larger settee.

"I see a change in you after your American experience Ed. Yours is a mind unsatisfied, unless it's exploring new fields." Oscar expounded.

"You're right Oscar. I've other projects on the horizon."

Oscar took a long sip of brandy and looked in my direction.

"Now Louis here, is a perfect candidate to succeed as a seer. Studious when he must be, charming when he wants to be, and well connected as he needs to be. I foresee a glorious future for our friend Ed, what do you think?" Oscar touted.

Ed shifted uncomfortably.

"I can't see any impediment to Louis achieving his goal, if that's what he desires." He replied.

"Exactly. Excuse my frankness Ed, but Louis has an extra quality which will undoubtedly catapult him to victory."

"And that is?" Ed asked, raising an eyebrow.

"Yes Oscar, what is it?" I asked.

"It's your unmistakable sex appeal Louis. A feature ensuring success in anything requiring human interaction."

"Whatever you say Oscar." I replied, rolling my eyes.

Swallowing more brandy, he continued.

"Ed is not unattractive, but you are akin to Adonis, Louis. Don't you agree Ed? Does Louis not possess that extra something?" He asked.

"Yes Oscar. Louis has been blessed with fine attributes." He replied.

"Blessed or cursed, it remains to be seen. Anyway, are you feeling yourself Ed? You seem a little distracted?" Oscar enquired.

"Sorry Oscar. Yes, I am rather. May I get your opinion on a matter of concern?" He asked, with a worried expression.

"I recently purchased a jewel which I believe is cursed." He told us.

Oscar and I were stunned into silence.

"I'm not imagining it. I was warned before I purchased it. In my mind, such things are often superstitious mumbo jumbo. However, the moment it was in my possession, strange things began to happen. I even gave it away to others. They were equally affected by bad luck."

"Have another drink Ed, and try to calm down. Tell us about this gem. What's the history of it, do you know?" Oscar asked.

Ed drank more brandy and continued. Reaching into his pocket, he placed the infamous piece on the coffee table.

"There, see for yourself. The Delhi purple Sapphire."

The amethyst-coloured stone sparkled in the lamplight. An ominous glow radiated from its meticulously crafted silver setting, engraved with mystical symbols. The pinpoints of light glittered off the gem, compelling me to reach forward and handle it.

"No Louis, don't touch it. Trust me, I'm not imagining the sinister energy hiding behind its beauty." Ed warned.

"Yes Louis, why tempt fate." Oscar agreed.

Ignoring the warnings, I placed the jewel in my hand. The gem released a calming heat, and my eyes grew heavy. Strange images appeared in the darkness. A sacred temple with a statue surrounded by flowers and praying Hindus, and a commotion forcing the devotees to flee. Men in soldiers' uniforms at the bronze idol. Between the eyes of the deity, lay the imbedded purple sapphire. One of the soldiers prized the gem from its place, and rushed from the temple. The returning Hindus placed a curse on the stolen stone. Until it was returned to its rightful home, disaster would befall all those who possessed it. The laughing face of the Indian from Paris overlayed the images.

"Louis, are you alright? Say something." Oscar shouted.

"Yes. Don't worry. I was overcome by a vision. I'm recovered now." I replied.

"What did you see Louis?" Ed asked, as Oscar fetched water.

"This gem was stolen from a much-revered God. It holds the energetic memory of those who treasured it, and the negative vibrations of those who cursed it. You are right Ed. Nothing but calamities will come to the owner of the stone." I explained.

Oscar returned with the water.

"Are you feeling better Louis?" He asked.

"Yes, thank you Oscar. My advice is to place the gem in a wooden box to prevent the negative energy from escaping. Using several boxes like a Russian doll, or an Egyptian sarcophagus would ensure protection. Lock it away and forget about it." I told him.

During dinner, the story of the stone was revealed. It was stolen from the sacred temple of Indra, Cawnpore, around 1857. A Colonel W. Ferris brought it back to England where a series of disasters followed. Ed took my advice, secreting the encased stone away in a bank vault with a note of warning.

***

The Delhi Sapphire experience increased my interest in psychic energies, and I became involved with a new organization known as 'The Hermetic Order of the Golden Dawn.' This society embraced teachings from freemasonry, alchemy, theosophy, astrology, hermeticism and Jewish qabalah. Joining the recently opened London Isis-Urania Temple, connected me with a network of like-minded people. Here, men and women participated equally in rituals and ceremonies. Away from the previous masonic temple, I was free to explore the new avenues of magic without the constraints of past theatrical connections.

Robert absorbed the masonic information whenever we spoke, but wasn't interested in participating in the rituals or becoming a member. As a secretive Scorpion, he preferred one-on-one interactions over group discussions on mysticism.

Early in 1890 he was introduced to the American journalist and playwright Harry Dam. As editor of 'The Star' newspaper,

Dam was invited to speak at the School of Journalism on writing techniques. After the session was over, Robert approached him.

"Mr. Dam, might I have a moment to discuss your theatrical works?" He asked.

"Yes of course. What would you like to know?" He replied.

"How does writing for the theatre compare to your work for a newspaper? Are there any special techniques one should employ when writing for actors?"

The journalist laughed.

"It's simple. Keep the language natural. Don't get too intellectual, otherwise you're making it hard for the audience. It's a fault of the English I'm afraid. We Americans like to be entertained, not subjected to long-winded monologues. Think of a newspaper headline; quick and to the point. That's what people want." He explained.

The following day, Robert recounted the conversation.

"What would Oscar Wilde say about Dam's philosophy?" I asked.

"I'm sure he'd deliver a long-winded and scathing monologue mocking Americans with short attention spans." Robert chuckled.

"I can hear it now." I laughed.

"Dam was an agreeable chap. After our conversation he invited me to the Star office to see how he operates. What do you say, would you like to come along?" Robert asked.

"It might be interesting." I replied.

***

The steely sound of typewriters echoed through the corridors of the Fleet Street offices. Tense journalists punched out words for the next day's edition of 'The Star'. We found ourselves sitting across from Harry Dam's huge desk.

"So, gentlemen, you've come to observe journalism in action." He smiled.

"Yes. I hope you don't mind me bringing Louis?" Robert asked.

"Of course not. Well, this is it. Where the words and stories are put together." He told us.

The desktop was covered with papers, and a piece about Jack the Ripper caught my attention. While Robert chatted with Dam, I read the article.

"What do you think Louis?" He asked, nudging my arm.

"Oh sorry, about what?" I asked, embarrassed.

"The Ripper certainly captures everyone's attention." Harry laughed, looking at what I'd been reading.

"Louis has a particular interest in the Ripper. He's certain he's met him." Robert explained.

Harry leant forward in his chair.

"Really Louis? What makes you think so?" He asked, excitedly.

"I'm a student of palmistry. Much can be gathered about a person from their hands. A trained eye can readily observe traits of murder and suicide, as well as cruelty and addiction. One evening last December, while walking in Whitechapel, I had the misfortune of encountering such hands. They were waiting in the darkness for their next victim. "

"You don't have to convince me of the validity of palmistry. I've experienced it in New York when attending Edward Heron-Allen's lectures on Chirology. I believe there is something to this curious science. Go on with your story Louis." He told me.

"It was late when I encountered the Ripper. When living in the East end, many unsavoury characters crossed my path. None compared to the evilness of this malevolent figure. A quick observation of his hand and the silver gleam of a blade confirmed my beliefs." I recounted.

Robert put his hand on my shoulder.

"Every time Louis relives the experience, I shudder. If not for his gift of intuition, who knows what might have befallen him that night." Robert suggested.

Harry's mind was racing. Sitting at his desk was someone who'd come face to face with the notorious serial killer terrorizing London. The Ripper murder stories and the dramatic headlines, increased sales. It was in his interest to continue the coverage of the murders, and anything associated with them. After our discussions, Harry encouraged Robert to submit anything useful to keep the public's focus on the murders. Harry was less enthusiastic when asked if I might contribute something also.

"Louis, you've an obvious talent for Palmistry. You should follow it my man. It's all the rage now. People cannot get enough of someone who's studied the art with conviction. You would make a lot of money, I'm sure." He advised.

We left Fleet Street and returned home. Robert was thrilled to work with Dam and wrote articles for the Star over the following weeks, as well as outlining numerous ideas for novels. After Harry Dam's words of encouragement regarding palmistry, I focused on building my career as a professional chirologist. Noting the finger topography of every acquaintance consolidated my study. Long fingers belonged to the careful, short fingers to the impulsive. The hands at the theatre, were of a different type to those collecting horse droppings on the street. There was no doubt; shape revealed personality. The birth physiology couldn't be altered, even if the hands were subjected to different environments. After studying many books, it was time to seek out others with interests in Palmistry.

***

Katharine St Hill was known for her research in the field of scientific palmistry. Born in New Zealand, she travelled to England and established the 'London Chirological Society'. After learning of the organization, I made an appointment for a reading. Katharine was middle aged and not a pretty woman by any means. She reminded me of Robert's spinster Aunt Agatha, who recently visited from Speldhurst, demanding we take her shopping. I hoped the palmist's personality was less abrasive.

In her premises in central London, the studious woman greeted me. Her long fingers were enhanced by knotty joints, signifying an organized person. A broad palm indicated logic and a methodical nature. I was confident of her knowledge and ability to decipher my palm, and thought it best to remain silent about my own studies. On the desk lay her recently published book, 'The Grammar of Palmistry,'.

"Oh, you've written a book?" I asked.

Katharine gave me a curious look.

"Yes. It's my new work. It's been out for some time. Please take a seat." She told me.

"I haven't seen it." I replied, sitting.

"Perhaps you should find better book stores. Shall we begin?" She asked, holding out her hands to take mine.

I leant forward, giving her my palms. The physiology and structure of the hand can reveal as much as the lines. This primary observation divulges important information before the closer inspection begins. The session lasted for about one hour. For the most part, her analysis of the lines and markings was taken from Heron Allen's book. Katharine spent many hours gathering palm prints from hospitals and institutions. This work enabled her to gain further insights relating to health and symptomology. Visiting a successful palmist and experienced her methods, only strengthened my resolve to continue in this area.

<u>Chapter Four</u>

(1890-1892)

Returning home after the reading, I found Robert busy writing.

"I've just seen Katharine St Hill." I told him.

"How was it? What do you make of her?" He asked, looking up from his papers.

"She reminded me of your aunt. I was impressed. She's definitely not a charlatan."

"Did her interpretation differ from your own?" He asked.

"Not really. Clearly, we've studied from the same sources. Katharine has additional information from hospital patients. Her interest extends to the medical side of the practice, and this knowledge is useful in recognizing illness. Her setup was encouraging, inspiring me to begin my own practice. I never let on about my own studies. It's time to receive payment for my services." I announced.

"I'm glad the contact proved helpful. Speaking of which, I visited Oscar Wilde last week at his editorial offices."

"Is he going to use your stories?" I asked.

"There were no promises made. I know you are fond of him Louis, but I find him a conversational narcissist. I believe he only agreed to meet because of you. His attitude came as no surprise."

Robert never warmed to Oscar. Whenever the two were together, Oscar dominated the conversation, resulting in jealousy from both.

"You never know, something may come of it." I replied, encouragingly.

"I'm not waiting for Wilde. The stories were given to 'Home and Hearth', and were accepted. Here's the payment." He told me, waving the cheque and smiling.

"Wonderful. Things are looking up for us."

Business cards for the palmistry services were printed, and a steady flow of customers came to Phillimore Place. Alexander Hood Nelson, the Duke of Bronte, was particularly impressed with his reading. He arranged a visit to White Lodge in Richmond Park to consult with Princess Mary Adelaide and her daughter. He was well acquainted with the Royals. Later, he became the Controller of the household and Equerry to Princess Mary. He continued the association as Private Secretary to her daughter Mary of Teck, after her marriage to the Prince of Wales.

***

Arriving at historic White Lodge was a significant occasion. It marked the beginning of connections to upper levels of society. Princess Mary Adelaide, a granddaughter of George III and therefore first cousin to the queen, was famous for her extravagance. Requests for a higher income from the Queen were unsuccessful. Debts increased, and the family fled abroad during the 1880s to escape their creditors. Recently returned, they hoped to procure lucrative marriages for their daughters. Accompanied by the Duke of Bronte, we were shown into the library, where we awaited the princesses.

"Remember what I've told you Louis. Follow my instructions, and all will be well." He whispered.

After some time, the two women appeared. The older Princess Mary arrived dressed in a sumptuous gown, looking nervous, and fiddling with a necklace of dazzling jewels. Her daughter sat quietly.

"Well Alexander, is this the gentleman you have been telling us about? He is so young to have such knowledge, is he not?" The older princess asked, with a heavy German accent.

"May I present Mr. Louis Warner. It's true, his knowledge does belie his years. I'm sure you will be impressed with his skill Maam." He declared.

"I do hope so Alexander. Young man, anything you uncover here is to be held in the strictest confidence you understand." She ordered.

"It goes without saying Maam. You can be assured of my discretion." I told her.

"This is my daughter, the Princess Mary. It would please us if you begin with her hands. You may sit beside her."

The young princess smiled as I took my position on the intricately carved sofa.

"Firstly, I will look at the overall shape of your hands and the fingers, including the nails. This tells me your personality type, and how you deal with life's challenges. I can see you are a logical and methodical person. Your finger length is equal to your palm, showing a balanced mentality. A large mount of Venus, denotes a love of beautiful things. The full mount of Mars, gives you an inner strength to cope with hardships."

"Hardships? What possible hardships could my daughter experience? "Princess Adelaide questioned.

The young Princess looked at her mother.

"Please mother, let the man finish before we ask questions." She begged.

The Princess Adelaide waved her hand to resume.

"Thank you, I will continue. You have an excellent lifeline. The marking is strong and clear without any lines crossing or causing impediments. I foresee a long life. Your health line does show periods of illness, but I'm confident the Mars energy will help you recover from these. The headline is well placed across the palm, and does not swoop too sharply into the mount of Luna. Your heart line signifies a happy marriage and a beneficial union."

"Splendid. Let us hope it comes to pass." Princess Adelaide announced enthusiastically.

The young princess seemed relieved.

"I'm most pleased the marriage will be a happy one." She sighed.

A closer look at the lines revealed other details.

"There is something which should be pointed out. Your fate line is decidedly strong on both hands." I continued.

"What does this mean?" Princess Mary asked.

"You are bound to a fulfil a destiny. Whoever designs our fates has bestowed a path which cannot be altered." I explained.

"You mean I cannot change what lies ahead?" She asked.

"It's my belief, individuals who are marked by fate must fulfil their karmic obligations."

The Princess looked puzzled.

"Did you not predict a happy marriage for me? Is this not my life, my destiny?" She asked.

"The palm knows nothing of marital ceremonies or contracts. I see an attachment to another before you are married. I believe you will fail to marry your first betrothed. This is the fate line at work. Perhaps you are spared the grief that union promised in order to marry another who shares your destiny?" I told her.

The young princess pondered the words.

"I would not welcome the heartache of a broken engagement." She replied.

"Your marriage is fated. The children lines from this union suggest they must also fulfill a karmic debt. Don't worry yourself. The signs on your hand indicate you've been given the tools to accomplish your destiny."

"It's strange to hear you speak of such things. I too have a sense of my future. I feel you are right when you say I'm destined to fulfill some purpose. You have given me much to contemplate. I thank you for your time."

Princess Adelaide sat in silence, processing the information. The plans she imagined for her daughter were confirmed by the reading.

"I must acknowledge the skill you possess young man. No doubt you combine intuition with a sharp mind. I do not require my hands to be read at present. Much has already been said regarding my daughter. Anymore predictions would overload the mind." She explained.

"Of course, Maam. I'm at your service, whenever you are ready." I told her.

The princesses left, and we were escorted from the library. Driving away in the hansom cab, the duke explained some details.

"That was a remarkable reading, Louis. You've given the occupants of White Lodge something to think about." He chuckled.

"The young princess has definite indications on her palm. I feel I've just met someone who is destined to live a life very different to the one she imagines."

"I will tell you something in confidence, Louis. There is talk of an engagement between Prince Albert Victor and the young princess. This could explain things." He told me.

Recalling John Saul's revelations about the Cleveland Street brothel and Prince Albert Victor's visits, gave the reading credence.

"I believe you're right. Please forgive Robert's gossiping. He's told me of your conversation with John Saul regarding Prince Albert. If this engagement does eventuate, what tragic event prevents the marriage? Perhaps the princess becomes aware of her betrothed's true nature, and refuses to go ahead with the union". I speculated.

"It's possible. I cannot see the Princess Mary Adelaide missing the opportunity to wed her daughter to a Royal heir, given the family's precarious financial position." He told me.

"Something else must occur then." I replied.

"Time will reveal all." The duke sighed.

"That it will." I whispered.

Later in the evening, I discussed what I'd seen with Robert.

"You know Louis, Prince Albert Victor is a loose cannon when it comes to the Royal family. Numerous scandals have placed him in a precarious position. I feel danger follows him on a cloud near." Robert said.

"What do you mean?" I asked.

"A lot of the Royal family's problems would be solved if the Prince of Wales's second son George were to succeed instead of his first born." He explained.

"That could only happen if Prince Albert Victor were to die, and he's a healthy young man."

"Exactly. Untimely deaths have occurred throughout history, altering the line of succession. Why should our time be any different?"

"It could explain what I've seen on Princess Mary's palm. Oh Robert, our writer's brains are imagining a sinister plot. They're not even engaged yet." I laughed.

"The duke feels the engagement will almost certainly go ahead.

He's privy to much within the royal circle." Robert told me, seriously.

"We'll wait for the announcement. If it happens, let us pray Prince Albert Victor has the protection of angels."

Most of us take for granted an existence free from public scrutiny. Many individuals are powerless to change their circumstances. I'd made a wise decision to alter my life's direction. Even though I'd experienced problematic times in the theatre, no obstacles stopped the advancement of a chirological career. It was surprising how easily I let go of my acting dreams.

***

The Duke of Bronte and Oscar, continued referring people for readings. The income allowed me to buy wonderful things. I visited high street fashion houses to outfit my wardrobe, and my hair was styled by elite barbers. Oscar's words regarding the importance of my appearance justified the expenditures.

At the same time, Robert's income from writing increased, and the world appeared rosy. My desperate arrival at Phillimore Place months before, faded into the past.

Most clients came to me for their consultations; however, the aristocrats of London were accustomed to people attending them. I found myself at a number of affluent homes reading the hands of the rich and titled. One day in the Spring of 1890, I received one such invitation. The envelope bore the Duke of Sutherland's coat of arms. It was a dinner invitation from Mary Blair, the Duchess of Sutherland, who lived close by in Hyde Park Gate. Oscar also received an invitation. No doubt, I'd be required to read a palm or two during the evening. Robert was home writing when the mail arrived.

"Another dinner invitation Robert. This time, the Duchess of Sutherland." I told him.

"You really are becoming the darling of the upper crust Louis." He smiled.

"Didn't I read something about the Duke and Duchess of Sutherland the other day?" I asked.

"You certainly did. It's quite a scandal. They've recently married. The duke's former wife died not so long ago. She was barely cold, when the two took their vows." He explained.

"Oh yes, I remember the story now. Didn't she have a husband who was killed in a shooting accident?" I recalled.

"Correct. Captain Blair was his name. He worked as a land agent and business manager for the duke. Apparently, his wife became the duke's mistress." Robert grinned.

"A cozy setup." I laughed.

"It may have been for the duke and duchess, but not for poor Blair. The new duchess has been shunned by society, but that probably doesn't bother her. I hear she is never short of interesting friends."

"Yes. I'm sure it was Oscar who initiated the request. He's been invited also." I told him.

"Oscar again. Be careful the gossip mongers don't start on the two of you." He snapped.

"Really Robert, you must get over these illusions about him. I can wear this new suit." I said, opening the closet.

"Be careful. You don't want to end up looking like a footman." Robert replied, irritated.

"Do you wish you'd been invited?" I asked, noting the sarcasm.

"By a vixen who's snatched a dead woman's title. God's teeth no. Conversing with a brazen social climber and your pretentious friend, is not my idea of an enjoyable evening Louis."

"Socializing with clients is part of my work Robert." I responded.

"I know Louis, ignore me. I'm having trouble finishing a story.

It's frustrating." He apologized.

"Perhaps you need a break. Let's take a walk, through Kensington Gardens." I suggested.

Robert agreed.

***

Oscar arrived in a cab to take us to the Duke and Duchess of Sutherland. Strolling crowds were enjoying the warmer weather, and Oscar seemed particularly animated.

"London is aglow this evening Louis. The sultry air does wonders for the soul." He told me.

"It's true Oscar. The city blossoms, along with the flowers. You seem particularly gay tonight. Life must be treating you well. How are Constance and the boys?" I asked.

"I cannot complain. The family is thriving. My writing is going well, and I'm being acknowledged as a literary genius." He gloated.

"I'm pleased for you." I replied, as we arrived at the townhouse.

"To top it all, I've recently met a young man who promises to stimulate my intellect even more." He added.

"Surely your intellect is not in need of anymore stimulation, Oscar." I jested.

Oscar cast me a defiant look.

"Here we are. I'm sure you will enjoy meeting the duchess. She is quite the entertainer."

"So, I've heard." I smiled, as we climbed the stairs.

"The Duke of Sutherland's wealth is astronomical. It would benefit you greatly to make a good impression on him and his new wife." He warned.

"Of course, Oscar. I will try to behave."

The door opened, and we were greeted by a grim-faced servant. The parlour was decorated with large paintings and numerous sculptures. Presently the duchess entered.

"Oscar, how nice to see you again." She announced.

"It's always a pleasure duchess. Allow me to present Mr. Louis Warner."

The duchess moved forward, extending her hand in a regal fashion. I kissed the appendage, disappointed an assessment of character was thwarted by the silk glove.

"Pleased to meet you, Mr. Warner. You've quite a reputation around town. I expect we will see if it's deserved." She told me.

The subtle warning was delivered with grace. It was clear the duchess was no fool. The duke arrived shortly after. His modest dress gave the impression of a merchant, rather than a titled aristocrat. With a trembling voice he addressed us, and we moved to the dining room. The food was impeccable. After finishing, the duchess asked us to retire to the salon where we took our various positions. The duke sat in a large wing chair, nervously smoking a cigar, and contributed little to the conversation. The duchess perched herself on a large silk-covered lounge.

"Oscar, why don't you go over there. Louis, you may sit here next to me." She instructed.

Oscar sat, flicking his hair.

"Yes Louis. You must sit next to the duchess. Time to uncover any secrets found on her lovely hand." He said, crossing his legs.

The duke began to cough. The duchess sent him a stern look whilst uncovering her hand.

"Which hand would you like first?" She asked.

"I begin with the left hand. This is what we've been given

from the planetary influences at birth, and the genetic traits." I explained.

"As you wish. What does the right signify then?"

"It tells us how we react to those influences."

"The right hand is the one in control of things then?" She quizzed.

"You could say that. It's true, the right hand attracts more attention as it shows us how we act."

"I've heard one reads the left hand of a woman, and the right of a man. Is this not so?" Oscar interrupted.

"That's a simplistic view, and outdated, Oscar. It comes from a time when women had little control of their lives. Fate determined their happiness. Marriages were arranged by others, with most women having no influence on their destinies. Life has changed for the fairer sex. In fact, one could say in many circumstances today, the woman is the one in command."

The duchess pulled her left hand away and uncovered her right.

"I agree Louis. Why not begin with my right hand then." She told me smiling.

"Very well duchess."

I noted the physiology of the duchess's thumb. The shape of this finger indicated a negative personality trait. It belonged to the club type. This was the mark of a cruel and violent person. Some references classified it as a murderer's thumb. Wondering how to proceed, I continued.

"A well-formed life and health line, tells me you take great care of your physical body. The robust colour, denotes good circulation. The head line runs straight across the palm, and is separated from the heart line. Your head rules your heart when it comes to decision making. You are prepared to take risks in life however." I told her.

"I agree, pray continue." She replied.

A cold shiver passed through me while holding the duchess's hand.

"Why are you shaking Louis? Do I make you nervous?" She asked.

"No, not at all. I feel a chill in the air, as if it were a Winter's night. I don't understand. It was warm when we arrived."

A breeze swept in from the open windows. The lamps began to flicker and cast strange shadows over the room. The same feeling, I experienced while holding the Delhi sapphire overcame me.

"Louis, are you feeling unwell?" The duchess asked.

Furniture swirled about me, and I fell into a trance.

"I see two men standing in an area surrounded by trees and bushes. One has a gun, while the other takes aim at a target in the distance. I can see the faces of the hunters. One of the men asks to see the other man's weapon. His companion hands it to him. The second man examines the interior of the barrel. He proceeds to show it to the owner while still holding the trigger. The firearm discharges, and the man lay dead and bleeding on the field."

"Stop this immediately. I knew this would happen Mary. I warned you. Why didn't you listen to me? We are done for." The duke shouted.

The duchess looked perplexed and angry.

"Be quiet George, you fool." She told him.

The duke sobbed into clasped hands. The duchess explained her husband's behaviour resulted from the strain of his previous wife's death. I regained my composure, as Oscar calmed the duke. The duchess showed little compassion for her distraught husband.

"That was unexpected. It seems your companion has psychic abilities, Oscar. How terrible for you Louis to have seen the accident in such terrible detail. Nevertheless, it was an accident." She insisted.

"The vision was clear Duchess, including the faces of the men. I failed to recognize the man who was shot, but I'm sure a photograph of your previous husband, would confirm his identity. There was no mistaking the other man as your new husband, the duke. When he wiped the rifle clean of his fingerprints and placed the weapon back in the arms of the unfortunate victim, I knew it was no accident." I responded defiantly.

The duke looked up.

"What do you want? I'll be ruined if this investigation is reopened. Think of poor Mary, think of my children." The duke implored.

"I am thinking of the duchess." I replied, scathingly.

After looking at the hand of the duchess, I'd no doubt she was behind the sinister plot.

Oscar intervened.

"Let us all calm down. What's done is done. Everyone has moved on. Why drag up the past again. Louis is a trustworthy fellow. Your secrets are safe with him, and you need not ask where my allegiance lies." Oscar told them.

We left Hyde Park Gate later that evening. Walking along the park, we discussed the night's events.

"Louis, you are a tricky fellow. I couldn't have written a better story myself. Those drama classes with Ben Greet were certainly not wasted. Do you realize what a trump card you hold over the Sutherlands?"

"I wasn't acting." I told him, indignantly.

"You mean you actually saw the scene?" He asked.

"Every detail was real. I believe Captain Blair's spirit was responsible."

"The extent of your talent continues to amaze me, Louis."

We parted ways at the Albert memorial. Oscar hailed a cab, and I headed back to Phillimore Place. It had been quite a night.

Oscar returned to Paris after leaving 'Woman's world', and I wondered if the young man he spoke about accompanied him.

***

One evening, I attended the London Chirological Society, and met other students of the science. Ina Oxenford, Katharine St Hill, and Gertrude Minetts were key figures in the organization. The Chirological review was a periodical published by the Record Press in London, and provided current research on the subject. The publishers were directly associated with the society and the first to publish my own work, 'Book of the hand' in 1892. Around this time, I began using the pseudonym of 'Cheiro'. Katharine St Hill believed such names degraded the profession.

"Why do you find it necessary to use the bizarre name of Cheiro in your work?" she asked.

"I accept others prefer to use their real names, but I'm establishing myself differently. It calls for a more exotic title." I replied.

"We let the science speak for itself, and leave the theatrical side to vaudeville actors." She replied.

"Having studied drama, I can assure you there is no acting used in my consultations." I told her, firmly.

Recognition altered the look in Katharine's eyes. She never asked me if I'd consulted her, but I'm sure she remembered me. I believe she felt intimidated and envious of my rapid rise as a London palmist. What had taken her years to achieve, came to me in a matter of months.

***

At the Phillimore place apartment, I continued reading palms. One woman brought a newspaper with faces I recognized on the frontpage.

"Might I have a quick look at your paper Madam?" I asked.

"Yes of course. The big news of the day is the engagement of Prince Albert Victor to the Princess Mary Teck." She told me, smiling.

Memories of the meeting with the Princess Mary and her mother came rushing back. It seemed the Duke of Bronte was correct in his belief the marriage would go ahead.

"You're not pleased with the match?" The client asked.

"Oh no. Yes. Anyway, shall we begin your reading?" I said.

It was difficult to concentrate on other people's hands. I kept visualizing the young princess and her lines. What could prevent the marriage?

Before long, news of the prince's influenza was made public. On the 14th January, the prince died, leaving the country in shock. How could a young and healthy individual of royal blood die in this way? Robert delivered the news.

"Louis are you here?" He shouted, opening the door.

"Aren't you working at the newspaper today?" I asked.

"Yes, but I had to come and tell you the news. Prince Albert Victor is dead." He told me, wide-eyed.

"No, is it true? I believed his illness to be a mild influenza. Did that really kill him?"

"That's what the royals are saying. Others, like our friend Alexander, know better."

"Have you seen Alexander?" I asked.

"Yes. He's always feared for the prince. It seems Albert Victor had syphilis. The Princess Mary Adelaide was made aware of this after the engagement. She conspired with others to alter her daughter's destiny by disposing of her betrothed. You see, his brother could easily take the place of Princess Mary's husband and claim all his succession rights. Princess Mary Adelaide had nothing to lose and much to gain. Her daughter could still provide them with a high position within the monarchy."

"But how did they do it?" I asked, in disbelief.

"The prince was receiving medicine for his condition. His prescription was obviously tainted to hasten his demise." Robert said.

"Poisoned? It seems our imaginative stories were not far from the truth after all." I told him, shaking my head.

"It's not the first-time a murder has altered the course of the monarchy, and it won't be the last. Who'd dare question the death?"

"The poor princess. I'm sure she is ignorant of the plot. Losing Prince Albert Victor weeks before her planned wedding, is a cruel blow. It was in her hand." I whispered.

"Yes, the innocent pawns. It remains to be seen if she consents to marry his brother." Robert said.

"She has little choice. Her hand showed a happy marriage, perhaps it's for the best."

"I hope you're right Louis. I must get back to the office. There are other stories needing my attention." Robert said, rushing off.

***

The weeks continued without a break. Hand after hand was read. Pound after pound was placed on my table. I was making money, but it was taking a toll on my health. Robert travelled to Maniace

Castle in Sicily to visit Alexander. The Duke of Bronte was a direct descendant of Lord Nelson who'd been given the property by the King of Naples. After his departure in June, I collapsed from exhaustion and entered Devonshire Lodge, a convalescence home for three months. I returned to Phillimore Place a week before Robert.

"Let this be a lesson, Louis. You must look after yourself, and take breaks from your readings." He insisted.

"You're right Robert." I agreed.

Soon after returning, Oscar paid a visit. I hadn't seen him since our dinner with the Duke and Duchess of Sutherland.

"I'm sorry to hear you've been unwell Louis. I trust you're better now. Would it be too presumptuous to enquire as to the nature of your illness?" He asked.

"It wasn't an illness, Oscar. I was overworked and exhausted." I explained.

"I'm glad. There are so many mysterious conditions afflicting people these days." He smiled.

"Yes, I've heard." I replied.

"Our friend, the Duke of Sutherland is not doing well. I met with the duchess last week, and was told her husband's nerves are not improving. She was sorry to hear you'd been unwell, and has offered you some help." Oscar told me.

"Help? In what way?" I asked, puzzled.

"She is prepared to provide you with a sum of money to get you back on your feet, provided she can rely on your discretion of course." He explained.

"You mean she wants to buy my silence regarding her husband's murder confession."

"Louis, do not look a gift horse in the mouth. The Sutherlands are extremely wealthy. This will set you up in business. You can get rooms, furnish them in style, and attract high paying clientele." Oscar told me.

"Was this your idea, or the Duchess's Oscar?" I asked, suspiciously.

"It came about naturally, after discussing your vision. I always have your best interests at heart Louis." He responded, with a nervous flick of hair.

"I'm reluctant to take money from such a despicable person, however, I feel the duchess should be made to pay for her treachery somehow."

"Excellent. I will inform her of your decision. You should expect the funds within a week." He smiled, departing.

This marked the beginning of life as a Bond Street palmist. Oscar helped select Indian rugs and exotic furniture from our favourite shop, Liberty's on Oxford Street. Queen Victoria, as Empress of India, made it fashionable to decorate with pieces from Asia, and there was much to choose from. The Sutherland's generous donation meant I could purchase numerous items necessary for an exotic ambiance. After finishing the fit out, a healthy balance remained.

Robert helping by writing reviews. The first appearing in 'Hearth and Home' magazine's August edition.

"I wish to tell my readers of a wonderful Palmist called 'Cheiro,''to whom I paid a visit a few days ago. He has had an eventful life, although he is yet quite young. When he was a mere boy, he began to take an interest in hands, rather than in hearts, and his fame so spread abroad that some adventurers, desirous of making money out of his strange powers, stole him away from his parents, and took him around with them on their wanderings. They were eventually clapped into prison, and Cheiro returned home. The nomadic spirit was, however, by this time strong upon him, and he crossed the ocean to America, still intent on the study of the future, as revealed in the hands of all those whom he encountered. After a prolonged sojourn abroad, he came back to England,

but soon embarked for India, where he spent a long time. Finally, having read thousands of hands in various parts of the world, he has come to London and settled in delightful rooms in Bond Street. Cheiro is a wonder. I have had my hand told before, but never so minutely, never so correctly. Every detail of my character, as I alone can know it, was given swiftly and unerringly. My relations with various people were described. My emotions were analysed and traced back to their beginnings. I was told my ambition in life, my hesitation in choosing a career, what I had imagined to be my true bent, and what I would eventually find my true bent to be. The exact state of my health now and in the past was given, and then Cheiro, having thoroughly convinced me of his claims upon my time and intelligence, proceeded to read to me some of the dark mysterious future. I know in what year I shall die, in what year I shall lose money, when I shall marry, and when I shall attain success- at least I feel as if I knew it, for if Cheiro can read the past, as he undoubtedly can, why should he not read the future? Cheiro does not pretend to be a thought reader, a spiritualist- anything, indeed, except a palmist. He explained to me by what means he knew so much about me- what line meant this, what star meant that, and he certainly made me know myself thoroughly. Really, when I come to think of it, I almost look upon Cheiro as a moral force! And then he accomplished a remarkable feat, which, however acrobatic we are in our tendencies, few of us can manage. He tells the unvarnished truth!"

As Robert read, my smile softened.

"The review sounds like an adventure story. It is fanciful and engaging, but don't you think a 'moral force' is going too far?" I asked.

"Absolutely not. A little embellishment never hurt anyone. There are many charlatans in your business. You should be proud of your good character and integrity. Look how the Sutherland's helped you. People admire you and want you to succeed." He professed.

Robert believed the Duke and Duchess of Sutherland's money was a business loan guaranteed by Oscar.

"Robert, I must tell you something. The money I received from the Sutherlands is not really a loan."

"What do you mean? Don't you have to pay it back?"

"No."

"I don't understand. Why would they give you money and not expect it to be returned?" He asked confused.

"It was not my idea, Oscar.."

Robert didn't let me finish.

"Oh no. I might have known. Don't tell me it's his money you're using. "He shouted.

Robert's anger was usually well controlled. When he was really upset, there was no stopping the fury.

"It's not Oscar's money. It came from the Sutherlands. I've learnt something about the duke and duchess, which they wish to keep to themselves. It was Oscar who organized the details of the money."

"What are you saying? Are you some kind of sordid blackmailer? He asked, looking disgusted.

"Of course not." I shouted.

"What do you call it then?"

Yes, I was a blackmailer. Oscar made the whole scenario appear respectable by not mentioning the word. I felt ashamed and angry. Robert's looks only heightened the pain. I tried justifying my actions.

"You don't understand what transpired. What those people did. They are not what you think. Don't feel sorry for them." I told him.

"No. I don't care. It's what you did. Were you so desperate? You never disclosed anything to me. What possessed you?"

"Captain Blair possessed me, if you must know." I whispered.

"What are you talking about?" He asked, angrily.

"I never told you what happened the night of the Sutherland's dinner. I entered a kind of trance, and witnessed Blair's murder. The duke panicked, confessing to the crime in front of Oscar and the duchess, who was none too pleased."

"It was no accident?" Robert asked, shocked.

"It was a staged suicide. Everyone felt it should be described as an accident to prevent any scandal. One lie covered another. The vision clarified everything."

"Because of their position in society, no one asked questions." Robert realized.

"If the case were to be re-examined with forensics, the outcome would be different. The testimonies of two witnesses who've heard the duke's confession is damaging. The scandal would blacken the Sutherland name for years. Buying my silence was a small price to pay." I told him.

Robert sat heavily, sighing.

"I've no right to judge you, Louis. I've not experienced the hardships you have. Hunger and fear can cloud a person's judgement. Let's not speak of it again. Here is the transcript of my review. It's being printed as we speak. I'm going out for a while. I'll see you later."

With a look of despondency, Robert dropped the paper in my lap. It was a turning point in our relationship. Things would never be the same.

***

Walking to the office, I passed Henry Irving's home. How life had changed since taking tea with him there. The 'Book of the Hand' was available in bookstores and included the address of the practice at 47 New Bond Street. I wondered if Mr. Irving had seen it, or any of the magazine reviews. To those acquainted with me, a photo left no doubt 'Cheiro' and Louis Warner were the same person. People knew where to find me.

The morning paper publicized the death of the Duke of Sutherland. The strain of recent events surely led to his demise. Those last few weeks with his scheming wife must have been torturous. His slow death differed greatly from the quick end he delivered to his wife's former husband. My heart felt no pity for the man.

Life became easier after employing a secretary to manage the bookings. There were walk ins off the street, and these people could be attended to without interruptions. One afternoon a woman sat with a large veil in the waiting area. As I said my goodbyes to the previous client, I took a closer look. The fabric did little to hide her identity from me.

"Why Mary, is it really you?"

"Yes Louis. Can you see me?" She asked.

It was Mary Eastlake. The sight of her brought back feelings of betrayal and emotional turmoil.

"Please sit." I told her.

"I heard you were working as a palmist under the name of Cheiro. I happened to be passing when I saw your sign." Mary said, uncovering her face.

"That was fortuitous. How are you keeping?" I asked, suspiciously.

Mary looked troubled. Stumbling across my office by chance was a lame story. I knew her ways too well.

"Where are you working?" I asked, not mentioning Barrett or his company.

"I retired from the stage last year." She told me, surprised.

"Really? I had no idea. I move in different circles these days." I explained.

"I want to know if anything has altered on my hand since you last saw it. Lines change, don't they? I remember you once told me it can happen."

"This is true. Lines do change, but only if the person changes first." I replied.

"I feel I've changed Louis." She smiled.

"Have you really Mary? In what way?" I asked, raising an eyebrow.

I found it difficult to hide my contempt for Mary's past behaviour.

"Louis, I'm sorry I hurt you. I didn't mean for it to happen. Wilson is such a beast, and has this power over me." She pleaded.

"Please Mary, I don't want to hear anything about Wilson Barrett. He's caused me enough trouble to last a lifetime. I don't need to be reminded of past offences against me."

"You don't wish to look at my hand then?" She asked, angrily.

"No Mary. Perhaps you can tell me what's troubling you, and the real reason you are here?" I demanded.

"Very well. I've been cast aside by Wilson. He's found another leading lady and I'm to make way for her. She is young and beautiful, just as I was when entering the Barrett Company." She explained.

"Surely, he's not so callous. What do you mean he's cast you aside?"

"Exactly that. I'm no longer his leading lady. I'm relegated to minor roles."

"Oh, I see. Your pride has been injured. How do you imagine I can help you with that? There's something else you're not telling me. Why does that not surprise me?"

"Louis, you must believe me. I'm truly sorry for not confiding in you before." Mary implored rising to her feet, dramatically wringing her hands.

"You're still a great actress Mary. How is your child?" I asked, with a deadly look.

"I see you haven't lost your scorpion sting. My son is well. He is what keeps me sane."

"Well, you've something of Wilson's that cannot be taken away."

"Yes, it's true. Wilson is providing for me. He's promised to look after our son without acknowledging him." She informed me.

"I see. That's why you're able to give up your work."

"But I'm lonely Louis. Wilson never visits. He's not interested in his son. He spends more time with his dead wife's children."

"And in your loneliness, you've sought me out, hoping I'll embrace you with prosperous arms." I laughed.

"We once shared such passion, Louis. Can we not resume the fire?"

"That fire burnt-out long-ago Mary. The wild waters of the Atlantic extinguished all feelings for you on the voyage home to England. Your performance at the Statue of Liberty ended what we shared."

"I see it was a mistake to come here."

"I'm afraid so Mary. Go home to your son. My affections are not to be trifled with. The person you once knew, no longer exists."

Mary covered her face and left without a backward glance.

***

The long hours I spent at the office with clients became tiresome. I needed time alone. I found a small apartment off Bond Street, where I'd escape during the day and return at night. Phillimore Place was Robert's domain, and I needed my own. We were still close friends, but the dynamics of the relationship changed after the truth of my financial windfall became known. Our backgrounds were different. Respectability and honour are constantly driven into the heads of the English, whereas the Irish are motivated by passions of the heart. We agreed to acknowledge our core values, and parted amicably.

In my new abode, there was a freedom to do anything. Many times, those who began their association with me as paying clients would find themselves there. Inevitably my professional life became intertwined with the private.

*****

Lady Arthur Paget contacted my secretary requesting a reading at her home in Belgrave Square. Arriving at the residence, she led me to a room where a male client sat behind a curtain. She left, and I read the mysterious palm. At the end of the reading, the identity of the man was accidentally revealed when he leant on the curtain causing it to fall. I found myself once again in the presence of the Prince of Wales. There was no indication he recognized me from our previous encounter at the home of Frank Miles. With a new hairstyle and gentleman's attire, I bore little resemblance to the young man of that time. Reminding him of our meeting would be embarrassing.

"I'm glad the curtain fell at the end of the reading. "The prince laughed.

"Yes. You can be assured I had no idea of your identity." I replied.

"You've given me some interesting insights into my future Cheiro. I'm much obliged to you. It was your reading with my future daughter-in-law which prompted me to seek you out. She was impressed with your predictions. The details you imparted have helped her cope with the loss of my son." He explained.

"I'm at your service your highness, whenever you require me." I told him.

We talked for some time before Lady Paget paid me, and I left.

***

Fate delivered a goddess to Bond Street that first October. I'd been in a strange mood for most of the afternoon. When she arrived, her captivating appearance left me spellbound.

"Please come through miss." I told her.

The elegantly dressed girl moved through the doorway like a gliding swan. The raw and sensuous energy was palpable. Her unflinching eyes met mine, without any trace of youthful nervousness.

"Good afternoon. My name is Maud Jeffries." She announced.

"Pleased to make your acquaintance. It's a pleasure to meet someone who carries herself with such style." I smiled.

"That's very kind of you. You come highly recommended by a friend." She told me.

"I'm grateful for the reviews, especially when they result in charming clients."

Who was this person? The accent was clearly American. Was she one of the many chorus girls who made their way to London each year hoping to snatch a wealthy aristocrat? Could she herself be an heiress? One thing was certain. This young lady possessed an uncommon charisma promising success.

"You're curious about your palm?" I asked.

"I'm open to the opinions of others regarding my future." She smiled.

"You've had your palm read before then?"

"Not by a professional. A creole woman back home in Mississippi once looked at my hand. She was taught by a gypsy many years ago. I'm eager to see what someone of your learning makes of it."

She produced a copy of my palmistry book, and placed it on the table in front of us.

"I've read with interest your recently published work. Would you be so kind as to sign it for me?"

"Of course. I'm flattered you have it. It's a rare thing indeed, to meet someone with any knowledge of the subject."

"I've not read it thoroughly. Time doesn't permit that luxury at present. I intend spending more hours studying it on the voyage back home next week." She informed me.

"Will you be returning to London again soon?" I asked.

"Perhaps you will find that information here." Maud replied, removing her gloves.

The hypnotic spell was broken after her hands were placed on the velvet cushion. She gave no clues in relation to her activities in England.

"We shall see." I said, taking the soft hands.

Impatiently, I read both, wanting to discover her secrets as quickly as possible.

"Your main lines are clear and defined. The line of the sun is extremely well developed, rising from the mount of the moon to the finger of Apollo. This denotes a creative life force which must be followed. It usually indicates fame and distinction in the arts." I explained.

I waited for any response, but she remained tight lipped.

"The lifeline is long and for the most part, unhindered. There are some areas crossed by lines of influence. These are attached to your relationship lines. I would say your lessons are to do with partnerships."

"How many relationships and marriages?" She asked, eagerly.

"The palm makes no distinction between marital unions and those lacking nuptial vows. There must be an intense connection for the lines to show. I see three powerful unions on your hand." I told her.

"Three. I certainly hope they are not marriages. What about children?"

"There are also three children marked here. One is attached to an earlier union, and two are attached to a later relationship." I revealed.

"I'm surprised by this information." She exclaimed.

"You're young, and have years ahead of you." I said, reassuring her.

"Will I be financially secure?"

"You will certainly earn money from the arts. Rewards from a partner are indicated. A money line attaches to your last relationship, with this union providing additional security."

"Will it be a happy relationship?" She asked.

"Like many unions, it begins well. Unfortunately, the line slopes downwards indicating tensions later in the relationship. Your fate line travels to Saturn. It indicates a love of the earth, animals, and nature." I told her, tracing the line with my finger tip.

"My people were cotton farmers back home. I grew up with animals, particularly horses."

"Your appearance led me to believe you'd be more at home in a drawing room, surrounded by fine things." I smiled.

"Heavens no. I love the outdoors and riding. I need to be

amongst the flowers and trees." She explained.

"Yes, your spatulate fingertips indicate a need for freedom of mind and body. Your palm indicates talent in the arts. Have you discovered this yet?" I asked.

"It's true, I'm an actress. I've been working back home in the United States for the past couple of years, and recently here in London. An English theatre company saw a performance of mine in New York, and offered me a position." She confided.

To learn this young girl was an actress surprised me. Her manner was less flamboyant and overt than the thespians one normally encounters. Her energy was fresh and genuine, exuding an intoxicating enthusiasm.

"With such a brilliant sun line under Apollo, you cannot fail. Do you have family with you?" I asked.

"No. My brother is a working actor back home. My parents are kept busy on their property. At present, the theatre company's actors are a substitute family.

"May I ask which company?"

"I'm contracted to the Wilson Barrett Company." She proudly stated.

Everything fell into place. This was the girl who'd replaced Mary Eastlake as leading lady. Had she also exchanged places with her predecessor, becoming Barrett's love interest?

Maud seemed disappointed with my silence.

"You're not familiar with Mr. Barrett? She asked.

Still processing the information, I hesitated. Maud continued.

"I expect you're too busy to get to the theatre. I was hoping you wouldn't recognize me. We leave for our tour of the States next week."

I regained my composure.

"The name of Wilson Barrett is known to me, as are many of his associates. I'm sure if time permitted, I'd have admired your performances. In the past, a great deal of my time was spent around theatres. I find such indulgences difficult to fit in these days." I lied.

I had no intention of revealing my past associations to Maud.

"You should make time for yourself. The stage is a wonderful escape from reality." She insisted.

"It certainly is Miss Jeffries."

"Allow me to invite you to our last performance of 'Othello' this Saturday. Could you possibly make time and come as my guest? I'll arrange an excellent seat in the front row for you. My role as Desdemona has been well received, and I'd value your opinion. Come to my dressing room after the show and we can talk further."

I found myself on the edge of a stormy lake. Should I stay on steady ground and decline Maud's invitation, or enter the volatile waters? Mary told me of Barrett's infatuation with the new actress, but Maud appeared interested in me. Perhaps his charms were failing to hit their mark where Maud was concerned. Was fate providing an opportunity to strike back at the man who'd caused so much grief?

"It would be my great pleasure, Miss Jeffries." I replied, smiling.

"Please, call me Maud. I look forward to seeing you at the theatre. Thank you so much for the reading. It was most enlightening and timely." She said.

"For me also." I grinned.

After Maud left, I returned to my office. Relaxing in the carved Indian chair, I closed my eyes. Wilson Barrett's enraged face appeared, destroying the serenity of the moment. Was it a premonition, or imagination? What would Barrett make of my association with his leading lady? Perhaps he'd never find out?

Bitterness still resided in my soul from his negative references affecting employment. The memories of those dark times in the East end, drove me to face the man once again.

***

Two days later, I was seated in the front row of the Princess Theatre. After my time working backstage, it was strange to look at the stage from an audience perspective. Examining the intricacies of the production was detrimental to the play's magic. Illusions of the theatre are lost when one has knowledge of the craft. Maud's charisma was unquestionable. Her portrayal of Desdemona dominated the stage from the moment she entered, captivating everyone. I understood the jealousy Mary Eastlake felt when Maud entered the company.

Awaiting the arrival of Othello was torturous. Had Barrett observed me from the wings? The glow of the stage lights reflected on the faces of those in the front row. Barrett often engaged the audience during his performances. What would he do if he saw me?

Maud was absorbed by her character, never making eye contact with the audience. At one point, Barrett scanned the upper area of the theatre. Anxiously, I waited for him to look to the lower seats, not wanting to miss his moment of recognition. The performance played out without detection. The play finished, and the final bows began. Hand in hand with Barrett, Maud bent low to the stage. I tossed her a red rose. When it fell at her feet, Maud picked up the flower and blew me a kiss. Barrett's eyes met mine. They narrowed when and I smiled. His face turned to Maud, then back to me in time to see the gesture returned. The restrained anger was delicious, as the audience continued to applaud and cheer. The thrill of the moment compelled me to stand, prompting others to do the same. Barrett and Maud stared as the cheering grew louder. Empowered, I gestured for the audience to continue, and the whistling began. Returning to my seat, Maud mouthed a 'thankyou'.

After the applause died away, Barrett delivered a short farewell speech. Still holding Maud's hand, he exited the stage. Slowly, the crowd left the theatre. Would Barrett try and block my entry to Maud's dressing room? By now, she'd have told him of the connection. Rushing to the backstage door, I was met by a burly fellow guarding the entrance. Barrett would have told him to prevent me from entering.

"Good evening. I'm here to see Maud. I believe she's expecting me." I told him calmly.

Maud had also given instructions to the doorman.

"And you would be?" He asked, suspiciously.

I handed him my card.

"The name is Cheiro." I smiled.

"Very good Sir. Maud asked me to watch out for you. I'm on the lookout for another fellow named Warner. Don't worry about being disturbed. I'll see he doesn't get in." He told me, proudly.

"Thank you. Maud must have many unwanted admirers. You need to be vigilant." I grinned.

"Yes. Mr. Barrett keeps his actors safe. Thank you, Sir, have a good evening."

Another victory over Barrett. Exhilarated I knocked on Maud's door.

"Who is it?" A muffled voice asked.

"Cheiro." I replied.

"Oh lovely, one minute please."

Barrett's door was closed. Part of me wished it would open. While Maud finished dressing, my eyes remained glued to Barrett's room. It opened, but no one passed through. I could see Barrett pacing around the room, oblivious to my presence outside. Looking upset and angry, he eventually saw me.

"Gods teeth Warner. How did you get in?" He shouted.

"Mr. Barrett. It's been some time. How good it is to see you again. Are you well?" I asked, smiling.

Barrett moved closer. He looked me over, taking note of the stylish clothing.

"I don't know what you're up to Warner. You think you can dress yourself up and play the gentleman, do you?" He smirked.

Barrett was unaware of the elocution training with Ben Greet. I was putting them to good use. Luckily, he was ignorant of my new name or vocation, allowing me to pass through the backstage guard.

"Mr. Barrett. You once told me; I never had the talent to portray any character convincingly. Therefore, if you now see and hear a gentleman before you, then a gentleman I must be. I thank you for the compliment."

Barrett moved closer in a vain effort to intimidate me. It only accentuated the disparity in our heights. I retrieved a gold pocket watch, placing it between our faces.

"I do hope Maud will be ready soon. I've a lovely supper planned for us back at my Bond Street apartment." I gloated.

"You were always smug Warner. I don't know what your new situation is, but I'm sure it's dishonourable. I've surpassed you before when it comes to the fairer sex, and I'll do it again. Have your supper with Maud. You've one night. I've countless evenings ahead in a country far away from you and your tricks. We'll see what eventuates." He smiled.

Barrett's exit speech was dramatic, and he strode away after delivering the lines. Maud opened the door on cue, as if the scene had been rehearsed.

"Sorry to keep you. Come in." She beckoned.

"I was eager to offer my congratulations on a magnificent

performance. You're a remarkable artist." I told her.

"Thank you for my beautiful rose. The fragrance is divine. It reminds me of home and my mother's gardens." She said, picking up the flower and smelling it.

"I remember your reading." I told her.

"Yes, I miss being able to wander through nature." She sighed.

"If it were earlier in the year, I'd take you through Kensington gardens. The aroma of the blossoms on a summer's evening is sublime. With the cooler weather, many of the flowers have disappeared."

"How lovely it would've been. One must take advantage of beauty before it passes."

"Yes, such opportunities shouldn't be ignored. Your hand tells me you're not someone to let a chance slip by." I explained.

"Oh Cheiro, you continue to fascinate with your insight." She giggled.

"Let us have a lovely supper and talk more on the subject."

"Perfect. I'm always ravenous after a performance. Where shall we go?"

"I'd be happy to entertain you at my home in Bond Street. I've something prepared." I told her.

Maud placed the rose in a vase, and took her hat from the chair. She adjusted it in a mirror, and sprayed a delicious scent of perfume.

"Well, as you rightly pointed out; I'm not one to let an opportunity pass me by." She smiled.

As the clocks struck midnight, we arrived at my apartment. Maud entered, removed her hat, and placed it on the rack beside the door.

"What a sweet home you have. How long have you been here?" She asked.

"Not very long. It's conveniently close to my office."

"Your taste is impeccable. Did you decorate it yourself?"

"For the most part. I'm a regular customer of Liberty's on Oxford Street. They've a wonderful collection of furniture and paraphernalia."

"Come and satisfy your hunger. I've a selection of sweet meats, breads, cakes, and biscuits. There's some excellent cherry brandy if you'd like a glass?"

"A small one." She replied.

Our conversation flowed freely. The chemistry between us was unmistakable.

"Thank you for this happy escape from my hectic world. I get so tired of living in hotels, and eating in dining rooms."

"In a way, it's the same for me. My days are spent meeting people for short periods of time. For the most part, they're only interested in whether they'll make or marry money. In the precious time between clients, I usually eat alone."

"Your life is similar to mine. It's difficult for people who've a regular profession to understand our situation."

"This is true. I don't want an average life though. Do you?" I asked.

"That's where we differ. You see, I eventually want a normal life with a faithful husband and children. A house and garden in the country somewhere, where I can tend my pets and flowers. This is my idea of happiness." She told me, wistfully.

"Why did you become an actress then?" I asked, puzzled.

"A woman from the theatre can find a husband and retire. That's the future I see for myself. I know you've told me my palm denotes a strange situation regarding my love life. I will remain optimistic." She smiled.

"Of course, Maud you mustn't be influenced by me."

"I went into the theatre because of my family's financial situation. They owned a cotton plantation and things were not going well. I was compelled to perform as a means of earning money. They rely on my financial support." She informed me.

"I see. I admire your loyalty."

"Don't misunderstand me. I enjoy performing and the accolades, but I believe most actors grow weary of living in a world of constant fantasy. Most people are ignorant of the hard work and gruelling schedules actors are subjected to. It can become too much. This happened to me once in New York."

"I can relate Maud. I drove myself into the ground when I first started reading palms. It took me three months to recover."

"Really? It's a horrible state of affairs. I never want to experience those feelings again."

"We've much in common Maud, even though our future goals differ."

"You don't wish to marry and have children one day?" She asked.

"No, I can't imagine it. The life I want for myself wouldn't be possible if I were married with children. Having said that, my palm does indicate a later marriage. It's something which puzzles and troubles me."

"Why should such a thing concern you?"

"I'm independent in nature. I couldn't see the marriage working."

"You say the lines can change. Your feelings towards marriage may alter."

"Anything is possible." I smirked.

I felt as if I'd known Maud for years. I'd never experienced a connection with anyone so quickly. Common traits emerged despite our different nationalities. Our success was driven by necessity. She engaged with the black population in her home state of Mississippi, empathizing with the trials of the workers. I compared it to the tenant farmers in Ireland, who'd been virtual slaves to the landed gentry. We were incensed by the injustice of life. We sat comfortably on the lounge together.

"Can I have your hand, Maud?" I asked.

"Do you want to read my palm again, or just hold it?" She jested.

"Both. Shall I show you a special marking?"

"Didn't you explain everything during my reading?"

"It's something I observe from time to time in individuals. I don't always tell my clients of it."

"How curious. Is it a bad sign?"

"On the contrary, I consider it an exceptional one. If you look here, underneath your finger of Saturn and Apollo, you'll find a looped line. It's only partially formed in many hands, but in yours it's complete. It's known as the girdle of Venus."

"What a name. What does it mean?"

"The owner is open to physical sensation. It denotes a powerful and creative sexual nature."

"No wonder you keep it to yourself. Do you possess the mark?" She asked.

I responded with a passionate kiss, which Maud reciprocated. Our love making continued for some time. In the morning, she prepared to leave.

"I can't believe we must part after such a night. When will we meet again?" She whispered, kissing me.

"Have faith Maud. Let's be grateful we've found each other, and trust in the power which brought us together. You must call me Louis. Cheiro is a name I adopted to separate my private and professional life."

"I've only known you as Cheiro. It will seem strange to call you Louis." She replied.

"Maud, before you go. Who was the person who referred you?' I asked.

"Of course, I never did tell you. I'm indebted to her. She was once an actress in the company. Before leaving, she convinced me to make an appointment with you. She also told me of your incredible charm and handsome features."

"And her name?"

"Mary Eastlake. She'd been in the company for some years, but retired soon after I arrived." She explained.

After a passionate kiss, Maud left. Discovering Mary was behind her visit, made things clearer. It was a cunning and calculated manoeuvre. Mary expected Maud to fall in love with me, disrupting any developing romance with Barrett. Mary believed her relationship with Barrett would continue, if Maud's affections were directed elsewhere. I refused to let the woman upset me. The girdle of Venus depicting Maud's impassioned nature, did worry me. She'd be away, working closely with Barrett on the American tour. A powerful union was consummated that night, and the thought of it ending was inconceivable.

***

<u>Chapter Five</u>

(1893-1895)

Thoughts of Maud and Barrett were pushed aside during the day. The dismal Winter nights were difficult, with sleep eventually coming after a few brandies. Spring brought the promise of new encounters, and made everything bearable. I'd just finished my readings for the day, when Oscar walked into the reception area.

"Louis my boy. I'm glad you're still here. I felt it time we caught up. Are you engaged for dinner?" He asked.

"I was just leaving. I'll join you." I replied.

Many weeks had passed, since the truth of the Sutherland's money was revealed to Robert. I'd moved on from the guilt, subduing the memory by avoiding my accomplice. The atmosphere of the Café Royal on Regent Street was colourful and opulent. The establishment was a favourite of Oscar's, and reminded me of the Parisian cafes we frequented during our trip. We found a table adjacent to a column with a carved nymph.

"How are you enjoying your new found wealth?" Oscar asked.

"I've no complaints. Plenty of clients, a published book, and another on the way." I replied.

"Your hard work has paid off. I'm pleased you've put the Sutherland's money to good use." He whispered.

"I prefer to forget that past association, Oscar." I told him.

"Of course. Like the poor duke, what's gone is gone. That reminds me. My new play, 'A woman of no importance' opens at the Haymarket theatre this Saturday. Will you accompany me?" He asked.

"You want me to go with you? What happened to that young gentleman you were so infatuated with?" I smiled.

"Oh Bosie. He's reluctant to show his admiration in public. I've invited other friends as well. There's no cause for concern, you'll not be alone." He explained.

"Bosie? What kind of a name is that? Who is this fellow? What does he do?" I asked.

"His name is Lord Alfred Douglas. He's the son of the Marquess of Queensbury."

Oscar flicked his hair and summoned the waiter. After ordering, we resumed the conversation.

"What about you? Who's been keeping you warm this winter?" He grinned.

"I've been too busy to become involved with anyone." I replied.

"You were never a good liar, Louis. I detect a change in you. Are you interested in someone? I know the feeling myself. A serious infatuation changes one's demeanour. Am I not a trusted friend? You can divulge your heart's desire to me."

"Very well. Anything to keep you quiet. I've met a young lady who's made quite an impression."

"Really? Is she a woman of no importance?" He laughed.

"Sometimes, you go too far." I warned.

Oscar was not the best person to be discussing my intimate thoughts with.

"Anyway, there may be little future in it. She's out of the country at present." I informed him.

"Oh Louis, the world is your oyster. You've become the talk

of the town. As I predicted some time ago, your charming personality and handsome features guaranteed success. Why waste time pining over something you can't have?"

"It's not in my nature to give up Oscar. I can't tell you more. It's possible you know this person."

"As you wish. I've an invitation to supper with Blanche Roosevelt after the performance on Saturday. I'm at liberty to bring anyone, and in your present lovestruck state, it might be a welcome diversion."

"I'll let you know on the night." I replied.

Feeling weary after dinner, I left Oscar to finish his coffee. Walking home, I considered Oscar's invitation. Meeting people away from palmistry work could be beneficial.

***

A crowd gathered outside the Haymarket Theatre. The excited conversations of London society could be heard for some distance. I'd arranged with Oscar to meet at a location along from the theatre, and found him surrounded by a group of young men.

"Louis, over here." He shouted.

Oscar introduced me to the five smiling faces, all wearing a green carnation on their lapels. Oscar produced another.

"This is for you Louis." He said, handing me the flower.

"Oh, I see. I'm to be a member of your entourage as well."

"Indeed. Part of an elite club. Come let's make our way to the theatre." He announced.

As Oscar and his flowered companions paraded through the lobby, people stepped back whispering. Once again, I'd fallen victim to Oscar's ego. I'd become an unwilling participant in his narcissistic performance. The thunderous applause at the conclusion of the play further inflated his vain persona, and he bathed in the adulation of the theatre goers. The play was a triumph, and Oscar consumed the attention like a hungry child.

Before long we were in the presence of Blanche Roosevelt, a remarkably charismatic woman. American by birth, she was blessed with intelligence, beauty, and although nearly forty, far from faded. Beginning life as an opera singer, her talents extended to works of literature, writing books, and journalistic pieces.

Blanche was married to Signor Macchett, Marquis d'Alligri. It was common knowledge she'd once been the mistress of the French author, Guy de Maupassant. Her glamorous appearance and refined personality, made her a popular hostess. The hotel suite was filled with interesting guests, and Blanche was quick to notice us.

"Oscar, how privileged we are. After your wonderful success tonight, I thought you may be too distracted to come. I've been hearing great things."

"Nothing could keep me away from a Blanche Roosevelt party, my dear. Allow me to introduce you to the young gentleman I've been telling you about. Cheiro, this is Blanche Roosevelt."

Blanche extended her hand.

"Very pleased you could come, Cheiro. You must tell me more about your special talents." She told me, smiling.

"I would be only too pleased." I replied.

"But Oscar, where is this other young man you've been singing the praises of? I thought he'd be with you this evening?" She asked.

"I expect he'll be here soon Blanche. Don't worry yourself, I'll not let him abscond without meeting you."

Blanche took Oscar's arm and moved towards the guests.

"It's going to be a splendid party, Oscar. Come and I'll introduce you to the others."

It seemed Oscar's new friend Lord Alfred Douglas was going to make an appearance after all. I expect 'Bosie' thought he'd be less visible in a hotel suite compared to a packed theatre.

"Everyone, I'd like you to meet my dear friend Oscar Wilde, and his mysterious friend Cheiro." She announced.

We were introduced to the Australian singer Dame Nellie Melba, the American theatre producer Henry Abbey, the well-respected painter Lord Frederic Leighton, Prince Colonna of Rome, Francis Pelham-Clinton-Hope, and his wife the American actress May Yohe. Dame Melba was the first to speak.

"Mr. Wilde, won't you tell us how your play was received this evening?" She asked.

"Oh, you were not in attendance? You missed a resounding success. I couldn't be happier." He replied, flicking hair.

"I'm delighted for you. Unfortunately, time doesn't permit me the luxury of enjoying the performances of others. These days, most of my time is spent on or behind the stage." Madame Melba answered.

"The lack of recreation time is a condition common to those who crave the spotlight. As an author, my work is done after the words are written." Oscar explained.

"Believe me, many actors wish they'd written the words they're reciting." Henry Abbey laughed.

"Behold the dilemma. If an actor wishes to change the dialogue, let him write his own play. He's only creating more work for himself and others, meddling with my words. I've no patience with those who feel they know better."

"It's true. There's nothing more frustrating than dealing with someone who feels they know better." I smiled.

May Yohe sipped a glass of champagne, and laughed, spilling the drink down her neck.

"Oh, Excuse me." She spluttered.

Oscar gave me a harsh look, which was returned. May wore a spectacular jewel around her neck. Feeling responsible, I found a napkin to dry her.

"Here take this." I said.

"Thank you. That's very kind of you." She smiled, wiping her skin.

Yohe's husband Francis looked embarrassed.

"May dear, I think you've had enough champagne for this evening." He scolded.

May's huge gem sparkled in the night light, and my gaze was still fixed on it when Blanche directed the guests to a table. We continued chatting before joining the others. The young actress was annoyed by her husband's reprimand.

"Francis is so easily irritated. Is it such a catastrophe to spill my drink, who cares?" She whispered.

"It's a curse of the English. They worry too much about what others think."

"Exactly. You're not English I take it?"

"No, I'm from the emerald isle. We're not so easily embarrassed."

"Oh, you sound English?" She questioned.

"A result of elocution." I explained.

"I see, as an actress I can relate."

"Have you been performing in England?" I asked.

"Yes, recently in 'The Magic Opal'. I didn't change any of the Isaac Albeniz's words though." She laughed.

The jewel on May's bosom continued drawing my attention.

"It's quite amazing, isn't it?" She smiled, holding it up.

"Yes, very hypnotic. Is it a sapphire?" I asked.

"Oh no. It's a diamond. Haven't you heard of the Hope diamond?"

"No, I haven't. A diamond of such size must be extremely rare."

"It was left to Francis by his grandmother. Legend says it was stolen from India, and some say it's cursed. Would you like to touch it?" She smiled.

"No, thank you. I've some experience in these matters. I wouldn't take the warnings too lightly if I were you." I told her.

May looked at me seriously.

"The story of the 'Magic opal,' revolves around an opal ring. It's said whoever touches the ring falls in love with the wearer."

"An interesting plot." I smiled.

"I don't believe in such things. How could something so beautiful, be evil?"

"In my experience, one cannot guarantee beauty and goodness are found together." I explained.

A servant showed a new arrival to the table, and Oscar stood to greet his friend.

"Everyone, I'd like to introduce you to Lord Alfred Douglas." He announced.

Oscar continued the introductions around the table.

"And this Bosie, is Cheiro, the great soothsayer."

Alfred's sly grin revealed his nastiness.

"Pleased to make your acquaintance. Any friend of Oscar's is of course, a friend of mine. You are, I believe, from the same part of Ireland?" He asked.

Young and fair, Alfred fitted Oscar's ideal vision of male beauty. His aristocratic background only enhanced the snobbish attraction.

"Yes, County Wicklow, God's country." I boasted.

"Well, that depends on which God you believe in." Alfred said, raising an eyebrow.

"I expect it's the same one you worship." I replied, refusing to be drawn into an argument.

"The only God Bosie worships is the one reflected in his mirror. Come and sit. Blanche has provided a wonderful spread for us." Oscar intervened.

May sat next to her husband sampling the fare. Smiling, she consumed another glass of champagne. After many enjoyable conversations, we thanked our hostess, and left.

Outside the hotel, Oscar and Alfred hailed a cab.

"Would you like to share a ride, Louis?" Oscar asked.

"No thank you. It's a lovely evening for a walk."

"As you wish. It's clear you're not in a hurry to return home." He smiled, with a flick of hair.

"Not at all. A quiet stroll after a hectic week will be much appreciated." I explained.

"Did you hear that, Bosie? Oh, to be so popular." Oscar smirked.

"Goodnight Oscar. And to you…."

"Lord Alfred." Douglas interrupted, before I could finish.

"Of course, my lord. I wouldn't dream of using Oscar's pet name for you." I told him.

"You really shouldn't dally about on the streets Cheiro. Don't you want a good night's sleep? After all, you've an important day of fortune telling ahead of you." Alfred snickered.

They climbed into the hansom, and the pretentious dandy had one last comment before the horse pulled away.

"Oh, before you go. Wont you take a quick look at this cabbie's hands. Can we trust him to deliver us home safely?"

They drove away laughing. What was the purpose of the evening? Oscar's actions were cold and calculated. I'd enjoyed the play, but the preceding parade of pompous youths was demeaning. My inclusion was an intentionally cruel act to put me in my place. I believe Oscar was jealous of my social success, and parading me as one of his boys in public was humiliating. Alfred's cynical comments reflected what this privileged snob really thought of my profession. From various conversations, it became clear I'd been invited to Blanche's soiree to entertain guests as a palm reader. Payment for my services was never discussed. Apart from a few quick looks, I managed to deflect those palms thrust at me between drinks. I spoke scientifically on the research and study of palmistry to the annoyance of Oscar and Alfred. In fact, most of the guests made bookings for private readings over the next few days. Oscar's attempt to relegate me as a 'party trick', failed miserably, and by the end of the evening, I'd secured a number of well-respected clients. It gave me great pleasure to inform Oscar of this, the next time I saw him.

***

Maud's romantic letters from America were heartfelt, and the separation hadn't altered her desire for a reunion. When the company returned to England, Barrett made plans to tour regional areas, preventing Maud from spending time with me. A worrying change in her letters prompted me to leave London for a few days to investigate.

The countryside was flush with flowers, but concern for Maud kept me from relishing the passing landscape. Her hotel was a short distance from the train station, and meeting her was at first tense, but after talking, we relaxed and spent a passionate day together. Conscious of avoiding any confrontation with Barrett, I stayed away from the theatre. The time with Maud was blissful, and I returned to London secure in our relationship.

Back home, a note from Robert requested we meet the following Thursday at the newly completed Shaftesbury monument in Piccadilly Circus. After so many weeks, I was eager to catch up on his activities. Robert stood with a cane under the statue of the naked god eros, and the disparity between the two figures was comical. The humour disappeared, when a closer inspection revealed his weak and fragile body.

"Robert, whatever is the matter? You don't look at all well." I asked.

"Thank you, Louis. Your flattering comments regarding my appearance are encouraging. Let us find a café, and I'll detail the events which led me to this sorry state."

Once seated, Robert proceeded to relay the story.

"I have to tell you, I'm most apprehensive about eating out these days."

"Why, what's happened?"

"Oysters Louis. They almost killed me."

"No. Tell me."

"I was having a wonderful night out with Edward Benson and Charles Powell. Well, I ordered oysters. The damn things were off. Can you believe it. They tasted fine. There was no hint of their insidious poison, and I ate them all. We went off to see Irving's play, and before long I was at death's door."

"Terrible. I've heard of similar instances killing people." I told him.

"Let me tell you, I almost joined them. I've never been so ill. I really believed I was going to die. Anyway, it's taken some time for me to recover. The doctors advise leaving England before the Winter." He explained.

"Poor Robert. Can you manage it? Where will you go?" I asked.

"Thankfully, it's all arranged. My mother came to the rescue and gave me enough to travel. You know Edward Benson, don't you?"

"Not intimately. I remember him from the literary gatherings at Hamilton Aide's home."

"Apart from his talent as a writer, Edward is something of an amateur archaeologist. He's planned a trip to Egypt later in the year, and I'll meet him there. I'm quite excited. The dry climate will help my recuperation."

"It sounds marvellous Robert. I envy you. Egypt is one place I've always wanted to travel to. Does he know many people there?"

"Apparently so. We plan to visit Cairo, Luxor, and Aswan. It's becoming the place to go during Winter. In fact, he's meeting up with a few of his London friends in Luxor."

"Really, anyone I know?"

"Probably. You seem to know everyone these days Louis. I do remember Edward talking about your friend Oscar." He told me.

"Surely Oscar is not travelling to Egypt at present, after his current success?" I asked.

"He won't be there when I arrive, but apparently this new beau of his, Lord Alfred Douglas will be there."

"Bosie? Really? Are you are going to meet him in Egypt?" I asked.

"Bosie? Whatever are you talking about? Don't tell me you know Lord Alfred as well?" He asked, rolling his eyes.

"Actually, I've met him."

"Where? Oh, of course, with Oscar no doubt."

"Yes, it was at a recent supper, after the opening of 'A woman of no importance.'"

"What's he like?"

"You can make your own judgement, but I wouldn't expect him to be interested in digging around in the Egyptian dirt."

"Not everyone who visits Egypt is interested in the ancient world, Louis. Edward informs me of several other activities on offer." Robert advised.

"I've no doubt, you'll discover those. You must educate me on your return next Spring. Will you stay in touch?"

"Of course."

After a light meal, we said our goodbyes. A part of me envied his upcoming adventure. I'd seen the Egyptian pavilion at the Paris Expo, but Robert was going to experience the real thing.

I made a mental note to avoid eating oysters. The possible consequences of a contaminated meal outweighed the desire to indulge in them. Besides, there were plenty of other luscious delicacies available.

***

It had been six weeks since my visit to Maud. Her correspondence once again dwindled. A letter was delivered one evening in July.

"My Dearest Louis,

How quickly the weeks have flown by. I remember our last time together with tenderness and love. The performances have gone well, with applauding audiences showing their approval. Wilson remains unchanged. Your name has come up in our conversations recently, and I cannot help but feel he suspects something of our meetings. He's decided to tour America again in November, and we'll be away until June of next year. I'm sure he's doing this to keep us apart. The thought of not seeing you for all that time is more than I can bear, but what can I do?

Your loving Maud."

I threw the letter down, cursing Barrett with every profanity known to me. Was there no end to this man's vanity and vindictiveness? I believed we'd been watched during our time together. Maud was not only the subject of Barrett's infatuation, but a major drawcard for his company. Losing her would not only hurt his ego, but his profits. I took pen to paper.

"Dearest Maud,

I was so very pleased to receive your latest letter. You deserve all the accolades. Barrett is abominable. I won't let him succeed in his efforts to separate us. I'll arrange to leave for the United States this September, and stay until June. There's been much interest in my work there, and I won't be put out by travelling abroad. Our separation is only temporary. Take heart my love.

Your Louis."

After the letter was posted, I began planning for the trip. It seemed a confrontation with Barrett over Maud was inevitable. After the latest turn of events, my anger knew no bounds. The excitement of working in America again was diluted by thoughts of what may occur in the future.

***

In September, I boarded the SS. Paris bound for America. After arriving in New York, I travelled on to Chicago. In 1893, the exposition buildings on the edge of Lake Michigan were completed. The event was due to finish in October, and the glowing accounts of those who'd visited convinced me to attend.

The bustling city of Chicago was impressive. The great fire of 1871 had destroyed much of the old city, and the new buildings were grand structures of stone and cement designed to prevent any repeat of the disaster. The Auditorium hotel on Congress

Street demonstrated America's tenacity to recover from adversity. My luxurious suite had a separate sitting area where I could see clients.

Much had changed since my visit with Barrett's Company in 1887. The Columbia theatre where we performed in January of that year, remained the same. Walking past the building allowed me to reflect on how much my life had changed in those six years.

I was amazed at the number of Americans wanting readings. Often, wealthy people found themselves in a bidding war to secure an appointment.

One successful auction winner was John A Logan. He was from a wealthy Chicago family. Tall and handsome, John's aura glowed with the light of privilege. His dark eyes glistened with the vitality of a good life, and the well-groomed hair and moustache only added to his charm. He was a man accustomed to getting what he wanted, when he wanted it. It didn't surprise me he'd gained an appointment ahead of others. As he entered my suite, the scent of sandalwood and orange blossom permeated the room. I was familiar with the fragrance.

"Please take a seat. I must congratulate you on your choice of cologne. I've sampled this new scent myself in the hotel store." I told him.

John smiled, revealing a perfect set of white teeth.

"I believe it's the finest, made specially for the Exposition." He replied, stroking his moustache.

"You've paid quite a sum for this half hour appointment. Is there something specific you'd like me to look for on your palm?" I asked.

"I'm curious about my professional life. Perhaps you can enlighten me on anything you may see regarding that."

"Very well. Please place your palms here facing upwards. I will see what secrets lie within." I smiled.

"I have no secrets." He told me, defensively.

"Everyone has secrets. It's a fact on which all psychoanalysts agree."

As John's eyes met mine, his breathing became heavy. Slowly, he placed his hands before me. I examined the palms with the magnifying glass.

"That glass is something extraordinary." He commented.

The magnifier was custom made for my work. A solid gold snake coiled around the lens, provided a stunning frame and handle.

"It's a design inspired from Ancient Egypt." I explained.

Holding the glass, I continued to decipher the network of lines. The physiology of the hand was interesting. A square palm with long conical fingers.

"You're a practical person. You balance your head with your heart when making decisions. This is shown by the equal length of your fingers to the palm. The close connection of your head line to the life line at its beginning, indicates a cautious approach in your dealings with others. You're not someone who rushes into things. You carefully assess every situation, much like you're doing now." I smiled.

"And my career?" He asked.

"Your fate line suggests a preordained destiny. Your right hand tells me your actions will not alter the outcome. Your designated path has already commenced and will continue."

The length of life indicated by the lines was not long. The health line or line of Mercury, cut across the lifeline fracturing it at an early age. Unless a client specifically asked about this, a short life was never divulged. Interestingly, those whose hands foretold a premature end, usually never asked about their lifespan. As in Maud's case, the girdle of Venus marking was evident in John's hand. Given his charisma and physical attributes, this came as no surprise. I returned to his career.

"In what area does your vocation follow?" I asked.

"I'm involved with the military."

"Then I predict this will continue until your end."

"Well then, what about a marriage?"

"There is an indication of a partnership. I would expect it to have already occurred, as it's low on the mount of Mercury, and this indicates an earlier time in one's life. You may have missed opportunities in your love life, given some other markings."

"You're quite right about the partnership. I've a charming wife. What are these other opportunities you speak of?"

John's breathing grew faster. His eyes wandered over my body, and he repositioned himself in the chair. My instincts regarding his secret desires were proven when he adjusted the lump in his trousers.

"Opportunities for physical pleasure. Certain signs are clearly marked. They're obvious to the trained palmist." I grinned.

John was accustomed to hiding his desires and deflecting situations which could lead to regrettable encounters. He ended the reading.

"Thank you Cheiro. It's been most informative. Tell me, have you been to the Exposition yet?"

"No. I do plan to visit. I gather it's quite large, and takes time to see everything. Perhaps I'll find a suitable guide to keep me from becoming lost in its enormity."

"You're welcome to accompany me. A friend and I are planning to go this Friday. Would that suit you?"

"That's a generous offer, and I'll be happy to take you up on it. Let me know the details."

On the appointed day, a pair of well-groomed horses pulled up at the front of the hotel. John opened the door to his carriage and ushered me inside. Smiling widely, he introduced me to his companion.

"Cheiro, this is Mr. Arthur Caton. After I told Arthur of our meeting, he's been eager to make your acquaintance." He explained.

Arthur was a well-dressed gentleman in his early 40's. As a Chicago lawyer, and the son of a prominent Illinois supreme court justice, he shared the affluent lifestyle of his companion. A substantial inheritance meant he spent more time following his sporting and leisure activities than practicing law. His hands signified a person of refined and artistic persuasion, and I felt an immediate affinity with the man.

"I appreciate you taking the time to show me your city and the exposition, Mr. Caton." I told him.

"Don't mention it, it's my pleasure. Please call me Arthur. You come highly recommended, not just from John, but many others. You've made an impact on Chicago society from your suite at the Auditorium." He explained.

We drove off in the direction of the Exposition's new 'White city'. In comparison to the Paris Exposition, the American version was much larger, with numerous fountains and classically styled buildings painted white to reflect the electric lighting.

Moving through the fair, I felt as if I were visiting an unreal world mirroring our own. Crowds moved within the exhibitions, delighting in the latest inventions from different countries. The sheer size of everything eclipsed the Paris Exposition, and a huge ferris wheel dominated the skyline, giving 2000 people an amazing view of Chicago. A hot air balloon floated above buildings, and people looked down on streets reflecting foreign towns complete with authentic inhabitants. In a matter of weeks, the structures would be torn down and the temporary world dissolved.

John made a logical suggestion.

"Right men, we need a plan of action. We've a day to achieve our objectives, and as the exposition is too large, I suggest each of us nominate a place we'd like to visit?"

I thought of Robert and his exotic Egyptian adventure.

"I believe Cairo Street is something spectacular. I'd like to spend some time there." I suggested.

John laughed.

"I've heard about the escapades of the Egyptian belly dancers. They are the talk of the fair. Do they interest you?" He asked, grinning.

"I've read something about them, but John, there are also belly dancing men. Such performances have been a part of the Arab culture for centuries."

John's smile faded.

"Is that so." He replied.

After referring to our guide maps, we headed off. What a triumph Cairo Street was. The sheer size of the exhibit added to the illusion, and I felt I'd been transported to another country with the authentic architecture, music and aromas. There were even camels, donkeys, and Arabian horses. We'd arrived just in time to view a mock wedding procession with costumed white horses. I've always had a love of this majestic creature, and often dreamed of owning one.

"Look at the magnificent horses. Are they not spectacular?" I declared.

Arthur stood next to me as the procession passed us.

"You've a love of horses then Cheiro?" He asked.

"I surely do, especially such fine specimens as these. Lucky is the person who owns these beauties?"

Arthur grinned and replied.

"Yes, I believe I'm very lucky to own these Arabs." He smiled.

"What did you say? The music is loud. I thought you said you owned these horses." I laughed.

He came closer shouting in my ear.

"But I do. They are from my stud. I'm loaning them for the duration of the Exposition at a handsome price."

"You own them? Unbelievable." I shouted.

"Yes, I too am a great lover of equines. I've several excellent thoroughbreds at my property in Ottawa, just outside of Chicago. If you're interested, I'd be happy to show them to you. It's a pleasure to meet someone who shares my passion. Unfortunately, my wife shows little interest in such things."

"I will make time." I replied.

"Excellent, shall we continue to explore Cairo?"

We walked in silence as the wedding procession passed us. It was the beginning of a close friendship lasting until Arthur's death.

John returned, after escaping from men selling pornographic postcards. The sound of a drum and Egyptian flute grew louder as we walked towards the stage. The rhythmic music was hypnotic, attracting a large crowd.

A group of girls, covered with sheer veils and dangling jewels, thrilled the crowd. People yelled and applauded as the pulsating abdomens and rhythmic convulsions sent them into a frenzy. Suddenly, the drum stopped and the dancers fell to the stage, motionless. The flute commenced its soulful tune, and the dancers turned to face a new performer.

Finding a space next to the stage, I became entranced by the beauty of this young girl gliding across the stage. Her face was angelic and flawless, and she danced with the energy and style of someone beyond her years.

The audience remained silent, paralysed by the scene unfolding before them. The raucous cheering stopped as the young girl made eye contact with the crowd, without any hint of nervousness. I wanted to see what lay beneath those dark pools of black, and she turned to acknowledge me. Had she read my thoughts? She stared for some time, before a drum broke the spell. In an instant, she transformed into a whirling extravaganza and people gasped as the performance intensified. Her astonishing athletic ability and unique choreography separated her from the other dancers. Images of her stayed with me for weeks.

John was happy to move on from the dancing, and enter his choice of the arms pavilion, where we found every conceivable weapon of death and destruction. Each country's canons and guns were on display to demonstrate their military strength. Arthur and I sighed at the size of the gun shafts, and were relieved to leave humanity's weapons of war behind. Our military friend was appreciative of our patience.

After the gun pavilion, we moved on to Arthur's choice, the Italian exhibition. He'd fond memories of travelling to the continent particularly Venice, and before long, we found ourselves in an authentic gondola with a young Italian. On the other side of the lake, an Indian village had been constructed, and it amused us when our gondolier blew kisses to a young girl on the shoreline.

"I believe our Italian friend has eyes for a beautiful squaw. There are no boundaries when it comes to love." John laughed.

"The Italians are a fiery race with little inhibitions, and rarely let an opportunity pass." I grinned.

"Rightly so, life is too short." Arthur declared.

Arthur spoke without realizing the prophetic nature of his remark. Both of my companions were dead within a few years.

After the exposition, I visited Arthur's stunning home and

opulent stables in Ottawa. He told me his wife was away in Chicago, and it seemed they were content to live separate lives. His wife spent a great deal of time with the millionaire Marshall Field, whom she'd marry in 1904. I eventually met Field when he came for a reading soon after.

The experience of Ottawa consolidated the love of horses, and I acquired thoroughbreds years later in Paris.

John went off to the Spanish American war, and served as an assistant adjutant general in the siege of Santiago. In 1899, he fought in the Philippine American war and was killed in the Battle of San Jacinto. He was only 34, and it was difficult to reconcile the loss of such a fine specimen of manhood. Just as I'd seen on his hand, destiny delivered its ominous promise. I hoped his fate would somehow be altered, but it was not to be.

***

In November, I expected to hear from Maud after she arrived for Barrett's tour. In the meantime, I continued seeing clients from my rooms on Fifth Avenue. I'd written to her with my new address in New York, and finally, a letter was delivered. With nervous anticipation, I opened it.

"Dearest Louis,

When you receive this letter, you'll expect me to be in New York.

Please don't be angry with me when I tell you, I'm still in England. I will not be touring America this season, and there's no point explaining the circumstances. Believe me when I tell you, I'm not up to the rigors of travelling and performing. I will return to the company in June once they are back in England. I know you've committed yourself to stay in the States until then. Be content, as we'll be together when you return. You can be comforted in the knowledge I'm away from Wilson and therefore free of his attentions.

Your loving Maud."

"Be content?" I shouted, tossing the letter on to my desk.

All my plans were thrown into disarray. I stormed out of the building, strutting up Fifth Avenue to calm down. Barrett was behind it for certain. How had he learnt of my trip to the United States? What tactic did he employ to convince Maud to stay away from me? The power he possessed over his actors was perverse. He was even prepared to sacrifice Maud as leading lady in order to win a point.

I found myself heading to the theatre where Barrett was performing, in the hope of confronting him. By the time I'd worked out the best way to get there, my temper had cooled. Taking the brisk walk helped me see things clearer. Remaining alone and focused on my work had its benefits.

***

There were numerous festivities for the 1894 New Year in New York, and the invitations allowed me to mingle with the cream of Manhattan society. These interactions led to readings in Boston and Philadelphia. I'd been approached by an American publishing company to produce a paperback guide on palmistry, and an elaborate leather and gold covered edition. The 'Comforts Palmistry Guide' was published in the middle of the year, just before my return to London. This was the second of my published works, following the Record Press Co's, 'Book of the Hand.' Given the success of these works, I self-published 'Cheiro's Language of the Hand'; a more extensive edition with prints of famous clients. The photographer, George Prince, took a portrait for the first edition. Subsequent copies of this book were produced through other publishers, and included a portrait by the New York Photographer, Aimee' Dupont. The first edition of 'Language of the Hand' was funded by the monies obtained from the Duchess of Sutherland. The last of the illicit money was used productively.

I returned to my Fifth Ave rooms in May. The readings and talks outside of New York provided a lucrative income, and everything was going famously. Barrett's plan to keep Maud away, was consuming, and for the sake of sanity, I decided to confront him.

Realizing he'd be returning to London around the same time, was problematic. It was better to deal with Barrett away from her.

I entered the lion's den during a rehearsal, wearing the finest clothes and accessories. If required, the silver tipped, ebony stick could be used as a weapon. The theatre attendant allowed entry, after I told him I was a dear friend visiting from London. In the shadowy section of the stalls, I waited until the right moment presented itself, and it came when Barrett called a lunch break. As the actors rushed away, I watched him write notes on a script. I wanted to set upon him there and then, but showed restraint.

"Mr. Barrett, may I have a few words?" I asked.

Barrett jumped to his feet, looking for the voice in the darkness. Slowly, I moved into the light.

"Warner, what in God's name do you want?" He shouted.

"Mr. Barrett, you shouldn't take the Lord's name in vain. Afterall, you've an image to uphold." I smiled.

Barrett glanced around nervously. We were alone. His anger was as intense as mine, and he moved closer.

"I've had about all I can stand of you." He bellowed, striking a warrior pose.

"Save your performance for someone who appreciates it. Stop the acting. You may be in a theatre, but without a costume, you cut a comical figure. You're nothing more than a conniving controller, manipulating others for your own sinful pleasure." I shouted.

"You speak to me of sins? I'm not the one portraying myself as an exponent of palmistry in order to seduce clients." He roared.

"No. You use your power as a showman to ravish your leading ladies, leaving them sad and sorry to raise your bastards. Yes, I know about poor Mary Eastlake. I wonder how many others there are? What do you think the world would make of such a man? Any number of publications would happily print the story. This is the last time you'll meddle with Maud and I."

Barrett lunged forward, grabbing my throat. He tightened his grip, choking me. Using my stick, I dislodged his hands and pressed the wood into his neck.

"You talk of bastards. What of your bastard? Why do you think Maud couldn't tour? She was away in Australia giving birth to your child." He spluttered.

"It's not true. You're lying." I shouted, dropping the cane.

Barrett collapsed, still coughing. Some actors returned after hearing the commotion, and helping him to his feet, demanded to know what was happening.

"This is far from over Barrett. What you say may be right, but you've far more to lose than me if your indiscretions are made public. Unlike yourself, I was never married. Be warned, I'll not be crossed again."

I'd been careful not to incriminate Barrett in front of the others and left. Knowledge of Mary's child gave me protection, and my thoughts turned to Maud. After Barrett's revelations, the contents of her letter made sense. Had she really gone to Australia to have her child? After some calculations, I realized I could be the father.

A week later in my consulting rooms, an attempt was made on my life. Not long after the session commenced, the covert client lunged forward with a dagger, thrusting it at my heart. His aim was meticulous and bore the mark of a professional assassin, and if it wasn't for the cigarette case in my coat pocket, I'd be dead. Luckily it deflected the weapon, preventing a serious wound. After answering the attack with one of my own, he fled. A scar reminds me of the encounter along with the words he shouted when leaping from his chair.

"This is for someone who wants you dead."

I'm convinced Barrett hired an assassin to remove me. As a result of the experience, it became standard practice to keep a loaded revolver close by.

***

In mid-June, after my near-death encounter, I returned to London. There was much to discuss with Maud regarding her pregnancy. The company was performing Hamlet in Blackpool at the newly opened Grand theatre, but I stayed away to avoid any upsetting altercations with Barrett while she was present. She agreed to meet me in my hotel after a performance. Did Maud intend telling me about the child? Had Barrett told her of our heated exchange in New York? Was she aware I knew of her trip to Australia to give birth?

There came a knock on the door.

"Maud my love, come in. How are you? After not hearing from you for some weeks, I've been worried." I told her.

Maud looked pale and tense, and there were no passionate embraces or kisses.

"I'm sorry Louis. So much has happened since our last meeting. I scarcely know where to begin."

"I was devastated when receiving your letter telling me you weren't coming to America. I planned the trip so we could be together."

"I know, it was terrible of me. How can you forgive me?"

"Well, in the end, the trip was profitable. What happened to change your mind?" I asked, innocently.

Hiding the knowledge of Maud's predicament was not easy. I wanted her to confide in me. Her eyes searched my face, looking for any sign I may know the truth, and it was clear Barrett hadn't informed her of our meeting.

"I cannot speak about it as it's too painful to recall." She cried.

"But you must. Am I not entitled to know? After all, I planned the trip to be with you."

Maud looked shocked by the words. Had her secret been exposed after all? Logic told her there was no way I could know the truth, and she continued her deceit.

"Entitled? What do you mean? You're not my husband. What right do you have to demand anything of me? This past year has been a trial for me Louis, and I've handled it alone. It's changed me, there can be no denying it." She told me, angrily.

Hurt by her inability to confide in me, I continued.

"What do I mean to you Maud? I thought we had a special bond. Has your love for me changed? Can you not share your secret with me, whatever it is?"

"And you Louis? Will you share your secrets with me?" She challenged.

Stunned and hurt by the remark, I retaliated.

"We're talking about you Maud. If you're determined to deny me any knowledge of something which concerns me, then I must ask the question. Did you or did you not travel to Australia earlier this year to give birth to a child?"

Maud began to cry.

"How could you know this? I've spoken to no one except Wilson?" She replied, though her tears.

"Exactly. You dare to confide in Barrett and not me. I'm the man who should be told. I had to hear it from him." I shouted.

Maud realized I'd seen Barrett in the United States.

"You deserve to be told? Wilson has as much right as you to be told. Perhaps he neglected to tell you that." She informed me, defiantly.

Grabbing Maud by the shoulders, I shook her. What are you saying? You don't know which one of us fathered your child?"

Maud pulled away.

"It's true. I'm sorry Louis, but there it is. I'm tired of thinking about it. Weary of you both. I cannot be responsible for the mistakes I've made with the two of you. I'm just a woman, who is at the mercy of men. My father sent me away to work in the theatre, and my brother instigated the contacts enabling me to earn money for the family. I was entrusted to a theatre manager in New York, who negotiated with Wilson to have me work tirelessly in his company. He packed me off to Australia where another man, arranged the adoption of my beautiful baby girl. Men and more men making decisions about my life without a thought for what I want. What's to become of this sweet angel who now lives on the other side of the world?" She wept.

"How could you allow Barrett to do that?"

"I had no choice. I don't want to discuss details of the experience. I must continue on as if nothing has happened. But it has."

"Barrett claims the child is mine." I told her.

"He said that to you?" She asked.

"You're the father of Maud's bastard, were his exact words."

"I'm not surprised he denies it, a man wishing to project a wholesome image to the world. The truth be known, I cannot be certain who the father is, although the odds suggest one of you more than the other. With two such egotistical men, my daughter is better off not knowing the identity of either of you. Don't pretend you'd be happy to become a father and provide for her Louis. I know you too well."

The words cut deeply. I'd never had the desire to have a family as other men do. It infuriated me that Barrett had succeeded in seducing Maud, just as he said he would. I should have understood, given the right circumstances Maud would succumb to him, as she bore the mark of the Girdle.

"You're right Maud. The child is better off with others. We're not the kind of individuals who can provide a wholesome upbringing to anyone."

"Speak for yourself Louis. One day I'll marry and leave the theatre, and my children will be loved and cherished. Until then, I'll continue on without any more dangerous liaisons."

"You're right Maud. Our destinies are different." I conceded.

As Maud left the hotel, feelings of betrayal surfaced. It was a milder version of what I'd experienced in New York after the debacle with Mary and Barrett. At the time, I vowed never to love as deeply, and it seemed I'd succeeded.

I returned to a rigorous schedule of readings. These included Lord Leighton, Lord Kitchener, Sir John Lubbock, and the Countess of Aberdeen. Many titled personages frequented my rooms, content to pay the high sum. Other affluent people made appointments, after hearing reviews from their aristocratic friends.

I remember a particular gentleman by the name of Charles Millar. He offered me a large sum if I'd see him immediately. It was his money rather than a title, which opened doors for him. Born in Ireland, he moved to Australia and involved himself with lucrative timber and railway projects. He acquired a vast fortune, and purchased the best yachts money could buy. He was friends with Lord Brassy and the Prince of Wales, who sailed regularly on his state-of-the-art Yacht, 'Saide, at Cowes.

Charles was an exception to the rule. Here was a fellow Irishman who'd become a member of the Royal Yacht Squadron. This was highly irregular for a commoner, let alone an Irishman. He'd succeeded in infiltrating the elite world of the aristocrats without a title. I remember his reading well.

"Welcome Sir, please come through." I told the well-dressed gentleman.

"Charles Millar's my name. You come highly recommended, from the Prince of Wales no less." He informed me, shaking my hand.

"His Royal Highness is too kind." I replied, smiling.

"He's most impressed with your knowledge, and amorous personality."

"Do I detect an Irish accent?" I asked.

"Right you are. Even though I've lived in Australia for some years, it seems I still retain traces of the homeland. I believe you too are from Ireland, are you not?"

"Yes, from County Wicklow. I've lost much of my accent."

"It's what happens when we're separated from our brothers and sisters."

"Shall we begin?"

"Of course, one hand or both?"

"If you'd place both hands palms up thank you."

I noticed how pale and dry Mr. Millar's hands were. It led me to examine his line of mercury or health line.

"You're having some health issues at present."

"This is true. For some time, my constitution has troubled me. I expect I've driven myself hard over the years. You must be frank with me, as I want the truth." He told me.

"Very well. Your left hand denotes a long life with an excellent health line; however, your right hand fails to support these hereditary influences."

"My mother is still alive at 84."

"Your lifeline and the lines which cross it from the plain of Mars, tell me you've been subjected to much stress and opposition in your life. The heart line is crossed at several points. Fine lines are descending from the lines of marriage and children."

The gentleman broke down and began to weep.

"You're right. I've made money and bought fine possessions, but the one thing I desired most of all, was a son to share it with. Many times, my prayers were answered only to be taken away, sometimes on the very day they were realized. I do have beautiful daughters, but no male heirs."

I looked closely at his marriages and children lines.

"I can see many pregnancies in your relationships. There are complete fine lines of three females attached to the first marriage, and these signify healthy girls. There are other lines indicating pregnancies which were not full term. This marriage was early."

"Yes, my poor wife died at 24 after trying to give me a son. The pain of her loss was unbearable."

The second marriage also has many children lines attached.

"Two children were born in a row. First a girl, which we lost the same day. Then within a year, the birth of my beloved son. All was perfect for two weeks until he died. The grief was unimaginable."

"There are two healthy lines attached to that union."

"My sweet girls Saide and Muriel came after another two deaths, and still no son."

"But wait, don't you have a son to your third marriage?"

"Sorry Cheiro, you're wrong. I've only been married twice, and the outcome of the second marriage prevents me from marrying again. The relationship didn't end well, and we've been separated for some time."

"It's very clearly marked. There's a third relationship which may not always be a marriage, but a union, nonetheless. There's a son attached to this line." I explained, showing him the marks.

"Are you sure? What if I became involved with someone who

already had a child? Could this be what you're seeing?"

"In my experience, no. It's a question that's often asked, and it comes down to the quality of the line. It's my opinion, the male child on your palm is of your body. The marking is too strong. It's something you've longed for."

Charles was elated. The desire to have a child of one's own is passion common to many. My thoughts turned to Maud, and her plan to have a child in the future. My ambivalence for children was in sharp contrast to the dreams of Maud and Charles. I couldn't reconcile it. The pain and heartbreak he'd experienced almost certainly affected his health, and I didn't tell him the fate and life lines gave no indication of him reaching the age of his mother.

"Does this make sense to you?" I asked.

"It certainly does. What a gift you've given me. For these past few years, I've been involved with a married woman, and she is the mother of a boy. He was born during the time I'd been intimate with her, but she was adamant her husband was the father. Your reading tells me otherwise. I've met this child, and I do feel a strange affinity with him. Today is the happiest day of my life, and I cannot thankyou enough."

Such meetings convinced me of those unknown forces shaping our lives. Everyone who crossed my path, did so for a reason. Usually, the information from the readings made their lives happier, and the power connecting us may never be understood.

***

Robert returned from his Egyptian adventure, and was eager to tell me of his escapades before I left for the United States. We met in Piccadilly Circus at our usual spot under Eros, and this time he looked much healthier.

"Robert, how well you look. The trip has done wonders for

you."

"I can't tell you how wonderful I feel, in body and spirit. Let us find somewhere to eat, and I'll reveal all."

"Shall we dine at the Royal?" I suggested.

"I'm quite strapped for funds Louis, after my time away. It's a little extravagant for me."

"Nonsense Robert. I've plenty for both of us." I gloated.

The situation showed how our circumstances had changed in a few short years. I was the one with the full purse, while Robert watched his pennies. He was making a living as a journalist, but his salary was far from lucrative. We arrived at the café and ordered our meals. Robert looked around at the other patrons.

"Do you think we may run into your friend Oscar here Louis? Is this not one of his favourite haunts?" He asked.

"It's possible. He is rather busy at present I believe, writing a new play."

"I must tell you, after Egypt, I'm well acquainted with his beau, Lord Alfred."

"So, you did meet up after all. Somehow, I knew you might. What is your impression?"

"He's a complicated fellow, young and immature. A product of his upbringing I dare say. We spent time together at the Luxor Hotel, and he accompanied Benson and myself on excursions down the Nile. Louis, if you could see these places, you'd be amazed. The temple of Edfu is sublime, and I had a profound experience there amongst the preserved ruins. It was only one of many. You must go one day."

"It's somewhere I've longed to visit. I've been to Cairo Street at the Chicago fair." I joked.

Robert and I laughed at the disparity of the experience.

"I feel so optimistic about things. Benson's company was inspiring. I mean to start writing novels. He's had such a success with his first book 'Dodo'. Why can't I do the same?"

"Of course, you must. You're just as talented. Have you an idea to work on?"

"Yes, I've begun work already. I'm writing about London and our times. As a result of my association with Lord Alfred, I'm frequently bombarded with the 'Oscar Wilde show', both in person and indirectly through him. It's generated much material for a novel."

"Is Bosie aware of your planned book and the subject matter?" I asked, raising an eyebrow.

"Lord Alfred is not. I refuse to use Wilde's name of 'Bosie' when discussing him, Louis."

I laughed aloud before biting into my croissant.

"Do you have a title for this novel?"

"I thought I might call it, "The Green carnation", in honour of your recent experience with the man."

I choked as Robert revealed his plan.

"But everyone will know who you're writing about if you dare use such a title?"

"I believe I will publish it anonymously."

Robert's scorpion eyes glistened with delight.

"Oh, Robert. You really don't like the man, do you?"

"Let us say, it will be interesting to see his reaction after he reads something written at his expense for a change."

"You must be careful. Have you not heard the recent stories regarding Bosie's father, The Marquess of Queensbury and Oscar? The feud is becoming very public." I cautioned him.

"Of course. Only last week Lord Alfred told me his father had gone to Wilde's home in Tite Street and accosted him there."

"What did Oscar do?"

"Nothing by all accounts." He told me.

"The story may be different if the Marquess attempts to defame Oscar in public. His ego would not stand for that."

"I expect you're right." He agreed.

"Does Oscar not realize he's little chance against a member of the aristocracy. They are a law unto themselves when it comes to getting what they want. The injustice of our society is endemic." I replied, angrily.

"You're right. Nothing has changed regarding the legal system for some time. Only yesterday I read about the inequality of the sentences for the different levels of English society. Not so long ago the average person could be transported to Australia for stealing a piece of rope, whilst an aristocrat who embezzles the government of thousands of pounds, gets to say he's sorry and make amends."

The mention of Australia with its dark convict history made me think of Maud's daughter. Would she be happy growing up there? If she were my child, then she must inherit a drive and tenacity to overcome obstacles. What if Barrett was her father? I preferred not to dwell on it any longer.

"You're right. There's still much inequality when it comes to the justice system." I agreed.

"Speaking of the justice system, are you aware of the Duchess of Sutherland's recent settlement? I read about it the other day. £750,000. What a sum. A fortune many times over." Robert told me.

The mention of the duchess was still a sore point between the two of us. I refrained from telling him about my recent publication, funded by her money.

"Yes, I did hear something about the trial recently. I'm not aware of the details. I was so busy in America." I lied.

"Your Duchess is quite a piece of work. She tried to wipe out any inheritance owing to Sutherland's children. When his papers were being read, she seized one, and after finding its contents damaging, destroyed it in the fireplace. She went to jail for her actions, but the experience of incarceration was quite different to that of most others. The Duchess didn't want for anything, and after a short time, was released to spend her fortune."

"The woman belongs in the past Robert. Let us change the subject."

"Then tell me of your plans. You're returning so quickly to America. When will you be back?" He asked.

"I've nothing definite booked for my return. The Americans are a wonderful race, so full of optimism. They don't dwell on the past, and the positivity is contagious. I need to be around that at the present time."

"It may be for the best anyway."

"What do you mean?" I asked.

"I dined with Alexander recently. As you know, he's a duke and privy to the gossip. He's of the opinion, the Marquess of Queensbury intends to make an example of Oscar."

"In what way?"

"He means to provoke Oscar to expose the relationship with Lord Alfred. This could potentially result in a criminal charge against him."

"That would be disastrous for Oscar, and he'd have no chance against such a conspiracy."

"Exactly. Alexander has warned Oscar's acquaintances of the

consequences if they are called as witnesses against him. A great exodus has begun across London. Alexander himself will be leaving for Sicily before the Winter, and doesn't expect to return until events are settled. He's invited me, and given my new connections to Oscar and Lord Alfred, I'm accepting."

"You may be right. Perhaps I will stay longer in America until, as you say, events are settled." I told him.

The memory of Oscar's fate line returned. I'd no doubt, any challenges to his reputation would be met with an arrogant reply. The current situation was tenuous, and I packed extra things before leaving in September.

***

I arrived back in New York during the fall of 1894, and the city was abuzz with the news of my return. There were appointments booked, and invitations to attend. At these events, I never felt pressured to sing for my supper, and people were genuinely interested in my work as a scientific palmist. Before long, I'd joined Manhattan's elite, taking my place amongst other self-made success stories.

My suite at 432 Fifth Ave provided a convenient location for the well healed clients passing through my door. Before leaving, they'd sign the visitor's book, allowing them to see other illustrious names. Often this was the time when identities were revealed. On one occasion, a Mrs. Frank Leslie was none too pleased when I failed to recognize her name.

"You've not heard of 'Frank Leslie's Lady's Magazine?" She asked, indignantly.

"Alas no Madam. I'm not a buyer of publications directed at the fairer sex. In fact, I'm only aware of one such magazine in London, 'A woman's world', because an acquaintance of mine was at one time, the editor."

"You cannot mean that scoundrel Oscar Wilde?"

Mrs. Leslie's knowledge of the publication and its editor impressed me.

"Well, yes. You're familiar with the magazine?"

"With the publication, no. With the editor, yes." She huffed.

"You've met Mr. Wilde?"

"My good man, I was married to his brother."

It wasn't something I expected to hear. Oscar had talked little of his relations.

"You certainly are well acquainted with the family then." I smiled.

"More than I care to remember. If you're able to read about mistakes one makes in life, then where was the line depicting that disastrous episode?" She questioned.

"I'm sorry the marriage wasn't what you'd hoped for."

"Willie like his brother, hid many secrets from his loved ones. My ex-husband's vice was the bottle, while Oscar's wickedness has been recently revealed."

"I see the American press sources the London tabloids."

"We like to stay abreast of any scandals in the world." She smiled.

"The frailties of humanity are universal, and appeal to all."

"London never fails to provide countless stories of impropriety." She continued.

"It's human nature to hunt for such things. I expect to be targeted at some point."

"But Cheiro, what negative reviews would you attract? I've only read positive stories about you." She replied, cynically.

"Alas, envious and spiteful individuals have always existed. Finding fault with others is a condition manifested from their unfulfilled lives."

Mrs. Leslie removed a postcard from her handbag.

"I thank you for an amusing hour. Clearly, your knowledge is to be commended. The reading was entertaining, quite theatrical actually. May I give you this postcard promoting a book I've recently published? Please don't be put off by the title, 'Are men gay deceivers?' I believe you may find it interesting given you're connected to some of the characters who inspired me to write it."

"Of course. What a fascinating title, and I'll make time to read it. Thank you for signing my visitors' book."

"It's the least I could do after the session. I do feel my book will leave more of an impression on you however, as it seems you've forgotten our previous correspondence. You wrote to my publishing house last May, with details of your work, and I published a notice in my magazine before you returned to London."

"Please forgive me. I was extremely busy at the time, and as a consequence, I failed to respond to all the press."

"You really must read my book. Good day to you."

Mrs. Leslie rolled her eyes, and departed.

***

In 1895, 'Language of the hand' surpassed all expectations. The fifth edition containing more prints of famous hands, created a great deal of interest in the subject. Self-publishing the book proved lucrative, and publishers like the Transatlantic Company offered me a healthy sum to reprint the work. The logical and scientific format impressed non-believers who'd been adversely influenced by charlatans.

The reputation of chirology was helped immensely by genuine palmists publishing their research. Readers were unaware a number of the handprints in my collection were taken by secretaries, and I'd not met many of the owners at all. In some cases, money was exchanged to secure the handprints, which I intended to use at a later date. I must admit this was the case for Lord Kitchener. My secretary met him at the war office and took the print. In my recent book, 'Confessions', I fabricated the meeting with Kitchener to add interest. Nevertheless, I was able to delineate the palm from the print, and that part of the story is true.

It was mid-January, when I learnt of the Barrett Company's return to the United States. According to the advertisement in the newspaper, the tour was due to open at the Boston Theatre on January 21st with 'The Manxman'. Reading the cast list, I found Maud Jeffries listed as Kate Creegan.

Apart from a note at Christmas, I'd had no correspondence from Maud. Concerned, I decided to see her. Why should Barrett have the satisfaction of destroying our friendship?

My plans were to arrive for opening night, and stay a couple of days. A surprise visit with Maud after the performance could be dangerous, as the animosity between Barrett and myself escalated. If the situation arose, I'd deal with it, as I wasn't about to be intimidated by a person who'd orchestrated an attempt on my life.

I purchased a book from an esoteric store dealing with the charms and curses of antiquity, and intended leaving it as a warning. When working in Barrett's company, I'd heard others speak of his superstitious beliefs. The effect of the evil eye, was particularly worrying to him. The power of suggestion is a formidable weapon, especially if the person is a believer.

***

The January wind swept through the train station. The six-hour trip through the brown countryside was broken by white patches of snow. As we entered each town, signs on rooves advertised an array of products. By the time I reached Boston, the latest pills for constipation, oil for healthy hair and tonics for depression were familiar to me.

The landscape bore little resemblance to the countryside around Britain, despite the name of 'New England' being applied to it. My desire to return to a bustling city grew stronger the further we travelled.

We arrived at Union Street Station on time, and passengers rushed from the platforms to find shelter. It took some time to secure a cab because of the inclement weather, and after settling into my room on Boylston Street, I headed out for a meal at Marston's on Brattle Street. The recently refurbished cafe was a popular meeting place for Boston's businessmen who patronized its dining room. A waiter informed me the café had a seating capacity of 800, and a staff of 300. There were prosperous looking patrons everywhere. I returned to my room for a nap, after consuming a delicious Irish stew.

***

The entrance to the Boston Theatre on Washington Street sat inconspicuously between two shopfronts, and the modest façade disguised the three thousand seat theatre.

When I arrived, streams of people were passing through the lobby towards the auditorium. On the walls, portraits of notable theatricals hung including a striking oil of Henry Irving. The promenade saloon, measuring forty-six feet by twenty-six feet, was paved with marble, and the theatre itself measured three hundred feet from front to back.

My seat was in one of the three balconies of the dress circle, giving me an unimpeded view of the enormous stage. The design of the building was remarkable, and I took special note of fire doors and stairways.

The curtain opened, and the story of 'The Manxman' unfolded. Maud performed her role as an abused woman without fault, and there were gasps during the violent scenes with Barrett. I remembered Mary Eastlake's experience of working with Barrett in these confrontational roles, and it angered me to think Maud would have to recover from the effects of the performance, just as Mary had done.

The two women had much in common. They both bore children to Barrett without the benefit of a close commitment or marriage, and both had been romantically involved with myself. In my heart, I believed Barrett had the greater chance of fathering Maud's child, and coming to this conclusion helped me deal with the situation. No doubt as time passed, the truth of the parentage would become apparent as the physical differences between Barrett and myself were obvious.

Watching Barrett perform in this wonderful venue filled me with jealousy, but it was comforting to know my current life offered more recognition and money than that of an actor. Barrett's inflated ego, and the manipulation of those around him, was at the heart of my disdain for the man. His need to maintain power regardless of the cost, was unbelievable.

I'd been a threatening and destabilising influence in his company, helping others achieve their dreams and break free of tyrants like Barrett. Reading the palms of fellow workers and identifying their strengths, gave them the confidence to leave his company and seek a future of their own. Barrett considered me an Irish insurgent, instigating rebellious mutiny in his world. My refusal to go away even after the threats, enraged him, and his intimidating behaviour would have ended the conflict for many.

Barrett miscalculated my character in fighting back when threatened, and I was in possession of information harmful to his reputation. His lack of accountability for Maud's pregnancy was disgraceful, and diverting responsibility, showed the man's true colours. My intimate associations with two women who'd shared their secrets with me, must have haunted him.

After the final applause, I remained seated.

"Sir, if you would make your way to the lobby, please." A young usher told me.

"I wonder if you might take this to Miss Jeffries? I'm a friend of hers. Tell her I will be waiting beside the stage." I said, handing him a card and a coin.

"Thank you, Sir, I will give it to her."

The boy rushed off smiling, and I waited beside the empty stage. Perhaps Maud would decide not to see me, but it wasn't her nature to run from problems. I knew she preferred to face her tribulations head on.

Maybe she'd changed. I was about to leave, when I heard her voice from behind the wings.

"Louis, what are you doing here? I thought you were in New York?"

I could barely see her face in the darkness.

"I thought I'd surprise you. Can you meet me later?" I asked.

Maud looked around nervously. It's strange how quiet a stage becomes directly following a performance. Everyone was away in their dressing rooms or taking a break from the night's work.

"Is that really a good idea? What do we have to talk about?"

"I'm here as a friend Maud, but if you feel you aren't in need of one, I'll leave you alone."

"Very well. I cannot stay for long. Please go now, as I don't want any confrontations here tonight." She whispered.

I gave Maud the address and she retreated to her dressing room. On my way back to the auditorium doors, I found the usher again.

"Young man, thank you for delivering my message to Miss Jeffries. There's one more task, if you could once again accommodate me?"

"Of course, Sir."

"Would you deliver this book to Mr. Barrett?"

"Most certainly Sir, I will take it directly."

"Oh, there's no hurry. Whenever you're backstage again." I told him, smiling.

I handed him another coin, along with the book of charms and curses carefully wrapped to hide the ominous title. Barrett would open it thinking it another gift from his adoring public. Once reading the title and my note, he'd realize his mistake. The note read,

'Mr. Barrett,

I believe this book may be of interest to you. There are many cultures that believe karma dictates the events of one's life. The trouble a person deliberately causes others will return threefold. If one is innocent of any malice, they can rest in peace. However, if one is guilty of any acts against another, they will surely answer for it. The content of this book reveals the tools which are used to expediate that retribution. Sleep well.

Louis Warner.'

***

I returned to Boylston Street and awaited Maud's arrival, and before long there was a knock on my door.

"Louis, I'm not sure this is a good idea."

"Why ever not? We're old friends Maud. Why should our friendship be destroyed by Barrett? Come sit a while and tell me how you're doing."

"I don't know how Wilson knew of your visit. He was furious, and ordered me to remain in my hotel. The audacity of the man, to think he has the right to dictate such things to me. His behaviour convinced me to come, if nothing else but to defy him."

"I won't be angered by that remark Maud. I hope you wished to see me on your own account, and not as a means to win points against Barrett. Anyway, let's not argue."

Maud relaxed on the sofa. The anger left me, and I was able to speak calmly to her.

"Apart from tonight, are you coping with Barrett? Is he treating you well?"

"He's still attempting to seduce me, but I'll never submit again. My bed won't be shared with anyone, except a husband."

"No doubt your past experiences and having your child, has made you a stronger woman."

"My daughter is about to turn one year old, and my heart aches to see her." She cried.

Leaving the child behind in Australia was painful for Maud.

"You must tell me what happened? It will help you to recount the experience to someone." I told her.

"You may be right Louis. Wilson knew theatrical people in Melbourne, and he told me I could go there and have the child under another name. These people gave me lodgings in a boarding house where I stayed until the birth. I used the name Bertha Jeffreys and told the couple who ran the house, I was from Tasmania."

"Did anyone ever suspect something was amiss, given your American accent?"

"I'm sure they realized I wasn't from Tasmania, despite my best attempts at an Australian accent, but they needed details for the birth certificate. The couple were not unfamiliar with unwed actresses giving birth to babes. The children were adopted out, and the mothers continued on with their lives."

"Did you name her?" I asked, gently.

"Yes, I called her Florence Beatrice."

I wanted to ask what the child looked like, but Maud went on to describe her without my prompting.

"Louis, she was adorable, a perfect looking child. She wasn't a large baby, making the birth easier."

"Are you in contact with the people raising her?"

"Yes, I made it clear I wanted to be informed of her progress. It's made it harder for me though."

"You must find comfort knowing she is well looked after, and will have a stable upbringing."

"I suppose it's some consolation, but it's painful to know she can never be a part of my future. She's a secret I must keep, not only for my sake, but for the father's also."

"Do you ever discuss Florence with Barrett?"

"I discuss nothing of a personal nature with Wilson anymore. He'll never acknowledge Florence as his child because of my past relations with you Louis. As I said at our last meeting, I've changed, and will no longer be entwined in the passions of a man who cannot commit. Our relationship will remain professional."

"He doesn't strike me as someone who'll give up easily."

"This is true, but I'm a stronger person now, and my compliant days are over."

As we talked, Maud relaxed. No doubt Barrett's spies would inform him of her late return, and he'd imagine the worst. The trip to Boston had been fruitful in repairing the relationship with Maud, and intimidating Barrett on a private and spiritual level. I'm sure my gift had achieved its objective. Whether he chose to read it or not, was unimportant.

***

Back in New York, the appointments continued, and by April, the strain of the long hours began to show, and fate stepped in. This time, it came in the form of an Indian guru, Swami Vivekananda, who visited for a palm reading.

I'd read about Swami, when in Chicago for the World's fair. His famous speech at the Parliament of Religions introduced Americans to the fundamentals of Hinduism. He was a charismatic figure, with a gift for oration.

Swami greeted me with engaging eyes, staring with a calm serenity over the top of my head, examining something unseen. His clothing consisted of a saffron yellow robe, and a tightly wrapped turban. When he spoke, it was in a soft tone, as if he were communicating with one's inner soul. His voice when lecturing on world religions and the brotherhood of man, was passionate and emotional. I'd not been present at his lectures, but was told they were delivered with a resounding and eloquent voice. Although exhausted, in Swami's presence I felt energized.

"Swami, it's an honour to examine the hand of such an enlightened soul." I told him.

"Believe me, I'm the fortunate one to have the knowledge of one so learned, looking at my hands."

"Surely you've had your hand read before in India?" I asked.

"Of course, but there are many charlatans in my country, as there are in yours. I'm curious to see what you have to say."

"If you would place your hands here Swami, I'll begin."

Sitting opposite an Indian in native costume brought back an unpleasant memory. At the Paris Exposition of 1889, my bizarre reading was terminated by the seer's collapse. The hands of the guru brought me back to the present.

"Your hands are fine and slender, indicating a sensitive and spiritual nature. The fingertips are conical in shape, with philosophical knots at the joints, showing your love of learning and analysis of ideas. You are methodical and structured in your research of topics, and your swooping head line indicates you undertake tasks with a spiritual bent, rather than a logical one.

The strongest line on your hand is the fate line running from the base of your palm to the mounts of Jupiter and Saturn. Because the line terminates between the two, it indicates great success and recognition for your work concerning the spiritual side of life. You are fated to achieve your destiny, which you must do as early as possible." I told him.

"You're correct my friend. You don't need to shelter me from the facts, as I know I'll not reach an advanced age. This is something which has previously been foretold."

"It's true. Your life line is fine and frail indicating a lack of vitality, and this is reinforced by the poor health line indicating many issues with your body. Your fate line is by far the most robust line on your hand."

"The prana is provided by spiritual entities allowing me to finish my destiny, as you've seen. This energy keeps me functioning. Without it, life is extinguished." He calmly explained.

Swami's life line was the weakest I'd ever seen. Why had fate decreed this enlightened spirit should die so young?

"Swami, this prana energy you speak of fascinates me, as I exhaust myself at times with consultations. How can I learn more about the subject?"

"I'm retiring from lectures. I've spent all my reserves over the past weeks delivering my lectures in Chicago and Boston, and intend limiting myself to private consultations here in New York over the coming months. I'd be happy to show you what I know on the subject." He offered, smiling.

"That would be splendid. Give me your contact details, and I'll arrange something before leaving on the lecture tour of Boston." I told him.

"You're to lecture in Boston as well?" He asked.

"Yes, like yourself. The Bostonians are great lovers of knowledge, and I've been advised lecture tours there are successful."

"I must give you the names of those who helped me when I visited. I'm sure they'll be as equally kind." He told me.

Swami departed, leaving his palm print and the names of John Henry Wright and his wife Mary Tappan Wright, both learned scholars and writers. The contact was invaluable for research, as Mary Wright organized entry to the Algonquin Club, providing access to books from their extensive library.

The techniques of meditation, yoga and pranic healing Swami taught me, would prove invaluable for the rest of my life. Sadly, he passed away in 1902, at the age of 39.

***

Just before I left for Boston, I received a letter from Robert updating me on the London happenings.

'Dear Louis,

I thought I'd write and let you know the latest from London. Even though I've been here at Castello Maniace in Sicily since December, there's constant correspondence from the London crowd. It seems all that we feared has come to pass. In February, Lord Alfred's father left a card at Oscar's club, naming him as a sodomite.

Our indignant friend has foolishly taken legal action against the Marquess of Queensbury and now Queensbury's counsel is gathering affidavits from various sources to prove Wilde's behaviour as a sodomite. We all know there are many places where this can be obtained. The trial is set for April 3rd, and there are not many of our friends left to relay anything further.

You were right to stay in the United States, and delay your return until this is over.

I feel particularly bad given my book, 'The Green Carnation', will do nothing to improve his chances of winning the case. Had I stayed in London, I'd surely be called as a witness as the book is a testimony to his behaviour.

Why could he not let things be and ignore the horrible fellow? You were right in your prediction Louis. Oscar's ego wouldn't allow the challenge to rest after such a public insult, and I feel he's made a fatal mistake.

I trust you're well. My new novel, 'An imaginative man', is due to be published soon, and I will send you a copy once it's available.

Robert.'

Looking at the date of the letter, I realized Oscar's trial had already begun. I could only imagine what must have been going through his mind entering the courtroom. In the beginning I'm sure he'd relish the attention, until the gravity of the situation took hold. As more witnesses came forward with damning testimonies, he'd display a defiant series of hair flicks.

From what I'd seen of his palm, the disastrous outcome was inevitable. It fitted perfectly with the sign of a cross on the mount of Saturn foretelling imprisonment, and scandal.

The American newspapers published the outcome of the trial in late May when Oscar was found guilty and sentenced to two years hard labour. I'd been lecturing in Boston at Chickering Hall in April, and when the trial ended, took some time away from my suite at the Brunswick Hotel to travel out of Boston.

***

An acquaintance of mine, Arthur Hurtt, had introduced me to the painter Jean Paul Selinger and his wife Emily. Arthur was a talented artist with experience designing scenic theatre backdrops, and well acquainted with Oscar. We decided to take a break and travel to the Selinger's art studio at Crawford House in the White Mountains of New Hampshire.

Jean Paul invited me to the beautiful resort when we first met. Crawford House was a stunning building set amongst a backdrop of cliffs and mountains, and a scenic train enabled guests to travel directly to the hotel. It became a white wonderland in Winter, and when the weather warmed, melted snow created sparkling waterfalls and streams in the surrounding ravines. It was a perfect time to visit and put the troubles of our friends in London behind us.

The path of the railway through Crawford Notch was an engineering feat, with passengers astonished at the narrow passages of sheer cut rock.

As we pulled into the station house, a lake with a fountain created ripples of reflection on the water's surface. The hotel gleamed white, and singing could be heard from the Crawford House choir. It was a magical, theatrical entrance.

Jean Paul and Emily were waiting for us. Jean Paul, a robust man in his mid-40's smiled and shook our hands.

"Cheiro, Arthur, how was your trip?" He asked.

I moved out of the way of other passengers and greeted our friends.

"Jean Paul, Emily, lovely to see you again. This is a spectacular location, and I can see why you come here. It's a wonderful escape from the hustle and bustle of Boston."

Emily stepped forward.

"It's wonderful you could come and visit. Arthur, of course, has been here before. Isn't that right Arthur?" She asked.

"Yes Emily, I believe it was a couple of years ago. It's a natural paradise, full of inspiring locations for an artist."

Jean Paul ushered us towards the Hotel.

"Let's get you settled first, and we can discuss our plans later."

Entering the hotel lobby, we found ourselves face to face with the choir. They were accompanied by a pianist on a Hans Richter grand piano, crafted from burl walnut and inlaid with mother of pearl. The singer's eyes surveyed the arrivals as they made their way through the building. New people provided a welcome change from the same faces.

I remained at Crawford House for the summer, and it provided a much-needed respite from my busy schedule. The mountain air was clear and fresh, and the many walks and donkey rides with Arthur and the Selinger's helped my physical body regain its strength. I thought little of Maud and Barrett who were due to return to England in June.

I practiced the spiritual techniques Swami Vivekananda taught me, opening a new area of poetic creativity. Within a few weeks I'd written several pieces on various subjects, and these were published in 1895 by F. Tennyson Neely under the title of 'If we only knew and other poems.'

Boston had a profound effect on my desire to write. Moving within the literary circles and meeting with people such as the Wrights, had inspired me to put pen to paper. The quietness of the white mountains allowed my imagination to flow easily, and before long I'd finished a work of fiction. This was also published in 1895, by F. Tennyson Neely in the United States under the title of 'A study in destiny.' It would later be published under another title, 'The hand of fate.'

During one of our dinners, Jean Paul and I discussed painting while our companions talked of other things. His portraits were sought after by the well-to- do, and I compared him with my other artist acquaintance, Frank Miles in London.

"Jean Paul, I admire your talent as an artist. Your work evokes a real sense of the person."

"I'm glad you appreciate my art. Have you seen portraits of people you've known in the past?" He asked.

"Indeed yes. I've met some of the artists as well. Lord Leighton is a particular talent, and someone I've great respect for. It's sad when an artistic light shines less brightly. I believe he's now at the end of his life and work." I told him.

"You've been blessed to meet such people. Have you ever

thought of having your portrait done?''

The question conjured images of Frank's painting, and his hideous defacing The beauty of it when first completed, and the hideous defacing after his mind became unhinged.

"An artist friend of mine did paint me once. It was a few years ago. Frank Miles was his name. Do you know of him?"

"I believe I do recall the name. A great society painter, wasn't he? Didn't he have a tragic end? Arthur, didn't you know the artist Frank Miles in London?"

Arthur and Emily had been chatting at the buffet, and returned with their cakes. I'd never discussed my association with Frank Miles with Arthur, but his expression told me he knew the story well enough.

"I didn't know him personally. Friends of mine were well acquainted with him. I believe Louis was one of them. Poor Frank ended up quite mad didn't he Louis?"

Arthur was part of an artistic circle travelling between England and America where such topics would frequently be discussed, and I knew the association with Oscar explained his sheepish look. I refused to acknowledge any accountability.

"Yes. As so often is the case, great artistic talent fails to survive in the real world. It's a sad story indeed." I replied.

"Very sad. The fragility of an artist can so easily be exposed." Arthur declared.

"Those cakes look delicious. Shall we partake Cheiro?" Jean Paul asked.

"Oh yes, you must try this angel cake." Emma agreed, plunging her fork into the dessert.

"Perhaps he'd like devil's food cake instead?" Arthur grinned.

"You're too witty Arthur. Be careful not to choke on the

crumbs." I told him.

Arthur's smile disappeared, as that morning we'd discussed his dire finances. After confiding in me, I made light of the situation by telling him he'd have to rely on crumbs from his friends' tables. It was an opportune time to repay his sarcasm. Jean Paul and Emma were oblivious to the subtext of the conversation.

At the buffet, Jean Paul offered to paint my portrait, and I wondered how another artist would capture my image. The experience of sitting for him was different to my time with Frank. The completed portrait was technically brilliant, photographic in its detail, and admired by all who saw it.

As wonderful as it was, it lacked the luminous, hypnotic potency of Frank's painting. There was some unexplainable mystical energy in the first portrait. It was a travesty Frank destroyed it before others had the chance to view it. Perhaps it was never meant to be seen by anyone except the painter and the subject. Maybe it was symbolic of how beauty can be corrupted and destroyed, after all, attractiveness is subjective. What one man finds tempting; another may leave.

The motivation behind the creator must influence the final product. Jean Paul's brush was directed by a man who admired me as a friend, where Frank's brush was in the hands of someone obsessed with possessing my body and soul for his own gratification. Every stroke of paint was infused with his sexual desire and lust. Such emotion, in the hands of a technically skilled artisan produced the extraordinary work.

***

On my return to the Brunswick Hotel in Boston, I continued with readings. The use of palmistry for vocational guidance was invaluable, with parents bringing their children for advice on career options. Why put your child forward for a musical career if their hands show little promise in that area? Finding other talents will save time and heartache. This was the advice offered to many parents. At this time, I used the smoked paper method to make palm prints and provided a detailed interpretation on a separate sheet of paper. Later on, I used the roller and ink method to make prints.

***

The next town on my lecture tour was Salem, Massachusetts, an historical town famous for its persecution of astrologers and palmists. Oscar's imprisonment gave me the strength to stay true to my beliefs. Any impositions encountered from antiquated laws regarding my profession, would be fiercely opposed.

It didn't take long for such animosity to show itself. After arriving in Salem, I was informed the lecture would be in breach of the law and illegal. After deliberation, the lecture was allowed to proceed under the condition no money exchanged hands. All proceeds of the night went to charity, and the lecture went ahead to great acclaim. It was worth forsaking any money to allow the 'witchcraft' to proceed, and infuriate the religious groups who'd tried to stop it.

The next day, I laid flowers on the graves of those unfortunate souls murdered by the puritanical tyrants. It's a sad fact, countless innocents were killed in the name of the Lord by those who called themselves Christians.

After Salem, I lectured in Syracuse and Buffalo, New York. The Iroquois Hotel in Buffalo provided a luxurious suite to meet with clients. My next stop was the city of Detroit, where the Cadillac Hotel offered the same hospitality, providing an ideal venue for my readings.

***

At the end of the year, I was back in Chicago, where an extraordinary woman was making a name for herself in Occult circles. After a light supper, the concierge hailed a hansom cab to take me to the local spiritualist church where she was delivering a lecture.

The building was full of animated people, all busy conversing with each other about this gifted woman, Betz Hermann. A vacant seat next to a gentleman offered a chance to make conversation.

"Pleased to make your acquaintance sir. The name is William Judge." The man said, offering his hand.

"Count Louis Hamon, a pleasure. It seems this young woman has quite a following. The crowd is large for a Spiritualist church gathering." I told him.

"Yes, I believe Miss Hermann has studied the Occult sciences voraciously for many years. I'm visiting from New York to hear her speak. I make it my business to seek out such rays of light."

"Are you somehow involved with the Spiritual world?" I enquired.

"Very much so. I'm head of the Theosophical Society here in the United States."

"Really? I've had some dealings with the London branch where I live."

"You too are involved in the Occult world?" He asked.

"Yes, I've been lecturing here."

"What spheres are you involved in?"

"Mainly Chirology, but also Numerology and astrology. You may have heard of me? Cheiro is the name I use for my palmistry career."

"But of course. Anyone at all interested in the science knows the name." He replied.

Before we could continue the conversation, our speaker appeared and addressed the crowd. Miss Hermann's appearance could only be described as plain, with round spectacles sitting studiously on her serious face. The hair was pulled back in a style usually reserved for those of a more mature age. There was nothing showy or glamorous about this woman, and I listened intently to the words she fervently delivered.

"Welcome truth seekers. I thank you for coming to hear me speak tonight.

My style of lecture can only be described as simple, as it comes from my inner most self, and the object sought is to open a way to the hearts of my fellow-beings. Observation and experience, the impulses of sentiment, deep thought and thorough knowledge make up the subject matter.

I have also as a diligent student, recovered and restored many things from the ancient scientists, penetrated their enlightenments, and particularly investigated astrology as a guide and reference to human affairs.

At the horizon of human reasoning there appeared a ball called occultism. This ball rolls slowly ahead while high up many obstacles bar its progress. The way does not form an incline which would facilitate a rapid rolling down into the valley of knowledge or perception. But the way is nevertheless level so that the ball, which has once been set moving cannot entirely be stopped, and therefore the prospect of it reaching the valley is but conditional."

There was a burst of applause from the audience before Hermann continued.

"Away and away over all obstacles it will roll and roll to its destination, leaving behind it ignorance, prejudice, scepticism, hypocrisy, egotism, and the stupidity of mankind, as a crushed mass in its wake. Hundreds of thousands press the ball onward, and millions resist, but all resistance is without avail. To roll the ball upward is beyond worldly power, and those that stand on top and work downward perceive with certainty that the opposing forces are gradually becoming depleted, and that a standstill is impossible. The ball rolls and rolls to its destination, accompanied by courageous and intelligent men, who consign the crushed masses to the sea of oblivion."

More applause and cheering followed.

"I see what all the fuss is about. What an inspiration to those of us who've questioned our spiritual paths." William told me, applauding.

I nodded in agreement. The power this unremarkable looking woman held over the crowd intrigued me. Without any elaborate costumes or scenery, she was able to capture the attention of the audience.

"The disciples of occultism distribute spiritual nourishment to all who are able to assimilate it. To the children of intellectuality, this nourishment lends a refreshing impulse. To the spiritual dyspeptics, however, it is an indigestible herb. The occultists do not distribute their spiritual nourishment to the latter, for they protest that it is poison. For spiritual nourishment, a spiritual stomach is required, that is, intelligence and reasoning power, adequate to digest such food. If not digested, it hardens into incomprehensibility, thus causing antagonism and jealousy. Let occult science be for you what it should be for every right-thinking person, allow it a place in your innermost self and you will find that Science and Truth go hand in hand, that old traditions lag far behind, and that Knowledge is about you and is your own. It only begins then where occultism begins."

Could this woman be some kind of occult saviour? Perhaps her life purpose was to create a bridge between the unbelievers in our world and those who'd chosen a life devoted to the spiritual sciences. As the night progressed, she answered questions from those in attendance, resulting in a change of mind on my part.

A woman asked her.

"Do you not tire from the multitude of people you see for readings?"

The question was of interest to me given I'd exhausted myself seeing people in the past.

"I can stand the strain because it is my calling madam. Advising and assisting has become second nature to me, and this is why I am lecturing here this evening. I can reach a great many people at one time." She told us.

Another asked if her work interfered with her private life. Miss Hermann launched into another lecture on the virtues of marriage and children.

"At the present time I am unmarried and without children. I intend to remedy this situation soon. I will not go against God's commandment to 'be fruitful and multiply.' In all spheres of society, we find bachelors and old maids. I do not intend to end up as one. Various circumstances contribute to this renunciation of the commandment. Such persons are mostly too careful, or they think themselves super-intelligent. But they never learn to know the happiness of life, which is only to be found in marriage. Only in marriage (providing it be a natural and good one) thou findest thy only sincere and devoted friend, the only person who shares sorrow and joy with thee. There are also persons among them who live for a certain cause and concentrate their whole thoughts upon it, forgetting their own self. Such persons are found among great scientists, warriors, and overzealous businessmen."

I looked over to William who was shuffling uncomfortably in his seat. It was the words she delivered next which changed my opinion of her.

"We also find it among persons who indulge in unnatural things, wherein they bury their sentiments in the sea of passion from which no love or human happiness can be derived. In all cases, they do not allow the course of their fate to wander according to the law of nature, which is the very reason that so few among them find their happiness. In old age they arouse our compassion; often they awake at an advanced age, plunging themselves into the fetters of marriage-fetters they are for such, but still it is better to be fettered than to be thrown by the storm of exasperation into the sea of isolation, where oblivion speedily buries them forever."

The words were harsh and judgmental. There must have been several unmarried men and women in the audience who would now be questioning their chosen paths. For them, the earlier words of encouragement had been obliterated by the later dialogue.

After the evening concluded William and I chatted for some time regarding what we'd heard. It seemed Miss Hermann's unsympathetic views were not shared by him.

"I have to say, I'm disappointed in our speaker's comments towards the end of her speech. Not the words of an enlightened spirit; more like those of a bigoted, religious zealot." He sighed.

"What started off as promising dialogue quickly descended into a self-absorbed rant. To say those of us who are unmarried are doomed to a life of unhappiness is extreme, and shows a sad lack of experience. Who is this woman to condemn those who choose not to have children? There are any number of reasons why loving couples do not procreate. In many cases the decision doesn't rest with them. Surely this is God's will." I scoffed.

"Yes exactly." William agreed.

"Her inability to see the love that two people can have for each other regardless of who they are, surprised me. I pity the people who consulted her, and were misguided by her ignorance."

"I'm afraid the ray of light only illuminated intolerance, and it will be disappointing for many, when I write my review of tonight." He concluded.

William departed and I returned to the hotel. Thirty years later, I came across Miss Hermann again. After her marriage, she used the name Josephine Schwimmer, and in 1929, her photo was on the front page of a newspaper. Her only son had been murdered with gang members by Al Capone in what would become known as the Valentine's Day massacre. It seems despite all her sanctimonious preaching; she'd raised a Chicago gangster.

The words of Miss Hermann continued to haunt me for some time after her lecture, particularly those relating to marriage. Her belief that the matrimonial union came later in life to those unfortunate 'unnatural souls,' worried me.

You see, my palm indicated I'd marry in my later years. My love of independence and unconventional lifestyle were reasons enough to never consider such a tie. The 'rolling stone' existence I found myself living would never sustain a marriage, and I didn't understand why two people had to be tied together by law, when love is the only tie that binds.

After Chicago, I travelled to Newport and Florida for the Winter.

Chapter Six

(1896-1897)

In New York, the Central Park trees sprouted new foliage. I received invitations to attend the Metropolitan Opera Season's performances of Edouard De Reszke, Jean De Reszke, Mlle Emma Calve and my old friend Mdme Nellie Melba.

I'd not seen Mdme Melba since July 1894, when she'd consulted me for a reading. After the meeting, her career flourished, and greatly influenced by what I'd told her, maintained correspondence. On the night of her performance, I left my card hoping we'd meet later. An usher escorted me to her dressing room, where Melba's assistant answered my knock.

"Good evening. Could you let Mdme Melba know, Cheiro is here." I told the young woman.

"Cheiro, come in my dear fellow." A voice yelled from behind.

Melba was seated at her dressing table, and extended a hand to me.

"How good it is to see you again Nellie. Your performance was thrilling." I exclaimed, kissing her palm.

"You're sweet Cheiro. Thankyou. Tell me, what have you been up to since we last met?"

"Well, my career, like yours, has taken off. I'm in constant demand for my readings here in New York and other cities, and my lectures and books have been well received. I cannot complain."

Nellie looked at her assistant and smiled.

"Mary, this is the great seer, Cheiro, who can foretell things from your hand. I met him at a party only a couple of years ago, when he was virtually unknown outside of London."

The young woman smiled while continuing to fix Nellie's hair. I'd forgotten Blanche Roosevelt's supper after Oscar's opening night in 1893.

"It seems so long ago." I replied.

"It was an interesting group of people, wasn't it? Things have turned out well for us. Other guests haven't been so lucky." Nellie sighed.

"It's true, the stars were less kind to them." I told her.

"Did you make any warnings to those unfortunates?" She asked.

"If you mean, did I see anything on Oscar Wilde's hand indicating his downfall? The answer is yes. Heeding the advice of others was not something Oscar was known for."

"And what of the other guests?"

"Of whom do you speak?"

"Were you not conversing with May Yohe for some time? Did you see anything foretelling the extravagant spending which resulted in her husband's bankruptcy after a year of marriage?" Nellie asked.

"I'm not aware of these events, and I didn't read her hand. If my memory recalls correctly, she wasn't open to it. Perhaps she wished to keep her secrets. I cannot believe the owner of such a priceless jewel is a bankrupt. Then again, owning such a jewel invites disaster."

"You mean the curse?"

"Yes."

"By all accounts, the marriage is over. How foolish men can be." Nellie exclaimed.

"Francis Pelham Hope wasn't the only man that evening whose life was ruined by obsessive love."

"You speak of Oscar again, and his companion?"

"Yes, Lord Alfred Douglas." I said, with venom.

"He seems to have emerged unscathed from the scandal."

"No surprise someone of his class remains unsoiled."

"As you say, destiny is responsible for those crossing our paths. Let us speak of happier things."

Dining together, we chuckled about our experiences touring America. Nellie spoke of her songs to cowboys from railway cars in Texas, while I recounted tales of pious women carrying crucifixes outside my hotel room in Boston.

"They failed to exorcise my demons" I laughed.

We eventually parted; grateful our colourful lives were free of confining romantic relationships. Sharing the companionship of another whose choice of lifestyle few comprehended, was uplifting.

Another soul who walked an uncommon path was Mlle Emma Calve. As part of the Metropolitan Opera Company, she'd recently toured with Mdme Melba. Heavily disguised in a black mantilla, she walked into my rooms on Fifth avenue one afternoon. I'd no idea who this mysterious woman was, despite the heavy French accent. Holding out her hands, she gave away little in conversation.

I was struck by the squareness of her palm and the spatulate shape of her fingers. The elegance and style of her dress were at odds with the type of hand one usually sees with the working classes, who carve out their lives with little thought of any artistic endeavours.

"I see from your hands you possess a great deal of energy to achieve your goals, and are not averse to hard work."

"But yes monsieur, everything I have is because of the toil I've endured."

"Your sun line rises to the mount of Apollo, indicating success in the arts. It's not due to natural ability however, but through perseverance and endeavour. Your hand is not of the artistic type, which tells me you've chosen your path rather than destiny choosing you. The line of the heart is strong and straight enabling you to overcome emotional setbacks in your life."

There was a whimper from under the veil.

"Two lines cross your life line and line of destiny from the mount of Mars, and these are periods of extreme unhappiness. The first occurs at a young age, around nineteen, when the line attaches to a relationship line, indicating a disappointment relating to a love interest. The second at around thirty-five, attaches to a child of that relationship. You've a second fate line rising from the mount of the moon, indicating spiritual insights and influences from a person from a foreign country."

"You're perfectly correct. May I take my hand for a moment mon dieu. Your words have caused me tears."

When a silk handkerchief was produced and the veil lifted, the identity of my client was revealed. Mlle Emma Calve was well known for her portrayal of Carmen in the operatic world.

"Now you are aware who sits here, yes?" She asked.

"Of course, mademoiselle. It's a privilege to read your hand."

"My secret sadness shows on the hand non?"

"Yes, I'm afraid the hand hides nothing. If you wish to conceal your true feelings, the veil should cover your palm.

"I spoke to no one of the loss of my true love at nineteen, and my only child at thirty-four. Why did heaven give this to me, then take it away Cheiro? It is too cruel." She cried.

"True Mademoiselle. They're hard losses to bear." I sympathized.

"If it were not for Swami Vivekananda, I'd have given up long ago. I'm amazed you saw this on my hand."

Swami Vivekananda's profound effect on Calve was unmistakable.

"You're strong and determined Mademoiselle, and you attracted a person such as Swami to help you understand the pain. Delving into the spiritual side will give you the answers you desire for peace."

"Yes, I moved forward using the pain to become a better artist. Many years ago, when living in Spain, I came across a group of gypsies, a camp of tsiganas, who'd arrived near our village. I was fascinated by their dances and strange customs, and it was here a woman read my palm. She began with smiles, and finished with tears. I was too young to fully understand all she told me, but the memory never left me, and I knew my life would not always be happy."

"I'm glad you've accepted your destiny Mademoiselle. You've much to give to the world, and ironically, your sorrow brings happiness to many people."

"I hope so." She whispered.

Calve left, and it would be years later before we met again in Paris.

***

Climbing the social ladder required the latest fashions, and a new suit made me feel as fresh as the Spring foliage in Central Park. This particular day, countless birds sang amongst the blossoms when strolling.

The park's magnificent openness was in stark contrast to the cluttered world bordering its edges, and after visiting the natural world, I ventured back into the city and the Eden Muse on Twenty Third Street.

The Eden Muse was an extravaganza of entertainment. Festooned with banners, the battleship designed building, housed a collection of wax works rivalling Madame Tussauds in London. After talking all day, I needed quiet stimulation, and little conversation was required with a wax figure.

As there were only a few visitors, I could take a leisurely stroll around the dioramas. The backdrops were well executed, and my scenic designer friend Arthur Hurtt, would be impressed.

The Roman section, with its figures dressed in togas, reminded me of my time working on Barrett's ancient dramas, and I half expected to see a wax figure of the man, dominating other figures.

There was a civil war diorama with men firing a huge cannon. John Logan from Chicago, would've been impressed.

I moved through other scenes and played chess with an automated Arab named Ajeeb. I'd seen automata in France, and was not fooled by the experience, realising there was a real person inside the elaborate contraption moving the chess pieces.

'The rulers of the world' was an extravagant diorama of figures in a regal room. The Pope sat motionless next to the Czar of Russia, and Queen Victoria in her finery was seated next to Princess Alexandra and the Prince of Wales. The President and first lady stood in the centre. With the exception of a young woman, the room was empty.

"Do you think it's a good likeness?" I asked.

"Oh sir, you startled me. I was away with the fairies. I can't comment on the likenesses, as I've not seen the real people. They do resemble their photographs." She told me.

"Well, the Prince of course, has put on a bit of weight lately, and the colour of his eyes is not quite right. Perhaps the fullness of the lips is a little overdone as well."

The young girl looked at me in disbelief.

"Really? Have you met the prince?" She asked excitedly.

"Yes, I've met the prince and his wife. Alexandra is much taller than this figure suggests."

The girl's expression changed, and I was sure I'd seen her before. The face and eyes were familiar, but the voice and accent were not. It wasn't American, English, or European. Different accents fascinated me after studying elocution with Ben Greet.

"Your accent intrigues me. Where do you hail from?" I asked.

"I was born in Australia." She replied.

"This is an accent I'm not familiar with."

"Not many people here in America have heard of Australia, let alone come across a native. My home is far away." She told me.

"I've met an Australian, Madame Melba. Her accent is quite different to yours. I expect her voice may have been modified during her studies." I explained.

"Oh, she is wonderful. We were born in the same town, Melbourne. Actually, the same suburb, Richmond." She boasted.

"What a coincidence. I've never been to Australia. I've a dear friend who was in your town not long ago, and gave birth to a daughter there."

I thought of Maud. Would her daughter be brought up in similar circumstances to this striking girl? I wondered.

"Perhaps she will grow up as pretty as you, under the southern stars?" I smiled.

"And then come to America and become famous?" She laughed.

"Is that why you're here? In what area do you seek fame?

"I want to be a successful dancer and travel the world."

When speaking, she raised an arm and twirled her skirt. It was then, the memory of her came back. This girl, dressed in American clothes, was none other than the young dancer who'd amazed everyone at the Cairo Street exhibition during the Chicago World's fair. It was three years before, and in that time, she'd blossomed into a stunning young woman.

"I remember you. I saw you dance at the Chicago Fair." I told her.

"As strange as it seems, I remember you too. At first, I wasn't sure."

"How is it possible? You must have seen thousands of faces."

"Yes, but none of the men looked at me as you did. I was accustomed to a certain look when I performed, and your gaze was different."

"You're very perceptive. How is it you ended up dancing at the Egyptian exhibition?"

"It was all my mother's doing. We were in San Francisco performing with another company when she received an offer to come to Chicago. Before I knew it, we were at the World's fair. I've been touring with the M.B Leavitt company in the 'Spider and fly recently.'"

"May I ask your name?"

"Clarissa Molony, but my stage name is 'Saharet'."

"Allow me to introduce myself. I too, am known professionally under a different name. Louis to my friends, and Cheiro to the rest of the world."

"What shall I call you?"

It was a relief knowing Clarissa hadn't heard of Cheiro. I wasn't in the mood to answer questions related to my work that afternoon.

"Please call me Louis. Where are you performing? I would like to see you dance again."

Clarissa's smiled and moved towards the next doorway.

"Shall we continue the tour?" She asked.

We braved the chamber of horrors, moved through a beheading in Morocco, a lynching in Alabama, and a scalping in North Dakota. Clarissa coped with the blood and decapitated heads, until we reached the Chinese street scene. A chained man wearing a heavy weight around his shoulders was being dragged through an alley and whipped savagely. His face was contorted in tortuous agony.

"Oh, this is horrible. I've had enough." She cried.

"Shall we take some tea in the café upstairs?"

"That would be lovely, thank you."

Sipping on our tea, we chatted away like old friends.

"You didn't tell me when you're next performing?"

Clarissa looked at me and began to cry.

"I'm sorry Louis. I came here today to forget my troubles."

I noted Clarissa's hands as she wiped away her tears. The delicate artistic type, characterized by pointed smooth fingers and a small palm. Emotions are heightened in these people, and relationship problems affect them deeply.

"I see you have no rings of marriage or engagement. Could it be your problems are to do with the heart?" I asked.

"You could say that. I won't be performing for months, and that's distressing when I live to dance. Why now, when my career has started to make great advances, am I forced to stop?"

"Have you fallen out with your 'Spider and Fly' company? Is this why you won't be dancing?"

"No no, quite the opposite. Mr Leavitt offered to increase my wages and time on stage."

"You don't have to tell me what troubles you. You've your mother to support you."

"I'm to be married soon and this is why….."

Clarissa burst into tears before finishing her sentence.

"I see, you're with child. Do you love your husband to be?"

"He's a driven man, a theatrical producer, Ike Rose. I've no choice, as my child is expected at the end of the year. It's not what I planned."

"Our destiny is not controlled by us, but we can choose how to deal with the circumstances. You must have faith in yourself."

I resisted the urge to look at Clarissa's palm, not wanting to see anything negative. If there were sinister forces ahead for this girl, I preferred to remain ignorant of them.

We parted ways without her knowing anything about Cheiro the palmist, and her only impression of me was as Louis the man, a deep thinker with a mutual love of dance and theatre.

***

In July, I received a letter from Ireland with the news of my father's passing, and found it necessary to return to Mount Mellick County to see to his affairs. After my mother's death, my father moved from County Wicklow to be closer to his relations.

Mount Mellick was known as the Manchester of Ireland because of the textile manufacturing. My relations were not affluent by any means, and contact was kept to a minimum to protect the truth of my lineage. I'd sent money to my father over the years, but received little correspondence in return. My family never understood the success I'd attained as 'Cheiro' the palmist, or appreciated the reasons for leaving Ireland. The William Warner Jr they once knew, disappeared long ago.

There was nothing familiar in my father's home, as he'd eliminated any trace of his wife and children.

The relatives' mediocre existences showed I'd been wise to leave Ireland, and I couldn't wait to return to my prosperous life in London.

***

In August, I was back in Bond Street, and the constant readings drained me to the point of exhaustion. I relied more and more on my secretary Thomas, to handle the book work, take prints and see people through to the reading room. One afternoon, a curtain was put up around me for a client who wished to remain anonymous. Stifling a yawn, the door opened.

"A young lady to see you Cheiro."

"Thank you, Thomas. Please take a seat next to the curtain Miss."

Thomas left. I waited for the hand of the young woman to be produced.

"Would you place your hand on the table through the opening in the curtain please miss." I told her.

I waited for the hand to appear, but there was only silence. Was the client a foreigner who hadn't understood my instructions?

"Just put your hand through the opening please miss." I repeated.

Still no hand, and a pungent smell filled the room. Surely this awful stench could not be from the young lady? Thomas would never allow such a person into my office. Something outside must be producing the odour.

"Do you speak English?" I asked.

Finally, a reply.

"Yes, I speak English." She whispered.

"Very well. You must speak up, and place your hand through the curtain. There's nothing to fear, as the future is never as bad as we imagine." I said, encouragingly.

The whispering continued.

"Do I have a future?"

"We all have a future Miss. Let me see your hand and we will know your story."

"You know me. You know my name."

"Then don't reveal it to me. We have the curtain so you can be sure of your privacy."

Puzzled, I continued. Who could this frightened soul be? The voice was unfamiliar. Maybe disguised, as it certainly was a strange sound, and still no hand was produced.

"How is it I know you?" I asked.

"You don't know my face, but you know my name. Emma Shears." She informed me.

The name was familiar to me, but from where?

"I'm sorry, I don't recall your name. I must insist we start, or else your session will end."

"Very well, read my hand. Tell me of my future, the future you took away from me." She shouted.

The whispering turned into a moaning, and then a terrifying scream as she thrust her hand through the curtain. The burnt arm smoked and dripped fluid onto the table. Bony fingers reached out to scratch my face, and claw my skin, and the smell of burnt flesh caused me to gag with revulsion. I screamed out for Thomas as the flaming apparition pulled down the curtains.

"Help me, I'm burning." She yelled.

Losing consciousness, I awoke to find Thomas standing over me looking worried.

"Are you alright Louis? What's happened?" He asked.

Another bad dream. They were becoming more frequent and intense. I realized Emma Shears was one of the victims I'd read about from the Exeter Theatre fire.

It took me some time to recover from the vision. If these dreams continued, I'd have to seek help, as the horrific images were pushing me into the realm of madness.

***

After Oscar Wilde's trial, Robert, like so many others, returned from abroad. I'd invited him to dine with me one evening in order to catch up on each other's news. I'd never told anyone about the Exeter Theatre fire, and perhaps this was the reason for the reoccurring nightmares.

Robert was looking healthy and robust after his time away in Sicily. He'd been writing articles for various London periodicals, as well as spending time on his fictional works, and was beginning to make a name for himself. The success made him especially animated at dinner.

"Sicily is an inspiring place, Louis. I've met many interesting people and the conversations were extraordinary. It's been a wonderful tonic after this nasty business with Oscar."

"I'm glad you've been the first to mention his name for once." I said.

"You're right, we should discuss other matters. Tell me how America was?"

"The United States is a world offering anything to anyone wishing to seize it. I was in awe of the many people I met there who started with nothing and made a fortune. No doors are closed to those who have money and are successful."

"Very true, it's a cruel twist of fate to be born into the lower social ranks here in England."

"My trip was cut short as my father passed away in July, and his affairs required attention. Which leads me to tell you something important Robert. It's time for me to reveal to you who I am."

"Whatever do you mean? I know who you are."

"I'm really a Count. My true name is Count Louis Le Warner Hamon, and I'm descended from French nobility."

"Whatever are you talking about Louis? Has something happened to you in America to cause this delusion? You're Irish. Furthermore, you've detested the concept of titles and the landed gentry for years. Now you want to be a part of it?"

"I know it's hard for you to accept Robert, but there it is. Our Irish roots descend from a Norman family and that's the truth of it."

"Call yourself what you like Louis, but don't expect me to start addressing you as a Count, or walking the required number of paces behind you."

This was how the conversation went all those years ago. Robert saw through the ridiculous efforts to authenticate the title, and we never mentioned it again.

***

Shortly after, Robert organized a dinner for a few people and asked me to attend. After arriving, I realized every person present with the exception of myself, had a real title. It was Robert's way of getting his point across regarding those who possessed such lineage. Most of his guests worked for a living, and were ambivalent of their inherited titles.

One of his friends in attendance was Gertrude Elizabeth Blood otherwise known as Lady Colin Campbell. She'd married Lord Colin Campbell, the fifth son of the 8th Duke of Argyll in 1881, and the marriage disintegrated shortly afterwards. She remained married but separated, until his death in 1895. Gertrude was a remarkable looking woman, possessing both charm and beauty.

"Louis, I'd like you to meet Lady Colin Campbell." Robert said.

Gertrude sent him an angry look.

"Robert, I have told you, I do not want to be known by that name. The man was a stain on my reputation and now that he's dead, I wish to be rid of it for good. My name is Gertrude Blood, Louis. I'm very pleased to meet you."

Robert smiled at me.

"So sorry Gertrude. I should realize by now; titles mean nothing to you."

There was great delight in Robert's eyes when uttering the words. I took Gertrude's hand and gently kissed it.

"A pleasure madam. Do I detect a hint of Irishness in your voice."

"Very good Louis. Gertrude is a fellow countryman of yours." Robert declared.

Gertrude's features were indicative of the 'black Irish'. The Gipsy-like dark hair and eyes were offset by the ebony paleness of her skin. I continued our conversation while sipping some wine.

"Where are your people from?" I asked.

"We are from County Clare. The estates have been in the family since the time of Elizabeth I, and you?"

"County Wicklow. I grew up mostly in Bray."

"Isn't that the same area where that 'white slug' Oscar Wilde lived?" She hissed.

Robert dropped his fork. I wondered what lay behind the nasty description.

"Yes, his family owned a house in Bray as well as Dublin. Were you acquainted with him?" I asked.

"Oh no, but my former brother-in-law Lord John Campbell certainly was."

"You knew Lord John well then?"

"We were together many times with his family at Inverary. They were enjoyable gatherings, before the murkiness of the people became apparent to me. I was not oblivious to the interests of both my husband and his brother. Whilst my husband preferred the company of prostitutes, Lord John spent an awful lot of time in the stables. Needless to say, he was not a horse lover. His interest lay with the groomsmen, literally. I continue to hear stories from my friends about him, and feel sad for his wife, Princess Louise."

The comments explained her hostile attitude towards Oscar. Gertrude felt contempt for any man marrying a woman, knowing it wasn't in his nature to do so.

"I'm sorry your marriage was not a happy one." I sympathized.

"The experience scarred me in many ways. Nevertheless, I've made a happy life for myself. Have I not Robert?"

"You most certainly have. What would I do without your articles?" He said.

Robert's connection with Gertrude was strengthened by their love of writing. The former Lady Colin created plays, books and articles for the London press under various names. Robert later informed me; her husband went through with the marriage knowing he'd contracted syphilis, and as a consequence, he infected her on their wedding night. She was granted a judicial separation three years after the marriage, but the peerage closed ranks, slandering her reputation to prevent a divorce. His death from the dreaded disease, freed her.

The ongoing friendship with Gertrude proved fortuitous. Later, I was involved with her former brother-in-law, Lord John, after he became the 9th Duke of Argyll.

***

The Lyric Theatre advertised its latest play, 'The Sign of the cross,' on giant posters.   Barrett's ancient drama became his greatest triumph, providing him with the financial security he desperately needed. Maud played the role of a slave, Mercia, and Barrett played the role of the Roman prefect, Marcus, who falls in love with her. Did he write these works to toy with the emotions of the cast?

Maud became famous for this role, and countless statues were made of her as Mercia. I'd not seen her since Boston, and wanted to be sure all was well in the Barrett Company. After sending her a note, she came to my office in Bond Street.

"Louis, thank you for reaching out to me."

"I'm always here for you Maud."

"It's comforting to know that."

"How are things with you? Are you happy to be back in London after your tour?" I asked.

"It's been a hectic time, but it keeps my mind from upsetting thoughts."

"Your daughter?"

"Yes, but there's been some light in my shadowy world."

"Come sit and I'll have Thomas bring some tea."

We made ourselves comfortable in the larger chairs. After Thomas left us, Maud resumed her story.

"In March, after a performance of Wilson's new play, I received a note from a young girl, wanting to meet me. Her name was Marian Read, and the words she'd written were so sweet and heartfelt, I couldn't refuse her. In the beginning, I thought she was interested in becoming an actress, but she's a gifted spiritualist, and needed to convey a message."

"She's a clairvoyant?" I asked.

"Definitely. She uses cards, not tarot, but playing cards to help her receive impressions. Louis, the things this young girl told me; details only known to me. She described my labour and birth in Melbourne, and the room where I shared those few days with my baby."

"There are such people. It seems the younger and purer they are, the greater the gift." I explained.

"Marian told me I'd see Florence again soon. I asked her if she were certain, as I couldn't imagine how it would be possible. She was adamant, describing what my child would look like when I held her."

"It won't happen Maud. Wilson will never let you go, especially now, with the great success of this new play." I told her.

"I know. Her comments caused me grief. Even though Marian was correct on many things, I thought her mistaken about Florence and I meeting again."

"No one is infallible. Perhaps she was getting an impression of your wish to go."

"No Louis. She was right. The following week, Wilson informed the company, he wants to tour Australia next year. Hiding my emotions from the other actors when told was difficult. Marian was right after all."

"Did you tell Barrett of this girl and her cards?" I asked, suspiciously.

"Heavens no. Wilson and I only speak professionally. As I told you in Boston; no matter how much he tries to regain my affections, I'll never confide in him again."

"Of course. I must learn to ignore my paranoid thoughts concerning Barrett. I still believe the man is obsessed with winning you, and will do anything to achieve his objectives."

"I cannot tell you how this news of the Australian tour invigorated me. It will sustain me over the next year." Maud said.

"This young girl Marian, is she in London?" I enquired.

"She is. I can give you her details if you like? Perhaps you should see her Louis? Who knows what her cards may reveal for you?"

"Indeed, I believe I will seek her out."

***

Three weeks later, I found myself knocking on the door of Miss Marian Read at her home in Greenwich. I was about to walk away, when a young woman in her early twenties answered. An oval table with a purple silk cloth, stood in the corner of the sitting room where she received clients, and on top, a wooden box sat surrounded by coloured crystals. She gestured to take a seat opposite her.

"May I ask how you came by my name?" She enquired.

"A friend of mine recommended you." I replied.

I made the appointment under the name of William, giving no further information.

"You must thank them for me. Is there something specific you'd like to know, or will I do a general reading and see what turns up?" She asked.

"A general reading, thank you."

Marian's hand shape verified her psychic gifts. The long-pointed fingers were typical of a sensitive individual. Opening her box, she produced a deck of unusual playing cards.

"I use these cards as a tool for my readings. They help me to unlock the past and future of the querent. As visions and impressions appear when deciphering them, please remain silent until I tell you to speak."

"As you wish."

"Take the cards with your left hand and shuffle them, then cut the deck into three piles and shuffle each separately."

Marian drifted off into a trance. Placing the cards into the piles, I watched her eyes flutter behind closed eyelids. Eventually, she opened them and arranged the cards into a defined pattern.

"Your past draws me. The ten of diamonds tells me you've made money through your own efforts. The knave of diamonds followed by the queen of diamonds tells me you've benefited through the patronage of a woman. The knave of clubs tells me the woman is deceptive and dishonesty surrounds her. I feel you will have more to do with this person, as the cards for the near future show it." She explained.

Marian could only be speaking of the Duchess of Sutherland, who I hoped never to see again. It was puzzling.

"The future shows the King of spades, indicating a dark-haired man. The nine of spades indicates a theft, and as the ace of diamonds follows, I predict this man involves you in his criminal activities. The cards tell me you benefit from the connection."

The future appeared complicated, but financially positive. During the reading, I realized how important financial security was to me, and I never wanted to be without money again. Marian looked away from the cards and into space, and her eyes began to flutter once more.

"There are souls here wishing to speak. A recent passing, a man, a father figure. William, he says to me. He is calling to William. Stay strong and do not follow the path of the wicked, he says."

Marian was receiving messages from the spirit world. Maud told me she was clairvoyant. Following her previous instructions, I remained silent.

"Another soul is here; John, and there are many with him. Their passing was not easy. Much pain and terror. Fire, Fire. Unfinished lives, unexpected departures." She relayed, moving in the chair uncomfortably.

As John and others from the Exeter theatre fire were present, I could no longer remain silent.

"John, I'm sorry. It all happened so fast. There was nothing I could do." I cried.

Marian listened to the voices.

"John tells you not to worry. Everyone around him knows it was an accident. Don't blame yourself for the disaster. The dreams you're having, aren't from spirit. They're from your subconscious."

"I saw a young woman, burning and screaming in my vision. Wasn't that real?"

"No. The woman you speak of died quickly. Crushed to death, she was unaware of her burning body. After you read a list of victims in the newspaper, the name remained in your memory. John tells me, be at peace Louis."

The words stopped the stressful episodes and freed me of the guilt I'd been carrying for so long. When Marian was fully present again, we discussed the events.

Unlike many clairvoyants who entered a trance-like state, Marian was aware of the conversations taking place. I left her home feeling uplifted and unconcerned that someone else knew my horrible secret.

***

In the Summer of 1897, London celebrated Queen Victoria's Diamond Jubilee. After sixty years on the throne, the Queen paraded her carriage before the cheering crowds. Frail and suffering from arthritis, Victoria bravely waved to the masses, and smiled into the faces of those who'd been angered by her absence.

How sad and miserable she looked. What did she really think of the pomp and pageantry? I read of Oscar's release from prison after his two-year sentence, and Robert wrote of the many 'so-called friends 'who'd shunned him after his internment. By all accounts he'd fled to Paris, attempting to carve out an existence in a city which held fond memories. There were no invitations to the Jubilee celebrations for Oscar.

***

By far the most memorable event of that time, was a fancy-dress ball held by the Duchess of Devonshire on July 2nd. Invitations were sent to the appropriate people, including members of the Royal family. Actors, musicians, and politicians were thrown into the mix to add spice to the evening.

Lady Arthur Paget was a good friend of the Duchess of Devonshire, and organized an invitation for me.

The ball's 'monarchs of history' theme, allowed for costumes from any period. Gods and goddesses were acceptable, as well as prominent figures from the ancient world, and London designers worked overtime creating elaborate costumes.

I knew a designer from my theatre days, Willie Clarkson on Wellington Street, who provided a suitable costume. Willie was a master craftsman, and his skill at making wigs and clothing was revered within theatrical circles. He'd provided disguises for well-known individuals, enabling them to mingle with the London crowds undetected.

Sir Henry Irving used a number of Willie's disguises to remain incognito. The designer told me of a lord who lived a secret life as a woman, and spent periods of time as a femme fatale before returning to his life as a man.

I had Willie design a costume for me as Cagliostro, the mystical figure who frequented the courts of Europe during the 18th Century. He clapped his hands and created a marvellous outfit. A long silk robe of vibrant purple, trimmed with gold, and black silk pants with a fringed sash of gold. Black velvet shoes, complete with sparkling diamond buckles, and a white silk shirt adorned with coloured glass gems encrusted in gold metal. The 'piece de resistance', was the elaborate gold turban sprouting a white plume of feathers.

Willie was beside himself with delight after the final fitting.

"It's truly magical." He exclaimed.

The costume gave me the confidence to hold my own with the other expensively adorned guests.

***

The carriages began arriving at Devonshire House later in the evening.

The Viscountess Raincliffe came as Catherine the great of Russia, followed by a stunning entourage of Imperial guards. She cut a regal figure in a white satin dress, decorated with real rubies and an ermine lined yellow velvet train.

Lord and Lady Tweedmouth were next to arrive. They received a royal welcome befitting their characters of Queen Elizabeth and the Earl of Leicester.

The ball gave the minor aristocracy a chance to surpass those whose titles were higher up the social ladder, but few succeeded in outshining those of greater rank.

I joined the line of carriages waiting their turn, and eventually, the cab door opened, and an attendant took the invitation.

Inside, a large orchestra played music. When entering the rooms, huge floral bouquets from the gardens of Chatsworth, delivered a sweet fragrance. Amongst the extravagant decorations, guests chatted.

Daisy, Princess of Pless, was dressed as the Queen of Sheba, and sat surrounded by black attendants in multi coloured outfits. Mrs. Asquith arrived as an oriental snake charmer with her winged headdress of gold. Lady Algernon Gordon Lennox, came as Princess de Lamballe, Marie Antoinette's ill-fated friend. Lady Gerard stunned as Astarte, Goddess of the moon, wearing a headdress of diamond stars and crescents. The duchess of Somerset came as Jane, Queen of England, and her husband the duke, as his ancestor, Edward Seymour. The duchess of Devonshire as Zenobia, Queen of Palmyra, and her husband the duke as Emperor Charles V, enjoyed hosting the event.

The music paused, as the Prince and Princess of Wales arrived with the royal entourage. The prince was dressed as the Grand prior of the Order of St John of Jerusalem, and the princess adorned herself in French couture as Marguerite de Valois. She wore her famous pearls as a collar, with strands falling around her waist, and daughters Victoria and Maud, were dressed in a similar fashion as Marguerite's ladies in waiting.

The Princess of Wales's daughter in law, Mary of Teck came as another lady of waiting, and her mother Princess Mary Adelaide cut a formidable figure as Electress Sophia of Hanover. I'd not seen this mother and daughter since visiting them to read the Princess Mary's hand, before she married the Prince of Wales's son, George.

During the night, people were curious to know my identity. It was Lady Alington who first approached me on her way back from the powder room.

"Good evening. Who do you portray in your stunning attire?" she asked, smiling.

"I'm Cagliostro, the infamous mystic, my lady." I replied.

"Cagliostro? Oh yes, was he not at the French court with Marie Antoinette? I believe I've read something about him and a diamond necklace?"

"There was a scandal involving diamonds, however he was

acquitted of any crime. It's a small part of his larger story."

"Why did you choose such a person? May I ask to whom I'm speaking?"

"I'm Count Louis Le Warner Hamon. You may have heard of me as Cheiro, the palmist. May I know your identity?"

"I am Lady Alington, and my character is a lady in waiting to Marguerite de Valois. I believe you may be familiar with my ladies already?"

Lady Alington nodded towards the group of Princesses who watched our conversation earnestly. The older Princess Mary Adelaide looked towards us with a worried expression.

"Have you not read the duchess of Teck's palm? I remember her telling me something of the sort some time ago, before her marriage."

The younger Princess Mary nodded and smiled.

"I see you are acquainted. Wont you come and pay your respects?" She asked.

"Thank you, my lady. It would be a pleasure to meet with the princesses again."

We approached the group as they watched the passing parade of people. Princess Mary Adelaide sighed, and her discomfort came as no surprise. I'd correctly predicted the outcome of her daughter's first engagement, and if I was able to see such things, what else might be uncovered?

"Ladies, may I present Cagliostro or Cheiro. I believe the Princess Marys are already acquainted with him."

"Cheiro, how splendid you look in your costume." Princess Mary Teck smiled.

"And how appropriate your choice of subject." Princess Mary Adelaide snapped.

"You are familiar with Cagliostro, Princess?" I asked, realizing she'd been informed of my presence.

"Of course. He was well known in the courts of Europe, and we are taught to beware such deceitful characters."

"Recognizing those who perpetrate acts of evil is an invaluable skill and should be taught with greater diligence in every court, including our own." I replied, glaring at the Princess.

The Princess Mary Teck then addressed her mother-in-law, the Princess of Wales, Alexandra.

"Mama, this is the man who read my palm before I was engaged to Albert. He told me the marriage would not eventuate and I would be betrothed to another."

The Princess of Wales looked deeply into my eyes.

"You foretold my son's death?" she asked, her face becoming flushed.

"No, your Royal Highness. Only the death of an engagement." I explained.

"You saw nothing else regarding his death?" she enquired.

"This is a sombre subject for such a night. Let us speak of other things." Princess Mary Adelaide interrupted.

"No Mama. Let the man speak. I believe he has the gift of insight, and I want to hear what he has to say." Princess Mary Teck insisted.

I observed the hostile expression of Princess Mary Adelaide. She returned my gaze with a defiant look, and her conduct convinced me she was hiding something. I was about to speak when we were interrupted by the Prince of Wales.

"I recognize this man. Fancy seeing you here Cheiro. You really are moving up in the world." The prince laughed.

"I expect Minnie Paget had something to do with it." He

whispered in my ear.

"It's an honour to have been invited your Royal Highness." I smiled.

"What do you predict will be the outcome of this evening?" He asked.

"I expect people will be talking about this ball for some years." I replied.

"It's been a wonderful Summer, let us hope it continues. I will call on you again when I'm in need of advice."

The Prince of Wales raced away, and the princesses retired to the powder room to indulge in private conversation. Infidelity, suspicious deaths, and controlling parents, seemed to figure deeply amongst the pomp and frivolity of the night.

After speaking with the Royals, I was tapped on the shoulder by Gertrude Blood, the journalist friend of Robert.

"I'm not a princess, but could you lower yourself to converse with a reluctant duchess."

"Gertrude, wonderful to see you. Are you here to get a good story for Robert?" I asked.

"Oh no. I wouldn't miss this ball for anything. If I happen to find something to write about, it may end up in print." She laughed.

As we talked, a striking young man in his early twenties, came by us with some refreshments.

"Could I offer you some drinks?" He asked, with a dashing smile.

I took a glass of champagne as Gertrude remained fixated on the man.

"Would you like something?" I asked her.

"Oh, thank you, yes." She replied, keeping her eyes on the man's face.

The young man stared intently at Gertrude and offered her his tray. When walking away, he glanced back at her.

"Quite a stunning fellow, don't you think Gertrude? You seem quite taken with him?" I smiled.

"No, it's not that at all. I believe I've seen this person before." She replied.

"Really where?"

"I'm certain he's someone I've met on the Campbell estate at Inverary. He spent a lot of time with my brother-in-law, John, hunting and walking around the grounds. I believe one of the staff caught them in a compromising situation. That employee was subsequently discharged, and later, we heard he'd disappeared under mysterious circumstances."

As fate would have it, John Campbell, the Marquis of Lorne, made his way across the room, as we spoke. Standing in a corner, he waited for the young man to pass. Taking a glass from his tray, the two smiled and laughed together. Gertrude was furious.

"There, I knew it. I was right. It is him. Obviously, they know each other. So brazen. The Campbell family have no regard for morality."

It was clear from the body language; the marquis and young man were intimate. Most of the guests were merry from alcohol, and oblivious to the flirtatious behaviour. When the marquis put his hand on the man, he noticed Gertrude watching.

"Oh bother, he's seen me. Let us move away. It causes pain to rest my eyes on any member of that family. There's my friend Kathleen, the Duchess of Newcastle. Come, I will introduce you."

Gertrude led me to a couple who'd just arrived. The duchess Kathleen, was much younger than her husband, the Duke of Newcastle, Henry Pelham-Clinton. He was the older brother of Francis, who I met at Blanche Roosevelt's party with Oscar and Bosie. Gertrude was a good friend of the duchess, sharing a common interest in horses and dogs.

"This is Count Louis Le Warner Hamon. May I present the Duke and Duchess of Newcastle." She said.

"Your costume is intriguing. It reminds me of the Indian Maharajas parading around London this week." The duke told me, shaking my hand.

"Cagliostro's attire is inspired by the mysterious East." I told him.

"Kathleen, how are you keeping my dear?" Gertrude asked.

"Very well, actually. You must come and see my new litter of terriers. They're just adorable"

"How would you like a little fox terrier to keep you company Louis?" Gertrude asked.

"Oh no. I prefer a larger animal. I feel more secure with a dog that can protect me."

"Do not underestimate the tenacity of the terrier Sir. Size doesn't always equate to bravery." The duke interjected.

The duke was a small man, and the disparity in our heights may have prompted the comment.

"You're quite right. One shouldn't judge the measure of any creature by its appearance. Actually, I've had the pleasure of meeting your brother."

The faces of the duke and his wife soured.

"Francis and myself have always been like chalk and cheese. Luckily, fate dictated I as the first born in our family, and we've the heavens to thank for that. Who knows what would've become of the estate had he inherited the title first."

"Let us not speak of Francis and his wife. There's only so much one can do to help one's relatives. They are their own worst enemies, and we must let their destinies play out." The duchess told us.

"Well-spoken Duchess. You're wise beyond your years." I said.

"Yes, forget about those who cause distress." Gertrude told us, casting her eyes towards John Campbell, still in conversation with the young man.

"Where are the drinks? I'm getting quite parched." Henry exclaimed.

Not wanting to interact with the young man again, Gertrude moved on.

"There's a fellow over there with some refreshments. I'll ask him to come over." I told them.

The duke and young man were still engaged in conversation when I approached.

"Sorry to interrupt, but could we have some drinks over yonder? My friends are longing for some champagne." I asked, smiling.

The young man scurried away, leaving the duke glaring.

"And who would you be?" He asked.

"You mean in real life, or as I am in costume?"

"I believe I'm unfamiliar with both." He replied.

"Count Louis Le Warner Hamon at your service. I attend tonight as Cagliostro."

"Again, I'm unfamiliar with both."

The cold remark did nothing to fluster me, as Gertrude had provided me with some interesting information on the duke.

"I expect there are several people here tonight who are unfamiliar to you, and perhaps others that are very familiar." I asked, looking back at the young man.

The duke's eyes narrowed, and I met his stare with a smile.

"Excuse me. I see some people whose conversation will be more agreeable." The duke told me, walking away.

A steady flow of new arrivals filled the ballroom. A man dressed in Shakespearean costume was talking with a tall figure adorned in ecclesiastical attire. As I approached the figure it turned, to reveal Henry Irving.

"Louis, is this dashing mystical figure really you?" He asked.

"Good evening, Henry. Oh, sorry, Sir Henry. I forgot about your recent knighthood."

"Forget the formalities. We're old friends, aren't we?"

"Indeed, we are." I replied.

"May I present the dashing Lord Hyde. Does he not make a splendid Romeo Louis?"

The young man was no more than twenty.

"Pleased to make your acquaintance Sir. And you are?" He asked, extending his hand.

I took the slender hand with its long smooth fingers, into mine.

"Count Louis Le Warner Hamon." I replied, shaking it.

"A fascinating character, I'm sure. You must tell us all about him, but I'm sure Lord Hyde would like to know your name?" Henry asked, smiling.

"That is my name Henry. I'm finally revealing my true lineage and background to everyone. My character is Cagliostro. What part are you playing this evening in your auspicious gown?"

"A count, how surprising, but then, somehow not. I am Cardinal Wolsey, from the court of Henry VIII."

"A man of intrigue and mystery. Are you enjoying the evening

Henry?" I asked.

"Very much. There are many interesting people here. Lord Hyde, I've known Louis since he arrived from Ireland a few years ago. He had a bag containing a few clothes and a lot of ambition to become an actor. For some time, he worked in my company until his real vocation became apparent."

"What do you do now?" Hyde asked.

Henry replied before I could speak.

"Have you not heard of the famous palmist, Cheiro of Bond Street? Louis reads the rich and famous from both here and abroad. He moves in the highest circles of society and is revered by many, and dare I say, feared by many more. You've received more fame as a palmist than you'd ever have achieved as an actor Louis."

"Fame and money Henry. I don't regret the decision to give up my dreams of the stage. I perform my own story now; not one written by another. When people see and hear my lectures, it's me they applaud, not an actor portraying someone else."

"I've never heard of a palmist having a successful career. I thought it the practice of gypsies and charlatans." Hyde remarked.

"You're young my Lord. In good time you'll learn, people aren't always who or what they appear. The highest professions in this land, hide some of the most insidious and ruthless characters I've ever met. I've also engaged with those on the lower fringes of society, who exhibit a genuine honesty and kindness towards others far surpassing those who parade themselves as redeemers. Regardless of rank, good and bad forces are found everywhere. There's as many fraudsters in parliament as there are on the street, and I know for a fact, in this very room tonight, there are so-called 'respectable' individuals who've plotted, schemed, and murdered to achieve their ambitions. Others have killed and seduced innocents for their own gratification."

Henry interrupted.

"I agree. Titles are no prerequisite for honour; however, they do add a certain air of respect wouldn't you say Count Le Warner? Why else would so many individuals' covert them? All this intrigue and darkness, you should write a play. It seems you've uncovered enough material for a thrilling story."

"Perhaps one day I will. Until then, I'll continue living life my way. If fate has decreed money and fame come as a result, who am I to argue? I must leave you now. Very pleased to have met you Lord Hyde, and Sir Henry, as always, an interesting conversation."

The evening continued with lucrative contacts made and promises of private readings. It was like no other event I'd experienced, and I found it difficult to relax and sleep on my return home. The colour and spectacle of the Devonshire ball was not surpassed for many years.

***

Robert visited the following week.

"Louis, you must tell me all about the Devonshire ball. Gertrude told me bits and pieces, but I'm longing to hear what you made of the event."

"It was amazing. The atmosphere, costumes, everything. I felt a part of some grand theatrical production. For the most part, people were friendly and happy, and I made many contacts."

"The press coverage was extensive. Gertrude told me she was with you for a time."

"Yes, until she spotted her ex-brother-in-law, John Campbell, the Marquis of Lorne. He was fraternizing with someone she recognized from the Campbell estate. A dashing young man who'd been caught in a compromising situation with him. Their intimate connection was obvious."

"Gertrude never told me that." Robert said.

"No? She was upset with Campbell's overt behaviour. Apparently, the employee who discovered them together, mysteriously disappeared. Gertrude dealt with the poor man's distraught family after the incident. Clearly, foul play was involved, and I may have given Campbell the impression I knew of these events."

"What? Did you speak to him?"

"Only briefly. You know me Robert, I cannot help myself at times. After Gertrude left, I was with the Duke and Duchess of Newcastle, and they needed a drink. It was then I seized the opportunity to approach the two of them. Campbell was less than impressed when I asked his plaything to serve drinks to the Newcastles." I explained.

"I'm sure. Did he know of you?" Robert asked, concerned.

"He took great delight telling me he knew nothing. I believe it was then I made some ambiguous remark regarding his closeness to the young man."

"What do you mean ambiguous?"

"I cannot remember exactly. It was a combination of words and expressions which conveyed the information. Believe me, he understood what I said."

"Louis you are too much. Gertrude has already told you how people who oppose these characters disappear."

"Exactly. It's the injustice that compels me. We're both Scorpios Robert. You use the pen to poison and exact revenge, and I've other methods at my disposal."

"Speaking of writing, my new novel is to be published." Robert told me.

"Excellent. What's the title?"

"Flames."

"Simple title."

"It's set in London."

"Will it be as controversial as 'The green carnation'?"

"Let us say it will not be as obvious." Robert grinned.

"Perhaps they'll be dragging my body out of the river before yours then. Anyway, I've a few weeks left in London before heading back to the United States. I'll have my thought machine with me this time."

"What's this thought machine you've been talking about?"

"It's an apparatus measuring the invisible vibrations of a person's mind. By force of will, a needle can be moved in certain directions. It was invented by Savary d'Odiardi, an accomplished man whose intelligence and inventive abilities are astounding. I can demonstrate it if you have the time?"

Retrieving the machine, I placed it on the dining room table. The small metallic object looked like a compass, until a closer examination revealed its finer details.

"Now sit here Robert. You must concentrate carefully." I told him.

"Is that it? Hardly a machine." Robert giggled.

"It may be small, but the sensitivity is large. You must try and move the needle in certain directions."

"Just by looking at it? Should I do something else?" He asked.

"Firstly, try and move the needle in a clockwise direction. Just concentrate on moving the needle as far as you can."

Robert looked intensely at the needle and after a minute or so it shifted slightly.

"It moved. I did it." He shouted.

"Try and move it further now."

After a few minutes Robert was astounded how far the needle rotated when his concentration became deeper and focused.

"You see how the mind has an invisible force which can affect exterior objects. Some people are naturally stronger than others. The way the needle moves gives an indication of the quality of the mind. Drunkards with damaged brains, cause the needle to move in a jerky fashion, while drug addicts find it impossible to move the needle at all."

"Intriguing. It explains the energy we feel around certain people when close to them." Robert realized.

"Yes, and the way their minds can direct an invisible energy on us. It's proof such a force exists."

Robert left thoroughly impressed with the thought machine. A few weeks later in August, I presented the machine to William Gladstone at his home, Hawarden outside of London. The former prime minister was suffering ill health at the time, and passed away the following year. Despite his frail condition, the old statesman moved the needle in a robust manner, demonstrating the power of his intellect and determination. Thankfully, I managed to meet him and examine his palm before he departed.

***

In September 1897, I was back in New York.

An advertisement for the young dancer, 'Saharet' caught my attention. She was performing at the Olympia Rooftop Garden theatre on Broadway at 44th street the following Sunday. Since our last meeting, Clarissa had married and given birth to her child. Intrigued to see how things had turned out for her, I arrived for the performance.

The Olympia was an architectural masterpiece. The massive grey stone building accommodated a theatre, music hall, concert hall, and roof garden. Completed only two years prior, the fixtures and fittings shone brilliantly. The beauty of the roof top garden theatre attracted performers from all over the world. Large spans of iron formed a decorative skeleton on which panels of glass were laid, and luscious trees reached for the sunlight.

I made my way to a small stage, complete with curtains and backdrops, as the rows of chairs began filling with people. Finding a single seat vacant in the front row, I settled myself. My thoughts wandered back to the Chicago Expo and the performance I'd witnessed on the small stage in Cairo Street. Even then, this young girl showed a quality outshining her fellow dancers. Performing her solo act somewhere like the Olympia in New York, was a natural progression.

As the music began, the audience erupted into applause, prompting Saharet to cartwheel onto the stage. Her frilled and layered dress rustled over the sheer material of her stockings. The acrobatic moves enthralled people, ignorant of the fact she'd given birth a few months before. Not yet twenty-one, she moved with the power and passion of a seductress beyond her years.

Whilst doing the splits at the front of the stage, she spotted me, and sent a delightful wink before flipping back in a flurry of fabric. Clarissa elevated her status from a child performer to a hypnotic temptress in just a few years. Like the rest of the audience, I fell completely under her spell.

After the music and applause stopped, people raved about the performance. Eventually, they began to leave their seats, and I was about to exit when a stagehand gave me a note. It read.

"To my wax works companion. Please meet me backstage before you leave.

Saharet."

I was delighted to receive the invitation, and met Clarissa in a curtained section of the stage. The young dancer was still recovering from her physical performance. Arranging her hair and placing a fresh red camellia in the dark streaks, she extended her hand for me to kiss.

"Louis, how wonderful we should meet again."

"Saharet the dancer, the now famous dancer. It seems your dreams are coming true." I told her, caressing the soft hand.

"Yes, I've done well since we last met. Shall we take some refreshments and catch up on our news. I've time before I leave."

"It would be a pleasure." I smiled.

The tea rooms were not overly busy and we found a table in a corner under a palm. Clarissa ignored the stares of patrons who recognized her. She seemed eager to start up the conversation.

"This reminds me of our meeting at the Eden Musee. I'm in a much better state of mind this time." She whispered.

"Yes, you appear much happier."

"It's because I'm dancing again."

"What of your husband and child? Don't they bring you joy?" I asked.

"My daughter Carrie is so sweet. She is a dear little thing. My husband Ike and I are fortunate to have her. I'm sad to say, as much as I love them both, my life wouldn't be complete without dancing. Artists must be able to express themselves or else their soul's wither. Didn't you tell me you had a stage name Cheiro? You must know what I mean?"

Clarissa never asked what I did; the mark of a self-absorbed performer. She obviously assumed I was an artist of some sort given our conversations. I felt it time to clarify this.

"I agree with you. I know many performers who'd die if they were unable to walk the stage or create music in front of an audience. My art is slightly different. I'm not an actor, dancer, or musician."

"Oh. I thought if you had a stage name, you must be a performer of some sort?"

"I work under another name, but it's rather like an author who writes under a pseudonym. My art is created on a more personal level, apart from my lectures where I have a larger audience." I explained.

"You're an authority on some subject then?" She asked.

"Yes. I'm a chirologist."

"A chirologist. I'm afraid I don't know what that is?"

"Hand reading and palmistry are other names describing my profession."

"A palmist. Surely not. You look too prosperous. You know my mother sometimes worked as a palm reader in San Francisco. She had a gypsy outfit and everything, but didn't earn much money. It was an easy income for someone with a talent for storytelling." She laughed.

"I'm sorry to say, such people only bring the science into disrepute. It's made life difficult for those of us who've undertaken a serious study of the art."

"She only did it for a short time. My mother's life hasn't been easy, but she managed to provide for us through the hard times."

Clarissa showed no interest in her hand; perhaps a result of her mother's questionable use of the art to earn money, and we moved on from the subject.

Her much older husband, was also her manager, and was conscientiously working to increase his wife's fame. I failed to see how the union could satisfy all the passion and love this fiery young woman desired. A few years later when living in Paris, I came to understand the soul of Saharet the performer, and the heart of Clarissa the woman.

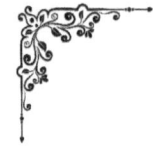

<u>Chapter Seven</u>

(1898-1899)

After another successful season in the United States, it was time to make my way back to London.

Robert returned from Morocco to join the London set again. His writing was providing him with a steady income, and I was proud of how we'd achieved our individual successes. His company was always welcomed, and there remained a close bond between us.

He was now a member of the Athenaeum Club on Pall Mall, a private exclusive establishment for intellectuals and creatives. Annoyingly, I wasn't eligible to join due to my dubious profession. We'd meet there, as I could accompany him as a guest. Knowing how sensitive I was about the membership rejection, he never referred to it.

"Would you like to eat first, or should we go straight to the lounge?" Robert asked.

"I'm not overly hungry. A drink in the lounge would be nice." I told him.

"What hours do you keep at your office?" He asked.

"I work from 11am until 5pm."

"Very civilized times. I'm glad you're not exhausting yourself as you did in the early days."

"No, I've learnt my lesson. I see fewer people and charge more."

In a quiet corner, we relaxed on leather armchairs. Presently a waiter brought us our drinks. Robert sipped his and placed it on a side table.

"You'll never guess what project I'm working on, and with whom." Robert told me.

"I thought you wrote me you were finishing another novel?"

"Yes, I have, 'The Londoners.' It's going to print. Actually, I 've written a play."

"A play? When did you become interested in the theatre?" I asked.

"I suppose I've you to thank for it. I expect I've absorbed your experiences through some osmotic process." He laughed.

"As a Scorpion that doesn't surprise me."

"I've written it in collaboration with Henry Duff-Traill. It's titled 'The Medicine man', and Henry Irving is producing it at the Lyceum in May."

"Henry Irving. I'm well acquainted with him. I'm sure you remember the stories of my time with his company."

"Of course. I mentioned your name when I met with him. It seemed to seal the deal. Is it not a strange coincidence?"

"Indeed. For a horrible moment I thought you going to tell me you were producing it with that scoundrel, Wilson Barrett. I realise that's impossible, as he's still in Australia on tour."

Robert picked up his drink and took a long swallow. A fearful expression prevailed when he'd something to hide.

"He returns in a few months. Now, try and stay calm Louis." He told me.

"How do you know when he's back?" I asked, raising my voice and slamming the glass down.

"Because he's written to me with a proposition. He wants me to adapt his play 'The daughters of Babylon' into a novel."

Just prior to Barrett taking his company on tour, 'The daughters of Babylon' was playing at the Lyric Theatre. Another ancient historical extravaganza in which he and Maud were key players. I'd heard about it from Maud before she left, and from the manager of the Lyric theatre, William Greet. William was the brother of Ben Greet, whose theatre school I'd attended.

"I don't believe it. Why did he approach you?" I asked.

"Lower your voice Louis, people are looking. Don't embarrass me at my club." Robert told me curtly.

"At your club. Of course, thank you for reminding me I'm not good enough to be a member. How could you contemplate working with a man who's caused me so much grief?"

"That's nothing to do with me."

"Of course, it has. Barrett's found out about our friendship. He's done it to spite me."

"Ridiculous. Did you ever think he may have approached me because of my previous work?"

"No, I don't believe it. You're ignorant of this man. He goes to endless lengths to find out information about people and uses it to his advantage. Are you not familiar with the narcissistic character?" I asked.

"I believe I'm becoming more familiar with every word." Robert replied angrily.

At that point one of the waiters came over to us.

"Gentlemen. I must insist you lower your voices. Other members are complaining. Could I get you another drink, or perhaps you're ready to eat now?" He asked.

I stood up enraged by Robert's news.

"I've lost my appetite." I said.

I left, leaving Robert and the waiter looking at each other. The waiter asked.

"Perhaps Sir, your friend needed something stronger to calm his nerves?"

"I don't believe such a drink exists. I'll make my way to the dining room after I finish mine. Thankyou."

The waiter smiled at Robert and moved on. The memory of that quarrel stayed with me for years.

Leaving the club, I strode angrily down the steps muttering. Oblivious of my surroundings, I collided with a young man, recognising him as the handsome waiter from the Devonshire ball.

"Terribly sorry, so stupid of me not to look where I'm going." I apologized.

"Don't trouble yourself, all is well. I believe I served you at the Devonshire Ball? Were in attendance?" He asked.

"Yes, I was. You've a good memory for faces." I told him.

"Only particular ones." He smiled.

"I remember seeing you with John Campbell, the Marquis of Lorne, for a period. You seemed very friendly and well acquainted." I probed.

The young man extended his hand.

"Frank Shackleton is the name. Pleased to make your acquaintance."

I returned the gesture, taking note of the long smooth fingers.

"Count Louis Le Warner Hamon."

"A Count. When I saw you at the ball, I thought you must be a toff of some sort."

The friendly conversation put me at ease. Frank's familiar manner was relaxed and unpretentious, and it was easy to become charmed by this dashing figure.

"You work in the Club?" I enquired.

"It's one of my jobs."

"I've just visited."

"It's a shame I didn't get to serve you. Perhaps another time?"

"I don't think I'll be entering the Athenaeum Club anytime soon." I informed him.

"Well then, have you a card?" He asked.

"I've a business card with my professional name."

Removing the holder from my breast pocket, I gave him a card.

"Cheiro. Palmistry. Bond Street. Very posh. Perhaps I'll pay you a visit and have my palm read." He grinned.

"You're welcome to make a booking. I get very busy, and I'm not cheap."

"I'm used to dealing with expensive characters. I don't see it as a problem."

"You're extremely cocky for someone so young."

"You're not the first to tell me. I'll take it as a compliment."

"Nice to meet you Frank, and sorry again for knocking into you."

"Meant to be I'd say. Bye for now."

Frank strode off smiling. It had been a strange day, and after returning home, images of the young man refused to leave. I knew we'd meet again.

Thoughts turned to Robert and his new venture with Barrett.

Was the actor intent on destroying my relationship with both Maud and Robert? Nothing would give him more pleasure.

There were still a few weeks before Barrett returned with Maud, and began working with Robert on the book. A plan of action was needed to counter his involvement with those who meant the most to me. My relationship with Maud had been repaired after a trying time. Why couldn't I do the same with Robert? The anger between us needed to subside before any reconciliation could happen.

***

Most of my clients were women, and made bookings with my secretary, Thomas.

There were those who came off the street, expecting an appointment straight away. These were the type of customers I could do without, as they were mostly impatient and difficult individuals. I rarely made an exception, but in June of 1898, an allowance was made. I'd just finished with the last person at five, and was showing them out, when a young girl walked into the reception area asking Thomas for an appointment. She was informed of the wait time, and accepted the situation courteously.

"You're in luck. I'm able to see you." I told her.

"Thank you. I didn't expect to get an appointment with you so soon." She smiled.

"Were you referred by someone?" I asked.

"Oh no. I'm down from Lancashire on a shopping expedition, and I noticed your sign. I thought I'd make an appointment for the next trip." She explained.

"Aren't you a little young to be in London on your own?" I asked.

The girl was no more than sixteen.

"I'm not alone. My aunt is with me and waiting at our hotel."

"Shall we begin?"

"I'm a little nervous at what you may find." She told me.

"Relax. It's better to be forewarned and forearmed in life. There's nothing to fear. Is there something you wish to ask?"

"I trust you'll tell me what I need to know."

The hands were extremely small, almost those of a child. I'd never seen such examples on an adult.

"Your hands are of the Venus type. The fingers are conic in shape, showing your artistic temperament, but unlike most examples, the head line is straight across the palm instead of sloping down to the mount of the moon. This makes the thought processes more logical and practical. You're tender, gentle and have a strong desire to be loved. The size of your hand indicates a dynamic and impulsive energy. I must investigate the other lines to reconcile these traits. Yes, a large mount of Venus here, showing your creative ability, and the fate line is clear and direct, terminating towards the mount of Jupiter. You desire position and recognition for your achievements. The marriage lines indicate an attraction to a partner who'll provide this."

"Marriages? How many do you see? I was hoping to have only one. If I should find someone like you, I'd be more than satisfied." She smiled.

"You pay me a compliment miss. I see two lines, therefore two marriages or strong relationships. There's one at a young age, in fact, I believe you'll be married before long. The other union occurs around the age of thirty-five."

"Are you married?" She asked.

"I'm afraid I'm not a marrying kind of fellow." I laughed.

"What a pity. If I'm to be married at a young age, what happens to my first husband?"

"The line ends in a fork, indicating the two of you grow apart."

"I'd never divorce. Perhaps something happens to him?"

"It's possible, however you'll have grown apart beforehand." I explained.

"Well, if I can't have you as my first husband, then I'll have you as my second." She told me.

The words shattered my train of thought, and as the reading progressed, the small hands became strangely familiar. Had I known them before in another existence, or would they play a part in my future?

As with Frank Shackleton, I was left dazzled and confused. Many years later, Katie Florence Bilsborough would re-enter my life.

***

In September, the sad news of Blanche Roosevelt's death reached me. What a tragedy this bright light was extinguished at only forty-four. Whilst travelling in Monte Carlo the year before, horses pulling her carriage bolted, and it overturned. The driver was killed, and the Marchesa was seriously injured. She never recovered from the accident.

I'd fond memories of her social gatherings, where the famous and talented partied the night away. Her supper with Oscar Wilde remained clear in my memory. How fate changes things in the blink of an eye, and there were many people from that evening whose lives took a turn for the worse. Blanche lived happily in the South of France for some time after the gathering, and like her I longed to return.

***

In October, the Parisian nightlife offered new excitements. As always, the artistic world was alive and thriving, attracting like-minded souls. The city was unique in its appreciation of artistic achievements over monetary gains. New York's business barons were worshipped for their millions, but Paris saved her accolades for the creators of beauty.

I recalled visiting the art gallery and studio of the renowned artist Gustav Courtois when in Paris with Oscar, and the memory compelled me to seek it out again. The building was just as I remembered, apart from a new selection of oil paintings in the gallery. The fragrance of the paints triggered memories of my time with Frank Miles in Tite Street, and I was reliving those scenes when Gustav discovered me.

"Monsieur Louis. How wonderful it is to see you again."

"Bonjour Gustav. I was just passing, and thought I'd call in. I'm not interrupting your work?" I asked.

"Non-Non. Of course not. Never too busy for an old friend, mon ami. What are you doing here in Paris? I hear you are a famous palm reader now. Tres bon."

"Yes. Things have gone well for me Gustav."

"I'm pleased for you Louis. It's good to know your life has not taken a turn for the worst, like your friend Oscar." He told me.

"We live in dangerous times Gustav. Fate can deal us a bad hand at any moment."

"It's true. I do not worry about such things. But tell me, have you seen Oscar?"

"I must admit, I haven't. I'm told he's here in Paris."

"Mon dieu, he is. You must see him. He comes here often to share his sadness with me. I paint, and he drinks absinthe. So many tears from one who was once so happy."

"Of course, I will visit him. Do you know where he's living?"

"Oui. He lives at the Hotel D'Alsace. You must not be shocked when you see him, as he is not the man you once knew. It is a tragedy to see where he now lives, and his appearance. To think he was once an icon of style and fashion...cést tres mal, tres mal."

After Gustav, feelings of guilt regarding Oscar surfaced. Like others, I preferred to deal with the events of the last couple of years by not thinking about him.

The Hotel D'Alsace was nearby. Gustav's description of Oscar's circumstances hadn't been exaggerated, and after discovering his room number from an unsavoury person, I waited outside his door.

Eventually, I knocked. If there was no reply, I'd console a guilty conscience with the fact I'd visited. About to walk away, the door opened slightly, and through the crack, a bloodshot eye peered out.

"Louis is that you?" He asked, weakly.

"Yes Oscar. Please open the door."

The door moved slowly, revealing what remained of the man I once knew. The long strands of hair were gone, replaced with a short grey matt of unwashed fibres, and his face was pale and puffy. The clothes were unkept, and his feet were bare. The most disturbing feature were Oscar's eyes. Gone was the sparkle; only glazed empty shells remained.

"Fear not Louis. I'm well accustomed to the shocked looks of my acquaintances." He told me.

"I'm so sorry Oscar. I'm at a loss for words."

"I'm pleased you found me. I thought you were the rent collector once again trying his luck. How did you find me?" He asked.

"I've been to visit Gustav Coutois at his gallery."

"Oh Gustav, of course. Was he glad to see you?"

"Yes. We reminisced about the times we visited during the Exposition, and he knew of my success as a palmist."

"I've told him about you. Like others, you made an impression on the man. Come sit for a while, and tell me your latest. I get so few visitors these days. I spend my time roaming the streets and living in the past. How long are you in Paris?"

"I'm taking a couple of weeks to recharge, and I plan to spend some time in Boulogne Sur Mer before returning to London."

"I believe it's the place to be seen. If of course, one wants to be seen." He wept.

I'd never seen Oscar cry. He'd always maintained his composure, even in the worst situations. Observing the tears, triggered an intense fear. If this could happen to Oscar, why could it not happen to me? One may be living a life of success and prosperity one week, and end up crying in a squalid hotel room, the next.

"Oscar, you mustn't give up hope. I know life hasn't been easy for you, but you have survived your trials. You must learn to live again." I said.

"Live again? Do you call this existence living? Louis, I'm done for. I've nothing left to live for. You were right with what you saw on my hand, and it's all my own doing. I blame no one but myself. I can accept the slings and arrows of those who despise me, as I don't care what such people think. I can move on from the taunts and sufferings of those who held me prisoner. My regret is, I've destroyed my life for someone who in the end cared nothing for me. What's been the point of it all?"

"You couldn't know how things would turn out for you Oscar. The emotions of others are beyond your control."

"Bosie did come and stay with me after I left prison, did you know?"

"No. I wasn't aware."

"Yes. I believe it was to ease his own feelings of guilt. It was a disastrous reunion, and when the money ran out, so did he. In the

230

end he cared nothing for me or what I'd been through for him. This realisation was the dagger causing the fatal wound."

Hearing Oscar speak of Lord Alfred Douglas only confirmed what I'd thought of 'Bosie' from the beginning, and I left my friend broken and empty, offering him little to overcome his predicament. There's only so much one can do regarding the emotions of another, but I left him some cash, and paid the outstanding rent. It was the least I could do for the man who helped change my life, all those years before.

I'd spent quite a sum on my French holiday, and was realising the lifestyle I'd become accustomed to, was beyond my means. Even with large fees, there was only so much I could earn in a week. Unlike many of my acquaintances, there wasn't any family money to sustain me. The cash from my dealings with the Duchess of Sutherland, was spent on the office and home furnishings, and publishing. Oscar's state of destitution affected me greatly.

***

The train from Paris to London passed through Amiens and Calais, with most tourists boarding the ferry at Calais to make the channel crossing. After an unexpected encounter, my plans to travel south to Boulogne Sur Mer changed.

At Amiens, the train stopped for a time, allowing passengers to buy refreshments and use the amenities. On my return, a familiar face stared through the window of a carriage. It was the Dowager Duchess of Sutherland, travelling with her new husband, the MP, Sir Albert Kaye Rollit. After sighting me, she gestured for her husband to go on without her.

Standing on the platform, Marian Read's message of further dealings with a dishonest woman, came back, and tempting fate, I boarded the carriage to confront my former patron. After counting the compartments, I knocked, but there was no answer. Opening the door, I entered to find the duchess looking flustered and angry.

"What are you doing here? How dare you enter my

compartment." She told me.

"Why duchess. Is that anyway to greet an old friend? Are you not pleased to make my acquaintance again?" I smiled.

"I am not. Our dealings with each other are over. I've a new husband now, and do not wish to be reminded of the past, and those who've caused me grief."

"I'm not the cause of your grief madam. I believe the origin of your distress, is your own guilty conscience."

"My conscience is perfectly happy thank you very much."

"I believe you, when you say you have no conscience. How could you live with yourself if you did?"

"Your slurs don't affect me, as I'm used to the sly comments of those who are jealous of my money and position."

"You may have money madam, but you delude yourself if you feel you have any position." I told her.

"And what position do you have? Your charade as a count is laughable. Call yourself what you want, but you're nothing but a conniving blackmailer parading yourself as a spiritual seer. Like your friend Oscar Wilde, you'll end up answering for your crimes in prison and receiving what you deserve." She smiled.

"I'm not the one in this compartment who's been to prison madam. You may escape one crime, but you were held accountable for another." I grinned.

"I will not stay here in the presence of such an infernal being. I'm going to join my husband, and you'd be wise to leave before we return, or suffer the consequences."

"Empty threats duchess. I and another, are witness to a confession proving you compelled the late duke to murder your former husband. One can only imagine what fate awaits your next spouse?" I shouted.

The duchess stormed out of the carriage. I watched her leave and disappear down the platform. I don't know what possessed me in the following moments, but I remember vividly the anger towards this woman who'd denigrated Oscar and myself with her words. This individual destroyed two husband's lives, yet she continued to prosper financially, even entering into another marriage.

Looking around the compartment, I noticed a small case with the duchess's initials. Without knowing what lay inside, I grabbed it, and returned to my empty compartment. No one was in the corridor at the time. Placing the case inside a bag of my own, I left the train.

Hailing a cab, I went to a hotel in the main street of Amiens. Still furious from the encounter, I ordered a brandy sent up to my room. On the bed, I contemplated what I'd done. I'd no regrets about causing the duchess discomfort when she failed to find her bag of accoutrements. Between smiles, I finished my drink.

Later that evening, I placed the case on the bed. Finding it locked intrigued me. Perhaps there was something of value inside?

It was my habit to carry a knife, and I used it to open the lock. Inside, there were creams, perfumes, and a bottle of fragrant water. Just as I'd hoped, the duchess would be without her sweet smells that evening.

Under one of the drawers, a black velvet bag caught my attention. Opening it, a cache of diamond rings, necklaces and bracelets fell out onto the bedcover.

What had I done? Next day, the newspaper headlines told the story.

"A DUTCHESS LOSES DIAMONDS.

A satchel containing $150,000 worth of jewellery believed to have been stolen from a car.

PARIS, Oct 17- The Dowager Duchess of Sutherland, while

on board a train for Calais, bound for London, lost a satchel containing jewellery worth $150,000. Her Grace left the train at Amiens and returned here to report her loss to the police. It is believed that the satchel was stolen, but there is no clue to the thief."

Is this what Marian Read meant when she told me I'd benefit from a past benefactor? The duchess may suspect me, but informing the police would be unwise, given my knowledge of her former husband's death.

Surely, insurance covered the jewels, meaning there'd be no financial loss for the duchess. It seemed ridiculous to ponder over such a point, given the amount of money she'd acquired. Nevertheless, it made me feel better about what I'd done. The next day, I disposed of the initialled case in the hotel's incinerator.

After this, it was onwards to Boulogne Sur Mer. Walking confidently around the town, I knew I'd never end up in the same state of poverty as Oscar.

The resort was a convenient location for people wanting to spend time away from familiar faces in London. Here, they could meet with strangers, or travel with companions in anonymity. At a café one morning, a handsome couple sat eating their croissants and coffee. Unfortunately for the lady, I knew her, and the man she ate with, was not her husband. After finishing my breakfast, I approached them.

"Good morning, Madam, Sir. Aren't the croissants superb?" I smiled.

The woman became flushed.

"They're not too bad at all." The man replied.

"If I'm not mistaken, I believe I've met you before, Mrs. Jennings?"

"Of course. Forgive me, I'm a little under the weather this morning." She replied.

"How is your husband?" I queried.

"He's quite well, thank you. Always busy with his work, and I end up going away on my own." She said.

"Well Boulogne Sur Mer is a wonderful place to meet people." I smiled.

I directed my attention to her male companion.

"Allow me to introduce myself. The name is Count Louis Hamon." I said, shaking his hand.

"Harry Jackson, pleased to meet you. Wont you join us?" He asked.

"Thank you, as long as I'm not intruding?" I said, looking at Mrs. Jennings.

"Not at all. "She replied.

"Have you been staying here long?" I asked.

"We've been here for a week. What about yourself?" Harry enquired.

"I've just arrived. I'm giving myself a little holiday before leaving on a tour of America."

"Are you an actor?" Harry asked.

"No, Harry. This is Cheiro. He's a famous palmist back in London, and that's how we know each other. He read the palms of my husband, and myself." She explained.

"A palmist. There's a gypsy woman on the pier here, reading palms. I was thinking of seeing her." Harry told me.

"I'm afraid you may be disappointed with the quality of the reading. Unfortunately, such people rarely know the science well."

"Are you doing any readings while you're here?" He asked.

"I wasn't planning to. I'm afraid I charge a bit more than your gypsy woman." I grinned.

"Sweetness, you'd pay to hear what my palm says, wouldn't you?" Harry said, rubbing his companion's shoulder.

The display of affection, and request for money, exposed the nature of the relationship.

"If you really want to know, yes." She told him, half-heartedly.

"When can you see me?" He asked.

"You can come by my hotel later today, if it suits?"

"Wonderful, we'll be there."

"You can go on your own Harry. You needn't have me along." Mrs. Jennings said.

"As you wish. I'll see you then." He told me, and the two departed.

Later that day, he arrived.

"Come in Harry. Take a seat and I'll get my magnifying glass." I told him.

Harry was eager to see what the future held for him.

"Your hand is of the mixed type. Long palm and shorter fingers indicate you make impulsive decisions, and the different shape of each finger demonstrates you're versatile, adapting to different situations. A strong head line and large mount of Mercury, tell me you're a shrewd character when it comes to money and business. What line of work are you in?" I asked.

"I have no particular profession. As you say, I make my way in life by adapting to each situation. At the moment, I'm enjoying the company of a woman who supports me." He told me, unashamedly.

There were signs of dishonesty on Harry's hand, and no doubt, he'd been involved in criminal activities. Perhaps the meeting would prove profitable?

"I can see you're a clever operator Harry, and no doubt, your skills have served you well in the past, even if they're not above board."

"Right you are. I make the most of every opportunity."

"The criminal world fascinates me. For example, what does a thief do with the goods after he steals them? I can understand small items, but what of these jewel thieves and suchlike? It must be difficult to unload those expensive items?"

"Not at all. It's a network, like all businesses. You learn who to trust, and who to avoid. There are always buyers and sellers in this game."

"Really? And do you have a network, Harry?" I asked.

"Of course. I can pretty much unload anything of value. Why? Do you have something?" He laughed.

The moment arrived naturally. Was this an opportunity to convert the jewellery into useable cash? Could I trust this person or not? Feeling lucky, I continued.

"Well yes, actually I do." I smiled.

"That's a surprise. What do you have?"

"Some jewellery. I can't go into how I came by it. Let's just say, I'd like to sell it quietly."

"I believe I can help you, for a small commission, of course."

"Of course. With your hand, I'd expect nothing less."

"When do you want to sell the items?"

"As soon as possible."

"Actually, I know someone here in town who can help. We can

meet him tomorrow?" He suggested.

"Excellent. Tell me where and when to meet you." I replied.

After Harry gave the details, I thought about the arrangement. It was a risk, but then I'd little choice. The jewels were useless to me as they were, and I needed the cash. I took only a few pieces until I knew I could trust Harry.

The next afternoon, we met outside a jewellery shop, on the main street of the town.

"Here we are." Harry said, as we arrived at the business.

"It seems legitimate." I told Harry, looking in the window.

"Now, the person I'm dealing with only knows me. You'll have to stay out here while I do the business." He told me.

"Oh really? I'm not sure about that." I said, concerned.

"Why? Don't you trust me?" He asked, annoyed.

"No, it's not that. How will I know if the price offered is acceptable?"

"I'll come out and let you know." He said.

"Very well. Here are the pieces."

"Wait here, and I'll return as soon as he makes an offer."

Nervously, I looked around as people passed, and everything seemed calm. I tried looking through the glass windows, but couldn't see anything inside. Ten minutes passed and Harry hadn't returned. I'd been watching the entrance the whole time, and went inside to see what was happening. A few customers were looking at display cases with the owner, but Harry was nowhere to be seen. Perhaps he was negotiating in the back with someone else, after all it's not something you'd do in public.

"May I help you Sir?" The gentleman asked.

"Just looking, thank you. I'm waiting for a friend who came in here a short time ago." I told him.

"Mon Dieu. He is a friend of yours?" He asked, surprised.

"Yes. Is he with someone in the back?"

"Non, non. He wanted to use the toilet, but he is gone, out through the window." He exclaimed, throwing his hands in the air.

Harry's departure with the jewels, hit me hard. How could I have trusted such a character after reading his palm? Foolishly, I believed Mrs. Jennings would provide some degree of security, as she wouldn't want her secret life exposed in London. There was no trace of Harry or Mrs. Jennings at their hotel, and the concierge informed me the two had an explosive row after Harry returned from the reading, and Mrs Jennings left for Paris. Had he told her of the jewels? Perhaps she wanted them for herself? The only consolation was, I'd only given Harry part of the cache. I'd make sure of my connections before trusting anyone again. Within a year, Harry was arrested in England after selling the gems. It seems the honourable Mrs. Jennings eventually betrayed him, as well as her husband. The papers told only part of the story. Later I'd sell the remaining gems through a more secure network.

***

Back in Bond Street, my secretary, Thomas, informed me the appointment book was full until the end of Summer. I told him of my plans to return to the United States in September, instructing him to keep the time free.

Conscious Robert was back in London, I debated whether I should meet with him, as we'd not communicated since our disagreement at the Athenaeum Club some months before.

I knew Barrett had returned from abroad, and was producing plays at the Lyceum, and I wanted to meet with Maud and Robert before leaving on tour.

I sent a message to Robert, at his infernal club, asking if he'd dine with me at our old haunt, the Café Royal. He agreed, and before long, we were chatting as if nothing had happened between us. I was careful not to bring up the subject of his work with Barrett, and he wisely did the same.

"Where have you been Louis? Your complexion has a healthy glow."

"I was in France a few months ago. I stayed in Paris and then Boulogne Sur Mer, where the weather was sunny." I explained.

"What did you get up to in Paris?" He asked.

"The usual things one gets up to there." I replied.

"Nothing is ever usual with you. Come now, details?

"You always know where to look, don't you Robert?"

"It's the journalistic training." He smiled.

"I visited galleries and met with artists I'd not seen for some time."

"You seem to gravitate toward creatives with a brush. Anyone else of interest?"

"Well, yes. I visited Oscar."

"Really? People told me he'd disappeared from the face of the earth."

"That's what he'd wish people to believe." I said.

"How did you find him? Don't tell me he's been corresponding with you?"

"Of course not. He's been occupied with Douglas, and the last thing he needed was another man denying his advances. It was Gustav Courtois who told me of his lodgings."

"Bosie back with Oscar? Is the man insane?"

"No, just a fool who's realised his folly. The pretty poison Douglas finally abandoned him."

"Is he well?"

"Quite the opposite, and I expect the worst." I told him.

"Your prophesy has finally come to pass."

"So, it seems."

"It will be a tragic end, more in keeping with a melodramatic Barrett play, than a gay Wilde production." Robert continued.

"Did you have to mention that name?" I asked.

"Sorry Louis. Ignore my stupidity. I'd forgotten how sensitive you are on the subject. I'll make it up to you by writing more glowing reviews in Hearth and Home."

"Saved by the pen." I replied.

"What are your plans for the season?"

"I'll be in London until September, and after that, I'm returning to the United States for another tour."

"You're keeping busy. Make sure you take your breaks."

"Yes, I realize that. That's why I went to France. Boulogne Sur Mer is the perfect place to rejuvenate."

"Oh, I almost forgot to mention the Duchess of Sutherland. Did you hear? Her diamonds were stolen whilst she was in France last October." Robert asked.

Caught off guard, I choked.

"Here Louis, drink this." Robert said, handing me a glass of water.

I wiped tears from my eyes with a napkin.

"Sorry Robert. I believe that was a bone." I lied.

"Nasty things. Another reason I avoid seafood these days. As I was saying, can you believe the audacity of the thief? In broad daylight. You must be careful Louis when travelling there, as obviously, there's a sly criminal element operating. Not that you've any diamonds to steal, but you need to be wary."

"Now that you mention it, I do remember reading something about it when I was there." I replied.

"You were in France at that time?" He asked.

"Yes. It was just before I left for Boulogne Sur Mer." I told him, avoiding his stare.

"You must have jumped for joy? I know how much you despise the woman."

"Karma takes care of things, Robert. Rejoicing in someone else's misfortune is fruitless."

"What hogwash Louis. This is another Scorpio you're talking to, and whether we like it or not; the spirit of vengeance courses through our veins."

"Alright, I may have been slightly bemused by the news." I conceded.

"Bemused? I bet you wished you'd stolen them yourself." He laughed.

"Can we move on from the duchess? It's a sore point I wish to forget. If you recall; my dealings with her changed your opinion of me."

"Yes, sorry Louis. I now realise, you were coerced by Oscar to blackmail the Sutherlands. It's not as if you planned it. That episode can't be compared to this recent theft."

Intuition and intellect are dangerous combinations in an individual. Add an intimate association, and the risk of discovery is increased. Escaping my friend's probing, convinced me I'd nothing to worry about from others who were less perceptive.

Relieved issues with Robert were sorted, my thoughts turned to Maud. The Barrett Company returned in September, playing Cardiff and other cities outside of London. Back in the city, Maud met with me in Kensington gardens.

Our reunion began with a gentle kiss and friendly hug.

"I'm pleased you could get away." I told her.

Maud looked prosperous in her tailored outfit.

"What a glorious day. I'm glad you suggested here. The scent of flowers and trees invigorates me."

"Isn't the park looking spectacular?" I declared.

"Yes, beautiful. I've missed the green. England is a fertile land with rich soils and plenty of water. Having travelled abroad I've come to appreciate it more."

"You speak of Australia? I've heard it's a harsh country."

"The land has a rough and rugged beauty, and the magnificence of the ancient landscape is something to behold. It's astonishing to see the desolation and dryness change after rain, but unfortunately, the great southern land is experiencing a drought, and this was evident in places." She explained.

"What about the cities? How did you find them?"

"The people are friendly, and the audiences in Sydney were particularly receptive. We had a wonderful time there, and the harbour is a natural delight, so clean and sparkling. Melbourne too, has a beauty of its own, and is more like a city one would find in England. The architecture and gardens are similar."

"I remember Nellie Melba telling me of its virtues one evening.

I've recently met another young lady in New York who was born there, a dancer named Saharet."

"Saharet? I've not heard of her."

"I believe you will before long. She's making a name for herself."

"A dancer? Where did you meet her?" She asked.

"It's a long story, Maud."

"No need to elaborate." She grinned.

"It's not what you think. She's a married woman, although if the right situation presented itself.." I stopped myself.

"Louis, you've not changed at all."

"Speaking of affairs concerning the heart, how did you handle Barrett on the tour?"

"There were situations when it became difficult. He's a persistent man, but I've told him many times; there will be no romance in my life with anyone but my husband."

"Would you contemplate a marriage with him, if he ever did ask you?" I dared question.

There was a long pause. Eventually she spoke.

"The idea is fruitless. Wilson will never marry again. It's clear he wears the memory of his dead wife as a shield around his heart, and this will never change. His children are important to him, and any new marriage would inevitably cause problems in their relationship. Anyway, my emotions have changed after his behaviour in Melbourne." She explained.

"To do with your daughter?" I asked.

"I met her Louis, and held her in my arms, just as Marian Read told me. Despite my requests, Wilson refused to accompany me. He's not acknowledging her at all."

"That's no surprise. He doesn't want to face the truth, and have to provide for another of his bas…." I stopped myself.

"Oh, Louis. You can say it. Bastard. That's the reality, isn't it? Florence bears a terrible title. When alone with her, I told her I was her mother, and wished I could keep her. Wiping my tears, her innocent face smiled, as if she somehow understood.

"That must have been hard for you?" I asked.

"There are no words to describe the emotion a mother feels when holding her abandoned child. It's an unbearable mixture of guilt, love, and shame. The performance that evening distracted my thoughts, otherwise who knows what may have befallen me." She cried.

Barrett is a cad for sure. Regardless of who the father is, he should have been there to support you." I told her.

"You're right. Something changed in me after that episode. I cannot continue to stay in his company."

"What will you do?"

"I plan to finish the season, and join Herbert Beerbohm Tree's company."

"Does anyone know of your plans?" I asked.

"Mr. Tree of course. He wants me for his production of 'Herod' at Her Majesty's. No one in Wilson's company knows, apart from Lillah Mc Carthy. She's a good friend, and I've discussed it with her on tour."

"You'll have to handle Barrett carefully, as he'll not let you go without a fight."

The news delighted me. Apart from the damage to his ego, Barrett would lose a major drawcard, and this time, Maud was determined to leave.

"I don't care what Wilson thinks, as there's nothing he can do or say to alter my plans."

"You can always rely on my help." I told her.

"Thank you, but these past couple of years have taught me to look inward for guidance."

"You speak with a new confidence."

"I've been reading material Lillah gave me from the Theosophical society."

"I'm glad you're connecting with your spiritual side."

"I found the information comforting. You know Louis, Marian Read has a remarkable gift. Her description of the visit with Florence was exact, and I intend going to see her again soon."

"She does have a special gift." I agreed.

"Did you have a consultation with her?" She asked.

"Yes, and it was disturbing in its accuracy. I try not to think of it actually."

The images and screams of the Exeter fire victims returned.

"Was it not helpful? It certainly was for me." Maud asked.

"Confronting as it was, it did clear something up." I replied.

"I'm glad." She smiled.

We found a park bench and chatted for some time before Maud left for the theatre. I watched my famous friend walk away and disappear into the crowds.

Strolling back to Bond Street, allowed me to ponder how fortunate I was to have Maud and Robert as friends. After visiting Oscar in his deserted loneliness, I'd not take such things for granted.

***

It was the last client of the day.

To my surprise, the young man I'd bumped into outside the Athenaeum club had come for a reading. It took me a moment to recall his name, Frank Shackleton.

"Good afternoon. The name is Frank, isn't it?" I asked, shaking his hand.

"Well done. You remembered." He smiled.

"Like yourself, I've a memory for certain faces. Won't you come through and take a seat."

It was our third meeting. The first was at the Devonshire Ball, the second, outside the Athenaeum Club. The intimate space of my office allowed me to survey the man in detail.

Like myself, he was tall, but lacked the solid bone structure of my frame. Immaculately groomed and dressed, his appearance looked prosperous and aristocratic. The large brown eyes were framed with dark lashes, and the full lips were accentuated by a carefully styled moustache.

"You've decided to tempt fate by coming to see me?" I smiled.

"I don't believe in fate, only the rewards of one's efforts." He replied.

"Were you born cynical, or has life made you that way?

"Perhaps you'll tell me?"

"Maybe I should only read your right hand? This shows what we make of our lives." I told him.

"Only one hand? Will you charge me half your fee?" He grinned.

"Sharp as your clothes." I laughed.

"Just a man who knows his worth."

"Let us discover where that worth lies shall we?"

"That's why I'm here."

Frank laid his hand on the cushion, and I inspected it with my glass.

"Your palm is longer than average. It's in proportion with your fingers, which are also longer than most."

"Do you believe finger size correlates to the size of other organs in the body?" He smirked, raising his middle digit.

"I'm not aware of anyone who's undertaken such a study." I replied, pushing the finger down.

"Well, if you decide to start one of your own, I'd be glad to participate."

"My study indicates long fingers with an equally long palm, denote a person who's cautious, and a careful planner. There's nothing impulsive or rash in your makeup. You're a clever strategist manoeuvring his way through life."

"That's true. I take my time making decisions, as I like to know what I'm dealing with before taking a risk."

"Your separated head and heart lines tell me you can take chances, but they're calculated ones. The fate line crossed in certain places, indicates struggles and trials which must be overcome, and at times, you'll encounter public scrutiny. This is shown by a line of influence extending from the inner mount of mars."

Frank looked concerned but remained silent.

"The heart line is marked by downward lines, showing hardship when it comes to emotional attachments. This marking here between the finger of Saturn and Mercury is known as the girdle of Venus, and I've rarely seen such a fully formed mark. It endows its owner with an appreciation of beautiful things, as well as a love of the human form. Your full mount of Venus and nail shape show you freely indulge in pleasures of the flesh."

"Amazing. You can see all this from my hand?"

"Of course. Is there anything else you wish to ask me?"

"I believe before long, I shall be appointed assistant secretary to the officer of arms at Dublin castle. Can you see whether this will be the case?"

"That's an excellent position. Your fate line indicates there's an auspicious connection in relation to your career around this time. Whether you believe it or not, it's part of your karmic destiny. I'm reluctant to confirm the position, as it indicates it will not be in a country foreign to your birth."

"I was born in Ireland. In Kilkea, County Kildare." My family moved to England when I was young." He explained.

"Then it's possible you will achieve this position."

"Oh, I know I will. I've been assured of it by people in authority." He told me.

Frank was referring to his connection with John Campbell, the Marquess of Lorne, was who was married to the Prince of Wales's sister Louise, and no doubt this association was proving beneficial.

"You're a fellow Irishman then? I cannot believe you were born in Kilkea. It's just a stone's throw from my father's people in Mount Mellick." I told him.

"It seems we have many things in common."

"Perhaps."

"Am I your last client?"

"Yes. I make a point of not overtaxing myself these days."

"Shall we dine together, and talk more of Ireland? I'm eager to gather as much information about Dublin before I arrive."

Frank was a lively character, and talking with him about Ireland proved a welcome distraction. In a rowdy hotel, we found a quiet corner to converse, and after many pints of stout, we headed back to my apartment. The memory of what followed is blurred, and next morning I awoke naked, beside my drinking companion. He left soon after.

Before leaving for America, I made another quick visit to Boulogne Sur Mer.

It was mid-September 1899, when I arrived back in New York as the trees along my favourite walk in Central Park, changed colour. When the cold winds of December did come, my spirits were not dampened. Furnishing myself with a new Winter wardrobe, I revisited familiar places.

One day I found myself in an area I'd stayed in when touring with the Barrett Company, and the Turkish baths I visited with Dauncey and Kersley still existed. No doubt the same shenanigans were taking place in the steamy rooms.

Chapter Eight

(1900-1910)

The new century was celebrated with extravagance, and the parties continued well into January. In February, I took in a play at Wallack's theatre on Broadway & 30th Streets. Clyde Fitch's production of 'Sapho', adapted from the novel by Alphonse Daudet, starred the young English actress, Olga Nethersole.

Newspapers were giving 'Sapho' a lot of attention, and the racy content, had New York's morality forces demanding the production be stopped. The controversy only increased people's curiosity, including mine.

The audience moved restlessly waiting for the play to begin. Countless men filled the seats, eager to experience the sensual delights of the production, as there were scenes of passionate kissing and groping. The story centred on a young man, Jean Gaussin, who loses his position in society after being seduced by Fanny Legrand (Sapho), a woman of scandalous reputation.

Sapho's notoriety is a result of her many past lovers. She eventually falls deeply in love with Jean, but must leave him to raise a child from those promiscuous days.

As the story unfolded, I thought of Oscar, who like Jean, had lost his position in society because of an infatuation. The character of Sapho, reminded me of Mary Eastlake who'd kept her illegitimate child as Sapho had.

The curtain rose, and the audience erupted into thunderous applause. Before us, a sumptuous, masked ball delighted the crowd, and the costumes and sets were of the highest quality. Olga Nethersole moved everyone with her emotional performance.

In the controversial scene, Sapho is carried up a staircase, where the passionate kissing and fondling continue for some time. The audience are still, and the sound of heavy breathing is unmistakable. The tension is finally broken when the scene finishes. When the play was over, the actors took their bows with standing ovations. 'Sapho' proved to be a success, despite the controversy.

The crowds dispersed up Broadway, and I headed to the Hoffman House Hotel at 25th Street to take supper. The hotel's sumptuous furnishings and decorations made it a favourite of celebrities.

When ordering a brandy from the bar, mirrors reflected an exquisite painting of a centaur surrounded by naked women, painted in 1873 by William-Adolphe Bouguereau and titled 'Nymphs and Satyr'. Moving to a table, I relaxed with a drink and admired the erotic image.

Two women and a gentleman entered the bar. Olga Nethersole was accompanied by Florence Striker and her co-star, Hamilton Revelle. The women sat at the next table while Hamilton ordered the drinks. Florence was the first to catch me staring, and smiled, prompting Olga to look my way. Hamilton returned with the drinks and found he was missing a seat.

"Would you mind if I take this chair?" He asked.

"Not at all. I'm not expecting company." I told him.

"Splendid. Lovely to meet another Englishman in New York." He smiled.

Hamilton was the archetypal actor, and his poise and cultured speech were typical traits of the English thespian. Although born in Gibraltar, he'd been educated in England, and his swarthy good looks were a gift of his Latin ancestry. I was flattered a theatrical star was talking to me.

"I've just seen your remarkable performance. Congratulations."

"Really? Well thank you. Wont you join us? I'm sure the ladies would like to hear your opinion of the show."

"Very kind of you." I replied.

Hamilton moved his chair, making room for me.

"Ladies, I've discovered a fellow Englishman who's just been to see our play." He told them.

"Good evening. I'm not really English, originally from Ireland. The name is Louis, and may I say how impressed I was with the performance."

"I'm Florence," She smiled, extending her hand.

"And this is….." She continued.

"Olga of course. There's no need for an introduction." I interrupted, taking Olga's hand.

"What no kiss?" Olga asked, raising an eyebrow.

"Don't you think you've had enough kissing for one night?" I replied.

The three erupted into laughter.

"Shall we drink to our success and the demise of those who would thwart us." Olga shouted, raising her glass.

"It's a comfort knowing there are others who feel as I do about those who oppose one's work." I added.

"Have you also experienced the prejudices of the righteous Louis?" Hamilton asked.

"I most certainly have. Many times, in many ways." I replied.

"What line of work are you in?" Florence asked.

"In my early days I was involved in your world of the theatre."

Olga leant forward in her chair, took out a cigarette and lit it.

"Did you actually act, or were you engaged elsewhere? You certainly have the looks for a leading man, don't you think Hamilton?" She smiled at her companion.

"He does indeed Olga. Can I offer you a cigarette?" He asked.

"Thank you. I don't usually smoke at this hour but tonight I'll deviate from my routine."

"Well chaps, I've finished my gin and I'm off to my room." Florence told us.

"Lovely to have met you, Florence." I said, standing.

"A pleasure Louis."

Hamilton and Olga waved goodbye. Walking through the bar, she glanced up at the painting of the Nymphs and Satyr.

"Did you see Florence take a sly look at the raunchy artwork as she left?" Hamilton laughed.

"Well, you cannot blame the girl. The women are voluptuous, and the half man half beast exudes a raw sexuality." Olga smiled.

"Like your play, the work has attracted criticism from those who feel it shouldn't hang in a public space." I added.

Olga puffed on her cigarette and blew out a trail of smoke.

"Phooey. What are those dried up women complaining about? It's not like it's hanging in their homes. Let them stay in their sewing rooms."

"Let's hope when this Victorian age is over, we can get on with our lives without all these constraints." Hamilton added.

"By all accounts we'll not have long to wait. I'm told the Queen is near her end, and the Prince of Wales is more than ready to take over. Knowing him as I do, I feel confident there'll be changes."

Olga's eyes widened.

"You've met the Prince of Wales? You never did finish telling us what it is you do?"

"I've had the pleasure of meeting with the prince. My work as a chirologist, has brought me into the company of many in the Royal household."

"A chirologist? What is that?" Hamilton asked.

"A palm reader Hamilton. It's a fancy name for someone who reads hands." She told him, putting her fingers on his shoulder.

Hamilton smiled and seemed surprised.

"Really, you read palms? I once had mine read back home in Gibraltar. You know we have many gypsies there, and that's mainly what they do. I'm afraid their reputation is not an honourable one." He told us.

"It's true. Unfortunately, the art has been exploited by charlatans. The knowledge of palmistry came with the gypsies when they emigrated to Europe from India centuries ago. There was a Frenchman, Stanislas D'Arpentigny, who when serving in Spain during the peninsular wars, met a gipsy girl who read his hands. She'd been taught the correct traditions, and he went on to write extensively about palmistry and formulate a scientific method of his own, based on his numerous observations."

"Have you studied his work?" Olga asked.

"Yes, and others. I've written and published works myself also."

"I've been told of palmists who work in London. I've never felt the need to visit, but by all accounts, they make a good living on Bond Street and such places." Hamilton said.

"Well, I'm one of those. I work under the professional name of Cheiro."

"Cheiro? I feel sure I've heard the name before." Hamilton told me, finishing his cigarette.

"I've also published a work of fiction and verse."

"Is this why you're in New York?" Olga asked.

"I've a practice on Fifth Avenue, which keeps me occupied from September until April. I prefer to spend the Winters in America these days." I explained.

"This is your chosen profession then? You don't regret leaving the theatrical world to follow this course? I couldn't imagine my life without the stage." Olga continued.

"Not at all. Each of us has a destiny. Fate guides us in the right direction by giving us open and closed doors. Let us say, my experiences in the world of theatre prompted me to make a change."

"I don't want to know anything about my future. My only interest would be the length of my life, as everything else is of no consequence. Is it possible to tell this from the hand?" Hamilton asked.

"Absolutely. There are definite signs on the hand to show this. I'd look at your hand if we were someplace else, but I don't wish to attract attention by reading palms here."

Hamilton finished a number of drinks by the time our supper was over.

"I've an idea, if you'd be open to it? Olga and I have a room upstairs. We could go and continue our conversation in privacy." He told me.

"Oh, you've a room together? It's no wonder your scenes on stage are so steamy." I grinned.

"We grew tired of rehearsing and thought we'd just live the part." Olga laughed.

When following Olga out of the bar, Hamilton looked up at the artwork and whispered.

"What do you really think of this artwork Louis?"

"I love it. The French artists have few inhibitions." I told him.

"Really?"

"In my experience, art and life often merge." I smiled.

Olga looked back.

"What are you two whispering about? "She asked.

"Just the artwork Olga." Hamilton smiled.

The hotel room was small and intimate, and Hamilton was eager to hear what his hand foretold.

"I'll only search for signs of longevity, and hopefully, the evening ends on a good note.

"Your heart line is strong and clear, and the line of Mercury or health line, is absent."

"Oh no. I knew it. I'm going to die young. At least I'll still retain my looks."

"No, no. The absence of this line is a good sign." I explained.

"Thank God." He gasped.

"Hamilton calm down. Let Louis finish." Olga told him, laughing.

"The life line is extremely long and well-marked with no lines of influence crossing it. Looking at the overall picture I predict you'll live a long life, into your 90's for certain."

"Oh, that's too long. My looks will be gone by then, and most of my work."

Having received the desired information, Hamilton lay down on the floor and stretched out. Olga came over and sat next to me.

"The vanity of an actor Louis. Are you glad you don't have to worry about such things? If only our looks could stay the same." She sighed.

"Don't wish for that, Olga. The concept has already been written about, and despaired over."

"Yes, true. I've read Wilde's story of Dorian Gray. The man has a fertile imagination. I expect he came across someone somewhere, who inspired the idea."

Olga cuddled into me and began stroking my hair. I'd desired her from the time I'd seen her perform as Sapho, and the sexual tension could no longer be restrained. What followed was a physical encounter between three highly aroused people lasting hours.

Hamilton and Olga were absolute creatures of Eros, engaging in the divine pleasures of the flesh, and I'd been a willing participant in their mutual desire for me.

The following days provided more opportunities with Hamilton and Olga.

On February 21st, Olga, Hamilton, and their manager Marcus Mayer, were arrested for offences against public decency and creating a public nuisance. Those dried up women Olga spoke about, obviously had influential connections. Olga and Hamilton were eventually released and the charges dropped.

The publicity only served to increase the popularity of the production. Unlike myself, Olga and Hamilton were following their destinies as children of the theatre, and as this was their karmic path, doors continued to open for them and provide successes.

***

In April, the season in America was over, and I returned to England onboard the SS Kaiser Wilhelm der Grosse. The magnificent ship was the first of the luxury liners boasting a crown of four funnels, and was unrivalled until the White Star's Olympic and Titanic overshadowed her a few years later.

Decorated with intricate details, the interior work and stained-glass features were beautifully executed by German craftsmen. The first-class passage was expensive, however, I felt justified spoiling myself after weeks of hard work.

I found it difficult to relax on the voyage, and the terrible night of the Exeter Theatre fire continued to play on my mind in certain areas of the ship. I was relieved when we disembarked at Southampton.

Not long after, I read about the massive multi ship fire in New York. The disaster damaged the SS Kaiser Wilhelm der Grosse and over one hundred lives were lost on her. Those poor souls had died in areas I'd walked around on the voyage, and the images were added to the Exeter Theatre victims. Once again, I'd escaped death by fire.

In a few weeks I'd be returning to Paris for the Universal Exhibition, but this time there'd be no travelling companion. I hoped the 1900 Exposition would be as thrilling as the 1889 one.

***

Arriving in June, Paris was alive with tourists walking the boulevards and enjoying the festivities of the Exposition. The moveable walkway brought visitors to the entrance, reducing the number of steps people were faced with. The atmosphere was as electric as the previous Expo, with many arriving from London to partake in the celebrations.

I was young and unknown when I came with Oscar in 1889; a mere companion and assistant for someone on the verge of becoming a successful author and playwright. Anyone engaging us back then, did so because of him. Walking the exhibition, I crossed paths with people eager to converse with me. I planned to lunch at a café near the Chateau d'eau overlooking the gardens of the Champ de Mars, and it was here, I came across acquaintances from London. Whispering to each other, they gave me a wave. Walking towards the café, I felt obliged to approach them.

"Good afternoon. Are you enjoying the exposition?" I asked.

"Very much so. Isn't the weather divine?" A woman replied.

"Paris this time of year rarely disappoints. I'm looking to have lunch, and this café has been recommended by my hotel concierge. Have you eaten here?" I asked.

"We intended to, but have decided against it. We are particular about the company we keep." Replied a gentleman, looking back at the café.

I surveyed the patrons, and at a small table, the sorry figure of Oscar sat peering into his coffee. Since our last meeting, his appearance had deteriorated further, and the once proud head was lowered to avoid the sour expressions of the glaring English. In all my life, I can recall no sadder image than my friend that day.

"You cannot mean poor Oscar? Is he your excuse for not patronizing this perfectly good establishment?" I asked, angrily.

"Well of course. Why would we want to be seen anywhere near such a person?" The woman replied with venom.

"I expect he feels the same about you madam. I for one, have no problem with him, and will happily join him for lunch."

"If you do, you need never associate with me or my friends again." She threatened.

"Believe me, I'm happy to avoid such narrow minds. Thank you for enlightening me on your true natures. Good day to you."

I left the group gasping, and approached Oscar.

"Oscar, how are you?" I asked.

He raised his head, slowly.

"Louis, my friend. How good it is of you to acknowledge me here."

"Why wouldn't I, Oscar? May I join you for lunch?"

The defeated face cast its fearful eyes around the café. He was like a cornered rat, waiting for the trap to snap. Looking around, I caught the stares of disapproval and forcibly returned them until they were withdrawn.

"What do I feel like? You must let me order something for you Oscar. Let us imagine it's eleven years ago. Remember the former exposition, when we indulged in the wonderful cuisine?" I asked.

Oscar's face reddened, and tears formed when handing him the menu.

"We've quite a history together Louis, haven't we? It's an honourable past, something I can be pleased about. You never wanted anything from me. Unlike most others, you accepted me for who I was. You never sought to pull me down, even when I was at my most arrogant. I left you alone, because I knew your soul was strong and independent, and there was a darkness around you. If I fell in love with you as our friend Frank Miles did, I too would have been destroyed by the lustful obsession. The irony is, the one who I thought of as an innocent angel, ultimately annihilated me. Maybe the bible is right, the devil does come disguised. Perhaps you are really an angel hiding behind a mask of darkness?"

"No Oscar, believe me. I'm no angel."

"Louis, I'm repenting my sins."

"What do you mean?"

"I'm embracing Catholicism, and making atonement for my sins in the eyes of God. My time is near, and I expect to depart this world before long."

The religious narrative was disturbing. What was happening to Oscar? People do strange things when faced with death. Perhaps he thought it would ensure his salvation. Oscar, like myself, was christened Anglican. It's the Catholic church however, that offers hope for those who consider themselves sinners. I could never imagine myself accepting such a thing, even if I was about to enter another world.

Nevertheless, I wanted Oscar to have peace before he passed on, and if he felt he'd be forgiven for what he considered a crime against God, let him have that belief.

"I'm sorry you feel your life has been a sinful one Oscar, but I believe your only sin was vanity, and not the sin of loving. If your love towards another was pure and honest, how can it be wrong? If God is Almighty, he will surely see it, and if He is the supreme being in control of creation, then this is how he made you. How can you be evil? There are those in this world who manipulate and destroy others for their own lust and pleasure. These are the demons God speaks of, and you're not one of those."

Oscar raised his eyes to the sky. Placing a hand on my arm, he continued.

"Do you remember the day we met in Bray? You were drinking from the fountain in the main street, and we were caught in a storm."

"Yes, and there was a crow, you were most distressed about."

"He was interrupting my attempt at befriending you."

"I remember."

"He was wise to warn you Louis. I'm not what you think. It's true I loved Bosie with all my heart, but there have been encounters with others where my only objective was to satisfy my own lust. So, you see by your own definition, I'm indeed one of those demons God speaks of. Are you forgetting my right palm, that which I make in this life? I'm responsible for destroying the world God planned for me. The left hand as you say, is my destiny. Surely this is God's plan, and it was a rich and successful design, but not to be."

Oscar was right, and in his sad state, the dark side was illuminated. There were elements of his life mirroring my own, and the reflection was uncomfortable to acknowledge. We ate our lunch, and strolled around the fountain in front of the Chateau d'eau. It was obvious Oscar's body was in a weakened condition, and I didn't want to exhaust him further. I left promising to see him once more before I departed France.

Regrettably, I never kept that promise, and on November 30th, I received the news of his death. Though expected, it came as a shock to know the life was finally extinguished.

***

The newspapers took pleasure detailing Oscar's demise and final days. His funeral was held at the Bagneux cemetery on December 3rd.

The service in the Church of Saint-Germain-des-Pres began early in the morning.

There were fifty or so people in attendance with Father Cuthbert Dunne officiating. He'd been with Oscar during his final weeks, as was Reginald Turner and Robert Ross. I'd not seen 'Reggie' for some time. I first met him at one of Hamilton Aide's gatherings during my early days in London. After the service, the solemn cross where Oscar lay buried failed to reflect the impact of the man. Reggie joined me.

"Who would've thought Oscar would end his days in such a manner?"

"Yes Reggie, life surprises us sometimes."

"Surely you weren't shocked? Did you not predict his downfall? He tortured himself with the knowledge you'd warned him, and still he ignored your words."

"Who of us ever takes the advice of others, when it means giving up something we desire?" I replied.

Making a final gesture, I placed a bouquet on the grave. Staring at the floral offering, I wondered what Oscar would make of the arrangement. Imagining him reciting a spontaneous poem to end the farewell, was macabre.

"Can it be true? Lord Alfred is heading this way. I don't think I'll be able to control my emotions if he addresses me." Reggie whispered.

"Perhaps you should depart, as I don't think it appropriate there should be any scenes at such a time." I told him.

"I will leave you to his Lordship then."

Reginald walked past Bosie without any acknowledgment, and Lord Alfred's expression showed no sign of offense.

"Louis, how good it is of you to come." Bosie said, reluctantly.

"Good day to you, Lord Alfred. I would of course, not miss paying my respects to Oscar."

"Yes. You were a true friend of his."

Holding a single rose, Bosie kissed the petals, and placed it on the grave.

"A small offering Oscar, I know it's overshadowed by these other bouquets, but at least it's something."

"I expect Oscar would be happy to receive anything from you, my Lord." I told him.

The fact Oscar was left destitute because of Bosie, meant little to the spoilt prat. He refused his requests for aid, and my words informed him I was aware of this travesty.

"You did see Oscar in his final days then?" He enquired.

"I met with him in June, at the Exposition. He was a man in need of much, mostly love."

"Well, I'm sure you made him feel better, you're such a loveable person, Louis. Let me tell you something. You were the only person who made me jealous when it came to the affections of Oscar. I believe he desperately craved your love at one time, until of course, he became infatuated with me."

"It seems we both failed him. At least I was honest with him when it came to my affections, unlike others."

"You are perfectly correct. I did deceive him when I said I loved him, as much as he loved me; when I said I was his boy. What else could I say? It was what he wanted to hear."

"You were thinking of his feelings of course. How remiss of me to not see that, and to be perfectly clear with you, I was never Oscar's boy."

"No, I never believed you were. That was the power you had over him."

"I never sought to dominate Oscar. I left that to others who called themselves his friends, and of course, his lovers."

"Our relationship was complex. I don't pretend to understand the nature of it."

"There are people who are meant to meet again in this world, and work through the karma of their past lives. I've no doubt your association with Oscar stemmed from a past connection, and you both had free will to decide how that would play out."

"You believe things could have been different then?" He asked.

"Of course, as you well know. If either of you altered your choices with regards to each other, the outcome of your lives would have changed."

"What do you think will happen to that karma, now Oscar is gone?"

"You're still here my Lord, working through your karma." I smiled.

Bosie's eyes returned to Oscar's grave.

"Perhaps one day in the future, I'll follow in Oscar's footsteps and visit you. You can see if the lines of my hand reveal this karma." He told me, walking away.

"No doubt, I'll still be here. The markings on your hand, would certainly be interesting."

I never saw Lord Alfred for many years, but he and his wife Lady Olive Douglas did eventually visit me to have their palms read. I believe Oscar was looking over my shoulder when I told Bosie his life was empty of love, and would remain that way. I encouraged his wife to find happiness elsewhere, and after the reading, he disappeared from my life. The karmic debt was paid.

***

Returning to London, I found a note from Maud, dated the previous week.

"Dear Louis,

I trust you are well.

Had you been in London I would have come to see you, but this note will have to suffice.

I've finally left Wilson and the company. You were right, it was not an easy departure. He flew into a rage, but I remained strong, refusing to be intimidated by him.

After a few weeks break, I will begin 'Twelfth night' with Beerbohm Tree at Her Majesty's. I plan to work until June and then travel to Memphis to visit family.

If you've any free time before I leave, let us meet.

Yours Maud."

I was overjoyed at the news. Maud had finally moved on.

Her life would be different away from Barrett, and I wanted to see her again before our paths moved us in other directions.

***

My visit to Paris reminded me of wonderful memories, and I needed to spend more time in a place I loved.

During my last holiday at Boulogne Sur Mer, I'd met two businessmen, Baron Eugene Oppenheim, and his brother Robert. As entrepreneurs and bankers, they'd made a considerable fortune in South Africa, and wanting to establish myself in Paris, I became involved in their ventures in France. They convinced me; it wasn't necessary to follow established business practices to become rich, and provided the means to turn the remaining pieces of my jewellery stash into useable capital.

Eventually, the Oppenheim's luck ran out, and the two brothers were sent to jail by a Belgian court for falsifying their accounts, and their Selati railway project in South Africa was found to be another source of corrupt funds.

Influenced to undertake illegal business practices, I'd convinced myself everyone who was rich, did the same.

The Oppenheimer's gave the names of business associates in Paris who'd help while they completed their incarceration. These included the socially well-connected Abbe de la Fresnaye, Madame Eugenie de Souris and her husband David. Madame Eugenie was the daughter of Harry Emanuel, a Bond Street jeweller who sold his business to Edwin Streeter, and David de Souris was a Paris banker, and knowledgeable financial adviser.

This was the beginning of a decade of opulence and extravagance, and for the next ten years, I moved between Paris and London operating my concerns. I owned several racehorses, a champagne business in Rheims, and in 1904, purchased "The American Register", an Anglo-American newspaper with the largest circulation of its type in Europe.

As Count Leigh de Hamong, I socialized with wealthy American tourists and European aristocrats, and as 'Cheiro' the palmist, I offered up services to those who could afford to pay the consultation fee. There were constant invitations to the best parties, as the wealthy and titled of Paris were fascinated by a Count who possessed a knowledge of the mystical. It was the ideal setting to gather investors, as people believed my gift of foresight ensured a secure return.

I lived in lavish apartments with sumptuous furnishings. Two favourite addresses were 5 Rue Clement Marot, and 6 Bois de Boulogne, and these locations convinced sceptics I possessed a magic power to gain wealth.

***

In January 1901, Queen Victoria died, and the Prince of Wales became King Edward VII. Having an intimate association with the new King seemed unreal at first, but the relationship continued on as before, with Edward seeking advice on occasions.

Increasing the consultation fees further, did nothing to deter the flow of clients with and one gentleman paying double, to obtain an earlier appointment.

His name was Walter Sanderson, the proprietor of the Parisian Diamond Company located close by on Bond Street. Unlike others, who preferred to remain anonymous, Walter made his identity known to my secretary.

"Welcome Mr. Sanderson. I often pass your beautiful shop and admire the merchandise." I told him.

"Thank you. Please call me Walter. I've contemplated coming for some time."

"What prompted you to finally decide?" I asked.

"Issues with my business. Perhaps there's something on my hand to guide me." He explained.

Unfolding his story was revealing, but something still troubled the man.

"Forgive me, but I feel your problem remains unresolved."

"You are right. Will what I tell you will remain confidential?" He asked.

"Of course. I'm known for my discretion." I replied.

"Five years ago, we had a robbery. You may have read about it in the papers?"

"I do recall something, but I believe I was in the United States at the time."

"We'd just restocked the showroom with new pieces. You know of course, we deal in the highest quality imitation pearls and diamonds, and it takes an expert to distinguish them from the real thing. Anyway, it was reported the thieves used a skeleton key to open the outer door, and then drilled through a panel to open the inner one. £6000 of stock was stolen and has never been recovered." He explained.

"That's a considerable loss. You must have been beside yourself?"

"The theft wouldn't have been successful had the outer door remained locked."

"These thieves are clever with their skeleton keys and suchlike."

"There was no skeleton key." He told me.

"What do you mean?" I asked.

"They had a perfectly good key. Once inside, they were able to work on opening the inner door without detection."

"How do you know they had a key?"

"Because I gave it to them." He whispered.

The confession left me speechless. Walter continued.

"A terrible chain of events led to my actions. Miscalculating

269

finances left me with virtually no capital. I'd outlaid a great deal on the new collection, overextending myself financially, and the creditors threatened bankruptcy. I knew the insurance payout would save me, so I planned the robbery, giving the men a key for the outer door to gain access. Once inside, they damaged the inner door to make the theft look credible."

"You must have been desperate." I said.

"I was. My family would have suffered terribly, and everything I'd built would've been lost. I couldn't let it happen."

"I'm not sure I understand, as it was five years ago. You obviously received your insurance payout. Why are you worried now?"

"Because one of the thieves is blackmailing me, and if I fail to pay him a large sum, he'll expose the fraud. If he does, I'll surely go to prison."

"There's no indication of this on your palm. If he exposes you, he exposes himself. Why would he do such a thing?" I questioned.

"I'm too confused to think clearly." He said.

"The best way to deal with blackmailers is to call their bluff."

I felt ridiculous giving advice to the man, knowing I'd been a blackmailer myself.

"Are you in contact with the other thief?" I asked.

"He's not a part of this. By all accounts he did well selling the items abroad. I believe I could contact him."

"If I were you, I'd seek him out. Let him know his accomplice is threatening to expose you both, and let nature take its course. There's no honour among thieves." I smiled.

"You may be right. I never thought of involving him."

"These people usually act quickly and without much thought, and I expect he wants to hold onto his freedom as much as you

270

do."

"Yes. I feel better about things, thank you. If there's anything I can help you with from my collection, I'd be pleased to offer it to you as a token of my appreciation. Your advice and discretion are invaluable."

"You're most kind." I replied, escorting Walter out.

My secretary Thomas turned to me.

"I hope Mr. Sanderson's reading was a good one. I've met him in his showroom, and he's such a nice man. I wish there were more honest and decent businessmen in Bond Street like him." He declared.

"Yes, he certainly deserves the rewards of all his hard work." I grinned, returning to my office.

At the back of a diary, another name was added to the long list of dishonest businessmen I'd collated.

***

The coronation of King Edward VII was scheduled for the 26th of June 1902, but was postponed until August due to his sudden illness. The ailment was serious enough to prompt the king to send for me. I received a note from his wife requesting I make haste to Buckingham Palace. I'd not seen Edward and Alexandra since the Devonshire Ball.

The king lay ill in his bed, and wanted confirmation nothing had altered on his hand. At Lady Paget's home years before, I told him he'd live until his 69th year. I reassured him the lines were unchanged.

The information alleviated his stress, aiding his recovery. The coronation took place a few weeks later.

***

Maud's run at her Majesty's was over, and she was packing for her trip to America. Wanting to give her something special before she left, I remembered the Parisian Diamond Company.

Walter Sanderson was only too happy to provide a stunning necklace, which he of course, would not accept any payment for.

Maud was thrilled with the gift.

"Louis, it's so extravagant. I love it, but much too expensive." She told me.

"Trust me Maud, my finances can handle it. It's from the Parisian Diamond Company on Bond Street. They're not real you realize, but who can tell the difference?" I confessed.

"Oh well, I can wear it without feeling guilty. The design is beautiful. Thankyou."

She gave me a friendly kiss, and we sat on her sofa.

"How did you enjoy working with Tree? It must be a relief to be away from Barrett?" I asked.

Maud ran fingers through long strands of hair, and threw her head back in excitement.

"What a breath of fresh air. I can't believe I stayed with Wilson for so long, and it's been a pleasure playing Shakespeare with Tree. He's a professional actor who doesn't intimidate his fellow performers."

"Have you heard from Barrett?"

"Oh yes. He's still trying to win me back. He's planning to tour Australia in August, and return there regularly. He knows I love the country and the people, but above all, he's aware of that piece of my heart residing there."

"His manipulating character knows no bounds. Using your daughter as a way to regain his star attraction is diabolical."

"If I return to Australia, it will be without him. There are other companies touring the colonies." Maud told me.

"My friend Robert Hichens, has been seduced into working with Barrett, turning his play, 'The daughters of Babylon' into a novel. In his letters he writes he'll be glad to finish."

"A brave man. I couldn't imagine Wilson co-writing anything with anyone but himself." She laughed.

"Robert is making his way as an author, and the idea of the project appealed to his vanity. I believe Barrett only involved him after he became aware of our friendship."

"Yes, I'm afraid he'd do such a thing. I hope your friend's confidence won't be affected by Wilson's malice, as I'm certain he'll experience his controlling behaviour."

"Robert is as clever as he is intuitive. Don't concern yourself with his well-being, as he's more than capable of looking after himself when it comes to such characters." I told her.

"Of course. He must be if he's a friend of yours."

"Maud, how I'll miss our banters."

"You'll have to wait until my return from the States. I'm missing my family terribly. You know my brother Norman is an actor, and I'm trying to convince him to spend some time with me on tour. He's wonderful company, and it would benefit him greatly."

"I'm sure you'll convince him, and I'll try not to miss you too much. Robert is the same these days; always away somewhere. Anyway, my days will be full of travel between London and Paris, and there'll be little time to dwell on absent friends." I sighed.

When leaving, Maud once again kissed my cheek. With a healthy bank balance and no encumbrances, there was nothing stopping me from continuing the decadent life of a European count in Paris.

***

I'd only been back a short time, when an opportunity to purchase a newspaper presented itself. The idea of writing what I wanted without any interference was appealing, after all, I'd been associating with writers and journalists for years, as well as contributing to London newspapers myself.

The American Register was a weekly publication catering to wealthy Americans in Britain and on the continent, and it was founded by the American dentist, Thomas W. Evans in 1868. Evans worked for rich and famous Parisians, and counted Napoleon III as one of his clients.

Thomas died in 1897, leaving patients to his nephew Dr. John Evans, who was also a practicing dentist in Paris. Dr. John and his wife moved to France to take advantage of Thomas's impressive social connections, extending as far as the Vatican. It was Pope Leo XIII who bestowed the title of Marquis d'Oyley on John therefore making his wife Marquise d'Oyley and their two sons count and viscount, respectively, and it was through Dr. John, I came to read the hand of the pontiff himself.

The Marquis led an affluent life riding around Paris in an elaborate coach emblazoned with his coat of arms, and footmen dressed in beautiful outfits including bright yellow stockings. The American was impressed by nobility, and having a title of my own, helped me to infiltrate the rich American socialites Paris attracted.

In July of 1902, I was invited to a garden party at a chateau in Bellevue, the home of the d'Oyleys.

Prominent citizens of the Anglo-American community were present, and it was at such gatherings, I ingratiated myself with individuals I'd eventually do business with. After my readings, single women and widows were particularly eager to increase their nest eggs by involving themselves in my bank. Holding the hand of a vulnerable woman, almost always led to her investing with me.

The gardens of the chateau never looked better. Needing a break from the conversations, I wandered off through the trees. The hedges were trimmed to perfection, providing private spaces to reflect on the beauty of nature.

Approaching a row of flowering oranges, the heady scent of neroli filled my nostrils, and the delightful fragrance calmed me. Somewhere close by, the sound of clashing metal disrupted the moment, and walking towards the noise, I came across two young men fencing. Swords gleamed in the sunlight, and the bare chests were wet with perspiration.

I recognized one as the twenty-two-year-old Viscount Ivan d'Oyley, younger son of our hosts. Upon my arrival, they ceased their duel.

"Good afternoon, Sir. Excuse us, we're at present practicing our sport." Ivan told me.

"Don't let me interrupt you. I was just taking a tour of the gardens." I said.

"Well, we've finished anyway, haven't we Malcolm?" He asked his companion.

The other young man picked up his shirt and wiped the sweat from his chest. He was of Middle Eastern appearance.

"Yes. Enough for today." He replied, in a cultured English accent.

The two were highly proficient at their sport. Ivan's duelling companion, Freydoun Malcolm Khan, was the first son of an Armenian aristocrat who held a position in the Persian Embassy. He'd been educated at Eton, and both he and the viscount competed in the 1900 Paris Olympics in fencing.

"You both appear skilled at your sport, and I wish I'd arrived earlier."

Ivan secured his sword.

"Are you the gentleman who's purchased the Register?" He asked.

"Yes, Count Louis de Hamong."

"I believe you are also known by another name are you not?"

"Indeed. Cheiro is the name many know me as."

"You read palms, don't you? Malcolm have you ever had your hand read?"

"No. Back home we are cautious of such things. We never let strangers know our birthdays, or see the intimate parts of us." He told us.

"I don't regard the hand as an intimate part. Would you take a quick look?" Ivan asked, smiling.

"Of course." I said, grinning at Malcolm.

"Excuse the sweat. Let me wipe my hands."

The young viscount opened his hands, and I was struck by the short length of the lifeline appearing on both palms, as well as a fate line terminating early at the heart line.

"Your palm is clearly marked. The lifeline is broad and red on both hands, indicating a vitality for life, and the mount of Venus is full and soft, indicating a love of sensual pleasures. Your fate line terminates at the heart line showing a sudden change in your fortune resulting from a love interest."

"Perhaps I will marry well and gain more money?" He asked.

"Changes in fortune don't always indicate a change for the better." I informed him.

"Oh, you believe the match will not be advantageous?"

"I believe you must be extremely careful when it comes to affairs of the heart. The heart line itself swoops down deeply into the mount of Luna. You must learn to distinguish reality from fantasy." I warned.

A heart line entering the area of the moon as Ivan's did, often indicated a depressive and escapist nature. In extreme cases, suicidal tendencies; the ultimate escape from reality. Such a nature would benefit little from this knowledge, so it wasn't revealed.

"Paris is full of gold diggers, and I believe I'm equipped to handle such temptresses." He gloated.

"You're young and healthy. Enjoy every moment and make the most of every day." I told him.

The health line of the young viscount was excellent, and the indications of a short life on both hands meant his death wouldn't be the result of illness. It was hard to comprehend why fate decreed this young man should leave so soon.

Within a year of Ivan's reading, he'd become involved with a Peruvian woman he'd met holidaying in Vichy. The infatuated viscount spent the following months with Madame Pfluker in Cannes, and other places on the Riviera. His father was appalled, demanding he return without his new companion. The two quarrelled, and Ivan was cut off from any funds.

On 22nd May 1904, the young viscount, in the presence of Madame Pfluker, shot himself at the Hotel Rivoli in Paris.

I continued to socialize with the d'Oyleys, and I don't believe they ever knew of the reading, or the warning I'd given their son. The Marquis refused to believe Ivan killed himself, blaming Madame Pfluker for his demise. Such a story absolved him of any responsibility for the tragedy, as the action of withdrawing financial support almost certainly allowed the sombre nature of his son to surface.

***

Association with the d'Oyleys and the American Register, led to a champagne business in Rheims, ownership of several racehorses, and an investment bank.

In addition to the already established 'American register' newspaper, I began another named the 'Entente Cordiale,' A journal in the Interest of International Peace.' It was an ambitious project proving costly.

My hope was to unite sentiment in Europe and in particular, promote a better attitude of the French people towards England, and it coincided with King Edward's visit to Paris in May of 1903. The King wrote and congratulated me on my efforts.

I corresponded regularly with Maud and Robert, keeping abreast of their news. Maud returned from the United States, and was about to tour Australia with Julius Knight. She wrote.

"Dear Louis,

Just a quick note to let you know I'm about to depart for Australia. I expect to be away for some time, and Mr. Tree has agreed to let me go. The arrangement has been rather sudden, but I feel once again, destiny is at work. I'm thrilled my brother Norman will perform in the company as well. I'll keep you informed of my travels in the wide brown land.

Love Maud."

The tour offered Maud a chance to visit her daughter in Melbourne, and her brother's companionship proved invaluable. Even though we corresponded, I never saw Maud again, and the jewellery I'd given her proved to be a farewell present. It was a treasured possession, displayed on her dressing table next to a pair of booties. Everyone believed the child's apparel belonged to her second daughter who died young, and only Maud knew they once covered the feet of her adopted daughter, Florence.

During her tour of Australia, Maud met her future husband James Bunbury Nott Osborne. The dashing young man came from a wealthy Australian pastoral family, and they became engaged in May of 1904. The news came as a surprise to many, including Wilson Barrett, and it shocked us all to learn of the actor's sudden death two months later. A complication after a routine surgery in London took his life. Perhaps the news of Maud's engagement contributed to his downfall. I'd not heard from her after the news was released.

Three months after Barrett's death, she married her farmer in a private ceremony whist on tour in New Zealand. Two years later, she retired from the theatre altogether, to live the life she'd always imagined.

Wilson Barrett's death and Maud's departure finally ended a tumultuous chapter in my life, and the karmic threads connecting us were broken. All that remained were fiery memories of anger, passion, and jealousy, and they too faded with time.

***

In Paris, great actresses such as Sarah Bernhardt and Eleonora Duse visited me for consultations, and it was ironic destiny continued to channel performers to me after I'd chosen a career away from the theatre.

Letters were forwarded by my publishers, from people who'd read my books and wished to make contact, and many of these were from those wanting to study the science of palmistry and needed advice. One such letter read.

"Dear Cheiro,

I'm currently on holidays in Paris, and have recently learnt of your presence here.

You won't remember me, as I'm a rather a non-descript woman. My name is Nellie Simmons, and I consulted you in New York a few years ago.

As a student of palmistry, I'd like to come and see you whilst my husband and I are visiting Paris.

Sincerely yours,

Mrs. Nellie Meier-Simmons."

The interesting thing was, I did remember this woman. It

wasn't because of her appearance, but rather her motivation for undertaking the study of the hand. She was a woman under no delusions about her plain appearance, and it was refreshing to meet someone who'd accepted what fate had given them, and didn't dwell on the injustice of it.

Nellie was someone who craved attention, and undertook the study after realizing the power an astute practitioner of palmistry could attain in social circles. I decided to meet with a kindred spirit, and sent word for her to come to my apartment.

"Nellie, a pleasure to meet with you again. I must commend you on your choice of outfit." I told her.

Nellie walked confidently in and removed her hat. What she lacked in natural beauty, she made up for in stylish clothing.

"I'm so pleased you found the time to see me. Thank you for the compliment. I'm fortunate to have a talented fashion designer as a husband. You've done well for yourself since we last met in New York." She said.

Nellie's eyes were quick to survey my apartment, decorated with fine antiques and works of art.

"My success doesn't lie with palmistry alone. I'm involved in a number of businesses here in France. Tell me, how are your studies with the hand progressing?"

"Splendidly. I've quite a following in Indianapolis where we live. George and I were married five years ago, as you predicted."

"Do you wish to ask me something else regarding your hand?"

"Oh no. I'm confident with my own knowledge, and have read other sources as well as yours. I was hoping to confer with a fellow practitioner of the science."

"Of course. It's rare to meet someone undertaking the study. I agree, it's beneficial to talk with others who follow the same vocation. Do you have rooms in Indianapolis where you consult?" I asked.

"We have a beautiful home, "Tuckaway," where I see people. My husband George designed the home. He comes to Paris regularly keeping up with fashion trends." She explained.

"A perfect arrangement. As a palmist, you can share the spotlight with your husband in his glamorous world."

"You've not forgotten my reading then?" She asked, surprised.

"Your logical approach to life amongst the egotism of New York, left an impression. I'm curious. Did you read your husband's hands before you were married?" I asked her, smiling.

"I resisted the urge, but succumbed once I knew I loved him. There was a dread of finding something to shatter the dreams."

"Would you have changed your course if you'd discovered something disturbing?"

Nellie paused in deep thought.

"By that stage, nothing would have stopped me from involving myself with him." She replied.

"Who takes the advice of others if it means giving up something we desire? Discovering it for yourself changes nothing." I told her.

They were the same words I'd spoken to Reginald Turner at Oscar's gravesite in 1900, when he asked me about Oscar's infatuation with Bosie.

"Luckily, my husband possessed a hand full of compassion, creativity and love. I admit, I was relieved."

"I envy you. A loving partner with a good profession, a career which engages you, and a home that will always be there for you."

"You're forgetting my holidays to Europe every year." She laughed.

"Of course." I grinned.

Did wealth make my life better than Nellie's? As I was forever on the move, buying property seemed ridiculous. Why would I want to be anchored to one place when I could rent beautiful lodgings wherever I desired? Nellie made me look at things differently, and I pushed away the thoughts.

"You must forgive me, I've another engagement. It's been a pleasure to see you again, and talk with another palmist."

"Thank you again. If you're ever in Indianapolis, please come and see us."

"I'll make a point of it." I told her.

Nellie left, and I returned to the sofa. I lied about having another engagement. For the first time, feelings of loneliness crept over me, and I missed the company of someone to share my thoughts with.

Lately, it seemed everyone was finding a partner and living a happy life. These unions were unlike the materialistic and political matches I'd been privy to in London. These were marriages of misery, and barriers to true love, and my own experiences consolidated the mistrust. Walking along the Paris streets, comfort was found on the boulevard of broken dreams.

***

In late August 1904, a note arrived. It bore the insignia of the Russian aristocrat, Duke Peter Alexandrovich of Oldenburg. Whilst visiting Paris, he wished to have a consultation.

This encounter with the Russian nobility eventually led to the Czar himself. I remember the expensive clothing and accessories of Duke Peter. He'd married the Grand Duchess Olga Alexandrovna, the youngest daughter of Emperor Alexander III. His brother-in-law was Czar Nicholas II.

"May I enquire as to how you came to know of me?" I asked.

"It was the Abbe de la Fresnaye who first sang your praises, but there've been others in Paris who've told me of you." He explained.

"I'm honoured to receive you. Is there something in particular you wish to know?"

"Yes. I hear you're skilled in other mystical arts besides palmistry, dabbling in astrology and numerology. This interests me. Is it possible to determine favourable times when one should speculate?"

"Such things can be calculated. Do you have business ventures concerning you?"

"To be perfectly honest, I like to gamble. I've had enormous wins and lost large sums. I want to increase the odds of winning. Can you help with this?"

"I can make observations and work out a schedule for you." I told him.

"Splendid. My marriage to the Grand Duchess resulted in more money than I know what to do with, but the thrill of winning is addictive. Gambling became an essential part of my day, along with other forbidden pleasures." He smiled.

There was no mistaking the duke's lustful look, and ignoring the signals, I continued.

"Very well. I'll spend time on calculations rather than examining your palm. The hand alone won't give you the information you need." I told him.

"As you say, it's the dates and times which will be of benefit." He replied.

Within a short time, I had the information.

"Based on the planetary positions relating to your second house of money, and the numerological equations, these are the profitable dates and times." I told him.

The duke's eyes widened as he held the paperwork, believing he was in possession of an infallible key to unlock his winnings. Witnessing the adrenaline boost he received from the information was disturbing. In a way, I believed I'd contributed to his addiction.

Before leaving, the duke invited me to Saint Petersburg, promising to organize other introductions. I'd heard the Russian court was the wealthiest in Europe, and gladly accepted the offer.

My arrival in Saint Petersburg coincided with a tumultuous period in Russian history. Not wanting to find myself in an awkward situation, I declined Duke Alexandrovich's invitation to stay at his mansion on Sergievskaya Street, and took a suite at the Hotel de l'Europe. I sent a note informing him of my location.

The next morning, a carriage arrived to take me to the duke's home. The mood of the people on the snow ladened streets was tense, and the strikes and demonstrations were unnerving. Passing through the city, angry workers shouted abuse and spat at the duke's carriage.

There was great relief when finally, I arrived at the 200-room palace, where a footman helped me out of the carriage, and escorted me to the front door. An impressive coat of arms crowned the entry.

Once inside, the splendour of the interior design became evident. The incredible wealth of the Russian aristocrats, hadn't been exaggerated.

The former Baryatinsky mansion was a shadow of what I'd experience in Russia. Guided into a drawing room by a servant, the next ten minutes were spent admiring the oil paintings and numerous wall hangings. A cabinet full of Fabergé eggs dominated the corner of the room, and I moved closer to examine the intricate work of the master jeweller.

"I see you've found my eggs." The duke smiled, entering.

"A beautiful collection. You must be extremely proud." I told him.

"The collecting of lovely things is one of my pastimes." He

grinned.

"I'm fortunate to view the collection."

"Shall I order some tea or coffee?" He asked.

"Tea would be lovely, something to warm me. Your city is beautiful, but icy." I laughed.

"Come and sit by the fire. Saint Petersburg in Winter is not for the frail of body. Most of us leave it for warmer places, but this year many have remained to oversee their interests. The current unrest is causing a great deal of anxiousness for the aristocracy." He explained.

"Yes, I noticed the demonstrations in the streets on my way here."

"The workers are complaining again. The same old reasons, more money for less work. What will they demand next? To live in our palaces." He scoffed.

"Your home is magnificent. How many people live here?"

"The Grand duchess has rooms at the other end of the palace, and there are the servants in their quarters. Olga spends much of her time away at her villa 'Olgino' in Voronezh. She keeps herself occupied with charitable pursuits and then of course, there is her painting." He told me, waving his hand dismissively.

A servant entered with a silver tea service, and she placed the tray on an intricately carved timber and amber table. As the tea was poured, we were joined by a young woman.

"Oh, forgive me Peter. I didn't realize you were entertaining." She said.

As the duchess entered the room I stood. The duke remained seated.

"Olga, you are back?" He said, annoyed.

"Yes, there are things I must attend to in Saint Petersburg." She replied, nervously.

"Well, I best introduce you. May I present Cheiro. This is my wife the Grand duchess Olga Alexandrovna."

The Grand duchess held out her hand which I kissed.

"Most honoured your highness." I said.

"Cheiro? I've heard that name before. Surely, you're not the famous palmist?"

"Indeed I am." I smiled.

"I believe my relatives in England have mentioned you in their correspondences."

"Yes. I've had the honour of meeting with various members of the Royal family."

"Edward and Alexandra hold you in high regard."

The duke stood up abruptly, and a cold look passed between the unhappy couple.

"Olga, let us not keep you from your activities. We've men's business to attend to." He told her.

Olga's face reddened.

"As you wish. A pleasure to meet you Cheiro."

"Likewise, your highness."

The Grand duchess left, and the duke asked if I'd like more tea.

"Thank you." I replied.

"I'm disappointed you didn't accept my invitation to stay here."

"Your offer was much appreciated, but I prefer to base myself in hotels when I travel." I lied.

"I suppose staying in hotels offers you a certain anonymity?" He probed.

"Not really. It's the convenience of location. This tea is excellent. What's the blend?" I asked, changing the subject.

"Russian caravan. Now, down to business. I've been approached by my brother-in-law, the Czar, and he wishes an audience with you as soon as possible. I've told him about my recent speculations, and the success I've had thanks to your information."

"I'd be honoured." I replied, restraining my excitement.

"Of course, you understand, everything you discuss with the Czar must remain confidential, as the information will be of a highly sensitive nature.

"Absolutely. That goes without saying." I assured him.

"Would you be able to meet with Czar Nicholas tomorrow? I could arrange for a carriage at ten o'clock?"

"Yes, thank you." I told him.

The duke's eyes wandered over my body, and I retrieved a watch from my vest.

"I'm afraid I must leave you. I've another appointment at my hotel." I lied.

"Another disappointment. I was hoping to spend a quiet afternoon with you."

"Terribly sorry. It's rather important." I continued.

"As you wish. You best free yourself of any obligations before meeting with the Czar tomorrow. I'll have the carriage take you back to your hotel. Leaving the duke, I approached the waiting carriage. Inside, the Grand Duchess Olga looked distressed.

"Oh Cheiro, please forgive me. I'm desperate to meet with you." She pleaded.

"Of course, your highness. I'm at your service." I told her.

The Grand duchess ordered the coachman to drive away.

"You're my last hope. Will you look at my hands, and see if life will change for me? I must know. Is there something better ahead, or am I doomed to remain trapped in this hellish existence with my husband." She cried.

I took hold of Olga's trembling hands.

"Let's see what awaits you. Your life line is deep and clear on both hands, and a strong line of fate runs from the base of the palm to the finger of Saturn, again on both hands. This is a good sign, as the longer finger of apollo signifies artistic ability and a sense of colour and design."

"Painting maintains my sanity." She replied.

"Your hands clearly display talent."

"I must know about my marriage." She asked, impatiently.

"Your hands show one marriage, a strong and clear line."

"No, it cannot be." She cried, pulling her hands away, and sobbing uncontrollably.

"Grand duchess, you must let me finish." I said, retrieving her hands.

"The timing of this union does not coincide with your current marriage. There's no line indicating your marriage to the duke. You see, the palm fails to recognize pieces of paper. When it comes to relationships, the lines only depict loving unions."

"You're correct. My marriage was never consummated, and there's no love between us."

"I assumed as much. Therefore, the marriage here on your hand signifies a loving and beautiful union, lasting many years. Happily, there's no sign of a fork at its termination, meaning your love remains strong." I explained.

"I believe I've met this man. He's a Blue Cuirassier Guards officer named Nikolai Kulikovsky, and my brother, the Czar, refuses to let us marry, despite his knowledge of Peter's inability to love me." She sighed.

"You'll marry this man in your early 30's, as the line of influence crossing your fate line from the mount of Mars, ends at this point. Opposition disappears, and you both fulfil your destinies." I smiled.

"Can it be true? Are you certain?" She asked.

"I've no doubt. Your troubles will be behind you. I see from signs on the mount of Luna, you'll die in a country away from your birth."

"I'll leave Russia?"

"I believe so. It's a curious thing. Many of the hands I've read lately of noble Russians, show the same signs. I foretell a change of circumstances resulting in them leaving here and never returning."

"I don't care where I live, as long as I'm with my Nikolai."

"Your love survives all obstacles your highness. I envy you." I said, returning her hands.

"Oh Cheiro, you've made me so happy, and I can cope with the situation knowing it will eventually change."

"I'm relieved your hand shows a positive outcome. You must be strong and patient."

"I will be, and I can't wait to tell Nikolai. He'll be overjoyed at the news."

A smiling Olga directed the coachman to the Hotel de l'Europe. Driving away, her happy wave lifted my spirits. Once again, I'd given light to someone in their darkest hour.

Next day, the coach pulled up at the entrance of the Czar's

Alexandra palace. Four enormous columns dominated the façade of the imposing neo classical building.

A footman directed me inside, where two guards stood each side of a semicircular stairway. These lead to a large wooden door, framed in ornate glass, and after a few minutes, a servant opened it, and I was led down a splendid corridor into a reception room. The walls of the hallway were decorated with silver bread trays, embellished with gold, gilt and enamel designs, and newly installed electric light fittings reflected the dazzling colours.

The room's opulent panelled timber walls and ceiling were impressive; a feature found in European grand homes of the time. The servant directed me to an enormous leather lounge, built into a nook beside a cozy fireplace. Making myself comfortable, I surveyed the countless tapestries and oil paintings around me. In the centre of the room, an electric chandelier, dripping with beads of amber produced a subtle orange light.

I'd not been seated long, when Czar Nicholas entered.

"Your highness." I said, standing.

"Cheiro, thank you for coming. At last, we meet in person."

"It's a privilege to serve you." I told him.

"You come highly recommended. In a way, we've met before. Some time ago, King Edward had you examine my details without your knowledge to whom they belonged." He informed me, smiling.

"It's a service I'm often asked to perform."

"Let us come into the study."

I followed the Czar into another heavily panelled room, and rather than placing ourselves at the formal desk, Nicholas asked me to sit at a small dining table. He looked drawn and worried.

"You've previously calculated certain events from my birth details. Will you now look at my hand to see if these things will come to pass?" He asked.

"Of course. If you would place your hands here, I'll examine the signs."

During the next hour, the Czar's palms were meticulously studied. There were clear indications of a violent death, as well as a period of imprisonment and isolation. Unlike his sister Olga, destiny had decreed an ominous future.

The negative signs and dark clouds following the Czar could not be hidden. Nicholas was born under the sign of the fishes, Pisces, and these natives have a natural intuitive ability to read others.

"Cheiro, you must tell me if I die in Russia or somewhere else?" He asked.

The question puzzled me, as I assumed the Czar wanted to consult me on matters of state, rather than his personal destiny.

"I can see from your fate line your end will be in the country of your birth." I told him.

"Recently, others have informed me of your readings with them. Many say, you see their fates ending in other countries."

"It's true. A number of your countrymen have signs indicating they'll not end their days in Russia." I continued.

"You've already deduced the length of my life from your previous calculations. Does my palm agree with this?"

My hesitation caused tears to form in Nicholas 'eyes.

"You needn't answer. I know, we're all allocated a certain number of years. I believe such things are predestined. I've had a sense of the end for some time, and it grows stronger with every uprising and demonstration." He replied.

I wondered what kind of demise the Czar imagined for himself. There was no need for me to elaborate on the negative signs the mount of Saturn indicated; the imprisonment and violent death.

Did he have a sense of this, and already accepted it as his destiny?

"We must all make the most of the time allocated to us your highness." I declared.

"My family are the dearest things to me, and as long as they're safe, I'm content for life to end. The Czarina and my children are what I leave behind."

I departed from the Czar, failing to reveal all I'd seen. The absence of a legacy through children, did trouble me. I always suspected Nicholas would be killed by an assassin's bomb, as such occurrences were common in Russia at the time.

Few imagined that in little over a decade, the Czar and his family would be murdered in such a notorious way. The method of execution is a testament to the evilness living in the hearts of some men. On July 16th, 1918, a moment of madness wiped away his legacy forever.

***

After my meeting with Nicholas, the relationship with the nobility and the people continued to deteriorate. Life would never be the same for the people and the Czar after the bloody Sunday massacre on 22nd January 1905. St Petersburg was deeply scarred when the striking workers and their families were fired upon by the Czar's army. The wound never healed.

Despite the troubles, I continued travelling between London, Paris and St Petersburg, and lived a rich life combining palmistry readings with business. Everything was wonderful in the world.

Occasionally, I caught up with Robert, who was now a well-respected author. After the success of his novel, 'The Garden of Allah', our lives drifted apart. Constantly travelling meant, we never seemed to be in the same place at the same time.

***

In 1908, Frank Shackleton made a surprise visit to my rooms in Bond Street.

"Frank, what are you doing here?" I asked, suspiciously.

"Lovely to see you too Louis." He grinned, shaking my hand.

"Sorry. I didn't mean to sound cool. It's just a surprise to see you again. Come through."

Frank looked as dashing as ever. It had been a few years since we last met, and I wondered what he'd been doing.

"What have you been up to since I last saw you?" I enquired.

Alone in my office I maintained an air of officiousness, preferring to ignore the memory of our past encounter.

"I have until recently been in Dublin working at the castle. What about yourself?" He asked.

"Life has been good to me. I'm constantly on the move between London, Paris and St Petersburg."

"I've heard as much. You were always a great networker."

"Yes, my businesses are doing well."

Frank looked agitated. Why was he really making contact again?

"You look a bit frazzled Frank. What is worrying you?" I asked.

"I need to tell you something Louis. I hope you can help me. I'm taking a risk speaking to you of this." He continued.

"Of course, Frank. You know you can trust me." I assured him.

"I'm in possession of some incredibly valuable items, the nature of which attracts danger."

"What are they?"

"Before I tell you, you must swear that you'll not reveal this to anyone. It will be another secret we have between us." He insisted.

Frank's comment made me aware the memory of our night's

encounter was clearer in his mind than mine.

"I swear." I responded.

"When working at Dublin castle, I hatched a plan, but it didn't seem plausible at the time. It was a bit of a lark actually. As things turned out, it was carried out successfully, and now I'm in receipt of some hot property."

As Frank spoke, I recalled reading about a theft the previous year from Dublin castle, and I dared not believe it.

"You cannot mean what I think you mean?" I asked.

"It's true. I'm in possession of the stolen Irish crown jewels." He whispered.

I sat stunned.

"Frank are you mad? I whispered back.

Jumping up from my seat, I opened the office door. My secretary was busy writing.

"Thomas, you can finish for the day."

Returning to the room, I paced up and down.

"I know it was a stupid act, but it was so easily done." Frank told me.

"I can't believe what I'm hearing. How could you think you'd get away with it?"

"Well, that's the thing. I have. As long as there's no evidence, I can't be charged. Of course, I'm a suspect. I'm constantly being watched. They know I'm involved, along with a couple of others, but there's no proof. I'm certain the King has been informed of the details. You know I've some influence over his brother-in-law, John Campbell, the Marquis of Lorne because of our liaisons together. The Royals don't want a scandal. John has already questioned me about the theft, and I've told him nothing, but he's not stupid, he knows I was involved. I'm sure he's explained the repercussions to the King if things were to go public." He explained.

"Were you followed here?" I asked.

"I believe so. But I'm just visiting a respectable palmist with royal connections. Where's the harm?" He grinned.

Sitting back in my chair I processed the information. The shock of the revelation was wearing off. After all, I'd unwittingly stolen jewels from the Duchess of Sutherland. Who was I to judge?

"Why are you telling me this Frank?"

"Because I need your help. I know you've a network of connections, and I need you to look after the jewels until I work out what to do with them. You can take them out of the country when you travel for business. No one will suspect you, and of course, I'd give you a share of the proceeds after we break the stones up and sell them."

Why was Frank asking this of me? With the exception of the Oppenheim brothers in France, no one was privy to the breaking up and selling of the Duchess of Sutherland's diamonds. How could he know of this? The most cunning criminals were those who possessed an uncanny intuition.

"I'd be taking a great risk."

"You must Louis. The King looks on you favourably, and if anything were to happen, you'd be well protected. The jewels are small enough to hide in your baggage. Here I'll show you."

"What? You have them here now?" I asked, shocked.

Frank produced a wooden brass-bound box from his bag, and placed it on the desk.

"Yes, they're all here." He said, opening the top.

"My God, they're priceless." I said.

"Aren't they beautiful?" He said, holding them to the light.

The pieces of jewellery were magnificent. A large diamond star of the Order of St Patrick consisted of brilliant Brazilian stones, along with rubies and emeralds. A diamond badge of the Order of St Patrick had a silver setting containing a trefoil in emeralds, and a ruby cross of rose diamonds.

"Absolutely stunning." I whispered, excitedly.

"We used to play with them at the castle during our parties, and no one ever knew."

"I can't quite believe it." I said.

"They must be worth a packet." Frank exclaimed.

"Very well. I'll look after them for you." I told him.

"Thank you, Louis. You won't regret it."

"I hope not."

The memory of Amiens returned. After discovering the Duchess Sutherland's diamonds in her case, I did have misgivings, but after they were broken up and sold, life became easier, and I never looked back.

Frank left without his treasure, and the velvet wrapped box was deposited in a bank account I'd opened using one of my pseudonyms. The plan was to leave the gems there until he made contact, but plans often go astray.

***

The moment I took possession of the stolen gems, my luck appeared to change. Back in Paris some investments lost money, which in turn affected other interests, and nervous investors withdrew their funds. It was the beginning of the end of my life in France.

One of the major investors, Count Festeties demanded his funds, and wouldn't be pacified, spreading rumours about my financial position. This resulted in more clients leaving, including most of the wealthy Americans, and before long, the French authorities investigated and I was summoned to court.

The tide had turned, and it was impossible to repay more than £500,000 in funds.

After selling my possessions, I absconded to England to avoid the fraud charge.

The affluent life in Europe was over, with the French courts sentencing me to a prison term. I'd never see my beloved Paris again.

Back in London, the press had a field day, and I was forced to declare bankruptcy and suffer the indignation of what followed. These were dark days indeed, and I went into hiding with what little assets I'd secreted away.

Now in my 40's, the good looks I'd traded on for years, were gone, as the decadent lifestyle in Europe prematurely aged me. The boyish charms had vanished, along with most of my money.

***

What of the Irish Crown jewels? As they were hidden away under another name, they weren't seized as part of my assets. What could be done to restore my fortunes once everything calmed down? There'd been no contact from Frank, until he'd heard of my predicament. I hardly recognized the man who sat on the bench in Kensington Park, where we agreed to meet. He'd made an effort to disguise himself with a scarf and hat.

"Frank?" I asked, reluctantly.

"Yes Louis, it's me. I need to keep a low profile at present." He said, keeping his   head lowered.

"You too?" I asked.

"Yes. I'm afraid like yourself, I'll soon be before the bankruptcy court. That's why I've contacted you."

"Things have taken a turn for the worse as far as my affairs are concerned." I said.

"I'm assuming you still have the diamonds safely hidden?" He asked.

"Of course. They're in a safety deposit box under another name."

"Now is the time to move them." Frank said.

"Are you mad? Now is the time to stay calm, and wait until everything settles." I replied.

"No. I can't wait; I need money now. I'm in a desperate situation Louis." He insisted.

"I'm sorry Frank, It's much too risky for me. I already have a prison sentence in France, I don't want one here."

"I insist Louis. The diamonds belong to me, and I decide when to sell." Frank said angrily.

"Things have changed Frank. Don't try and dictate what's to be done. You don't own the diamonds. They belong to the crown; they're not yours." I responded, rising from the bench.

"I thought you could be trusted, and I see I was wrong. Despite all your talk of a spiritual nature, you're nothing more than a petty criminal. I'm not surprised you're a fugitive from France."

"Remember, I'm not guilty of stealing the jewels, only hiding them. It could even be said, I held them for you without opening the satchel and seeing the contents. In the eyes of the law, I'm an innocent accomplice. If I went to the police, after uncovering the jewels, you'd never see the light of day my friend." I told him, firmly.

"I won't forget this, and I'll be back to claim what's mine. No one crosses Frank Shackleton and gets away with it." He said, walking away.

Witnessing Frank's desperation, triggered memories of past poverty, and I had to find a way out of my own financial struggles.

Sitting back on the park bench it came to me, and a plan was hatched to safely move the jewels. In their current form, they were instantly recognizable, but changing their appearance, would eliminate any trace of their origin.

***

The Parisian Diamond Company was less busy just before closing time, and the owner, Walter Sanderson, was finishing up when I entered.

"Good evening, Walter." I said, smiling.

"Well hello Cheiro. Nice to see you again. I was just closing up. Can I help you with something?" He asked, nervously.

"Yes, sorry to be so late, but I wanted to catch you when things were less busy. I've a custom order for you, if that's something you do?" I asked.

"I'm afraid it isn't our usual practice to design pieces for customers. You see we have specific designs, and if you want a custom-made piece, you'd do better to try one of the other jewellers." He told me.

"Oh, it needn't be a different design. I'd like to discuss it further with you in private, if you have the time."

Walter looked anxious, telling his staff he'd finish closing up, and showed me into his office.

"Well now, what is it you have in mind?"

"You see Walter, I've some stones which I've acquired, and I'd like them set in different pieces." I explained.

"What kind of stones?"

"Diamonds, emeralds and rubies."

"You mean real stones?" He asked, surprised.

"Yes. I know your designs are synthetic and made to look like the real thing. Let us say, I'd like the real thing to look synthetic. By using your pieces and labels I can safely hide them in plain view. As you once told me, it takes an expert to tell the difference."

"I'm beginning to understand you, given the state of your affairs. It would be ridiculous of me to pretend I'd not heard about your unfortunate change of luck."

"Can I see these stones?" He asked.

"Before I show you, do I have your word you'll keep this to yourself?

"Of course. It's but another secret between us." He replied, smiling.

"The stones are already in settings, and I wish to preserve these; in the event I want them put back together. Do you understand?"

"Perfectly. Given what you know of my past indiscretions, what choice do I have?" He continued.

"Excellent." I said, removing the wooden box from my bag and passing it to Walter.

"Oh no. You cannot be serious? The stolen Irish crown jewels. I won't be involved in such a scandal." He protested, after opening the lid.

"Walter, calm down. There's no reason for concern. Once the pieces are reset, they're untraceable. It will seem as though I'm acquiring these items as my fortune changes for the better, and no one would expect them to be real, especially with the marks of your establishment, and the receipts." I explained.

"It's true. The stones can be easily incorporated into our current range of designs."

"I'm not asking you to do anything without renumeration. I can pay you for your trouble, as I still have some assets which I've been able to keep from the bankruptcy courts."

"It would be naïve of me to think I've a choice in the matter. God help me if I'm discovered." He said.

"Believe me, the theft of the Irish crown jewels will probably remain unsolved, especially if the pieces stay separated."

"Why then do you want the original settings kept?" he asked, puzzled.

"Call me a sentimental Irishman, but I'm not comfortable destroying such items of historical value, and there may come a time when they're returned, for the right price. I don't wish to be responsible for their irreversible demise."

"You're a strange character Cheiro."

"No different to many who walk these streets, Walter."

***

After leaving Walter, I walked to the local market to buy some fruit. Looking up from the produce, a familiar figure caught my attention, and I moved closer to the sad looking woman, rummaging through the cheaper items. She caught me staring, and averted her gaze, continuing to fill her bag with potatoes.

"Mary? Is that you?" I asked.

I'd not seen Mary Eastlake for some time, and was shocked to find her in a sorry state.

"Yes Louis. I'm surprised you know me. Few people do these days." She said.

"Oh Mary, what's happened to you?" I asked.

"What do you think has happened? Wilson has been dead for over six years. I gave up everything to look after our son, and came to rely on his support and overnight it disappeared, leaving me in a desperate situation." She explained.

"How is your son?"

"He's what keeps me going, and quite the young man now. We're living with family. Life has been hard Louis."

"I'm sorry to hear things haven't turned out well for you. I can empathize with your situation, as my luck has run out lately also."

"Oh Louis. Don't compare your life with mine. You cannot imagine how bad an existence can be when one is destitute." She said, angrily.

"Don't presume to know everything about me Mary. There was a time after I left you and Barrett in New York, that life was far from easy. In those dark times, I made a pact to never end up in such a way again, no matter what I had to do." I told her.

"A pact with yourself, or the devil?" She grinned.

"Mary, your appearance may have changed, but your heart hasn't. Here take this. It will help you to buy some decent produce." I said, handing her money.

"I'll take it for my boy. Why should I deny him what the devil offers?" She said, walking away.

To think I'd once been in love with Mary seemed unimaginable. She'd changed so much, but then so had I. Was my intimacy a curse? Many acquaintances did find themselves worse off after our unions.

There were others like Maud Jeffries and Robert Hichens whose lives prospered. Would things change for them in the future?

Thoughts of my new venture with the Parisian Diamond Company filled me with hope. I'd been handed a lifeline and intended to use it, even if the devil had given it to me.

***

As news of my dealings in France faded from the press, I began to see clients for palmistry readings again.

At the back of my mind, there was the fear that one day I'd find myself in a French prison. Oscar Wilde's experience showed me only too well, what jail did to one's body and soul. The unexpected changes in fortune prompted me to seek spiritual guidance of my own, as I wanted confirmation life would continue to get better.

Once again, I found myself at the home of Marian Read, the psychic who'd read for me so accurately in the past.

"Welcome Cheiro. Lovely to see you again." Marian said, opening the door.

"And you Marian. It's been some time since my last reading."

"Yes. Well come through and take a seat. I'll be with you in a moment."

The room was as I remembered. Unlike myself, Marian's life remained unchanged. A sense of calm resonated from the space, and I felt at ease to discover whatever might be uncovered. A few minutes later, she returned and took a seat opposite me.

"Is there something you wish to ask?"

"Yes. I'd like to know if my future plans are successful."

"Very well. Take the cards and shuffle, concentrating on the topic which concerns you the most."

I closed my eyes, visualizing the diamonds. I wanted to know if anything would guide me in this area.

"Now cut the cards into three packs."

Marian took the cards and began to lay them out in a defined pattern. She closed her eyes and remained silent for some time. Eventually she spoke.

"The reversed tower shows plans have gone astray in the recent past. Loss of money and power, and the devil card follows you. A tie to someone who brings you unhappiness and creates disturbances in your future. The page of wands shows a man with dark complexion who takes risks. The ten of coins, money comes. The moon follows, gains from deception and secret sources." She told me.

"Can you see the nature of this money? Will it be from my work? I'm planning to write and publish more."

Marian once again closed her eyes.

"I'll try and focus. No, I don't see this money coming from books. I see a man. He is working at a table. He wears glasses of some kind. Fine work, he is making something. Sparkles, shiny, silver, diamonds. A jeweller. He is removing the gems. The jewellery is special, a large star shape. There is writing. I can see it now."

Marian opened her eyes suddenly. I sat watching her with an expression of disbelief. Was it possible she could see such a thing? Did she know what she was looking at? She smiled at me and gathered the cards together.

"You will gain money Cheiro. There'll be some income from your writing and your palmistry, but the majority of your wealth will come from something else." She smiled.

"Something else?" I asked, carefully.

"We both know what I've seen. The images of the jewels are unmistakable and instantly recognizable. In your current position, the temptation is too great."

"It's true Marian. I cannot lie to you. Through an acquaintance I've become an accessory to a crime, and this is the tie you see to the dark man. Will I be discovered?" I asked.

"Your secret will never be uncovered. Fate has determined you benefit from this scenario. In your lifetime, there'll be five people who know the truth of the jewels."

"Five people?" I asked, puzzled.

"Yes. The man who stole the jewels, yourself, the jeweller, another woman who you'll meet in the future, and of course, me. You need not fear, I'm not interested in the intrigues of the world or becoming involved in them."

"You're a remarkable woman Marian, with a powerful gift."

I left Marian astounded by what I'd heard. Despite her knowing the truth, she'd remain silent. As a spiritual being, a quiet life was important to her. A weight was lifted from my shoulders knowing all would be well.

***

Chapter Nine

In 1912, the brother of my partner in crime, Frank Shackleton, paid me a visit. He came for a reading, but I knew he'd approached me for other reasons. Had Frank confided in him? Did he know the details of his crime? After initially disguising his identity, he revealed who he was.

"Thank you for examining my palms, and your observations are quite accurate. I was referred here by my brother Frank, who I believe, you're well acquainted with." He said.

"Yes. I've known Frank for a few years. I haven't seen him for some time. How is he?" I asked.

"Not too good, I'm afraid. Are you aware of his bad luck? He declared bankruptcy a couple of years ago."

"When last we met, I believe there was a conversation about his financial troubles."

"Poor Frank has got himself into some hot water. Did you know, there are pending fraud charges against him?" He asked.

"No, I was not aware of that." I replied.

"For the past couple of years, he's been working as a plantation manager in Portuguese West Africa. It seems, the authorities want him back in London to stand trial." He explained.

"Poor Frank. I can sympathize." I said.

"He told me of your similar predicament with the French authorities. For some reason, he believes you can help him. He didn't elaborate on why I should come here, but gave me the

306

impression you may owe him something?" He asked.

"Really? I don't know why Frank would imagine such a thing."

"I'm afraid, I don't have the funds to help any longer, and if there's anything you could do to help him, I'm sure he'd appreciate it. I'll give you his address should you wish to contact him."

"Of course. Thank you."

Frank hadn't divulged the nature of our relationship to his brother, leaving him to believe Ernest and I were intimate acquaintances. Frank's predicament meant I could continue replacing the jewels into the new pieces, without interference.

The original settings were hidden away in a travelling writing desk which always accompanied me, and the secret draw held the items for many years.

***

After the death of King Edward VII in 1910, all protections for Frank and myself disappeared. It was a new era, and the old alliances were buried along with the king. After the scandal of France, invitations from the Royal circles of London vanished, and my glory days with the monarchy slipped into the past as quickly as they'd arrived.

Not long after Ernest Shackleton's visit, his brother was arrested in West Africa and extradited back to London to face trial. A year later he was found guilty and sentenced to fifteen months hard labour.

I continued to correspond with friends and acquaintances in Paris, despite never being able to return.

During this time, a business relationship with the publisher William Rider of London developed. William was involved with members of the Golden Dawn Hermetic group and produced the famous Rider Waite tarot deck in 1909; a collaboration with Arthur Waite and Pamela Coleman-Smith. Pamela had drawn the images under the guidance of Arthur to produce the famous deck.

I remember meeting young Pamela during my first years in London, when I worked at the Irving theatre company. As a child backstage, she'd watch the actors, and create her own performances with dolls. Our conversations were much deeper than one would expect with a child her age. Her connection to spirit developed early, and never left.

In 1912, the first recollection of my younger days was published under the title of 'Cheiro's memoirs'. I'd not write of my life again until 1932, when 'Confessions, memoirs of a modern seer', was produced.

***

In the Summer of 1913, I was introduced to Prince Felix Yusupov, a Russian aristocrat studying at Oxford. I'd been invited to give a talk at the Oxford Russian club on palmistry, and was met by a flamboyant young man in his mid-20's, dressed in a combination of men's and women's clothing. Prince Yusupov's family were part of the Russian elite, and well acquainted with the Czar and his inner circle. The children of the two families had been playmates in their younger years.

"Good evening Cheiro. We're very excited about your lecture this evening, and you've been the subject of endless gossip this week." He told me.

"I was delighted to receive your invitation to speak. I trust the gossip hasn't changed your mind?" I smiled.

"Oh no, not at all. It's made you all the more interesting. After the lecture, I'd like to speak with you further, in private." He said.

"Of course, Prince Yusupov."

The presentation went well, with many of the attendees asking intelligent questions. Prince Yusupov offered his congratulations and invited me to take supper with him in an adjoining room. The small dining table was filled with Russian delights in which we indulged.

"How do you find the food Cheiro?" He asked, drinking his vodka.

"Delicious, I feel as if I am back in St Petersburg."

"My Russian cook is a treasure. It took some convincing to get her here, but I couldn't do without her. I believe you're familiar with St Petersburg, and I'm told the Czar and his family?"

"Yes. I've had the honour of meeting with him. He's extremely interested in my work."

"Both he and the Czarina have an obsessive thirst for metaphysical knowledge, and I believe it may be the undoing of them." He declared.

"How so? I've found studying these areas provides one with extra insight and guidance." I replied.

"Of course, if it comes from the right source."

"I see your point. You're referring to the monk Rasputin?"

"Yes. A controlling imposter exerting an unhealthy influence over the Czar and Czarina."

"I agree with you. He's a narcissist of the highest degree, and an overpowering presence of evil surrounds him. I believe his fate lies in the destruction of others."

"Have you met Rasputin?"

"In 1905, at my hotel in St Petersburg. I was introduced to him by Heliodor and Hermogen, the bishop of Saratov, and his hands confirmed what my heart already knew."

"What did you see?" He asked.

"A demise befitting such a character." I told him.

"When? His power has increased since you met him. Perhaps the people he's fated to destroy are the Imperial family. The situation is becoming intolerable, and if he's not stopped, I believe it will be the end of the Russia we know."

"For many years I've read the hands of your countrymen, in both Paris and St Petersburg, and the lines indicated the owners would not die in Russia. Others showed a violent and premature death in their homeland, and I've come to the believe some event will change the fabric of the current system. You're right to question whether the privileged lifestyle you know will continue."

"Never. I'll not let it happen. I'm prepared to do whatever is necessary to make sure our life remains as it has for centuries." The prince declared.

"Would you like me to look at your hands and see what fate decrees for you?" I asked, grinning.

"I'm not afraid. You may examine them." The prince replied, defiantly thrusting his hands out.

"Long conical fingers indicate a creative and artistic nature. Your apollo finger is spatulate in shape, which tells me you have a strong feeling for a particular dance or movement art."

"I'm famous for my tango performances." He replied, smiling.

"The line of life is strong and deep with no impediments, and the headline is straight, giving you a balanced outlook on life. The creative side of your nature is ruled by logic, a trait uncommon to many artistic types. A strong girdle of Venus and mount indicate your passionate physical nature. The fate line is one of note. On both hands it indicates you'll be instrumental in changing the lives of many."

"You see, I told you I'd return to Russia and make things right. I feel I've a destiny to fulfil."

"I'm afraid your hand indicates you belong to that group of your countrymen who die in a foreign country, my prince. You should be grateful you escape the fate of many of your friends."

"We'll see Cheiro. Time will tell."

"That's one thing we can be sure of."

"I'm returning to St Petersburg shortly, and expect to marry soon. The wedding will be everything a Russian of noble birth would expect."

Prince Yusupov did marry Princess Irina of Russia, the Czar's only niece, in Anichkov palace in 1914. It would be the last grand wedding of the Russian Empire.

Two years later on the night of December 29th 1916, he murdered Rasputin. His accomplices were the Grand Duke Dimitri Pavlovich, Vladimir Purishkevich and the British secret intelligence officer, Oswald Raynor. The prince had fulfilled his destiny to rid the Imperial family of a destructive influence, but ultimately failed to save the aristocratic world in which he hoped to live.

***

On the 4th August 1914, Britain declared war on Germany. Unlike the Boer war, the 'Great war' impacted us much more. From the loss of loved ones, to the attack on home soil, no one doubted this war was serious.

British travellers returned from abroad seeking the security of their families, and I reconnected with London friends from earlier times.

The year after the war began, I moved into new premises at 72 Regent Street. I told Walter Sanderson to sell some of the spare diamonds, enabling the setup of a new office.

One morning, Frank Shackleton appeared. He'd been released from prison and was using the name Frank Mellor. The dashing good looks were gone, replaced by angry lines on his face.

"Frank, this is a surprise. How have you been?" I spoke, calmly.

"Forget the niceties, Louis. I've no time for cordial conversation." He said.

"Well, what can I do for you then?" I asked, sitting at my desk.

I remembered those times in the past when I'd been confronted with a hostile individual, and as I edged closer to the drawer where the revolver lay, Frank jumped across the room and pulled me away from the desk.

"No, you don't Louis. "He shouted.

Still on my chair, Frank wrapped his elbow around my neck.

"Frank. What are you doing?" I spluttered.

"You've forgotten the things you've told me in the past Louis, including the practice of keeping your little friend in the desk drawer. My time in prison has made me less patient with people. Here you are in your fancy office, while I settle for the crumbs of generosity given by my brother Ernest. I'm working away in his establishment doing mundane tasks, while you sit here playing the successful businessman."

"It's not what you think Frank believe me." I implored.

"Tell me how a bankrupt claiming to have only £50 to his name, can afford all of this? You've sold the diamonds, haven't you?" He asked, his anger increasing.

Frank's grip tightened around my throat. The strength I once possessed in my younger days was gone, and I believed he'd kill me if I failed to calm him.

"Frank, I don't have the diamonds. They're in France."

"You told me they were in a bank here?"

"No. I told you they were in a safety deposit box under another name. They're in France. I moved them after things calmed down, and before I fled Paris. I can't get to them now." I lied.

Frank's grip began to loosen.

"Well if you can't get to them, I can. There's nothing stopping me from going to the bank in France, if you give me a signed authorization to collect the contents of the box." He demanded.

Tied to this devil by virtue of our crime, I needed to think quickly.

"Once I couldn't return to France, I contacted an associate. I believe he may have left the country with the diamonds." I told him.

"Did you inform him the jewels belonged to me?"

"Of course. As I told you before, it was imperative I keep out of trouble."

"Tell me his name and where he's gone to?"

Hesitating for a second, Frank's grip began to tighten.

"Alright, stop choking me. He's one of the Oppenheim brothers. Baron Robert Oppenheim. I'm told they've emigrated to America to escape another failed business venture."

"You better not be lying to me Louis. I swear if you are, I'll be back to finish what I started."

"Believe me Frank, it's the truth. The money I'm making now is from my readings and books. I'm still struggling."

Frank released my neck, but grabbed my face between his hands.

"Let me tell you Louis. You don't know what struggling is until you've spent time in prison." He whispered, looking into my eyes.

Releasing his grip, he left. I'd lied convincingly, and Frank believed me. What would he do now? I'd no doubt he'd track down Baron Oppenheim, but by the time he'd return, I'd have upgraded security.

***

Robert contacted me in the Summer of 1916. He was doing his part for the war effort by volunteering as a special constable. We strolled through the streets, laughing about old times. Both of us were in our 50's, and feeling the effects of time.

Walking returned us to happier days, when as young men we shared our dreams and aspirations for the future, and it seemed incomprehensible, the greater part of our lives had passed.

"You know Louis, I don't feel any older. When I speak with you, it's as if we were back in Phillimore place." Robert said, pensively.

"I agree, but my body keeps reminding me those days are long gone Robert. Also, seeing these motor vehicles. They're getting faster and faster."

Crossing the street, we laughed as Robert jumped aside avoiding a truck.

"I see what you mean. I do miss the horses, Louis."

"I miss my horses too. Losing money was bad enough, but the loss of my French beauties was painful." I sighed.

"You've had an interesting life my friend. It was never going to be average."

"And you. What a success you've made with your writing. Novels and now plays. A life of travelling and experiencing exotic places and people."

"It's what I wanted when I was young. I find myself longing to be with people more these days. A family was never something I wanted before." He told me.

"Do you regret not having children?" I asked, searching his face.

"Well, you know, it was never really in the cards Louis." He laughed.

"Many of our friends had children. They've lived a certain kind of life as well."

"It's not in my nature to be deceptive. The arrangement wouldn't have suited me."

"That's your English ecclesiastical upbringing rearing its head again." I smiled.

"No, just a desire to avoid hurting people." He replied.

"Perhaps you'll find a ready-made family who'll adopt you as their wise old patriarch."

"Perhaps I will." He grinned.

We'd just made it to the end of the street, when the sound of gunfire signalled an attack. London was facing a new terror, the German airships. The zeppelins floated over the city's night skies, and the ominous ovals of destruction, dropped their bombs indiscriminately.

The aftermath, was unimaginable. Raging fires lit the blacked-out streetscapes, exposing injured bodies and twisted corpses. People ran for shelter, and cars and omnibuses were left abandoned, as the deadly sounds came closer. Robert directed people to the shelters, urging everyone to hurry. When the street appeared empty, we joined the huddled masses.

"I feel like I'm hiding in a cave, waiting for the enemy tribe to pass." I whispered.

"Yes, humanity hasn't progressed much at all has it? The only advances are the machines we kill with. The greed and power struggles are still the same."

Another explosion rocked the street. Involuntary screams joined the muffled cries of children as their terrified mothers held them close. Eventually the danger passed, and we were able to return to the devastated streets. Robert and I continued to help rescue many victims that night, and eventually, we parted for some well-earned sleep.

These raids damaged the morale of the people. How could such a thing happen to invincible Brittania? It was nothing compared to the tales later emerging from the front in Europe. Stories of young lives lost and shattered, were recounted by grieving families, with whole generations wiped from the face of country villages. It was four years of suffering which seemed to last forever. Never again would the English believe they ruled the waves.

Relief came in 1918, when the war ended. Life gradually returned to normal even though a great number of individuals were gone. I changed my name by deed poll to Louis Le Warner Hamon, and continued to see clients for palm readings. I fell back into my old habits of overtaxing my body, and needed times to recuperate at Devonshire House.

It was whilst I was recovering, I read about the unfortunate death of Baron Robert Oppenheim. The newspaper article from the New York times read as follows.

'Fatal fall to Paris Banker who was ordered deported in 1916.'

Baron Robert Oppenheim, a banker of London and Paris, who came to this country in December 1916, died on Thursday in his apartments in the Hotel Le Marquis, 12 East 31ˢᵗ Street, as the result of injuries he received when he fell a month ago while romping with his dog on the roof of the building. He slipped on ice which had incrusted the roof, and had been in a serious condition since that time. He was 55 years old.'

The death was suspicious to say the least. It was a bizarre end to a man I knew took few risks with his personal safety. Somehow, I knew Frank had been involved. No doubt he'd do anything to retrieve the stolen diamonds. Once I left Devonshire House, further enquiries revealed Frank had indeed been missing for some time.

Increased security measures at my premises meant I'd no longer fall prey to anyone off the street, as all visitors were screened before entry.

It was during this time, a former acquaintance of mine reappeared. Miss Katie Florence Bilsborough consulted me as a young girl in 1899 at my Bond Street office. It was there I read her hand and told her of an upcoming marriage. The young girl took a fancy to me and declared if she couldn't have me as her first husband, then she'd have me as her second.

Her husband Henry Hartland was a sailor who disappeared at sea years before. She'd a son Jack, who'd been born within a year of her marriage.

Katie preferred to be called Mena, and soon became involved in the running of my business. Mena was a great asset helping with the office, and looking   after me when I became overworked. I never understood what a blessing it was to have someone care for me until Mena entered my life.

After a severe case of pneumonia which almost killed me, my attitude towards marriage changed. Inevitably, as my hand predicted, Mena and I married on April 15th 1920 in St Helliers, Jersey. She became Countess Mena Hamon, a partner sharing a dubious title.

<u>Chapter Ten</u>

Mena came from a prosperous Lancashire family. Her father made a fortune in timber, enabling her to travel and pursue interests abroad. Her son Jack was a gifted musician, who played the piano and organ exceptionally well.

Waiting for Frank Shackleton to show himself began taking its toll, and we moved to Ireland. Mena never knew the source of the influxes of money, or the real danger haunting me. Whenever we needed money, I told her an investment had matured. Being a shrewd woman, I often wondered if she believed me. As her own fortune was diminishing, she never asked questions.

Walter Sanderson was no longer able to help sell the stolen gems, as the strain of the involvement caused his passing. The remaining stones in their new settings stayed in the bank, and I still had the original box which held the jewels. I knew it was dangerous to have the old settings, but they were hidden in a secret drawer. I wanted to keep them to restore the star if needed.

We moved to my father's village of Mount Mellick, and began manufacturing peat briquettes. The area of Bally cumber was a rich source of the product, and we developed new practices to improve the process. During this time, my palm reading activities were virtually non-existent, as we put all our energies into this new venture.

Ireland was going through upheavals during this period. Eventually in 1922, our factory was burnt and destroyed by rebels. All our dreams and plans were wiped out overnight, and our only option was to return to London.

One evening, Mena in her desperation revealed some startling information.

"Louis we mustn't let these setbacks deter us. We'll find a way. You can begin your palmistry readings again." She said, encouragingly.

"Yes, and I'll write more books, and rework old material. It seems Cheiro is coming out of retirement. You're right, we can't give up."

"Our coal and peat business will have to wait. I believe I'll take a trip to New York. No need for you to come. There's someone there who may be interested in investing in our business." Mena explained.

"Oh, really who?" I asked.

"My first husband." She replied.

"What did you say?"

"I must tell you the truth Louis. It didn't seem to matter before, but we're in a desperate situation." She told me.

"What are you telling me? The husband who was lost at sea is still alive?" I asked, confused.

"Yes. I'm afraid so."

"How long have you known?"

"Don't be angry my love, he was never lost. Henry and I parted ways in 1902, in New York, when Jack was young." She casually informed me.

"1902. That was only two years after you were married."

"Had I not been pregnant, we'd never married. It was a

disastrous union."

"But we are married. Did he agree to a divorce?" I shouted.

Mena was silent.

"I need to sit down. Did you get a divorce Mena?" I asked again.

"No, we didn't. We were in different countries and living separate lives."

"Do you realise what this means? We're not legally married, and you're a bigamist."

"I can claim ignorance. Many men are lost at sea, it happens all the time."

"But you left him." I said.

"There's no proof." She grinned.

I began to see Mena in a different light. Had Henry been the victim of emotional desertion in New York, like myself all those years before? The memory of Mary Eastlake choosing Wilson Barrett over me came flooding back.

"Why did you leave him?" I asked.

"I wanted more Louis. I wanted you. After we arrived in New York and I found you working there, I believed it was our fate to be together. I wrote Henry a note, and told him I was leaving with Jack. I planned to visit you before returning to England, but Jack fell ill and my plans altered. By the time Jack was well again, you'd left."

"And you never saw Henry again?"

"No. Time passed and the story of his loss at sea became real."

"And now? You plan to ask him for money?"

"Jack was told some time ago about his father, and he's visited him in Jamaica. By all accounts Henry is a prosperous man."

"What makes you think he'll give you money?"

"For all those years I never received anything from him. As his lawful wife, I believe I am entitled to something."

"Mena. I can't understand it. You've never wanted for anything. Perhaps if you had, I could make allowance for your behaviour. God knows, I've been tempted to engage in immoral things, but it was because I was destitute and hungry."

"Oh Louis. When were you ever destitute? You were the epitome of decadence, when first we met." She laughed.

"It's a time only few have knowledge of Mena. Go to America. I'll continue my work here." I told her.

Was this my karma, finding someone to marry, only to discover the union is not legal? As I've often told people, the palm knows nothing of contracts, only the intent in one's heart. On our wedding day in Jersey, I believed I'd found a loving companion. To find I was an object of infatuation, resulting in a young woman leaving her husband, was troubling.

Born under the sign of taurus, Mena could be headstrong and stubborn. Perseverance and a dogmatic tenacity can either help or hinder a situation. Who was I to judge honesty in a relationship with my secrets Mena knew nothing of.

We were a team, aiding each other to survive in a harsh world. A powerful union, strong enough to repel any opposition.

While Mena was away, I concentrated on writing a new book, and saw few clients for readings. Previous books on palmistry were reprinted in different forms, providing income, but if I could write more, the financial situation would improve. During this time, I completed 'World Predictions', focusing on future events for various countries and people.

Mena returned from the United States without any investor funds. Not surprisingly, her former husband wasn't interested in parting with any money. There were other relations who proved more helpful. Her aunt Felicia, had been born in Illinois, after her English mother married an American from Kentucky, and although not rich, she was able to help Mena with her finances.

***

Remaining in contact with the French jeweller Marcel from Paris, was critical. As part of the Oppenheim circle, he visited London regularly, and if money became an issue, he'd help by converting loose gems to cash.

Mena went back to the United States to visit her aunt again in 1925, and while she was away, I reworked my previous published material to produce 'You and your hand' and 'Palmistry for all'. I also wrote 'True Ghost stories' which was published in 1926. Mena created the artwork for the front and back cover of the edition.

We were now living at 13 Nottingham Terrace in London, and it was during this time I was engaged in a legal battle with the Irish Free state in relation to the destruction of the Bally cumber property in 1922. I was not happy with the outcome, and at one point, fell into a coma and almost died. Mena also suffered from nervous strain, especially after an unwelcome visit from Frank Shackleton whilst I was in hospital.

It happened one afternoon as she was writing in her study. Unwittingly, she answered a knock at the door without realising who Frank Shackleton was.

I'd warned her numerous times, to be wary of dangerous characters from my past, but my involvement with Frank and the nature of our association, was unknown to her.

"Good afternoon. Can I help you?" She asked, answering the door.

"Good afternoon, madam. I'm looking for Louis Hamon.

Would he be in?" Frank asked.

"I'm sorry. My husband is not well at present, and is recovering in hospital. May I ask the nature of your business?"

"I'm an old friend, Frank Mellor. May I come inside to discuss some matters?"

Mena saw no reason to be suspicious of the gentleman, inviting him into the parlour   to continue the conversation.

"Well, what's this business concerning my husband?" She asked.

"Some time ago, Louis and I entered into an agreement regarding an investment which I entrusted to him. I'm afraid your husband hasn't been forthcoming with the proceeds of that transaction."

Mena shuffled uncomfortably in her chair.

"Oh, you were involved in his banking business in France? I'm afraid I know little about it, only that things didn't go his way, and there were people who lost money. I'm sorry if you were one of them. Unfortunately, such things are never guaranteed to be secure."

"No. I wasn't involved with his investment banking. It was an unrelated venture."

"I'm sorry Mr. Mellor. You'll have to be more specific, if I'm to be of any help to you."

"It seems you're doing well. How do you finance your life? Are you fully aware of your husband's assets and income?" Frank asked, becoming irritated.

"Of course. I'm his wife, and have been involved in his palmistry work for some time now. What are you inferring?" She asked, annoyed.

"Only that you may not be fully informed of some of his hidden assets."

"Mr. Mellor. I fail to see what my husband's private financial affairs have to do with you. I'm sorry if you've lost money, but I'm afraid I can't help you with any more information on this matter. I must ask you to please leave, as I've work to attend to."

Mena stood up and walked towards the front door. Frank followed her, and as she turned to open the door, he grabbed her from behind.

"Sorry Countess, I'm not quite finished with you yet." He told her.

Mena gasped, and tried to pull away, realising her mistake letting this stranger into her home.

"Please don't hurt me. I've told you all I know. You need to speak to Louis if there's unfinished business between you." She cried.

"I intend to. What's this lovely pendant you wear?" Frank asked, holding the small diamond.

"It was a gift from Louis on our first anniversary."

"Of course, it was." Frank seethed.

"And you know nothing about where he acquired it?"

"He had it made by his French jeweller who visits London regularly. That's all I know."

Frank ripped the pendant from Mena's neck and pushed her away.

"I suggest you ask your husband about his cache of stolen jewels. I'm not going away until I'm compensated. Tell him, I know the truth. Baron Oppenheim revealed it to me before he died, and if he doesn't want to suffer the same fate, he better transfer money to this account."

Frank took out a business card with his bank details written on the back, and placed it between the bosom of the countess before leaving. Mena fell back against the wall and retrieved the card. She looked at it for a second and then threw it on the floor. Still breathing heavily, she returned to her study, weeping uncontrollably.

Apart from the frightening encounter, she'd been told something about her husband she was unaware of. A cache of stolen gems? Could it be possible? The more she thought about it, the more sense it made. It would explain how money suddenly appeared at desperate times. Her own resources were almost depleted, and this knowledge threw a different light on our financial situation. There'd be much to discuss when I returned from hospital. My near-death experience weakened me, and I was in no state to lie or deceive Mena anymore. The day after my return she approached me.

"Louis, I must tell you what's occurred whilst you were away."

"Yes, of course. I can see you're on edge."

"I had a visit from an old acquaintance of yours, Frank Mellor."

"Oh no. You didn't invite him in did you?"

"He caught me off guard. I know we've discussed not letting anyone in without an appointment, but he told me, he was an old friend."

"Once a friend, now an enemy I'm afraid. I must tell you a story."

Mena sat and held my hand.

"Louis, whatever it is you must confide in me. It will be the end of any secrets we have from each other."

"The man you saw as Frank Mellor is really Frank Shackleton, the brother of the late explorer Ernest Shackleton. I met him some years ago. In the beginning, he was a nice chap and we were happy friends. Frank worked at Dublin castle during the theft of the Irish crown jewels, and told me he was in possession of the stolen gems. I agreed to look after them for him without realising what would transpire over the next few years. We both had protection from the royals at the time because of our personal connections to members of the family.

With the death of King Edward in 1910, our immunity disappeared, and Frank ended up in jail. With my fortune compromised after France, I had the gems reset in costume jewellery. My French jeweller Marcel sells the gems for me when money is needed."

Mena touched her neck, naked of jewellery.

"And he made the pendant you gave me on our anniversary?"

"Yes. I'm sorry Frank stole it from you."

"How many gems are left?" Mena asked.

"I'd been keeping enough to replace the diamond star, if the jewels were returned, but after our disappointing negotiations with the Irish free state, I've little sympathy for the idea."

"Louis, we must get away. We cannot stay here amongst all of this drama with Frank Mellor. He told me to remind you of what happened to a Baron Oppenheim. Does that mean anything to you?"

"I'm afraid Baron Oppenheim met a tragic end, a suspicious fall from his rooftop in New York. I sent Frank there telling him the Baron had the jewels."

"Oh Louis. We have to leave. He'll be back, I know." Mena said, frantically.

"I'm afraid you're right Mena."

"I'll book our passage to California, and escaping the English Winter will aid your recovery. Aunt Felicia is there with Jack in Pasadena, and we can start afresh away from this murky past."

***

In January 1927, we set sail on the SS Cardiganshire for California, and arrived in Los Angeles on February 17th. The sea air and Californian climate, helped me regain my strength. We met wonderful people and made lucrative contacts with publishers in Hollywood, and I read the hands of famous film stars including Mary Pickford, Irene Rich and Douglas Fairbanks.

Mena's musician son Jack, was finding success in America. After investigating our options, we'd no reservations about leaving everything behind in England.

After some months, Mena, Jack and myself returned to England to organize the documents needed to apply for residency, and I applied to the supreme court to have my name legally verified as Count Louis Le Warner Hamon. We sold everything in preparation for the move.

At this time, I made contact with the Irish free state government via Marcel in Paris, offering to sell them the crown jewels. We waited, but heard nothing. It was then, I instructed Marcel to send the wooden box back to show we were legitimate.

When our offer was ignored, I collected the contents of the safety deposit box and arranged to meet Marcel who was in London. I informed him I was leaving England permanently, and needed the gems sold. The original settings were melted down at his London workshop before returning to Paris. The Irish crown jewels were gone forever.

I kept a few pieces of the Parisian Diamond Company's collection to take with us to the United States. Mena's favourite piece was a modest diamond tiara.

With the influx of cash, my wife was able to add to her

wardrobe, and she indulged herself with the latest fashion shoes from Pinet of Bond Street, and Pluchino of Walton Street. Designer gowns were accessorized with stunning jewellery, but it was important to emphasis the stones were fake despite their real appearance. There is nothing more covert than the overt.

During this time, I met the astrologer Richard Harold Naylor. As R.H. Naylor, Richard contributed to newspapers and magazines making forecasts and predictions. I began to co-author my own books with him, which combined astrological information with numerology, and the first of these was my Year book for 1929, in which I made specific predictions for people and countries. This edition had a more defined timeline than the 'World predictions' edition I'd published with Herbert Jenkins in London. 'True Ghost stories' was also published in 1928.

Mena had written a romantic novel, 'Outlawed for Love', published by the London Publishing Company in early 1929. She'd skilfully designed the artwork for the covers.

In 1934, I adapted the story and wrote the film script. Mena was good friends with the actress Jane Winton, who'd married the screenwriter, Charles Kenyon, and we hoped to take advantage of this connection on our return to Hollywood.

***

On the 4th August 1929, the SS President Garfield pulled into the docks at Los Angeles and we began our new chapter in California. Filled with optimism Mena, Jack and our Spanish nurse Lusia disembarked from the great vessel.

I'd finished the manuscript for the 1930 edition of my year book before leaving England, and it was now available to purchase.

My 1929 predictions for the Stock exchange in America noted there would be 'great excitement caused in Stock Exchange circles by the rapid movement of stocks and shares, and large fortunes will be made and lost during the course of the year'. In the 1930 edition concerning the United States, I stated, *'crises would occur in her great centres of exchange'*. How could I have known the full extent of that prediction? Within a matter of weeks, the stock market had crashed and the unstoppable chain of events which would lead to the Great Depression commenced.

In 'World Predictions' of 1925 I analysed the chart of the Prince of Wales. In conjunction with Richard Naylor, I deciphered the chart and its indications. I wrote

'The present Prince of Wales has piqued curiosity many times by rumours of marriages that have faded away in the air. Even before the war, when he was a mere youth, he was affianced by rumour to a German princess, one of the Schleswig-Holstein family. I said at that time that the astrological indications for the prince put the marriage practically into the background.

Since then, Princesses from Italy, Russia, Sweden, Norway, Bulgaria and Greece have been confidently spoken of as future Princesses of Wales. Rumour says that Queen Mary, and in a lesser degree, King George, have worried themselves seriously over this problem of the prince who may be fond of a light flirtation with the fair sex but is determined not to "settle down" until he feels a grande passion, but it is well within the range of possibility, owing to the peculiar planetary influences to which he is subjected, that he will in the end, fall a victim of a devastating love affair.

If he does, I predict that the prince will give up everything, even the chance of being crowned, rather than lose the object of his affection.'

These words were not appreciated by those forces controlling the Royal family's public relations, and it was under pressure; I retracted this prediction in my 1930 Year book.

I wrote.

'I take this opportunity of correcting a widespread impression concerning the destiny of the Prince of Wales, who will certainly eventually succeed to the throne and nobly carry on the great traditions associated with that exalted office.'

Current events regarding the Prince and Mrs. Wallis Simpson demonstrate the accuracy of my original prediction, and I regret my weakness in succumbing to the pressures forcing me to write the latter. I believe everything I wrote in 1925 will come to pass as first stated.

***

In California, we found a beautiful home to rent at 401 25th street, Santa Monica. I employed two servants, William Darcy as butler and his wife Mary as cook. The surrounding homes were well appointed and the tree lined streets led to small boutique shops and businesses. Not long after we'd settled into the house, I bought an Alsatian dog. He'd been surrendered by his former owner who'd moved overseas, and the morning walks allowed me to meet other residents exercising their canine friends.

Unfortunately, Jack and the dog didn't get along. There was something in Jack's nature which troubled me. The canine intelligence felt it also, and the growling episodes around Jack contributed to the friction between us.

Soon after we arrived, Jack decided to move back with his aunt, who was living in Pasadena. Knowing he'd no longer be sleeping in the house was a relief.

We still saw a great deal of Jack, and there were elements of his musical personality that reminded me of Robert. My friend's book, 'The garden of Allah' was adapted for the screen, and was playing as a silent film in Los Angeles.

Jack's music completely ruled his life, while Robert changed his path to follow a literary career. Unlike Robert, Jack was completely obsessed by music and was interested in little else. Growing up without his father, impacted his personality in a negative way, and reconnecting with him later in life left him with mixed feelings towards his mother.

Jack could be aggressive at times, and his violent outbursts were becoming more frequent. Mena would trivialize these moments by explaining he'd suffered a blow to the head resulting in changes of behaviour.

Jack's hands were a mystery to me, and he guarded them with a stubborn defiance. If he'd any secrets, he was intent on keeping them to himself.

Music greeted me one afternoon when coming home after walking. Jack was visiting, which meant the dog would have to spend some time in the backyard. There was a tense feeling in the house, and the loud music caused me to pause before entering the parlour. I walked in to find Jack alone, playing like a madman on the grand piano. Sensing my presence, he looked up and grinned.

"Louis, you've returned."

"Yes Jack. Where's your mother?" I asked.

"I've no idea. I used my key. I hope you don't mind?" He grinned.

"No, why should I?"

"That's right. You've no reason to keep me away. After all, this is my mother's house also."

"Jack, let me be frank. Of late, I find your attitude towards Mena disturbing."

"Disturbing? In what way?"

"You're becoming more hostile, and we've endured enough stress and tension recently. Please don't create any more for us."

Jack became angry. He pounded the piano keys in time with the words.

"Tension, drama, lies, selfishness, greed, money, more lies." He shouted.

"Jack Stop."

Jack cupped his face and sat silently for a moment. His head was lowered in despair. Slowly he raised it and began to speak.

"You've no right to reprimand me. You're not my father. How I treat my mother is my business."

"I'm her husband. That makes it my business." I told him.

"Listen Louis. Don't make excuses for my mother. Wake up. This is a woman who lied to me my whole life, and to you. She told us my father was lost at sea, and I grew up never having Henry in my life because it suited her plans. She forced him to marry her after she became pregnant, and then left him. I was never wanted."

"Mena did what was best for you."

"What was best for her. She stole me away from my father. Why? To follow her own selfish desires, to marry another man who was equally as self-centred as herself. A fantasy man. Someone she thought she'd benefit from."

"A fantasy man? I'm no fantasy, Jack."

"And I'm no fool Louis. You married my mother because it suited you. You were at a stage in your life when you needed care. Do you expect me to believe you were swept off your feet by a romance at this stage of your life?"

"Jack, you've no right to judge what's in my heart."

"I believe I know what's in your heart." He replied.

"Your bitterness comes from a lack of love Jack. Perhaps you should not deny your own feelings?"

"Don't project your secret desires onto me. I'll be able to love someone when they show themselves to be worthy."

"Worthy of you? Poor fool, no wonder you hide your hand. I'm glad I never discovered what lies within your sad palm."

Mena appeared through the doorway.

"Jack, Louis, what's going on?"

Jack stood up closed the piano lid.

"My mother will drive you into the ground Louis. You're just a money maker for her. You'll be writing tall stories and reading palms until you die. And you mother, have tethered yourself to a fading celebrity. I'll make a prediction of my own, without consulting your hands or the stars. In the end, neither of you will find the fortune or fame you desire. Happily, I won't be around to see it."

Jack stormed out of the room. Mena stood motionless, watching her son exit. Walking over, I held her shaking hand.

"Don't worry my love. As you say, the head injury plays havoc with him at times."

~~~~~~~~~~~~~~

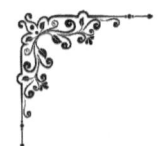

***

<u>Chapter Eleven</u>

I began lecturing again to stimulate interest in private readings. The cost for a half hour reading was $100.00, and after seeing one client, the rent and household expenses were covered for more than a week. Mena continued as my secretary and before long, there were many Hollywood types arriving, happy to pay the exorbitant fee.

After meetings at the Santa Monica Masonic Lodge, profitable connections were made, and clients increased steadily during those first couple of years. Many were too young to remember the controversy of France and the negative press which followed.

Marion Davies was an American actress at the height of her popularity, and would become a dear friend. It was through her, many of the current Hollywood celebrities came for readings. I always knew her as Marion Randolph as that was the name she used when contacting me.

I first met her in January 1932, after being invited to a party at her home on the foreshore of Santa Monica beach. Her stunning residence was completed four years earlier. The 110-room mansion was the biggest beach house in the area, and was built for her by William Randolph Hearst. After William spotted her performing in the Ziegfield follies in 1916, she became his mistress.

Hearst financed her film production company and was instrumental in providing the media support which made Marion a film star.

In 1932, she'd just finished her film, 'Polly of the Circus' co-starring the young Clark Gable. Her party was a lavish affair, with an assortment of film people attending. There were directors, writers, designers, as well as the recognizable actors.

Everyone who wanted to be a star or keep their light shining, would come to a Marion Davies party, and after talking with people at these events, I decided to write my own screenplays and have them produced. Marion was the perfect contact to make this happen. The theme of one party, 'Kiddies', did not thrill me at all, and realising I'd end up reading palms at the event, I didn't feel obliged to partake in the children's costume theme.

The taxi took me to the front entrance of the beach house where a butler and his staff were 'processing' the arrivals. I was surrounded by women in short skirts and bonnets, as the recent Shirley Temple films were a source of inspiration for many. I showed my invitation to the butler who smiled at me.

"Yes Cheiro, the palmist. We've been expecting you. Miss Davies has instructed me to show you through."

"Thank you." I replied.

There were excited whispers as the guests were told a famous palmist had arrived, and presently one of the 'Shirley temple' girls came over to me.

"You must be Cheiro. Very pleased to meet you. I'm Marion Randolph, your host."

The fresh-faced blond, reminded me of another American from my past, Blanche Roosevelt. Her large expressive eyes and happy smile projected a genuine warmth to those engaging her. Like Blanche, Marion was a perfect hostess and the life of the party.

"Thank you for thinking of me. May I ask how you came to know of me?"

"That man over there in the boy scout uniform, told me about you." She smiled.

Marion shouted to him.

"Hey Clark, come over here and meet the palmist fellow you told me about."

He came over, and Marion straightened his scarf.

"Here Clark let me fix this. It's leaning off to one side."

"Well, that's never worried anyone before." He chuckled.

"Behave yourself. This is Cheiro. He's going to look into your hand later, and let me know all your secrets."

"You mean all the others you don't know about?" He smiled.

"Cheiro, this is Clark Gable. He's a very naughty boy most of the time. I know, because I've just finished a picture with him."

Clark smiled and shook my hand.

"Don't listen to her. Marion's definition of naughty may not be the same as ours. Nice to meet you."

"In my experience, someone with such looks is almost always forgiven for any foolish behaviours." I smiled.

"You men always stick together. Tell us Clark, how you came to know of this lovely man?" Marion asked.

"Joan Crawford knew of Cheiro from her husband, Douglas Fairbanks jnr." He told her.

The recommendation thrilled me.

"Yes, I'm acquainted with his father Douglas Snr. I read his hand in 1927 when I first came to California."

"I see. You started with our Hollywood royalty. A wise move." Clark grinned.

Marion sipped furiously on her champagne.

"Well, Cheiro. Would you like to begin with Clark? I'm sure he's dying to know what the future holds for him."

"Of course. The hands of such men always intrigue me."

Clark seemed reluctant.

"I'm not sure if I want to know Marion. I'm kinda nervous all of a sudden. You go first."

"Oh Clark. Don't be such a scaredy cat. You're a boy scout, be prepared." She giggled.

"Alright. I hope I don't live to regret this night."

"Where have I heard that before. I'll leave you boys to it."

We sat, and the nervous actor gave me his palms. Producing a magnifying glass, I surveyed Clark's hands.

"Your hands are square in their physiology, and this gives a practical side to your nature. It makes you level headed and respectful of laws and conventional views. Perhaps all the talk of frivolity is exaggerated?" I smiled.

"It's true. There's that side to me, but to survive in Hollywood, one must learn to curb such traits."

"The line of success is strong and clear rising to the mount of Apollo, and your practical nature helps you attain goals in the world of film. Money lines are clearly marked indicating financial benefits from the arts. I see from your fate line, branching and weak at its start, that you failed to find your true path until earlier. From this point onwards, the line is defined and straight, and you'll not deviate from this course."

"You're right again. I had many jobs before I took up acting. You're pretty good at this aren't you? What about my personal life?"

"Your marriage and relationship lines are confusing."

"Tell me about it."

"You have a number of liaisons, some producing children. There's one relationship line standing out from the others, and I believe you'll meet this person before long. The line is unclear at its start, which tells me there is a delay in the commencement of this union, but it will eventuate, as you and this person share a karmic bond. You're meant to be together." I explained.

"That sounds ominous, but exciting. I never believed I'd be with one person my whole life."

"The line indicates you'd happily spend the rest of your days with this person."

"Is that what my palm really says?" he asked.

"The line ends after a short period unfortunately. Lines of influence from your heart line indicate a tragedy which impacts you greatly. Unlike your other marriage or union lines which all end in a fork, you don't grow apart from this person."

"Damn it. I knew it was sounding too perfect. What happens? I'm not used to women leaving me. It's usually me who does the leaving."

"Perhaps that's why fate has designed it."

"You mean to pay me back for my hurtful behaviour?"

"It's not for me to judge the reasoning behind the creator's master plan."

"Ok thanks buddy, I think I've heard enough. Great to hear I'm on the verge of artistic success in films. I'm happy about that." He said.

Clark left me contemplating the tragedy awaiting him. The positive aspects of his hand helped to counteract the negative ones, and I knew from his makeup he'd handle the information.

Exhausted from the work, but glad of the contacts, I left the beach house.

***

I'd made many friends at Marion's party, who eventually came to see me for more detailed consultations.

The first of these was Marion herself, who arrived at my door a few weeks later on March 4th.

The butler showed her into my study.

"Miss Marion Randolph is here to see you sir." He announced.

"Marion, lovely to see you again. Thankyou William."

The butler stood mesmerized by the iconic star, and reluctantly left.

"It's wonderful you live so close." Marion told me, smiling.

"Yes. The area is beautiful and convenient for everyone."

"Did you enjoy my party?" She asked.

"It was marvellous. It's been some time since I've attended such a gay affair."

"You've made quite an impression on people, and no doubt they'll be coming to visit you. I wanted to see you privately, as Hollywood actors have the uncanny ability to find out things after a few drinks."

"Of course. You know I'm the soul of discretion."

"For sure. Someone in your position couldn't risk the damage to his reputation if people didn't believe that."

"I've calculated your natal chart based on the information you've given, and we can compare it to your palm for a greater understanding." I explained.

"I'm so excited. I want you to tell me everything, don't hold back. I'm like Clark, I can handle anything you tell me."

"I see Mr. Gable has been confiding in you." I smiled.

"Clark and I are similar in many ways. We understand this business, but we don't let it mess with our heads. This world of actors and make believe can destroy you if you let it."

"You know Marion, many years ago I wanted to be an actor. In my younger days, this was a dream, and it took a while for me to realise it wasn't what I wanted. You're right. I saw the negative effects the world of the theatre had on many, and I found another road to follow."

"I bet you've had some kinda life Cheiro. Someone should write the screenplay."

"Do you think people would believe it?" I grinned.

"For sure. People can see through a story that's made up. It might be entertaining, but it's truth that grabs people's attention. That's the story they'll remember."

"Shall we find out your truth Marion?"

"Ok, hit me with it."

Marion gave me her hands. "I see why you relate to Clark, as you both have the same type of hands, square and practical. Your headline is straight across the palm indicating the same logical nature as Clark. Your sun and moon conjunct in the first house in Capricorn, signifying patience, planning, an ambitious nature to acquire security, as well as a natural business ability."

"You know Cheiro, I play the dizzy blond from Brooklyn, and some people say I've no talent as an actress. They say, I'm only where I am because of William's money. You're right. I wanted security and my ambition landed me a guy who'll always be there for me, no matter what."

"Yes, there's only one strong line in the relationship area of your palm. There's another earlier one with a child attached to it, and a faint line later in your life."

"I have an adopted daughter?" She said, softly.

"The child is yours, Marion. The hand doesn't lie."

"You're right. What's the point lying to you? I'll tell you because I trust you. The rumours my child's father is William are just that, rumours. As you've seen, that's not the case. I intend to stick with William no matter what. I've had many flings, but they don't mean anything."

"The girdle of Venus." I smiled.

"The what?" She asked.

"Girdle of Venus. Here it is, clearly marked on your palm. The sign of one who indulges in physical pleasures." I explained.

"You can tell that from my hand? That's some party trick I'd like to know. Show me again."

"Here, this loop formation between the Mount of Jupiter and the Mount of Mercury."

"I see. Well anyway, as I was saying. William and me have something together. It's not about the physical pleasures. I trust him to look after me, and I need that."

"Does the father of your daughter know about her?"

"He does. It's our secret. No one else knows about our little adventure on the set which resulted in her coming into my life. I went to Paris to have her." She told me.

"He is an actor then?"

"Yes, the best, and very famous. I worry one day someone will take the time to look past who they think the father is and discover the truth. She looks so much like her father and nothing like me or William. She's a darling, here take a look."

Marion produced a photograph of the young teenager. Psychometry or visions from holding objects, was something I'd dabbled with in the past. As soon as I held the photograph, the face changed to a well-known celebrity. I handed it back to Marion.

"Your daughter is lucky to have such talented genes. One day she may exhibit some of his comical traits." I grinned.

"Amazing. You are gifted Cheiro."

The face I'd seen overlaying the face of the girl was Charlie Chaplin. The resemblance was unmistakable, but I didn't feel the need to speak his name.

"I predict you'll stay with William, and other lines indicate you acquire wealth independently of your partner. You're definitely not a dizzy blond." I told her.

I went on to read Marion's hand in detail showing how the position of the planets in her chart mirrored the lines on her palm. When I told her of my plans to write more screenplays, she encouraged me to submit them to her production company. Despite my failing health, I wanted to prove myself as something more than a seer. Succeeding as an author would complete me. There were lucrative deals to be made if a story was accepted as a screenplay, and the lure of money continued to dominate my ambitions for the next few years. Marion would remain a trusted friend during this time.

***

Mena was intent on finding another avenue of money. After speaking with people in Ecuador, we started a business developing a method to preserve bananas. Under the name of Hamon Laboratories, we hoped to attract investors. Renting a more impressive building at 7417 Hollywood Boulevard, helped raise our profile.

Despite our best efforts, we failed to gain enough capital for the project, and the only benefit, was a couple of boat trips to South America.

My health deteriorated, and the response to my screenplays was disappointing. I used my experiences in Russia to write a play titled 'Revenge, a Russian drama in 5 acts'. I also adapted Mena's novel, 'Outlawed for love', for the screen, but no one was interested.

It seemed the only way to make money was to continue with my readings, despite the toll it was taking.

There were less stones to sell, and Mena's anniversary pendant and precious tiara, were all that remained. I'd replaced the original pendant Frank stole, before we left London.

Last year, my final book was produced. 'You and your star' published in mid-1935, is an astrological work detailing other branches of my esoteric studies.

I take long walks with the dog around Hollywood streets. No one recognizes me, and strangers never stop to talk.

Returning home, rich food and alcohol console me. The taste is reminiscent of a former life on the avenues of Paris, and in the palaces of Russia and England. The end is near; the clocks have been stopped, but my heart continues to beat, depleting the quota of time allocated.

Last night, I saw my death and funeral in detail. I will recount my vision here, as proof I still retain the power of precognition.

At 1 am, the grandfather clock struck its hour, three times. The clocks were restarted after I took to my bed in a sad state. Mena was at the bedside with a worried expression. As I drew a last breath, the dog placed his sad face beside me; ears standing up, and mouth whimpering. The clock incorrectly chimed three times, one for mind, one for body, and one for the spirit which slipped into oblivion. The nurse felt for a pulse and comforted Mena.

The vision continued. An impressive coffin rested on a pedestal surrounded by sumptuous arrangements of flowers. A death mask was placed beside my body, with a collar of purple orchids, and a floral arrangement from the masonic lodge depicting a star.

The music began to play and a soprano sang the song I requested, 'I hear you calling me'. It was a beautiful rendition, and prompted many tears. This song I'd loved, since hearing John McCormack sing it, not long after reading his palm. I felt as if I were flying above, looking down on the scene below.

Mena sat clutching her diamond necklace, with her aunt and son, beside.

In a corner sat Prince Yusupov with other members of the displaced Russian aristocracy. There were people from Paris, New York and England. Robert Hichens sat in the second row next to Marion Davies and other Hollywood people. To my great surprise, Maud Jeffries made the trip from Memphis to attend my funeral, after reading about my death in the papers. She was in the United States at the time visiting relatives.

In the end, the souls who'd made the most impact on me, were present. After a lifetime of people, there were but a few who mattered. In my last days, the divine force lifted the veil, allowing me to view those faces. There was peace and contentment for a life lived, and if other's judge me, let them. It's of no consequence, as only I know what lay in my heart when embellishing the truth. Only I know, the motivation behind the readings given to countless individuals, and only I know, what could have been.

"So ends the tale-go thou and see

The weeds and lilies in Life's stream;

Thy heart may tell thee more, my friend;

Go, think it o'er- 'tis not a dream."

Cheiro 1895

✱✱✱

<u>Epilogue</u>

What became of those closely connected to Cheiro?

Were any benefits gained from the man who promised to reveal the secrets of their lives?

Did their situations improve with the knowledge of foresight?

It seemed many of those who sought his wisdom, were powerless to stop the tragic events.

✱✱✱

Robert Hichens became a wealthy author, with many of his bestsellers adapted for the screen. One of his most successful, 'The Garden of Allah', was based on his own experiences whilst living in Sicily. After years of searching for a meaningful relationship, he entered into a romantic union with an Italian man of the cloth. Like the female counterpart in his novel, Robert enjoyed a blissful time with his lover. Despite his pessimistic outlook on relationships, he'd found someone to share his life, and after experiencing the reciprocated love of another man, he'd never be the same.

One day, his companion told him he could no longer continue the relationship, and intended returning to the monastery to make amends for his transgressions. Robert was plunged into a deep depression and loneliness, lasting years.

In the end Robert did find a substitute family with the writer

346

John Knittel.

Knittel's wife and children became close to Robert, and they travelled the world together. In 1950, amongst the Swiss Alps, he died at the age of 86. Although surrounded by the Knittels, thoughts returned to the love of his life, as they were the arms he'd wanted to die in.

***

Maud Jeffries left the world of theatre to find happiness in Australia.

The ideal life she dreamed of with James Osborne, only lasted a short period. The birth of her son James Jeffries in 1908 gave her the child she'd wanted, however, the death of their daughter at five weeks in 1911, signalled the end of that joy.

Maud blamed herself for the death, believing the tragedy was retribution for the abandonment of her illegitimate daughter Florence. In later years, she found solace in her garden and son's family. James married into the Wolfcarius clan of Sydney, who were active members of the Theosophical Society, along with Maud.

Whenever there were lectures on palmistry, she'd discreetly leave the room.

***

Lord Alfred Douglas continued his selfish ways. On 4th March, 1902, he married the bisexual heiress, Olive Custance, and the stormy marriage produced a son on November 17th, 1902. Douglas followed Oscar Wilde's repentant behaviour by converting to Catholicism a decade later, and denouncing his former friend, declaring Wilde, "the greatest force for evil that has appeared in

Europe during the last three hundred and fifty years." In 1913, he separated from his wife, but never divorced, blaming others for his failings, and growing more bitter with every year. In 1920, he founded the right wing Catholic and anti-Semitic magazine, 'Plain English'. In 1924, Douglas's karma sent him to prison for six months on a libel charge, and the incarceration affected his health and looks. The beaklike nose and twisted mouth mirrored the nastiness of his soul. His only child, Raymond, was diagnosed with schizophrenia in 1927, entered a mental institution, where he stayed until his death in 1964. When Douglas was 67, he met 27-year-old, poet and novelist, Samuel Steward. No doubt, his karma diminished the relationship. He continued to denounce individuals, projecting the cause of his miserable existence onto others. His last years were spent in reduced circumstances, and on 20th March, 1945, he died of heart failure. Unlike Oscar Wilde, Bosie's funeral was attended by only two people.

***

Ed Heron-Allen fulfilled his karma with Cheiro after writing a book on Cheirology. His translation of an earlier work by D'Arpentigny, was used by Cheiro in the early years. After a lecture tour of America, Heron-Allen returned to his law practice in London. Later he used his linguistic talents to translate the 'Rubaiyat of Omar Khayyam' from the original Persian script. Like Cheiro, the association with Oscar Wilde influenced his literary aspirations. He wrote books on archaeology and Buddhist philosophy, as well as a number of novels of science fiction and horror, using the pseudonym, Christopher Blayne. In 1891, he married Marianna Lehmann, who died in 1902. The year after her death, he married Edith Emily, with whom he had two daughters. After the first birth in 1904, Heron-Allen sent the purple Dehi sapphire to the bank, with instructions to lock it away and never let his daughter touch it.

After his death in 1943, his daughter donated the stone to the

Natural History Museum, along with a note on the accursed history of the gem.

In 1974, a curator at the museum chanced upon the stone whilst looking in the mineral cabinets, along with Heron Allen's note.

"Whoever shall then open it, shall first read out this warning, and then do as he pleases with the jewel. My advice to him or her, is to cast it into the sea."

***

Princess Mary Adelaide secured her position within the Royal family, when her daughter Mary, married Prince George, Duke of York in 1893. Her involvement in the death of the duke's brother was never uncovered. Despite the plotting, she never lived to see her daughter become Queen. She died on 27th October, 1897, at White lodge, following an emergency operation.

Her daughter, Queen Mary, led a happy and fulfilling life. Innocent of any involvement in her first betrothed's death, she was granted a happy marriage, and the knowledge her children would rule England. Despite her eldest son abdicating in December of 1936, she continued her role as grandmother to the future Queen Elizabeth. Did she ever read Cheiro's 1925 predictions for her son, when he was Prince of Wales?

'I predict that the prince will give up everything, even the chance of being crowned, rather than lose the object of his affection.'

Edward's abdication speech a decade later, confirmed Cheiro's words.

'I have found it impossible to carry the heavy burden of responsibility,

and to discharge my duties as king as I would wish to do, without the help and support of the woman I love'.

***

After Grand Duchess Olga Alexandrovna's marriage was annulled in 1916, she married her cavalry officer, Nikolai Kulikovsky. During the first world war, she served as an army nurse, and was awarded a medal for personal gallantry. After the Russian revolution, she fled to Crimea, and escaped to Denmark in 1920. She raised her two sons on a dairy farm in Ballerup, near Copenhagen, and continued with her art, producing over 2000 pieces. The creativity Cheiro saw on her hand, provided additional income for her family.

In 1948, forces within Stalin's regime threatened the last of the Romanov line. Olga and her family relocated to a farm in Campbellville, Ontario, Canada. In 1958, her husband died in Cooksville, Ontario, and Olga moved into a small apartment in Toronto. Two years later, the last Grand Duchess of Imperial Russia passed away at the age of 78.

After the revolution, her first husband, Duke Peter Alexandrovich, fled to France with his mother and a collection of Faberge eggs. He was known to attend parties in Paris wearing imperial dresses and jewellery. He died in Antibes in 1924 at the age of 55.

***

After the death of Rasputin, Prince Felix Yusupov and his wife, boarded the British warship HMS Malborough, which took them to Malta. From there, they travelled to Italy and Paris. Lacking visas, they bribed officials with diamonds. After some time in London, they returned to Paris in 1920, and founded a short-lived couture house.

Despite escaping Russia with considerable assets, the Yusupovs fortune dwindled due to Felix's bad financial management and the wall street crash. In 1928, he published his memoir detailing the killing of Rasputin, and in the same year, Rasputin's daughter Maria, unsuccessfully sued him in Paris for damages of $800,000. In 1932, he successfully sued MGM for libel and invasion of privacy in connection with the film 'Rasputin and the Empress' and received £25,000 in damages. Felix and his wife were married for over fifty years. In 1967, Felix died in Paris, followed by his wife three years later. Cheiro's account of the killing of Rasputin in his 1932 memoir, must have escaped the prince's attention. Perhaps, he preferred to ignore the book, given the past association.

***

Clarissa Molony or Saharet achieved success as an innovative dancer in Europe from 1898. Her relationship with husband Ike Rose deteriorated, but he remained her manager until their divorce in 1912. Soon after, she married the German born US millionaire, Fritz Von Frantzius. Lasting only a few days, Clarissa abandoned Fritz for her co performer Jose Florido, a young Spanish dancer. They maintained a relationship until 1917, when she married her German born theatrical agent, Maxim Phideus Lowe. Clarissa's daughter, Carrie, grew up in a convent school, and followed her mother onto the stage with the name, Dorothy Siddons. Later in the 1920's Carrie performed using the name, Madeline La Varre. Saharet no longer danced, and her life changed dramatically after divorcing Lowe in 1930. Eventually, in 1947, Carrie found stability managing an occupational therapy clinic in Battle Creek, Michigan. Clarissa moved to a trailer park to be near her daughter. In 1950, Carrie was involved in a serious car accident, which left her with permanent injuries. Unable to cope with the disability, she committed suicide, and in 1964, Clarissa's body was found in a bathtub with cut wrists. Cheiro made a wise choice avoiding Clarissa's hand. The girdle of Venus and indications of a grim death, would have been evident on her hands.

***

Marian Read continued providing spiritual support to Cheiro until her departure for Australia in 1913. She kept his secrets, and her association with the London Theosophical and Chirological societies. Arriving in Sydney with her husband and young daughter, she lost Cheiro's gift; an emerald brooch over the side of the ship. She took it as an ominous omen, never warming to her new country. Although continuing to involve herself with spiritual societies in Sydney, she longed for the life she'd left behind in London.

***

Clark Gable's film career flourished. His relationships for the most part, proved unstable. The one relationship predicted to be his best, did end in tragedy. Shortly after his reading with Cheiro, he met the actress, Carole Lombard, and they were married in 1939. Three years later she was killed in a plane crash.

Ironically, she'd visited the Indianapolis palmist Nellie Meier shortly before her death. In 1904, Nellie met with Cheiro in Paris. Carole remained flippant about the warnings Nellie saw in her hand. It was a trait she shared with her new husband.

Clark Gable never recovered emotionally from the loss of his greatest love.

He drank copious amounts of alcohol to deaden his pain, and passed away in 1960 at the age of 59.

Marion Davies remained with her newspaper baron, William Randolph Hearst until he died in 1951. In the late 1930's her astute business sense rescued Hearst from bankruptcy, when she used a million dollars of her own savings to keep his empire safe.

Her daughter's father, Charlie Chaplin, continued to play a part in her life, but Marion was never able to reconcile sexual temptations with the need for security. The girdle of Venus on her palm contributed to the numerous empty liaisons she entered into with aspiring actors.

Lacking the respect she craved, Marion turned to alcohol to comfort the emptiness overtaking her life after the loss of the man who 'made her feel special'. Later, she married a poor substitute for Hearst, and passed away at the age of 64. It was less than twelve months after her friend Clark Gable died.

Frank Shackleton failed to benefit from the theft of the Irish crown jewels, and drifted from place to place using his new identity of Frank Mellor. Eventually, he opened an antique shop in Chichester, where he crossed paths with Mena once more in 1941. After returning to England, Mena sold the last of her possessions, and ironically, it was Frank Mellor who came to look at the items. The war was raging in Europe, and both were too exhausted to engage in hostilities.

They were left contemplating the strangeness of the meeting, and what divine hand orchestrated it after so many years.

Shortly after, Mena walked by the antique shop, displaying a permanently closed sign, where she learnt Frank Mellor had passed away soon after their meeting.

***

Mena's world began crumbling after the death of Cheiro. Along with her aunt Felice and son Jack, they tried a new life in Jamaica, but her son's mental outbursts became severe and violent, and they returned to England. Jack moved to Yorkshire, and was killed in 1942, during a raid. Afterwards, Mena learnt he was playing on his piano when the German plane dropped its deadly package.

Mena inherited the copyright on her husband's books and set about having the titles reprinted. After Jack died, she unsuccessfully sued his father Henry Hartland for support. During the court battle, a farewell message to her husband was produced, and despite her claims of desertion, Mena was clearly the one who'd left the marriage. She'd underestimated Henry and his foresight in retaining the note.

After Jack's death, Mena purchased a gravesite in the Meltham Cemetery, near Huddersfield, Yorkshire, to lay her son to rest. Three years later in 1945 she had the ashes of her husband buried in the same plot. For nine years she'd travelled with Cheiro's remains. Less than one year later her, 92-year-old aunt passed away, leaving Mena completely alone.

Shortly after Cheiro's burial, she came across a woman placing flowers on the grave. The woman introduced herself as Edith Halford-Nelson and told Mena she'd been an important person in her husband's life.

In fact, she'd written a book in 1940 titled, 'Out of the silence', in which she made ridiculous claims to do with their relationship.

Her belief that Cheiro's ashes lay at Tewkesbury Abbey demonstrated the weakness of her material. Edith was the wife of the stage manager at Terry's theatre in London when Cheiro worked there. They'd attended the same acting classes at Ben Greet's school until Edith's obsession with Cheiro forced him to leave.

Her compulsive behaviour hadn't waned over the years. Writing a book after his death infuriated Mena, who warned Edith to stay away from her husband and son's grave.

In 1946 Edith passed away at castle Malwood, Minstead, after writing a couple more works of mediocre fiction.

Mena survived on the royalties of Cheiro's works and a small pension, and her life as a 'Countess' was over. The year before she died, Mena gave away her amazing wardrobe to a friend, Mrs Winder, who'd visit her in the nursing home in Emsworth, Hampshire.

She'd given instructions for her ashes to be buried with Cheiro and Jack after her death.

Mena grew older and poorer, but refused to let go of some possessions. On the night of the 24th August, 1969, the countess joined those souls who'd departed years before. The frail 87-year-old lay on her bed, in an eternal sleep.

Before passing, she'd placed a silver tiara on her head. The once beautiful headdress, was devoid of its precious gems. Around her neck, she wore her last piece of jewellery; a single diamond pendant. Her withered arm lay outstretched, in a loving embrace around the death mask of her husband.

***

About The Author

Stephen was born in Sydney, Australia, and is a graduate of the University of New South Wales's drama program. Since then, he's written and designed works for theatre and screen. An interest in history, led to the research of esoteric and mystical traditions, providing a rich source of inspiration for his writing. He now lives and works in Queensland.

You can find Stephen at www.stephendundonsmith.com

www.ingramcontent.com/pod-product-compliance
Lightning Source LLC
Chambersburg PA
CBHW032135190626
46814CB00005BA/1705